DEATH DANCE

To Sarah —
Keep dancing

1/28/99

DEATH DANCE

A NOVEL

by

Berton D. Garey

SLG Books / Cetusaurus Publications
Berkeley • Hong Kong

First published in 1997 by Commonwealth Publications Paperback

This first trade paper edition published in 1999 by

SLG BOOKS/Cetusarus Publications
P.O. Box 9465
Berkeley, CA 94709
Tel: (510) 525-1134
FAX: (510) 525-2632
email: dance@slgbooks.com
Website: www.slgbooks.com
email: Cetusaur@PacBell.net

Cover Design and Photograph by Berton D. Garey
Cover Layout by Leticia Valdez
Title Page Design and Drawing by Berton D. Garey
Title Page Layout by Doug Wordell
Typography by Mark Weiman/Regent Press

Color Separations and printing by
Snow Lion Graphics
Berkeley/Hong Kong

Library of Congress Cataloging-in-Publication Data

Garey, Berton D., 1944-
    Death Dance : a novel / by Barton D. Garey.
        p.   cm.
    ISBN 0-943389-29-1
    I. Title.
PS3557. A7148D43   1999   98-35294
813' . 54--dc21   CIP

DEATH DANCE is a work of fiction, as are the names, characters and events that take place in it. Any resemblance to actual events or persons, living or dead, is entirely coincidental. But if you think the shoe fits, wear it.

Dedicated to Earl Palmer
whose warmth, intelligence and joy calmed the waters;
and to George Bowen for always being there when it counted.

Acknowledgements:

I'd like to thank Marianne Callum for her early, thorough and thoughtful reading of the first version of Death Dance I let anyone see, and for her detailed suggestions.

I'd also like to thank Deborah Kemp, Kay Cavan and Jenny Vega for their reading and editing. It seems there is no end to the typos one can find, and they found many long after I thought I'd gotten them all. Any that remain must have grown overnight.

Chapter 1

My brother died violently. A gunshot to the head. The West Los Angeles Police Department spokesman said it was suicide. I wasn't so sure.

A couple of month's before he died, he and his oldest daughter came to Berkeley to see the UC campus. She'd been accepted here and at Yale. Until his divorce, he and his daughters were close. There was a distance between them now that he seemed to have resigned himself to. It appeared to be unwanted by him and unwanted by them, but fused to their relationship like an evil spell. I suspected their mother had cast it.

Maia seemed sullen and Marty, not so much aloof from the college considerations Maia was wrestling with, as distracted.

This was the first time that Marty had seen one of my houses. He was impressed. Dumbfounded, actually. He'd thought of me as a hippie-carpenter working small jobs, avoiding risks, avoiding successes or failures of any consequence to escape the plague we all thought privately, but never spoke about, might be genetic. Waiting there, lurking like some incipient cancer that would inevitably rise up and if not strike us down, humble us and snatch away both the financial and psychic rewards of pride in what we'd accomplished, and our conviction that no one else could have done it. In my family, from my great grandfather down, we were born to tempt the fates. We stand and announce ourselves, call our shots, and under the watchful doubting eyes of those who'd never dare, we succeed. "Don't tempt God," goes an old Jewish saying. Don't make a dare of your boast, don't let your pride out-run His grace. But there's no harm in amusing Him. Marty saw the house and I think he saw me for the first time.

It was ambitious, complicated and demanding, but compelling and successful in the sense of simplicity it evoked. It was nestled among Live Oaks in the Berkeley Hills overlooking the campus, the Bay and the City. Sculptural and graceful. But I think what pleased and surprised Marty the most was his intuitive understanding that it began with daring and confidence. There was in his eyes as he looked around the house the knowledge that I had publicly stood on the high-wire and said I would cross. And then crossed. I was his brother after all.

Maia went out on the deck with the glass of cranberry juice I'd given her while I poured us each a glass. He smiled a pleased I-knew-it smile that on someone else might've seemed smug, but on him was gentle and gracious. "Kurt," he looked around again, "this is wonderful." He hugged me. He was a very private man and usually kept his thoughts and feelings to himself. But he was also his father's son, sentimental and emotional. I was a little taken aback and at first stiff in his embrace then hugged him back. He kissed the top of my head as you would a child. His eyes were wet and he cleared his throat.

"I'd like to ask a favor."

"Sure," I said.

"I want to set up a trust for the girls, and I'd like you to be the Trustee."

"Sure."

"There's a little more to it."

"Like what?"

"It would be helpful if you'd also act as my executor." He saw the blank look in my eyes and said, "Of my will."

Why the hell didn't I see anything in his eyes? Was I just too busy basking in his approval of my work to see worry or pain or even fear? It was there. It had to be. I might have tried to be his big brother. Make him tell me what was wrong, help him gain some perspective on it, something. Now, I'd give anything just for the chance.

I must have looked at him a moment too long I suppose, because he added, "Don't worry, everything's fine. The executor on my current will is one of my ex-partners, and we have certain conflicts, so it's no longer appropriate."

"Yeah, that's fine," I said, embarrassed that I might have forced him to explain something that otherwise he wouldn't have explained. I thought I was letting him off the hook. Maybe I was letting myself off by not hearing any more. He looked out to the deck where Maia was absorbed watching a squirrel in the oak tree. It was a naked passionate look, a look of lost time and lost connections that made my heart ache for him.

He felt me watching him. "We'd better be going," he said, then to Maia, "Maia, we have to go." Then to me again, "We have an appointment to see an apartment for her."

I don't know what else I saw or didn't see, but I'll always remember his melancholy look, his melancholy smile as we shook hands and he hugged me again.

Then they left.

Chapter 2

WEDNESDAY

―――⟫⟩⟨⟨⟫――

Six weeks later my helper Paul and I had cleared and laid out the new site, dug it, and called in Wildcat Drilling. We'd poured the lower set of pier holes, formed and poured the lower wall, gotten Jerry and his rig back and drilled and then poured the upper piers and footings. We'd also finished pouring the upper walls and the rest of the foundation grade beams. It'd been a hell of a busy six weeks. I'd promised Paul that he could take a whole week off in exchange for working the seven days a week, twelve or fourteen hours a day we'd been logging ever since Jerry's banana-peel-on-the-clutch-pedal escapade had sent his truck mounted drill rig lurching backwards and almost collapsed the embankment between the upper and lower levels. It had set us back more time and money than I wanted to think about. We'd almost made up the time. The money was another matter. The last of the concrete trucks was pulling out of the driveway and I could see that the pump truck guy had cleaned up his rig and was ready to go. He waived the invoice at me, needing a signature. I was on top of the forms of the newly poured wall placing the last of the anchor bolts in the wet concrete. Paul was cleaning up spilt concrete, spreading it out thin with a shovel so it would be easy to break up and get rid of after it hardened.

"Hey Paul, sign for me, okay? I want to finish with these bolts."

"Sure," he said.

As he finished signing, and the guy got in the pump truck and started it, I saw Paul run to the garage, next door, at my house. I couldn't hear what he was saying when he came out over the noise of the truck leaving. I held my hand to my ear and shrugged. He pantomimed a telephone call and pointed to me. I finished setting the last bolt and climbed down. I passed him as he returned to his cleaning up. "For yooou," he said, as though it might be for someone else, being pretty silly, for him. I thought it had to be the anticipation of a week's vacation.

"Who else?" I teased, "It's my phone."

We were both so delighted with ourselves, having gotten as much done in the month and a half as we had. We were on a high. Lots of work, lots of food, little sleep, and lots of good vibes. Life was good. I walked to the garage and picked up the phone.

"Hello," I said.

"Kurt," it was my father. "Are you sitting down?"

"No," I laughed, "that'll be the day! How are you? What's up?"

"You better sit down." His voice was flat. Somber.

An ill-defined sense of unease swept through me, a tingling in my hands and near my elbows, then anger with what seemed the theatrical approach he was taking. "What's the matter? What's going on?" I asked, impatient and annoyed.

"Are you sitting down?" he asked me again.

"No! Dammit, just tell me."

"Marty's dead."

"What!? What did you say?"

"Marty's dead."

"Oh no! No! God no!" I felt light-headed and the edges around my vision turned bright yellow. I sat down on the garage floor with my back against the wall and just held the phone to my ear listening to my father cry. I started crying too, trying to cover my face and muffle the sounds that were beginning to escape me, but I wasn't doing a good enough job of it because to my left I sensed Paul approaching, cautiously peering in, investigating the sounds he was hearing coming from the garage, coming from me.

He asked me, "Are you okay?" I held up a hand for him to stay back, to stay away, to leave me alone.

"Kurt? Are you all right?" my father said. Deep choking sobs punctuated his words. I didn't think I could speak. My mind was a flood of anger and confusion and disbelief. And questions, but I didn't think words would come out of my mouth. I could hear this awful groaning cry coming from somewhere and I thought for a moment it must be from the phone, from my father. But then I saw the look on Paul's face and I realized it was coming from me. I was embarrassed by it, horrified by it, but I couldn't make it stop. It kept getting louder and more wracking. I wanted it to stop. I put the phone down and put both my hands over my mouth trying to hold it in but it wouldn't be held. I closed my eyes as tight as I could, hoping that might somehow help. Make it go away. For a few moments I felt as though I might as well stay like that forever. It seemed like there was nothing else to do and nowhere else to go.

Then I heard my father's voice coming from the phone on the floor.

"Kurt? Kurt?" he said. "Are you there?"

I looked at the receiver, wishing it would disappear. I didn't want to touch it. Finally, I picked it up and held it to my ear. I'd calmed down some, maybe become numb. "How?" I asked him, expecting car crash or heart attack in response.

"He shot himself," my father said. And then he began to wail. An anguished sound, pained and tormented, poured out of him. It was never going to stop. Never. I began to cry again too, both for Marty and for my father. We stayed on the phone like that for a few more minutes, and then I managed to say I'd talk to him later and I hung up.

Chapter 3

THURSDAY

My sister and I arrived at Burbank Airport just after noon the next day. I rented a car and we drove through the ugly, tacky, eastern part of the San Fernando Valley west along Vanowen, past the ramshackle assortment of Presto Prints and World Gym and Butterhorn Donuts and Adult Video stores to Laurel Canyon Boulevard and south over the hill to Sunset. The Canyon was hot and dry and looked like it was holding its breath against the likelihood of fire. The trees, the houses, even the people had a look of impermanence. As though the fire they all seemed to expect would be a relief, an excuse to finally pick up and get the hell out. We drove west along Sunset, through the seedy part of Hollywood, the strip joints and bars that catered to the daytime patrons, the sloppy, disheveled men and women of stringy unwashed hair and unshaven whatevers, past the run-down old movie palaces now fallen on hard times, and watched as the street and storefronts changed to upscale decorator's shops and expensive fashion stores and a smattering of sidewalk bistros, their gaily striped Cinzano umbrellas shading the rich, the idle, the unemployed-with someone-else's-credit-card-in-their-pockets, and around the curve just past Doheny where the very rich and very green of Beverly Hills begins. This is where we grew up. Not rich. Not even close. Neither of us talked. We just thought our thoughts as we headed to Marty's house in Brentwood.

She's three years older than I am, five years younger than Marty. When we were kids, she and Marty were close. I was an afterthought. An intruder in the world they'd created together. Marty read to her and taught her to read. He did more than just let her tag along with him and his friends; he took her with him, made her a part of what he was doing when he could, more often than his friends really liked, but he saw the need and took on the responsibility.

We passed Sepulveda and the 405, then Barrington and turned right on Seascape. It was still hot as a pistol and clammy, but here, closer to the ocean, a slight breeze and the lushness of trees and manicured lawns and well-tended gardens helped. Half a block away the street was choked with cars. Huge Mercedes, Jags, a few Rolls', the kind of cars, the kind of people who announce themselves in every way they can. At the best of times, I wasn't very social. I had the nagging thought that I was now the oldest brother. That there were responsibilities and duties that fell to me. I'm going to hate this, I thought. We drove past the house. The driveway was full, both sides of the street were full and there were even two cars parked on the well tended lawn. A couple of *machers* too important to waste time looking for parking, or walk back half a block to the house. Further up the block I parked and we walked back to the house. My younger brother, Nick, stood outside the open front door sipping Coke from a can. My sister's eyes began to tear half way up the walk. Neither of us had spoken to him since receiving the calls from my dad. He looked like he wanted to take a few steps towards us, but was afraid to move for fear of breaking. He was rigid with suppressed emotion. His normal coloring, like mine, strawberry blond hair and reddish freckled skin, was drained away. He reached out to shake hands with me. His lips were compressed to colorlessness. He was every inch a dam, holding, but ready to crack and burst. I looked at his eyes and we hugged. We're both powerfully built, but he's much bigger than I am, six-three to five-ten, a hundred and ninety-five to one-fifty five, and he wears a suit well. He fills it with muscle and pride, but as we hugged, his body began to tremble and shake, and he began to shrink down smaller and smaller, to become my little brother. He choked back sobs. Tried to swallow them, and after a moment, he did. He stepped back from me, contained and controlled again, his eyes red-rimmed. He hugged my sister and let her cry into his powerful arms. I stepped into the house to look for my father.

He was sitting next to Roberta on the couch in the living room. Maia and Eli were on the other side, Eli with her arm around him, her head resting on his slumping shoulder. The girls' mother, Ellen, stood next to them, absently stroking Maia's hair. My eyes met hers and we exchanged a silent greeting. Her eyes were wet, her pain real. I hadn't seen her in years. There was warmth and depth there now. She'd matured. Maybe I was wrong about who'd cast the evil spell. His whole life my father had been physically powerful, but now he looked old and beaten and used up. Roberta looked drained of any real color, but had over-compensated with heavy, clownish make-up. Something overly white on most of her face, bright red rouge spots on her cheeks and heavy eyeliner and lash mascara. She sat motionless, arms at her sides, but seemed preoccupied and somehow out of herself. Her eyes looked a little manic. Maybe she's worried about whether or not everyone was having a good time. Ever the hostess, I thought, then chastised myself for the unkindness. But there was something manic about the feeling throughout the house. There must have been sixty or seventy people moving with seemingly purposeful energy, as though they were launched on some crucial mission in one direction, only to return from wherever they'd been with the same intensity headed in exactly the opposite direction. Coming to rest momentarily, ready to be launched again. But after watching a moment, I decided this was a party where the guests were agitated and unsure of what to do since the presumptive host had had the bad manners to kill himself. When she saw me she jumped to her feet. I thought she was offering me the spot on the couch next to my dad. It was clear he couldn't easily stand to greet me. Instead, she grabbed my arm and pulled it tightly between her breasts and stage-whispered, "We have to talk." I felt awkward, and off balance.

"Let me talk to my dad first," I said as I retrieved my arm.

Her face hardened and her eyes tightened, then as quickly began to dissolve, and as I turned back to my father, she sobbed once or twice and suddenly shrieked, "Oh God Oh God...Where's Marty! Where's my Marty!" I knew it was unkind and unfair, but I couldn't help thinking not only was it a performance, and a bad one, but elicited by the movie crowd gathered here. Her husband just blew his brains out and she's auditioning for the film. I scolded myself for being mean. Roberta had never been one of my favorites. The first time I met her, just before they were married, she and Marty and I went out to dinner. A little tipsy, she launched into talk of sexual exploits. It was covered with a veneer of playfulness and teasing, but with a lewd harshness that made me uncomfortable. Roberta was closer to my age than his, and probably sailed through the sexual revolution with banners held high. Marty had missed it the first time around, and it was my guess she was his second chance. But his discomfort that night was greater than my own. He wasn't cut out to be a revolutionary.

The sound went through the house like the terrible screeching sounds just before a train wreck. Like a thousand fingernails across a thousand chalkboards. Hair must have been standing on end for blocks around. Mine was. A well decked-out woman about forty-five put her arm around Roberta's shoulders and supported her as they walked out of the living room. Stage right, I thought. Then reminded myself, jeez, give her a break! I heard her say something else to the woman, quietly, and then let loose with another blood-curdling shriek that was mercifully muffled by the kitchen door closing behind her.

"Dad?" He looked up at me listlessly, his eyes red and wet, huge puffy pouches below them.

"Kurt," he said, and sobbed, holding up his arms to me. I sat next to him and let him hold on while he cried. My sister and brother came in. Eli stood to let Sara sit next to him on the other side. Nick squatted down in front of him and put a hand on his knee. Someone tapped me on the shoulder.

"Kurt?"

"Yes?"

"I'm Victor March," he said, "Marty's accountant. I'm sorry to break in on you, but we need to talk." My father continued to sob against my shoulder.

I looked up at this March guy and then at my father and said, "It'll have to wait."

Nick stood up from his squat and looked at the guy like he was something on his shoe that stunk. Victor was not completely successful trying to ignore him. His voice quavered and he watched Nick apprehensively, but persisted.

"I'm afraid it can't."

I stood up and Nick took my place next to my dad.

"What is it?" I said.

"Let's go outside."

We stood across the street from Marty's house in the shade of one of the huge poplar trees that lined the street. It's a good house, I thought, about forty-five hundred square feet of nicely done ranch-style on about an acre; pool, pool house, screening room, four bedrooms and a maid's quarters. Comfortable. Nothing remotely ostentatious. Nothing even vaguely commensurate with the kind of money Marty made. Ya done good, Marty, I was thinking. Being broke as kids in Beverly Hills hadn't had the same impact on the rest of us because we were too young to understand or care much, and besides, we moved before it had a chance to sink in. But for Marty it'd been excruciating. He'd worked hard and forged a place for himself in this crowd based on his brains and talent and drive, not on family money or connections that were so common with these people. He was known as the best and brightest. In a town where a person's word is just so much talk, his word was bond. A commitment. Bankable. He put people and deals together, actors, directors, producers, and studios with a handshake. He made it all work on the strength of his reputation. A reputation well deserved. If he said a thing would happen, it would happen.

"Things are a mess," Victor said. His voice was tinged with a trace of panic. That caught my ear and struck me as odd, and my reverie about the house and Marty evaporated and I focused on him for the first time. Victor was about my age, a little taller and very slender. Dark hair and a dark neatly trimmed beard with flecks of grey that looked like he had it done once or twice a week at a barber shop. More likely a salon. Well dressed. "How soon can you come to my office?"

"What are you talking about?" I said irritably.

"You've got to get up to speed. I'll help you - tell you what you need to do."

My look must have conveyed my confusion. I had no idea what he was talking about or why he was talking about it to me.

"Wolf and Marshall don't think you should worry about First American Bank. They'll take care of it...at least that's what they told Thorne to tell me to tell you....but I don't trust...don't think that's wise...you should be in on it...and the Pyramid group wants to meet on Monday. Bob Thorne and Wolf wanted the autopsy done today, and Roberta agrees, but your dad overheard and got upset....I've gotten them to agree to postpone until tomorrow...but they say absolutely no later. Wolf's really going nuts...the others pretty much follow his lead...I don't know what to tell you about Danny Sutton and Faustini and Millennium. Wolf wants to tell them Marty was...you know...sick..and they can't hold the firm responsible...hope they don't try to screw you too bad..that's a mine field. They say Perry's ...well, really crazy on the subject...you know...goes nuts if Faustini mentions Marty's name or Sutton's....but even so...you'll have to meet with Wolf and Marshall and the rest of the partners, about that. What else can you do?" He took a breath and looked at me as though I knew what he was talking about. As though now that he'd told me all this, I'd start supplying him with the answers.

My head was spinning. None of it made any sense to me and I had no idea why he was telling me these things, but the part about the autopsy registered. "What do you mean, autopsy?"

It wasn't the response he was looking for.

"Forget about that," he said impatient and annoyed, "you've got to focus on the-"

I poked my finger into his chest and held it there firmly. "You focus," I said. "What autopsy? He shot himself. There's no fucking mystery here. What are you talking about?"

"The INSURANCE!" he yelled in exasperation. He expected and waited for a look of understanding to come into my eyes, for the fog to suddenly lift and for me to come alive with comprehension, to grasp the situation and leap into action and start barking orders that he could follow. To relieve him of the tremendous burden he was under. To lift it from his weary narrow shoulders and thank him for bearing up for the approximately twenty-four hours Marty had been dead. To bless him and grant him absolution. To take the baton and run with it. His eyes begged me.

"What insurance?" I said. "What's the problem?" His disappointment was near total. "And why are you telling me all of this?"

His mouth fell open. Now it was total. "Are you kidding?" he shrilled. "You're not kidding! You're Marty's executor for Christsake! His will. You. It's for you. You have to decide. You have to act in his place in all of it. Don't you remember? He asked you last May and the trusts for the girls and you agreed and he added a codicil to the will that I sent you myself. You signed it and sent it back to my office."

My look of dim recognition was apparently not inspiring.

"Oh for God's sake!"

He looked as though he were going to cry. He held his hand over his mouth and looked up at the poplar trees for counsel. Nick was approaching from the house. He looked at Victor, then me.

"Everything okay?" he said.

"Victor was just reminding me I agreed to act as executor for Marty."

Nick shrugged, "So?"

"There are a lot of problems," Victor said. Then as if inspired he asked Nick, "You're a lawyer too, aren't you?"

"So?" Nick repeated.

"There are going to be problems: legal, financial, very involved and complicated. And almost all of the people involved are going to be lawyers."

"What's your point?" Nick said impatiently.

"Kurt will be in over his...at a great disadvantage. You, on the other hand..." Victor let the words hang. His face brightened with the possibility.

"I practice criminal law. I don't know a thing."

"But you'd be better able." He looked from Nick to me. "I don't mean to offend you, but you've no idea what's involved here."

Nick cut him off, "Neither do I. If Marty asked Kurt to do this, he had his reasons."

I smiled slightly at Nick. "Gets you off the fucking hook."

Nick lit a cigarette, inhaled contentedly, smiled at me and said, "How right you are."

Victor was not amused or deterred. "But it makes such good sense. Kurt could resign in your favor. This is going to get difficult. Being a lawyer, used to the confrontations and combat, would-" He stopped suddenly as another of the well dressed, power-tied types approached.

"Victor," he said, "have you informed Marty's brother about the urgency involved here?"

He had looked briefly at Victor while he spoke, but almost immediately focused his attention on Nick. His voice had the deep rhythmic, almost hypnotic timbre of a courtroom giant, a commander of men and situations, a respected and listened-to arbiter of contentious issues. I might as well have been a dead leaf from the poplars fallen at their feet. My mother and Marty used to rail at me for my inability or unwillingness to dress appropriately to the occasion. The chickens come home to roost, she would have crowed. I was wearing khaki pants and a collarless white soft cotton shirt with three-quartered length sleeves, no buttons, open at top, and my best Mexican sandals. Considering the heat, I thought I was dressed about right. The guy was a little taller than me and heavier, but had the bearing of a former military type. He lit a cigarette in adult camaraderie with Nick and Victor. I wished I had some bubble gum to complete the picture.

He stuck out his hand to Nick. "Bob Thorne. I'm representing Roberta. You're Marty's brother, the lawyer, right?"

Nick nodded and took an extra second before shaking his hand.

"We need your signature on the autopsy request right away." He took a paper from his inside jacket pocket and held it out towards Nick. He glanced at Victor with thinly concealed contempt. "As a courtesy to your father, and against my best judgement, we've agreed to delay until tomorrow. But absolutely not a minute longer. Too much is riding on this." He noticed Nick hadn't made any move to take the paper. "You'll need to sign this. I'll take care of everything myself. Someone from my office will keep you informed."

Nick took a long drag and blew the smoke past the cigarette in the corner of his mouth and out his nose at the same time and tipped his head in my direction. "You should be talking to him." The words came with little puffs of exhaled smoke.

Bob Thorne looked at me like I was black and had just told him I was going to marry his daughter. He then made a show of sizing me up, finding me more than a little wanting, dismissing me, and at the same time smugly relishing the sudden and unexpected gift to the unimpeded furtherance of his cause that I seemed to represent to him. Nick looked over his shoulder from behind Thorne, smiled at me, raised his eyebrows up a notch or two, and pursed his lips, the short butt of his cigarette still dangling there. Your move, he seemed to silently say.

With no preamble, Thorne took a pen from his inside coat pocket and held it and the paper towards me. Came prepared, I thought. "Sign and date it on the back at the bottom."

I looked at it liked he'd just wiped his ass with it and still expected me to take it from him. I stared at him for about a three count before responding. To let him know I'd at least thought about it. "Not a chance," I said.

Victor groaned.

Nick smiled, relishing Thorne's discovery that he had just embarked on 100 miles of bad road, as someone once called me. Then looked at me as if to say, you sure?

Thorne looked at Nick for help, lawyer to lawyer, comrade to comrade. Nick shrugged.

Thorne decided to get tough right away and nip this in the bud. He faced me squarely, got his face close to mine and held the paper and pen even closer. In an angry, actually very convincingly outraged voice, he said through clenched teeth, "I don't think you've got a clue here, buddy. There's more than two million riding on this and we've got to move fast. If you think I'm going to let some-" he stopped long enough to give me another searing once over, "piss-ant fuck this up-" he stopped again, apparently having decided to be merciful and spare me the full force of his wrath, to let me off the hook. A kind of one-man good-cop, bad-cop routine. He looked to Victor and Nick for acknowledgement of his kindness. A once-in-a-lifetime deal. He smiled and offered the paper and pen for my renewed consideration.

"Why would you want to do an autopsy on a man who committed suicide? And how is two million dollars riding on it?" I asked, trying to keep the shock and rising anger out of my voice.

He took a deep breath, probably deciding whether or not to even talk to me. Apparently I'd gotten him on a good day. His largesse knew no bounds. He'd explain. "Goldman Marshall & Wolf, your brother's recently formed law firm, borrowed money from First American Bank to start up the partnership. Your brother was critical to the success of the firm. In fact, the loans were made primarily because your brother was involved. To protect themselves, the bank required a life insurance policy, a Key Man policy on your brother's life. Two and a quarter million dollars worth. The policy, like most insurance policies, excludes suicide during the first two years. It was in effect only twenty-two months at the time of his death. Therefore, if it were suicide, no payoff. Therefore no way to pay off the First American Bank loans. Therefore bankruptcy for the firm and possibly each of the partners, who jointly and severally signed for those loans. In the case of your brother, now Roberta, everything coming to her, and more, would be swallowed by the First American Bank demands for repayment. You can probably imagine how anxious the other partners are. They have all pledged everything they own against those loans." He took another deep breath. There, now you know, he seemed to say.

"He shot himself. That seems like suicide to me. Whatever his reason, it was his decision to make. An autopsy won't change that." I said.

"First: It's not legally suicide if we can show, if we can find something, anything to demonstrate he wasn't in his right mind. To be legally suicide, he must have had the intention to kill himself. He must comprehend the consequences of the act. He must..."

"He put a fucking gun to his head and pulled the trigger. I'd say he knew what he wanted to do." I was beginning to get angry, which by itself was not unusual, but it was accompanied by an unusually temperate voice in my head warning me to go easy here. If he had known, Nick would have been stunned. He was convinced I had no such voice.

Thorne smiled at me, indulgently now, like a teacher to a particularly dense or obstinate student, willing to continue to edify, but mostly for the benefit of the other less recalcitrant students. He looked at Nick, knowing the legal implications would not at least escape him. "If we find anything, anything at all to pin his actions on, we can put the insurance company on the defensive. They will have to prove what we've found did not lead to his death. Did not cause him to take his life without meaning to. In short-" he smiled again, too pleased with himself to not share it, "the burden of proof will be theirs, to disprove a negative. A formidable task!"

"And if you don't find anything?" I asked.

"Oh, we will. We most certainly will. There's not a person alive that if looked at closely enough doesn't have some abnormality, some physiological defect. It will be their burden to prove it did not cause his death."

"If defects are so common, why would anyone believe it had an effect?"

"Take my word for it, we will have them on the run once we come up with a hook to hang this on."

"Assuming you're right about any defect and the burden of proof, which I find hard to believe, what if there just isn't anything?"

"The next step would be to examine his medical records. And any psychiatric records that may exist."

"But that's confidential! That's no one's business but his!" My voice rose in alarm. I looked to Nick for help. "Doesn't the doctor or shrink have to keep them private?"

Thorne looked at me sternly. The bad-cop had returned. "Roberta has decided she wants the autopsy done and wants the records opened immediately. She was his wife for Christ's sake! It's her decision."

"Then take this shit to her!"

"You, as executor, can and must authorize the release of any and all records having to do with your brother. Beginning with this autopsy request." He held out the paper and pen again.

A short wiry guy, maybe fifty or so, with wavy absolutely white hair and a Club-Med tan approached us. Nothing casual about him. He came at our little gathering like a heat-seeking missile to a forest fire. I saw him coming and thought, in case anyone else decides to join us, it's a good thing the street is wide.

He looked at Bob Thorne, ignoring everyone else, and asked, "Is everything set for tomorrow?"

Suddenly Thorne was no longer in charge.

"Which one of you is the executor?" he asked, not caring if it were me or Nick. We were both equally insignificant to him. So much for the dress code.

Victor started to say something. Thorne cut him off in an attempt to regain some lost ground. "John, these are Marty's brothers. Kurt is the executor of Marty's will. It's this other brother that's the lawyer." The reasonable and probably smarter one, his voice implied. "John Wolf," he introduced.

"Then why isn't he the executor?" he asked Thorne, as if asking the question insured that someone would instantly supply him with an answer. And one to his liking. "Are we all set for tomorrow?"

Thorne swallowed hard and hesitated a moment longer than Wolf was prepared to tolerate. He saw the paper and pen in Thorne's hand and took them without so much as a by-your-leave. He was clearly not a by-your-leave sort of guy. They were back in my face like a fly you just can't seem to shoo away. His hands were amazingly clean and manicured. Like gloves of incredibly real looking but simulated skin. Even his fingernails looked plastic. Machine made. If for no other reason, I thought to myself, I wasn't going to take the papers and risk touching them.

Wolf had a menacing way about him. There was a Darth Vader energy emanating from him that counseled caution. Before he could speak, another suit approached. Tall and heavily built, his clothes expensive, but hanging on him, wrinkled and dusty looking like elephant skin, he ambled up to our little men's club. Behind him a few steps, a lithe good looking blonde also approached. The street may not be wide enough after all, I thought. Dark blue snug fitting suit and white silk blouse, her hair up in a French braid of some sort, and small uncomplicated pearl earrings. The skirt came only a little below her knees. Long tan legs. Medium high heels. Little or no make up. She walked as though the others didn't exist. Maybe she wished they didn't. We'd have that in common. Maybe we'd become great friends based on it. She hung back behind the others.

Up close the elephant-man had a warm sloppy smile and sad brown friendly eyes. He came straight to me, passing by Nick, probably sensing a kindred spirit in my sartorial un-splendor, or maybe having asked someone which brother was which before he left the house. He ignored John Wolf and the paper and pen and offered me his hand and his condolences.

"You're Kurt? Sandy Marshall-one of your brother's partners-I'm so sorry. It's a horrible shock for all of us." We shook hands. He turned to Nick and they shook hands. "It's a terrible loss."

Wolf couldn't stand it another second. He was six or seven inches shorter than Marshall and at least fifty pounds lighter, but cut between him and me with a move a skilled cowboy herding cattle would envy. "I assume Bob Thorne has told you this is important. I also assume you think you can jerk us around about this. You can't. Sign it now."

Marshall tried to intercede. "John, for Godsakes! His brother's just died. He's just got here. It'll keep until tomorrow."

"If he thinks he's going to jack me around - angle for some pay-off." He looked back at me. "Is that it? You want something for yourself?"

I hadn't noticed, but Nick had managed to slip around and now stood next to me. He put a hand on my right forearm just above my clenched fist. I may have been caught off guard and off balance and it had produced a wave of confused indignation and frustration, and I knew I'd never get any words out, but anger welled up with it, sweet and pure and uncomplicated. Nick's grip on my arm tightened. "The first thing you have to do is hire a probate lawyer." He looked down almost a foot at Wolf like he were going to piss on him. "In the mean time, you don't have to do or sign anything."

"You're fucking with the wrong guy!" Wolf said to me. He threw the paper and pen on the ground at my feet.

Thorne picked them up. "I wouldn't take too long finding a lawyer," he said. He tucked his business card in my shirt pocket and returned to the house.

Marshall said, "He's under a lot of pressure just now. I'd like to suggest you come to the office for a discussion of some of the issues facing us. You're welcome to bring an attorney with you. Tomorrow afternoon?"

"I'll call and let you know," I said. We shook hands again and he also returned to the house.

Nick and I and Victor March and the blond watched as he caught up to Bob Thorne and John Wolf on the porch. Marshall seemed unperturbed, but Thorne and Wolf were snapping at him, Wolf waving his arms and shouting. He stalked off to one of the two Mercedes parked on the lawn. It figured. He backed across the grass violently with no regard for the deep gouges he was leaving behind. Once on the street, he floored the blimp-sized car, headed for Sunset. Roberta came to the door and Thorne put his arm around her protectively and herded her away from Marshall who went back into the house. Thorne and Roberta talked next to the other Mercedes on the grass. They kissed cheeks and he got in his car and more gingerly than Wolf, backed out to the street and also took off towards Sunset.

Chapter 4

The blond smiled a small friendly smile, shook hands with Nick and turned to me as she introduced herself. "Tina Cox. I worked with your brother." Her eyes welled with tears. "I can't tell you how sorry I am. I just can't believe it." She stood there hugging herself trying not to cry. Her slender body shook from time to time, then she took a deep breath and wiped her eyes with her fingers and tried to smile again. "It's just not believable." She looked from me to Nick and back again as though maybe one of us could tell her it wasn't true.

She took another deep breath and nodded towards Nick's cigarette. "Could I have one of those?" He gave her one and lit it for her. "Thanks." She inhaled a few times. It calmed her. She took a card out of a little front pocket in her suit jacket and gave it to me. "I know this must all be overwhelming." She looked at Victor. "Victor, would you excuse us please?"

Victor seemed relieved. Maybe the baton had been passed. He was off the hook. At least for now. "Oh, sure. No problem. Call me, Kurt, as soon as you can. There's so much to discuss. I have the names of some very good probate attorneys I can give you." He took a business card from his jacket pocket and a pen, wrote on the card and handed it to me. "You call me at home or at the office, anytime."

"Thanks," I said. "I'll let you know."

He headed for the house.

Nick said, "I'll talk to you later. I'm going to check on dad and Sara." He gave me a one armed hug around my shoulder. He nodded to Tina Cox. They exchanged a look of tentative mutual respect like I imagined he would with a co-counsel he found himself working with and had to trust.

"I hardly know where to begin," she began. "First," she said, very lawyer-like, "Roberta said you were going to make all of the funeral arrangements." It was news to me but not completely unexpected. From what little I'd seen of Roberta since she and Marty married seven years before, in difficult situations she was either useless or hysterical. Usually both. I figured Marty had had a greater need to be at center stage alone than he had for a true partner. Roberta fit that bill. But I thought it wasn't just center stage Marty was after, it was a sense of control.

When my mother died Marty took care of everything. Almost every-thing. He was the oldest, the big brother, the adult. I was twenty-nine then. My son was two, I was just squeaking by, and had bought the first lot to build the first house. I hadn't yet put together enough money to make it happen. But I was close. He was thirty-seven and was making money like an Arab oil-sheik, like the US Treasury during the Eisenhower years, so he paid for everything. With one small exception. To do some-thing, so he wouldn't think he was in it alone, I insisted on paying for a funeral plot for my dad next to the one Marty had bought for my mother. I had to use-you should pardon the expression-the lay-away plan, and it took several years at $30 a month, but I finally paid it off.

What he didn't take care of, what he couldn't take care of, was dealing with my dad. About money. My dad's talent for financial disaster was without limit. For years before my mother died when things got bad or worse than bad, she'd call Marty and ask for help. He'd write a check and mail it. He could easily afford the money. But it took a heavy emo-tional toll on him. When he was a teenager and saving the money for college he knew my parents couldn't give him, my dad would have one emergency or another and have to borrow Marty's savings. It fed us, paid the overdue bills and a thousand other things that Marty gladly would have done. It was never repaid. But what really hurt was the sense that my father believed it was his to take. That his dreams, his needs, his failures placed this inescapable obligation and responsibility on a thirteen, fourteen, fifteen year old kid living in Beverly Hills work-ing day and night to have a dream.

But the green '37 Packard Convertible was the killer. I know Marty never stopped loving my father, but he never felt close to him in the same way after that. Out of his college savings, ravaged by my father over the years as they were, Marty bought this beautiful dark green '37 Packard Convertible from an ex-movie star neighbor. This guy had known and liked Marty from far back when as a kid Marty mowed his lawn and did odd jobs for him and other neighbors. He knew how hard Marty was working now. He knew Marty was going to commute from home to UCLA and to his assortment of part-time jobs in an endless circle. The car was in mint condition and he offered it to Marty at less than a third of what it was worth. Marty was so proud of it! He washed it and waxed it relentlessly and even bought a war surplus parachute to cover it at night, since he had to park it on the street. My dad drove cars into the ground, until they begged for mercy. From dust to dust was his motto. His car in those days was on its last legs. So he commandeered the '37 Packard from Marty. The look in Marty's eyes when he gave my dad the keys was heartbreaking. For my dad too, I'm sure. He was a sweet, talented man, but he had a lot to cry for when it came to Marty. So when my dad called Marty about money, it triggered emotional shock waves that ran deep.

Marty and I walked up this same street the day we buried my mom. He was weighed down with his recent divorce and my mother's death, but what was really eating at him was his dread of no longer having my mother as a buffer between him and my father. He had so much anger and was so guilty about it he could hardly breathe. It didn't last long, but it was the only time I'd ever seen him out of control.

"Remember the time in the garage?" he asked me out of the blue. We shared a smile. When I was twelve, my dad, frustrated and hurt by his father and brother's betrayal in a shared business, had gone off on all of us. At considerable risk to my own well-being, I'd pointed out the unfairness of it. It was a near-death experience. But Marty knew that I could always do that. Confront him without lingering hard feelings or ill will.

Marty bit his upper lip and bit back his feelings. His eyes watered and he looked away from me and said, "I just can't deal with him alone. I can't." He looked at me for some sign that I understood and could help.

"It will be my mission in life," I joked. He wasn't smiling with me. "Look, it's not just your responsibility. I can take care of it."

" It's not the money-not at all. I know you and Nick are struggling and you know if you ever need help, or want help..."

"I know, I know," I said.

There are all too few times when you can do a thing for someone you love that really matters to them, and you never know how long you might have to do it, but I knew then that I'd been able to do it at least once for him. His face completely changed and his sense of relief and liberation and gratitude were childlike.

Marty put his arm around my shoulder and gave me a hug. He'd rolled both lips back in between his teeth, biting back his emotions, raised his brows and nodded a silent thank you.

"I'd like to help if I can. You're going to be very busy with all of this," Tina Cox was saying.

"Thanks for offering, but I think I can manage." I said it with more confidence than I felt. "What I really need is some background. What's going on here? This partnership obviously wasn't a marriage made in heaven. What in the hell's going on? What was Marty doing in bed with these creeps?" She looked at me wryly. "Present company excluded," I added, but thought, for the time being.

I gave her a once-over. Nice body. Marty, I wondered? Not a chance.

"I still work with these guys, okay? I'm a partner. I'm not sure-"

"Thanks for nothing, then."

"You don't understand!"

"Right," I said. I started back for the house.

She stood there motionless. I got half a dozen steps away when she called out. "Wait. Wait a minute. Please."

I turned back to her. We'd have met there in the middle of the street, symbolic as hell, except I took a step back, adding one to her side as she approached. Petty, but I amused myself with it.

"This is very complicated and very difficult."

I waited.

"Where are you staying?" she asked.

"I'm not sure. Probably at a friend's house in Laurel Canyon."

"Could we meet later?"

"Name it."

"Do you drink?"

"Not much. Coffee. Maybe beer. Know a quiet coffee house? Good coffee?" You can take the boy out of Berkeley, etcetera.

"Sandy's in Venice. It's a coffee and beer place. Some nights a jazz trio. Do you know it?"

"No, but I'll find it. What time?"

"You tell me. I have a feeling you're going to be much busier than you can imagine."

I looked a why at her but she just looked down at the ground to avoid my eyes and an answer.

"Ten tonight. Better make it ten-thirty."

"Okay." She reached out to shake hands, her face clouding up again, but before I could react she impulsively put her arms around me and awkwardly hugged me and said, "It's just so wrong!"

She walked quickly up the street ten or twelve cars to a nicely kept old silver-grey Alfa Veloce, but before she could get in another suit called to her from the front porch. She waited impatiently for him. When he got there he put his hand on her shoulder and leaned close to whisper something. He looked up at me and back to her and said something else. She pulled back angrily. He reached for her arm to hold her but she forcefully pushed his hand away. She jerked the car door open, got in and closed it. He knocked repeatedly on her window. I could hear him demanding she open it. She ignored him and started the car and pulled away from the curb with no regard for his feet. He quickly back-stepped to save them.

"Dammit Tina!" he shouted after her.

Unlike everyone else so far, she headed away from Sunset.

I looked at the card she'd given me. Goldman Marshall & Wolf in the middle. Then in smaller letters below that, Christine Cox, Partner. In the right upper corner the phone and fax numbers for the firm and her extension number, and across the bottom the address: 81436 Ocean Avenue, the Penthouse Floor, Santa Monica, California. I turned it over. In pen and underlined heavily was written, John Goodman, Goodman, Winters Callan and Street, Probate Attorneys, and a phone number. I put it in my pocket and returned to the house.

As I stepped through the open front door, Victor March ceased talking to a tall guy with wiry steel-grey hair and what was likely his wife, the over dressed, over made-up and over-bejeweled woman in her mid-forties, looking every minute of it, who'd helped Roberta earlier. It was a safe bet he was a lawyer. Everybody else was.

"Kurt," Victor motioned for me to join them. "This is Barry Malovitch and his wife Dotty. He was a partner of Marty's at DBS."

"I'm deeply sorry," he said. "Marty and I have been close friends for more than twenty years. We were like brothers. It's just not possible."

We shook hands.

"I understand you're Marty's executor."

So much for the social graces.

"That's right."

"I hate to burden you with this right now but it's important that we get together."

His wife gave him a contemptuous look, which he ignored. She walked off without a word. I was beginning to like her.

Malovitch continued. "Marty and I had just about concluded his separation agreement from the firm. Do you know about that?"

"No. Enlighten me."

He gave me a funny look, not sure if I were being sarcastic or not. I think he gave me the benefit of the doubt. "Well, you know Marty was a senior partner at DBS when he decided to leave and start his own firm with Wolf and Marshall?" I nodded. "Certain clients that were his at DBS would naturally want to go with him. And deals he had negotiated while a partner with us would continue to yield income, some for several years more. The agreement we were concluding allows for some of that money to stay with us; some to go to GMW. There are also issues the firm is involved in for which Marty may have financial liability, IRS demands, old partnership problems. Others where he is, was entitled to, and now his estate is entitled to share in. We'd pretty well come to an agreement to resolve all of our differences. I'd like to familiarize you with it and get it signed; get it behind us."

My eyes moved to Victor. He looked as nervous as a virgin in a whore house.

"When would it be convenient to get together?" he asked.

"I'm not sure. I'll call you."

"How long will you be in town?"

"I don't know yet."

"I'd really like to conclude our agreement. I can make myself available almost anytime in the next week."

He took a business card from his wallet and wrote a number on the back of it.

"That's my back line. Comes directly through to me. Feel free to call me anytime. I'll tell my secretary to expect a call from you to set up an appointment, or you can call me on the back line. So sorry to meet you under these circumstances. I'll just get Dotty and say good-bye to Roberta."

We shook hands again. I had the urge to wash mine.

Victor watched him disappear. "I think you should meet with me soon. You've got to get familiar with everything Marty was involved in. It's all so connected. I need to know how you want me to proceed." He took out a second card and handed it to me. Must've forgotten the first. "I get to my office by seven every morning." He left quickly without another word or a look around.

Malovitch and his wife and Roberta came towards me saying good-byes. As soon as they stepped out through the door, Roberta planted herself in front of me and said, "I MUST talk to you NOW! In the kitchen." I followed like it were a trip to the woodshed.

"You HAVE to sign that autopsy request. I demand it!"

I said nothing. Sometimes that's best.

"Do you hear me!" she yelled. "DO YOU!?"

Most of Los Angeles did. From this close, the skin of her face was gaily colored, the texture of an orange, but turning definitely towards red now. She waited less than a second for an answer before letting me know, "It may NOT have been suicide." She waited for that to produce an effect.

I still said nothing, supposing she had in mind the legal intricacies Thorne had suggested.

"It could have been murder!" There was a ghoulish pleasure she seemed to take in having shaken me out of my silence.

"What!? What are you talking about!?"

Now that she had my attention she savored it and my shock. Over her shoulder I could see the maid at the kitchen sink. She looked at me until our eyes met and then away. Then she did it again. Under other circumstances I would have assumed she was flirting with me. Hell, even then. But the teary red-rimmed eyes were for Marty. She caught my eye again. Roberta noticed me looking and turned suspiciously, saw the maid and yelled something in Spanish that had to mean 'Get out!' because she did, and in a hurry. But she gave me one more look as she rushed out.

"Were the police here?" I asked.

"Yes, of course."

"Did they suggest that to you?" I asked incredulously.

"They said he did it himself. But he couldn't! He wouldn't!" she hissed at me.

I couldn't tell if she meant this to be a tribute to his strength of character, his desire not to leave this life and her, or a challenge to the suicide clause in the insurance policy.

"Bob says it's as possible as anything else." She actually seemed willing to believe it.

"You're out of your fucking mind!" I said.

"How dare you!"

She started to cry. It seemed genuine.

"I'm sorry, Roberta, I just think that's-" I looked for the right word, "absurd," was as inoffensive as I could come up with. I had the beginnings of a massive headache. "I need to make some calls. Where can I use the phone and have some privacy?"

"In his office." She pointed to a closed door past the breakfast room off the kitchen. "That's where he...it happened."

No one had said anything about it and somehow I'd imagined it happening at his office office. I looked at the door at first with a sense of horror, as though going into that room would somehow make me a participant or an accomplice. Roberta felt compelled to add with what I sensed was not shock or horror, but distaste, that the pool of blood had ruined the rug. She made it sound like the cum spot of a masturbating teenager on sheets she had to change. She confided she'd had the live-in Guatemalan maid, Maria, and her brother remove it just this morning. I'd been suspended in time and in my thoughts until I heard that. Then suddenly the room no longer seemed forbidding. On the contrary, I hoped I could embrace his spirit there the way you might comfort a terminal patient before they let it go.

"You MUST sign the autopsy request. I have to look out for myself and Lucy now." Lucy was her fifteen year old daughter by a previous marriage. Roberta stalked out of the kitchen.

The maid came back. She carried a large tray with dirty dishes from the crowd in the living room. She began to load them into the dishwasher. She was crying softly. She looked over her shoulder at me.

"No good English," she said. "Mister Goldman so good man...so good to me...so sorry..." She turned back to the dishwasher but it seemed like she wanted to say more.

"Thank you, gracias," I said, waiting for her to say something else.

She seemed about to speak when Roberta and one of the caterer's people returned. Roberta saw me and Maria and threw up her hands and yelled at the poor girl, "I told you to get out of here!" Repeated it in fluent Spanish. Maria glared defiantly at Roberta as she went to her room, which was just off the kitchen. Roberta and the caterer took hors d'oeuvres from one of the boxes and placed them on a tray, then the woman took the tray back to the living room. I turned and went down the couple of steps to the office door. My back was to them, but I heard someone come into the kitchen and a man's voice say to Roberta, "There you are!" followed by a muted exchange of words. It sounded like Roberta was crying.

"I'm so lonely!" I heard her say. "I don't know what to do!" The man's voice took on a comforting tone. I had a wave of sympathy for her. A small one, but it was there.

I went into the office and closed the door. As it closed, I could hear Roberta saying in exasperation to whoever he was, "Oh don't be ridiculous! Woodman's gay for godsakes!"

It was dark in there. The switch just inside the door turned on several recessed lights in the ceiling. The three large windows and sliding glass door were covered by closed mini-blinds. I opened the blinds and then the windows. A slight breeze stirred the room. On the left there was a large roll-top desk and a tall four-drawer file cabinet, both dark oak. Two of the lights were directly over the desk and lit it well. I'd forgotten that the office was separated from the screening room. I'd remembered them as one big room. This part was probably eighteen feet square. On the right, against the wall across from the desk, was a couch and coffee table. On the wall opposite me was a door to the screening room. Along that same wall was a large oak trestle table covered with distinct groups of papers neatly stacked.

I sat in the chair behind the desk. I was slightly ashamed but I looked to see if there were blood stains on it or the desk or on the floor or the walls near me. There weren't. Jesus, poor Maria, I thought. But I silently thanked her. On the floor to the right of the desk was a large black open briefcase. It looked new. It had a flap that locked into a brass catch with a cylinder with numbers on it requiring a combination. Marty's initials were just below the catch in bold gold letters. I thought it good luck that it was open. I looked in and saw it was empty. Maybe some of the papers on the trestle table had come from his briefcase. Marty's keys and wallet and an appointment/address book were on the desk near the phone. I put the keys in my pocket and looked through the wallet. There was about three hundred dollars in cash and half a dozen credit cards. I took out a magnetic card that read, Pyramid Parking, 81436 Ocean Ave. on it and put it in my wallet. I looked through the little drawers at the back of the desk under the roll-top. I went through the file cabinet looking for a phone book, but decided to read each of the index names on the files to log them in my mind.

Seascape Escrow
Autos:450 SL Purchase/MB Sedan/Wagon
Kurt:Copyright/Zak's Hill
DBS: issues; proposals (office comp.)
GMW:lease; parking; improvements to indiv. spaces.(office comp.)
Divorce: Alimony; child support.
Client list (1965-1975 DBS)

Client list (1976-1980 DBS)
Client list (1976-1980 DBS/GMW; office comp.)
Client list (1980-July 1982 GMW[printout]:see office comp.)
Merlon/old issues:
    Oak. PO Assoc. Suit
    Tahiti
    Millennium suit
    20th Cent. Suit
Merlon: $50k gift(office comp.)
International Distributors/notes; motions; original findings.
International Distributors/Judgement; Appeal; Calculations (office comp.)
DBS/ID: Distribution; Interest/Current Balance (office comp.)

In another drawer were dozens of old quarterly printouts from DBS with Marty's hourly billings against client accounts; records of studio payments to DBS on behalf of Marty's clients, Partnership Agreements and records of partnership profit distributions for all of the years from 1965 to 1980. These weren't in file folders, but stacked and rubber-banded in the bottom of the drawer, something I assumed he no longer needed ready access to.

In the bottom drawer I found the phone book.

From the yellow pages, I called the Temple Beth El and asked for the rabbi. A much too young sounding man came on the phone.

"Are you the rabbi?" I asked.

"Yes, I am. May I help you?"

"My brother has died and I need to make arrangements."

"Can you come see me?"

"Things are a little chaotic. I'm not sure when I'll be free. The problem is we're Jews, but I'm uneducated as a Jew. I don't know what should be done."

"Was your brother a practicing Jew?"

"I know he was bar-mitzva'd, but I don't think he goes to temple at all."

"So he would think of himself as reform, not conservative?"

"I couldn't say."

"Well, can you tell me this then: where is the body?" His voice was gentle and kind, but the question took me by surprise, making a reality again out of what had been an abstraction for the last half hour or so, and I stammered, "I don't know," I felt tears welling up. I hadn't planned on it being so difficult.

He was quiet for a while. I was crying as quietly as I could, but he must have known, because he just started telling me the things I needed to know and to do.

"I think you should do this first," he said. "Call Groman Brothers Mortuary. They will make all the necessary arrangements with the county authorities to move your brother to one of their locations for preparation. You must decide on whether he is to be buried or cremated. You'll have to make an appointment to go in and talk with them. You'll have to sign a release either with the county or sign one for Groman's to use, so they can begin."

He told me Jewish law required burial or cremation by the sixth day after death. He told me I should find out if my brother had any relationship at all with a particular rabbi. If he did, I should contact him and ask him to preside at the services and burial. If not, I should locate one and familiarize him with Marty, his history, and ask him to synthesize a service from information he could get from family members and close friends. The rabbi would know what to do.

"That should get you started." He paused. "I'm sorry for your loss." Then added, "Let God help you with your grief; if you wish to talk to someone, if you feel the need, I'd be glad to see you in person, or we could speak again on the phone."

I thanked him and hung up.

I called Groman. The guy I spoke with had the smooth practiced solicitousness of the truly professional, truly detached. As legal next of kin, it should be Roberta's signature on the Release of Body form for the county, but he told me they'd accept mine as executor. He gave me the address. It was downtown, on Washington near Figueroa. Could I be there before close of business today? Yes, I told him.

Some business.

I looked in the yellow pages under Probate Attorneys. There was no shortage. I scanned the long list, but then on impulse, I put aside the phone book and took out the card Tina Cox had given me. John Goodman, Goodman Callan Winters and Street. When I got through to him, I told him Tina Cox had given me his name.

"How is Tina? She probably told you I'm a friend of her father's, but I haven't seen Tina, well, in years, really," he said. His rich smooth baritone and his unhurried confident delivery were reassuring. A sea-anchor in rough waters. For the first time that day I didn't feel completely adrift.

I told him a little about the situation and asked if I could come meet with him to tell him more. I said I was going to Groman Brothers' but would be free after that. He said he'd be in his office until at least six. He gave me the address. I wrote it down: 304 Broadway, Suite 512 to 522. I was surprised and pleased that it was in downtown LA. Not only wasn't it far from Groman, but it was a pleasant million miles away from the Beverly Hills crowd I'd been ass-over-eyebrows involved with so far. I said I was sure I could get there before six.

I put Marty's wallet in the top desk drawer and found the key on his ring to lock it. I shut and locked the roll-top and the file cabinet. I took the keys and the appointment/address book with me, figuring I'd go through it later. I left the windows open but turned off the lights and left.

I found my dad and Sara and Nick standing together on the grass in front of the house under a shady tree.

"I've got to start making some arrangements." To Nick, "Can you get dad back to his place?"

"Sure."

"What are you going to do?" I asked Sara.

"I'm going to stay here with Roberta. She's upset and sort of... disoriented. I think she needs someone with her."

"Do you remember who the rabbi was that buried Mom and Ellis White? That big wild-haired guy?"

"He also married Marty and Ellen and me and Jim. William Krasznik."

"That's right! I'd forgotten that. Wild Bill Krasznik! Do you know what part of town he's in?"

"No, well, I don't remember. I could find out. Would you like me to find out?" She smiled a little. Wild Bill Krasznik had that effect on just about everyone, even years later, just remembering him.

"Yeah, I'll check in with you here, either by phone or I'll stop by," I told her.

Roberta came out of the house, looked at me and Sara and Nick uncertainly, and then threw herself into my father's arms. "Oh, Dave, I don't think I could bear all this without your help."

My dad did his best to support her as she clung to him sobbing.

Then she turned to me, her voice suddenly level and probing. "What are your plans now?"

"I'm going to Groman Brothers' Mortuary and then to meet with a probate lawyer, then on a few other errands."

"What lawyer?" There was an edge to her voice a sushi chef would have envied.

"John Goodman."

"Never heard of him. You should be talking to Bob Thorne and his firm."

I let it pass. I gave my dad a hug and shook hands with Nick. Sara kissed me on the cheek.

As I turned to go, two more suits stood there waiting for me. A third, the guy who'd chased after Tina Cox, just a step behind. The guy that approached me was big and solidly built under a little too much good food. Nice looking like a model from a Macy's ad, with short soft looking light brown hair and chiselled features slightly softened by the high living. He had glasses with thin dark stylish frames. His eyes were red-rimmed and tear filled. The other guy was very young looking, small and chunky. Baby-fat came to mind.

"I'm Joe Woodman," the bigger one said, "and this is Mel Davidson." We shook hands. I was expecting more about the autopsy request.

He suddenly broke into wracking sobs, covered his face with his hands and mumbled how sorry he was.

"He was a BROTHER to me! A BIG BROTHER!" he moaned. Davidson put a comforting hand on Woodman's shoulder. He couldn't reign it in so Davidson took over.

"Marty brought me and Joe and Gary and Tina in at DBS. He recruited us right out of law school and took the four of us with him when he started GMW. He's been good to all of us. He's been our guiding star. The rock. Now this. It's just not possible." He looked on the verge of tears himself.

They both seemed genuine in their grief and affection for Marty. But the guy back a pace seemed restless, anxious to get down to some business he had on his mind. He stepped forward from what seemed like an invisible on-deck circle, ready to take his first at bat. I had the feeling I was supposed to be the ball.

"Gary Weiselman," he announced. "Sorry about Marty." He looked briefly at Woodman and Davidson with unconcealed distaste. Then back to me. "I hope you'll show up at the office tomorrow as Sandy suggested. We've got to go forward. We've got to protect ourselves. We've got to get you up to speed."

Woodman came to life. "You callous ass. Marty's DEAD! This is his family. The rest can wait!"

"No it can't! You can weep and wail and wring your hands if you want, but I'm not going down in flames! I'm sorry about Marty, but we've got to take care of ourselves now!" Weiselman turned back to me. "Just be there!" Then he eased up a little, "It's important for all of us. You have to see what's at stake. I hope you won't disappoint us. Tomorrow then?" A command.

He was thin and very dark. Very intense looking. Black hair, deep tan skin, and eyes so brown they seemed black, almost no distinction between the pupil and the iris. He was agitated from head to toe. He fiddled with his hands as he talked, working thumbs on first fingers in small circles, fingertips to palms like they had sand that he was ridding himself of a few grains at a time.

"As soon as I can," I said evenly.

He took that like a called strike, eyes going wide, about to protest to the ump, but for whatever reason changed his mind. He gave me a look, then turned and left without a word more.

Chapter 5

I took Sunset back to the 405 and headed south to the Santa Monica Freeway east. It was slow and slower across town. Still hot and muggy. I couldn't imagine living here. This is the way the world ends, I thought, not with a bang or even a whimper, but in gridlock. I finally got off at Venice Boulevard went left to Figueroa and right on Washington.

Washington Boulevard near Figueroa was a black town now. In the twenties and thirties and early forties it was a Jew town. The real thing. Orthodox Jews with long beards, forelocks, yarmulkes, prayer shawls, Hasids in their long black garb and black hats busily going from place to place, mumbling prayers in Yiddish or Hebrew, no one speaking English. Groman Brothers was a holdover from those days. There were only a few Jews on the streets there now, mumbling prayers as they used to, but praying now only to reach their destination unmolested. Jews died and Groman's prepared them according to Jewish law and the State of California, and they were buried in the Eden Memorial Cemetery nearby. At least it used to be near-by. In the late forties and early fifties, after the war, the housing boom in LA made a fifteen acre parcel of land downtown too valuable for the stiffs then occupying it. After much hand wringing and an Eminent Domain suit threatened by developers with City Hall connections, Eden's owners took the money offered and moved, lock, stock and dug-up caskets to a place in the then, nearly empty, hot and dusty San Fernando Valley. Too bad. At least it had been green open space. What they'd built here then was now ugly and rundown, storefronts and a few small manufacturing buildings, most of them abandoned. Trash was everywhere along the street except in front of Groman's. Someone there took the trouble to clean their section of the street and sidewalk. The building was noticeably cleaner than its sooted neighbors.

There were bars over the windows. Probably not against the possibility of someone wanting to get out. It looked fortress-like and forlorn. The religious symbols on each side of the front door had been taken down or stolen, leaving two six-foot-across dark shadows of Stars of David on the wall. The two doors were dark mahogany, carved with a Star of David in the center of each. They were in beautiful condition. I wished I could look at them a little longer and then just leave. There was a bell but I tried the door first and was surprised to find it unlocked. I opened it and went in. There was a bored looking woman of sixty or seventy or maybe a hundred behind a desk.

"May I help you?" she asked.

"I'm here to sign some papers. Kurt Goldman."

"Mr. Kaplan is expecting you. Follow me."

She struggled to her feet and I followed her down a hallway. There were lots of deep red or maybe maroon curtains hanging from the walls, to hide the barred windows, I supposed. The rug was thick and red too. A theme. She knocked on a door and ushered me in. She pulled the door closed behind me. A guy much younger than I had anticipated sat behind a desk smiling at me like I'd brought him news he'd won the lottery. He stood.

"Kurt? Aaron Kaplan."

We shook hands.

"Sit, please." He rummaged through some papers and found what he was looking for. "Normally, if there's a spouse living, they should sign, but I think we can prevail upon the county to accept your signature." He held onto the paper to underscore the favor he was doing me. I had the feeling you get when you walk unexpectedly face first into a huge spider web.

"Good," I said. "Thanks." I reached across the desk and he handed it to me. Grudgingly, like some hold on me was being relinquished. I was scanning it.

"There," he said pointing, "in the middle. Odd place, but that's where you sign and date it." I took a pen from a holder in front of me and signed and dated it and handed it back to him." I shifted, ready to get up and get out. "I've already spoken to the coroner's office. No one has officially identified the body. They can't release it, him, even with this, until that's done."

I don't know what showed on my face, but a wave of dread and despair hit me and for the first time a clear image of Marty's dead body crept into my mind. I tried to push it down, the way you might burp and have something come up by accident, and quickly try to swallow it down. It leaves a bad taste.

"His widow should do that too, but I imagine she's not in any shape for that again. I understand from the coroner that she found him."

That was news to me. Everything was.

"Do you think you could spare her that?"

"Yes." My throat was tight and the word just managed to get out. One word at a time for a while, I thought.

"Do you know where he's being held?"

"No."

"Coroner's Suite, West LA Division; they share facilities with Santa Monica." He wrote while he talked. "Here's the address. There's someone on duty there twenty-four hours a day. If you could manage to get there tonight or very early tomorrow, we could go get him early tomorrow."

I put his card with the others in my pocket.

"Fine."

"I think we should step down to the casket room." There was a note of anticipation in his voice. We were about to kick the tires and look under the hood. We both stood. "They range in price from $1200, our cheapest unit, to, well," he smiled, "almost unlimited." He noticed I was not as excited as he was. "Right this way," he said, very business-like. He led me out of his office, down the hall to a double-doored room at the end. He opened the door with a small flourish, his excitement returning. Inside, the lighting was soft, the caskets displayed with the panache of a classy luxury car showroom. I never did step all the way into the room. In his renewed excitement he'd gone on ahead to a $4800 'unit'. He put his hand on it and smiled at me wordlessly, as if to say, this is the one! Am I right? Hey! Do I know my caskets or what?! It was very nice. Put some wheels on it, and you'd have had something.

I stayed at the door like the room was hexed. "I can't say yet if he'll be buried or cremated."

He was momentarily crestfallen, then recovered a little. "Well, when might we know?" He managed a small hopeful smile, his hands pressed together as though in prayer.

"I'll call and let you know," I said as I backed away from him down the hall. He started to follow me. I held up a hand. "No need, I can find my way out." I left him with the open caskets and his hopes of what might yet be.

It was five forty-five, the sun high and it was still hot out. At least the traffic was beginning to thin. I drove up Figueroa, right on Third Street for a few blocks to Broadway and then right again, looking for 304. When I found it I was amazed and thrilled. 304 Broadway was the Bradbury Building! I hadn't seen or thought about it in thirty years. Maybe more. It was an historic landmark now, a handsome late nineteenth century brick and wrought iron building five stories high, meticulously cared for, survivor of numerous earthquakes, hungry wreckers' balls, and not least of all, me and Nick.

This late in the day I easily found parking in a lot across the street.

I pushed the handsome wood and brass and glass door open and entered the lobby.

For five years before my uncle screwed him out of it, my dad and his brother Bernie had their factory there. They had the offices from 412-422, opened up to one huge space, about ten thousand square feet of cutting tables, sewing machines and pressing tables staffed by Mexican seamstresses. My dad was fluent in Spanish and women. And they loved him. He chatted them up, he flirted outrageously, and he paid them as well as the Anglos. Probably better. Unusual in those days. They knew his was a shoestring operation and because they liked him and because he made them feel that they had a stake in what he was doing, they cheerfully worked against his improbable deadlines and inadequate capital. Not that any of his competition were unionized, none were, but few worked on Saturdays or Sundays or holidays. He did. And so did Nick and I. On Saturdays it was our job to clean up the entire floor. Depending on how much business he'd been doing and how much work the girls had done, it could take us anywhere from two hours to six or seven. I was six when we first started going down with him. Nick was three and a half.

There were wheeled carts with cloth sides about three feet wide and four feet long, maybe three feet deep. We'd push one of those around and picked up all the cloth scraps and cut up templates from the floor. And lots of thread scraps. Whole hair balls of it. When a cart was full Nick and I would push it close to a cutting table, climb up, then take turns jumping off the table into the cart to squish down what we'd collected. And then we'd collect some more and jump into it again. We had a ball. My father was always busy and pretty much just turned us loose. Sometimes some of the girls were there and he was occupied with them, and other times it was just him and us, and he'd try his hand at cutting goods to save money on a professional cutter, or he did office work. We usually only saw him when we first arrived and he told us what he wanted done and again around lunch time when he gave us some money and sent us up the street to a deli and at the end of the day when he came looking for us.

There were other tenants in the building, mostly small manufacturers like my father, and a few salesman representing larger manufacturers, with single offices scattered throughout the building. But few of them were there on week-ends, so with my dad and maybe some of his workers tucked away, Nick and I had the building to ourselves. Except for Chester, the old black maintenance man. If we'd finished cleaning up, or even if we were just taking our lunch time break, Nick and I ran around the building chasing each other, screaming our heads off just so we could hear the echoes. And dropping paper airplanes, tennis balls and string balls gathered from the factory floor, over the railing to watch them drop four or five floors to the lobby.

The building was a five-storied rectangle with the offices around the perimeter surrounding a completely open atrium from floor to sky-lit ceiling. At each end of the long axis there was a large open staircase going up and down the five floors. At each floor there was an eight foot wide walkway that ran in front of the offices all the way around, defining the atrium. The walkways were supported by ornately done wrought iron fluted posts, and they stuck out about six inches past the line of the wrought iron railings. The railings were particularly beautiful and were well anchored to the posts, so that even though they ran the whole length of each floor, the long way and the short way, they were both rigid and delicate. There were two bird cage elevators opposite each other at the mid-way point of the building in the long direction, also beautifully delicate and graceful. From railing to railing across the atrium was probably forty feet. In the long direction, maybe a hundred and twenty. The skylights above spanned that whole area, supported by more of the ornate wrought iron fashioned into roof trusses.

Throwing things over the railings to watch them fall was only one of our tamer pastimes there. With Nick to dazzle and scare, I'd play daredevil. The object of the game was to work my way around the entire perimeter of the atrium on the six inch ledge-like portion of the floor that stuck out past the railing. I'd climb over with difficulty because it was higher than my crotch, and once I had one leg on top of the railing neither foot was close to the floor. I'd ease myself over, hanging on to the top of the railing until I felt my foot touch the little ledge. I'd hold on to the railing and scootch one foot over the other and move hand over hand as I proceeded around. It was tiring and my arms would begin to ache, but a successful run had somehow been defined as not having to climb back over the railing to rest on the walkway itself.

There were three problems to overcome on a successful run. The two elevators and Chester. When they combined, that would end the run. The bird-cage elevators were mounted against the edge of each walkway and stuck out into the atrium so that where the railing intersected the bird-cage there was no more ledge. That meant working my way around the wrought iron lattice work of the bird cage by hanging on with my fingers and wedging in my toes. The trip around the first cage was always exhilarating. By the time I'd worked my way around to the second cage only dogged determination was left.

"You boys cut out that yellin', hear!?" Chester yelled up to us from the lobby floor the first time he heard us. "You don't stop that right now, I tell your daddy to whip your butts!"

We went running off to the staircase to go a floor higher.

"I still see you. You ain't foolin' nobody. Cut that out now, people tryin' to work here!"

After he realized we were a permanent Saturday fixture, he tried to steer the course of our activities.

"You boys need some paper for planes?" he offered. He even showed us several different folds we'd never seen before. Planes that would circle slowly and gracefully from the fifth floor all the way down. We were transfixed by the long slow flights, and more importantly to him, quiet. The first time he caught me going over the rail, he turned white. His mouth dropped open and his lips moved but no sound came out. Maybe he was afraid a sound might disturb me and I'd fall. I'd just gotten both legs over the railing and my toes onto the ledge when I saw him. I stood there and balanced with no hands for a moment, then held the railing and rocked back, pulled myself towards the rail, only to let go and rock back and catch myself at the last moment. I repeated this six or seven times until Nick started crying and Chester started screaming.

"You nuts!? You nuts!?" his voice cut through the building like a factory whistle at closing time. "Mr. Gooooldman!" Mr. Gooooldman!" he called.

Whatever my dad had been doing, his concentration on it was no match for the agitated Chester. He came flying out of 412, stood with his hands on the railing and looked down to Chester in the lobby.

"What the hell are you yelling about, Chester?"

Chester pointed wordlessly up to me hanging on the railing from the fifth floor. My dad twisted around to look up. Since he hadn't seen them yet I did a couple more of my release and catch maneuvers for his benefit. I even waved once before the catch part. I thought I could see steam coming out of his ears. His face was bright red and I knew I was in real trouble because he didn't swear at me. He didn't say anything at all. His face contorted in a combination of anger and fear and he pointed a finger at me that said, don't move. He was up to the fifth floor before I'd clamored back over the railing. He carefully grabbed hold of me by my arms just below my shoulders and when my feet were back on the floor he kneeled down next to me and looked me right in the eye. He was about to spank the shit out of me. I could tell.

"Pretty neat, huh?!" I said.

He sputtered between tears and laughter and squeezed my shoulders so hard I had tears in my eyes. Then he hugged me to his chest so tightly my breathing stopped.

"Don't you ever do that again! Ever!" he both demanded and pleaded. "And don't tell your mother."

I stopped for a while, but soon was at it again. I'd made lots more successful runs before the time Chester actually saw me making one, elevators and all. That was the last time we got to go to the Bradbury Building with my dad.

When Chester saw me he was so shocked he froze where he stood and was unable to make a move to get my dad. He may have been afraid of breaking my concentration by calling out. So he watched. When I got the toe of my tennis shoe stuck in the lattice work surrounding the second elevator it was too much for him. As I was struggling to free it, holding on with one hand so the other was free to pry at my stuck shoe, my hands and arms fatiguing, he was struggling for breathe. He watched as long as he could, I suppose in moral support, until he collapsed in a heap on the lobby floor. One of the other tenants entered the building about then, saw him and tried to revive him and when he couldn't, called an ambulance. I'd finally gotten my toe unstuck and was just finishing the run when they got there. While they were getting Chester on a stretcher, one of the ambulance guys noticed me. He started yelling at me and then the salesman did too. I only had to go a few feet more to get back to my starting place, and with all the difficulty of the second elevator crossing I was determined to finish the run. All the yelling brought my dad out of 412, and brought this and any future high wire acts to an end. He took one look to where I was perched and I heard the familiar deep grumbling sound of trouble coming from him. I didn't wave. But I did finish the run. I was so spent I couldn't immediately climb back over the railing. I stood there on the little ledge resting. To my dad, I was rubbing it in. I might as well have waved.

I was doing this run around the fifth floor walkway for maximum dramatic effect, the distance down to the lobby floor probably seventy feet or more. When my arms stopped trembling from fatigue and I finally felt I could safely climb back over the railing, I climbed into his waiting hands.

And I got the worst spanking I can remember.

I decided to ride up in the bird cage elevator. Walking would have been faster. As it went smoothly and slowly but noisily up, I looked at the little ledges sticking out past the railings of each floor and I looked down the increasing distance to the lobby and hoped Chester had survived that day. I'd never heard.

The building was completely unchanged, except there were no small factories or manufacturing sites there now, just nicely done offices of lawyers and accountants and sales representatives. The elevator stopped with a slight clang and an abrupt short bounce at the fifth floor.

The late afternoon light poured in through the canopy of skylights, dramatically silhouetting the graceful wrought iron trusses. I came out of the elevator through the accordion-like door and instinctively turned right and walked to the corner set of suites to the large double doors of Suite 512-522. I was one floor above the exact location of my dad's old space. I was surprised to see that the owners of the building had allowed even so modest a change as widening the doorways, because it involved removing some of the sacred brick work. But it had been well done and if you hadn't seen the building before you'd never know it had been changed. In thick shiny brass letters screwed to the wood at eye level were the names Goodman Callan Winters and Street. I pulled a strapless wrist watch from my pocket. It was a couple of minutes to six. I tried the door on the right.

Inside was a large carpeted reception area about forty feet across with a couch and coffee table on both the left and right walls and a circular reception desk in its center. It was unoccupied. Behind it and slightly to the left was a glassed-in library. The three walls were lined with books from the floor to a glass ceiling which was supported by horizontal wrought iron joists about ten feet up, designed to look like the trusses above them, and let the light from the skylights pour in to the library during the day. I wondered if it got too hot in there. Slightly to the right, adjoining the library was a glassed-in conference room with a moderate sized oval conference table surrounded by eight comfortable looking tan-leather swivel chairs. The table wasn't huge and it wasn't rosewood or koa or any of the other exotic woods lawyers and accountants and their decorators find so fashionable and necessary. It was a medium light oak, with meticulously inlaid ebony designs around its perimeter. I guessed it had to be at least sixty years old. I went into the conference room, mostly to get a better look at the table. I ran my hands over the inlays. Smooth as a baby's bottom. I got on my hands and knees to look underneath and see how the surface was joined to the elaborately molded perimeter. Mortised glue blocks. I revised my estimate. At least eighty years old, I thought.

"Beautiful, isn't it?" It was the same rich baritone. His pleased look suggested that my crawling under the table to examine it was the most natural thing in the world.

I got up and we shook hands. "John Goodman," he said. "And you're Kurt?"

"Yes. It's wonderful! It must be, what? Eighty years old?"

"Ninety-two. It was made in New York in 1890. There's a little plaque under there somewhere. My dad bought it in the thirties. Had it in his offices over on Spring, just a few blocks from here. When he retired, we moved over here and there was never any question it was coming too."

"When did you move in here?"

"Six years ago. I've admired this building since-I can't remember when. When we had the chance to move, we jumped at it."

I told him about my dad's having been here, just one floor down. I also told him about my high-wire act. He loved it.

"Let's go back to my office. My partner, Bob Winters, stayed to meet you. From what you told me on the phone, this is going to get into areas of the law that Bob specializes in."

As we walked down the hallway I noticed the same wrought iron joists supporting a glass ceiling throughout, allowing the light in from the skylights above. It also provided a view of the sculptural wrought iron trusses.

"Any women working here?"

"Several," he said as we entered his office. "Why?"

Bob Winters was in a wing chair in front of Goodman's desk. He reached up to shake hands as I sat in another like it next to him. He was short and bulldog stocky. He had a Marine buzz-cut about half an inch long. His shirt collar looked three sizes too small, his thick neck ringed by it, his face a deep red because of it.

"Don't they complain about the glass ceiling?"

"No, not so far. Oh! I see what you mean." John smiled.

"Christ, if they thought about it they sure would! We'd never hear the end of it. I'm surprised it hasn't occurred to them. Mary at least," Winters said.

"She's an associate. Very good. Very serious," John said.

"Humorless!" Winters said.

"Doesn't it get too hot in here? With all the skylights and glass?"

"No, it's a special light sensitive glass: the more sun that hits it, the more it screens it out. It works very well," Goodman said. He paused, then took a small newspaper from his desk and handed it to me.

"This is the Daily Journal. It's LA's legal newspaper, much the way Variety is an entertainment paper. I didn't know your brother, but there are long articles in this and Variety about him. He was very well thought of. Well respected."

I glanced at the article. MARTY GOLDMAN SUICIDE. I started to hand it back.

"Keep it if you like," Goodman said.

I put it on the floor next to me.

We spent the next two and a half hours discussing what little I knew and the discussions I'd had and where I needed to go from here. Goodman asked the questions but it was Winters that seemed to take it all in. His complexion reddened more, if possible. He looked like the poster boy for high blood pressure. Goodman told me what he'd need to get started. The highest priority was the original of Marty's will. He said he knew Victor March and the Gravettz firm he worked for. They were good. He said before I met with any of the partners at GMW, he and I should meet with Victor. He said Winters should be with me when I met with any of the partners. Winters seemed preoccupied and unhappy. He hadn't said a thing. He listened intently and the more he heard the less he seemed to like it. He was tapping his fingers furiously on the arm of the chair by the time I thought we were just about done.

"What's the matter?" I asked him.

"This is going to be a god-awful can of worms, that's what's the matter. I can just feel it."

"Now Bob..." John soothed.

"Don't 'Now Bob' me! For Christsakes, you know as well as I do what could happen here-No," he corrected himself, "what will happen here."

"What?" I asked.

John interrupted, "If Tina Cox gave him our number, that's good enough for me."

Winters squeezed his face in his right hand like he could reshape it. Then he rubbed his hand vigorously front to back across the bristle of his hair.

"Jesus!" he mumbled through clenched teeth.

John looked at me benevolently, like a priest granting sanctuary from a howling mob. "What Bob is worried about is how contentious this is

likely to be. The more contentious it is, the more time we spend on it.
And there are rules to probate fees. Set by the state legislature. There
are ordinary fees based on percentages of the value of the estate itself
and then there are provisions for extraordinary fees when situations become complex. The probate court must approve all fees. They are no-
toriously stingy about extraordinary fees. So the more complex it gets,
the less likely it is that you are fairly compensated."

I looked at Bob who seemed ready to throw me to the mob.

"What happens if you guys take this on and it gets complex...or ugly?
Can you just bail out? And then I'm stuck trying to find someone else,
when it's already ugly?"

"Legally yes. But we won't." He looked at Winters. "Right?"

Winters threw his head back against the top edge of the chair-back,
his elbows resting on the arms, his hands steepled above his lap, fingers
drumming. I thought he must be consulting the ceiling, looking for a
way out. Apparently Goodman was the senior partner and there was
none.

"Right," he agreed without enthusiasm.

"How soon do you think we could meet with Victor?" John asked me.

Bob Winters got to his feet. He rolled his shirt sleeves down from
mid-forearm and buttoned them, then got his jacket off a coat rack near
the door and put it on.

"I'm outta here. Kurt?" He shook hands with me, then took a pen off
Goodman's desk and wrote something on the back of a business card.
He prodded me to take it from him. I took it. He pointed to the back of
the card. "That's my home number," he said, "don't even think about
calling me there." "John..." He stuck his tongue out, then said, "I'm
gonna love telling you I told you so."

After he was gone, Goodman said, "He's the best, Kurt, the absolute
best. Ah, about Victor?"

I got one of the cards Victor had given me. "If I can use your phone,
I'll call him now."

He pushed the phone to me and I dialed. On the first ring, Victor
picked it up.

"Were you sitting on the phone?" I kidded him.

"Who is this?" His voice was apprehensive.

"Kurt."

"Jeez, where are you? I've called the house a dozen times. I'm glad
you called. Wolf's called twice and Weiselman and Thorne - you've got
to sign that autopsy request." He sounded frantic.

"Victor, Victor!" I told him to settle down.

"Can you meet me and John Goodman in your office tomorrow morning?"

"John Goodman will handle the probate? He's going to do this? I
know John Goodman!" His voice brightened.

"Yes. Can you meet with us?"

"Absolutely, what time?"

"The earlier, the better." I looked across the desk for confirmation from Goodman. He nodded.

"I'll be at my office at six. I'll need a little time to prepare."

"Victor, what time?"

"Anytime after six-thirty," he said.

"Six forty-five?" I asked them simultaneously. Goodman rolled his eyes, then smiled and nodded yes again.

"Fine, fine!" Victor was suddenly on a high. I was glad someone was.

"See you then," I told him and hung up.

"I hate to sound as stupid about this as I am, but what does it really mean? As executor," I asked.

Goodman had a way of slowing things down and letting them come to rest in a natural way. Round pegs found round holes and square pegs found square ones under his watchful eye. He thought for a moment, looked at me, uncle to favorite nephew, and gave me a brief rundown of the duties and responsibilites of the executor.

"To begin with, you must be your brother, act in his place, a stand-in for all practical purposes. Your first task will be to get the original copy of his last will and testament and any codicils he executed to it, and bring them to us. We will have the probate court duly appoint you as executor. Once that is done, the court will issue letters testamentary, certified copies of which you will use to open a bank account in the name of The Estate of Marty H. Goldman. You will close all of his other bank accounts and transfer the proceeds to the estate account. If he has been doing business as a professional corporation-Victor will be able to tell us that-there will be accounts that will probably have to stay open until issues relating to your brother's corporation are resolved. You must file personal income tax returns for him, corporate ones as well if he has been doing business as a professional corporation; you must marshall all his assets and determine all of his liabilities, and give public notice that he is dead and that anyone who thinks they might have a claim against him, and therefore, now his estate, must file such a claim in the proscribed time before the probate statutes bar them from doing so; you must approve or reject these claims, and submit a list of those you wish to pay to the probate court for approval, and then pay those you intend to honor; give notice of the ones you decline. And once these basic items have been accomplished, it is your duty to impartially carry out your brother's wishes as he has made them clear in his will, if you can. Does that help?"

There was a deep persistent ache coming from behind my eyes and I pressed hard and rubbed the corners of them with the middle fingers of each hand. It might have been just too long a day and contact lenses gone way way past any semblance of comfortable use, but I suspected that that was the least of it.

"How long do you think all this might take?" I asked him.

"Well, it's hard to say. From what you've said, the business side is going to be difficult, maybe even contentious. And I'd really need to see his will before I could judge whether there might be conflicts on the personal side. You said he was divorced from the mother of his two daughters?"

"Yes."

"And he's remarried...was remarried at the time of his death?"

"Yes." He made a gesture of helplessness. "There's really no way of telling, at this point.

"Well, if everything went well, how long? And if it went badly, how long? Just, roughly."

"If everything went as well as it could, at least a year. Maybe a little more."

I felt like he'd just kicked me. When I caught my breath, I asked, "And if it all goes to hell?"

He smiled. The good uncle not wanting to trouble me unnecessarily. Why borrow trouble, my mother would have said.

Cup in hand, I tried again. "What's the longest it's ever taken you to settle an estate, the worst one you've ever had?"

His smile suggested I retract the question. I waited him out.

"Six years."

"Six years!!"

"But that was very unusual." He smiled his best soothing smile and with that rich, deep voice working for him, added, " It won't be anything even close to that, I can promise you. Besides, if it were, Bob would just kill me!" He laughed heartily.

Christ, what had I gotten myself into? I thought of one of the times Marty tried to persuade me to go to law school and I'd smugly told him that no matter how noble your motives, no matter how much money you might make, being a lawyer ultimately meant haggling over other people's problems, and that if I were going to haggle, I preferred that it be over my own. What a snooker job he'd done on me! Wherever he was now, he was having the last laugh.

Chapter 6

It was quarter to nine and my head was pounding and my contact lenses felt like they'd been glued to my eyeballs for a month. They had that dry, achy-itchy feeling that begs you to take them out. When I left the Bradbury Building I didn't know where to go or what to do next. I was drowning in thoughts and fragments of thoughts. People, faces, problems, meanings, and what seemed like subtle and not so subtle threats. I couldn't control the rush of them or sort them and I was completely unable to focus on any one at a time. What finally, intuitively, forced its way into my consciousness and brought some relief, my one and only clear thought, was of the ocean. I had to get to the ocean. Once I got a glimpse of it in my mind the rest began to fade away. So I got back on the 10 heading west. There was no traffic to speak of, by LA standards anyway, and it had cooled a little, and the closer I got the nicer it got. Santa Monica. Will Rogers State Beach. The Beach Club. I focused on them and pictured them each in turn and said the words in my mind like a mantra.

The 10 comes to an end and goes off to the left through an underpass tunnel, heads north and becomes the Pacific Coast Highway. If you go right, it dumps you on 4th Street in Santa Monica. Without thinking I took 4th Street to Colorado then left for a couple of blocks. 4th ends at Ocean Avenue and the Santa Monica Pier.

There's a long skinny park that runs for about a mile from the pier, north along Ocean Avenue. It has tall palms, a slightly meandering jogging path, a width of well groomed grass and some wrought iron benches painted a dark peaceful green. I turned right, driving slowly along Ocean. The park and the palms run along shear crumbling sandstone cliffs above the Pacific Coast Highway, and I could hear the surf, regular as a heartbeat, soothing as a lullaby, as I drove. My headache had disappeared. It was dark enough for the light of the moon on the water to silhouette the palms. The air smelled clean and good. It struck me that if I'd taken the Highway exit instead of 4th Street, I'd have passed The Beach Club and Will Rogers State Beach. I'd have treated myself to thoughts of the

thousand days we'd spent there as kids. But instead I found myself looking at street numbers on the buildings and it dawned on me I was looking for 81436 Ocean Avenue. The offices of Goldman Marshall & Wolf.

It was on the corner of Ocean Avenue and Arizona Street. There was
a café on the ground floor to the left of the lobby, set back from the
street first by landscaping, then outdoor tables. The building was white
stuccoed concrete with stepped-back tiered levels, pyramid style, and
balconies that ran the length of the building on the ocean side across
each of the twelve floors. Maybe half of the lights on each floor were on
but there seemed to be no one there, no one moving across windows or
going in or out of the lobby. The spaces in front of the building were
metered but mostly empty and I parked there. I could smell coffee as I
approached the café and it triggered the hunger I'd either repressed or
just hadn't had time to think about. I was very hungry. There were
more tables and booths inside. Inside and out the place could probably
seat a hundred and fifty or so, and I guessed at lunch time with a building
this size and all the people that must work in it and with the view of the
park and the ocean across the street, it probably did, with plenty more
people waiting for tables or sitting on the low concrete walls that defined
the landscaping. Now, there were eight or ten people outside and about
the same inside. It was set up cafeteria style with a long warming table.
You were supposed to push a tray along a shelf that ran its length and tell
the workers what you wanted starting with breads and salads, then en-
trees and finally desserts and juice drinks or coffee or tea. Only now
most of the pans were empty or being removed for cleaning, and the
salads were limp and desultory. The bread rolls and croissants had had a
long day too. My stomach was less discriminating than my eyes, growl-
ing in protest. There was a separate counter where they made espresso
coffees and the breads and cakes looked fresher. I settled for two brioche,
a café-latte and a piece of apple pie three inches thick. I took these
treasures outside and found a table away from the few other customers.
    The latte was hot enough but had too much milk, too little coffee. Ah
Berkeley, I thought. How I miss you. Can I come home now? I'm tired
and I don't want to be here any more. The brioche and pie were good. I
tried to think only of the food. I looked at my little pocket watch. It was
quarter after nine and I was supposed to meet Tina Cox at ten thirty.
What was the point in coming here? What did I expect to see? What
could I hope to find? I probably wouldn't know it if I saw it, or find it if
I tripped on it. What ever it was. There was nothing here for me to see
or find, not really. I wanted to feel something. I wanted to feel Marty. I
hadn't felt him in the house on Seascape. I hadn't felt him in any one I'd
talked to. Maybe Tina Cox. Maybe. I admitted to myself I'd hoped to
find something of him here. I finished the pie and brioche and only

enough of the latte to wash it down. I stood and took keys from my pocket. I looked at the rental car by the curb, but it wasn't calling to me. In fact, the keys in my hand were not the car keys, they were Marty's.

I entered the lobby. At the back, there was a lit board with the names in alphabetical order of the tenants and the various suites or floors they occupied. I scanned it and found Goldman Marshall & Wolf and across from it, Penthouse Floor. In front of the board was a reception station with one uniformed security guard seated, another standing, looking over his shoulder at something on the desk. The two elevators were on their left. My right. They stood open and ready and I had the urge to run for the nearest one and try to get the door to close before they could stop me. They were both black, the seated man in his late fifties. The other was about forty-one or forty-two and powerful looking. His clothes fit him like they were painted on. Muscle everywhere. He seemed to be in charge. I stifled my urge. He looked up, said nothing for a moment and then smiled perfunctorily. I approached them. In for a penny, I thought.

"The Penthouse," I said matter-of-factly. I made a show of searching through the keys in my hand for the right one.

"Are you expected? I don't think there's anyone there now, is there Gil?" he asked the older guy. They consulted a sign-in sheet.

"No. Everyone's signed out."

"I have an office there now." I'd found a key marked Master and one marked Off. I singled out the one marked Off and raised it to show him.

He stepped forward and looked at the key. I half expected him to grab it from me with one hand and my shirt with the other and demand to know where I'd gotten it. He looked at it and very politely asked for some ID. I showed him my driver's license. He looked at it, then me, then at the license again. He said the name out loud. He handed it back to me and I returned it to my wallet.

"You're his brother?"

"Yes."

His face clouded up with genuine emotion. It seemed odd a security guy would know Marty well enough to have any emotion about him one way or the other. I thought he was going to cry. This guy and Tina Cox and Sandy Marshall had had the only genuine responses I'd seen. And Woodman. Maybe too overwrought and overdramatic, but I credited Woodman with being sincere. And Davidson.

"I can't tell you how sorry I am. He was a hell-of-a-guy. A truly decent man. One in a million." He reached out to shake hands. "Ron Lawton." He looked closely at me, searching for some sign of Marty in me, I thought. "Would you sign-in, please. Everybody coming and going has to." he half apologized.

"Sure," I said. I signed in and put the time at 9:20.

Inside, the elevator was mirror-like chrome all around with thick gray carpet on the floor and a black waffled ceiling with much too bright light coming from each of the waffled recesses.

The door opened with a bong sound, and when I got off at the Penthouse, Goldman Marshall & Wolf in brass letters three feet high greeted me from the wall across from the elevator. Below them, a dark gray granite reception desk curved concavely like arms spread wide to embrace me. It would be a cold embrace, I thought. I looked behind it. In the center was a huge central phone station and a chair for the operator, and to each side of it smaller work stations and chairs identical to each other. On the granite surface facing the elevator in front of the smaller station on the right were brass letters indicating FILM, and on the other side, MUSIC. A house divided sprang to mind. There were several large white couches forming a U shape around a huge glass-and-chrome coffee table. There were a few lights left on for the night in every direction I looked. I prowled the hallway to my right. It ran in both directions, north and south, on the east side of the central reception area with offices and rooms for support services. A copy room with copiers and fax machines and several computer printers in it, a kitchen/lunch room that would seat a dozen or more at one time, with coffee machine and microwave and refrigerator, and then offices marked, Files: Music; Records: Music; Secretarial Support: Music all on the south side, and Files: Film; Records: Film; Secretarial Support: Film on the north side. Most definitely divided.

On the west side and south of the reception area, the hallway was about twelve feet wide, half of that to accommodate secretaries' stations near each of the offices that got progressively larger, starting with one for a Mathew McCord, then A. Bruce Hamilton, then Sanford Marshall and finally what was more of a suite than an office, in the southwest corner, John Wolf. It had a double-doored entry with clear but wavy glass block widows on each side of it. From its position along the hallway and distance from the end of the building, it was at least two times larger than Marshall's space. At the very end of the hallway was a wide single glass door to a conference room. I pushed the door open but didn't go in. There was a blond wood Scandinavian-looking conference table and ten chairs. There were skylights but no windows. No shelves, no bookcases, no file cabinets. There was a side table against the left wall with a multi-buttoned phone on it.

I tried Wolf's door. It was locked. Just for the hell of it, I tried the key marked Master. It fit, and the knob turned with almost no help from me. I went in.

This was the Taj Mahal of offices. The main room was thirty feet across to the west facing windows. It was fifty-five feet long, maybe even more, from left to right. The south end of the building's outside wall returned along the west side for twenty-five or thirty feet, I supposed for structural reasons, but in any case, cutting down the possible glass area that faced the ocean to fifteen feet or less. Where the glass ended another section of outside wall began and ran for about ten feet, where perpendicular to it was the wall that separated Wolf's from Marshall's office. The balcony ran past the room but there was no access to it. The large U-shaped south end of the office was a law library on three walls of handsomely done shelves, closed off by locked glass doors to within two feet of the floor. If you didn't often need access to the books it was probably fine, but then again, if you didn't often need access, why have them at all? Below the glass doors were huge wooden-faced file drawers that coincided with each segment of the book shelves above. Each drawer had a keyed lock. The three-walled library surrounded a desk of a massive irregularly shaped slab of deep red granite, two carved granite gargoyles, hands raised, palms up, heads flattened, all to support it. The three pieces together must have weighed a ton or more. I thought it was beautiful until I noticed the tortured expressions of the gargoyles, which lent it a macabre, Purgatory presence, ruining it for me. The north end of the room had four large white leather couches facing another similar granite slab coffee table six feet square. Wherever possible on the walls hung paintings. Not mounted or nicely framed posters, but real paintings. One huge colorful abstract landscape that I liked and several other brooding abstracts that would unnerve the dead. On the wall shared with Marshall were two doors, one in the middle, and one closer to the hallway wall. I peeked inside the first one. It didn't go through to Marshall's office as I'd thought. It was a huge bathroom. There was a hot tub and clear glassed shower stall on the left, and double sinks with a toilet on one side of it and a bidet on the other to the right. Across from the door was a walk-in closet about eight feet wide and eight feet deep with built-in drawers and shoe racks and tie holders and at least twenty very expensive looking suits. The floor throughout was a light green granite tile, as were the steps going to the raised hot tub and the area surrounding it and the shower. The fixtures were all gold plated.

I tried the second door. It opened on a short hallway that ran the depth of Wolf's bathroom with another door at its end. I opened it. Marshall's office. No bigger than a half of Wolf's, neat, business-like, tastefully but sparingly furnished with modern well crafted rosewood desk, file cabinet and computer station. Fifteen of the twenty feet of his west facing wall was glass, looking out to the ocean, but with no access to the balcony.

I went back to Wolf's office and out to the main hallway, checking to make sure the door was locked. I went back the way I'd come, past the reception area, and past doors marked: Joseph P. Woodman and Melville J. Davidson, Gary Weiselman and Christine Cox. They all opened with the Master key, and they were all pretty much the same size as Marshall's. They were obviously decorated individually, if not by the occupant, at his or her discretion. Woodman's was soft and pastel, Davidson's looked like a student's dorm room at an expensive college. Unlike any of the others, he had framed posters from a host of movies, standards like *Casablanca* and *Citizen Kane*, but he'd gone after and found posters from John Huston's *Sierra Madre* and *The Quiet Man*, and Howard Hawks' *Red River* and John Ford's *The Searchers*. Maybe he was a John Wayne nut. But there were off-beat posters from *Alfie* and *Morgan, Seven Days in May* and *From Here to Eternity*. I decided he was genuinely interested in movies. Film, I corrected myself. Really loved it. Cox's office looked like this was her apartment. Couches and tables and chairs and her desk all comfortable, colorful, but unselfconsciously messy in a busy well lived-in almost organized way. I could imagine her secretary and the building's cleaning people dying to straighten it up for her, but being ordered not to touch a thing.

Weiselman's was a surprise. Like a monk's cell, I thought. Wide, blond, white washed pine planks on the floor, and absolutely nothing on the white walls. There were two desks, and six five-drawer file cabinets, all white washed pine. One desk was really a U shaped affair made up of waist high bookshelves crammed with tax codes and IRS procedures, declarations and rulings, all within easy reach, incorporating a computer station. The other desk had a phone and desk calendar and yellow legal pads arranged and waiting. There was a beer mug with pencils and pens in it.

The last office at this end of the hallway was Marty's. I could tell it was bigger than Marshall's and the others', but nowhere as big as Wolf's. Past it in the northwest corner of the building, there was another conference room, much bigger than the one near Wolf's office. It had double glass doors and when I poked my head inside, I saw an enormous granite table and sixteen leather swivelling arm chairs. The west wall was entirely glass with a ten-foot sliding glass door that opened onto the balcony. The other three walls to the right of the entry doors were lined with bookshelves filled with law books. The room was at least twenty-four feet wide and maybe forty feet deep. On the east wall the bottom thirty inches or so of the bookshelves became wide and deep file drawers, so that they formed a long table top the width of the room. There were phones there and a computer station and a desk top laser printer. It seemed clear this room also served as the main library and research station for the firm. I closed the door and stood in the hallway trying to decide if I really wanted to go in Marty's office or not. It seemed for a moment that if I didn't, I might just leave open the possibility that he was in there working late, that the rest of this nightmare was a mistake. While I was debating it with myself, I heard the bell of the elevator bong as it arrived at the reception area. I didn't know exactly why, more on instinct than anything else, I didn't want to be seen. I quickly let myself into Marty's office and closed the door, easing the latch into place, careful not to let it click shut. I listened at the door and thought I heard footsteps lead away from the reception area, south, towards the MUSIC side. I thought I could hear a door down there opened and closed, but I wasn't sure.

Marty's office stunned me. It was all glass and chrome, clean and cold. There were paintings by nobodies about nothing, pale pastels without rhythm or feeling. The overall effect looked as though it had been done by a computerized decorating service told to spend a lot of money. Expensive and without character. I stood motionless, disturbed and disappointed and vaguely pained. I'd imagined I'd find a sense of him here. I'd hoped to feel his presence. I thought of him working here and another wave of sadness swept over me. I sat in the comfortable chrome and leather swivelling arm chair behind the thick glass-slab desk in the corner to the right. It was eight feet long and four feet wide. An inch thick. It was supported by legs at each end formed from intersecting rectangles of the same sturdy looking glass making an X cross section. There was a phone with fifteen or twenty lines on it, and a battery powered four inch square quartz desk clock, chrome and glass with inset brass pieces held in place by tiny brass screws at each rounded corner. The more I looked at it, the louder it got, the second hand clicking away noisily, until it seemed it could probably be heard all the way down to the lobby. I flipped through a desk calendar with appointments and notes written on it in Marty's firm, graceful handwriting, at an up-tilted angle to the spaced lines, as though he must have reached across the desk to write them rather than bringing the calendar to him and turning it to a more comfortable angle. I looked at the entries for the week. "Monday 8:30 retrn calls to Sykes, AHall re: checks, studio sheets; 10am: Victor; 11:30 Wilder; 1:30 Besser/MP Insur.; Tuesday 10am Faustini/Sutton @ Millennium. Wednesday 10am Victor @ Gravettz; 1pm Besser/MP Insur/ File?" The desk was set caddy-corner to the two walls behind it, in front of low, wide-drawered file cabinets of ash or birch that ran two drawers high, three wide, ten feet long in each direction forming the northeast corner of Marty's office. I tried a couple of them but they were locked. There was a computer on the one behind me to the right. My eyes roamed around the room. Against the south wall on the left side of the door was a couch with coarsely loomed off-white fabric, a matching armchair, deep and comfortable looking, at right angles to it and in front of it another glass-slab coffee table with similar, but shorter legs than the desk. My initial shock at the incongruity of the decor and the Marty I knew finally began to wear off, and the forty-five foot expanse of glass across the west wall, and the huge sliding glass door in the middle of it, sank in and became visible to me. I could see the upper portion of the tall palm trees in the park across the street from where I sat, standing watch, and past them, at the bottom of the sandstone cliffs, the westmost lane of the Pacific Coast Highway and the expanse of sand and the moon shimmering on the calm water. Of all the offices, in this room alone was there access to the balcony. I knew why this room was Marty's.

I knew why they were in this building, across from the ocean, and it pleased me.

When we were kids, this was where we came. No matter how broke we were, my mom would always scrape up enough money for gas for a trip to the beach at Santa Monica. Every day during the summer we'd come to the southern-most part of Will Rogers State Beach, right next to the oldest and most exclusive of private beaches at The Beach Club, the province of the rich and richer Beverly Hills crowd. In the twenties and thirties it had been the beach house mansion of Norma Shearer, and somewhere along the way she and then her estate had taken on partners and turned it into a Beverly-Hills-Hotel-at-the-beach.

"It's the same ocean, the same water," my mom told us.

Except that our side of the twelve-foot high, green-chain-link-and-wooden-slat fence separating the public from the private part of the beach, was without the wooden duck-walks that kept your feet from getting fried when the sand was scorching hot. It also lacked the tennis courts and paddle-ball courts and the tilted Merry-Go-Round and little canvas-backed beach chairs, and the colorful umbrellas that shaded and kept them cool. Our side was without the dark-skinned, hair-slicked-backed young Mexican and Italian guys in dark pants and white jackets serving cold drinks and sandwiches trimmed of crust, for which you didn't pay, just signed. Even the six and seven and eight-year-old kids our age signed. But what their side had that we truly envied was the clubhouse shower-room.

We'd fool around in the water for hours and then crawl through the hot sand like snipers to get warm again, then walk the beach collecting abandoned soda bottles for the deposit so we could get hot dogs and cokes across the Highway at Gert's Hot Dog Heaven. By the time we were ready to go home, we were encrusted in sand. We had it in our hair and in our ears and sand rubbing in the crotch of our swim suits. On the trip home we were usually sun-burned and uncomfortable and we bickered and complained a lot. We used to go back in the water to rinse off, but fooling around would insure that that took at least another hour, even with my mom standing near the water's edge yelling at us to get out, while we pretended we couldn't hear her. So, instead, my mom just rubbed us with a damp, sandy towel, the prime effect being to grind the sand into our sun-burned bodies. Nick was too young and too small to object much, and Sara submitted to it, complaining, but I usually ran. If Marty was with us my mom used him like a bounty-hunter, sending him to track me down and rub me raw. He was fifteen, long legged and gangly, and fast. If I couldn't get a good head start on him, he'd get me every time. But for a while, until we had to move to the Valley and didn't come to the beach as often, I solved the problem.

I'd been in the water trying to body surf like the bigger kids and had drifted south with the current in front of The Beach Club. I hung around, riding small waves with three of the kids from the Club. They all had rubber rafts with The Beach Club logo on them, and the rafts made catching the waves easy.

"Wanna try it?" one of the guys asked me. I wasn't doing very well body surfing.

"Sure," I said.

I caught three good rides in a row and after the last one, out of breath and exhilarated, I reluctantly led the raft by its rope back to the kid.

"Thanks," I told him, "that was great!"

"Why doncha check one out at the equipment window? They got about a million of 'em. Just sign for it."

"Maybe next time." I said.

"Come on, I'll go with ya."

"Well..."

"Come on!"

He left his raft just out of reach of the waves and we ignored the duck-boards and ran across the hot sand to the clubhouse equipment room. It had a dutch-door with a shelf on the top of the lower half. The kid rang a little bell. A black man wearing the black pants and white jacket attire responded.

"What you want, Eric?"

"He wants a raft," Eric said jerking his thumb towards me.

"And who might you be?" His palms were spread and braced as he leaned over the shelf towards me.

"I..."

"He's new here, Fred," Eric said.

I was afraid to meet his eyes. I was about to bolt, just run like hell for good old Will Rogers State Beach when he smiled and shook his head and his voice took on a light musical rhythm.

He said, "My man, my man, my man, you want a red or a blue one?"

"Blue," I mumbled.

"Now just sign for it!" Eric said, "Meet you back at the water." Eric took off to retrieve his raft, leaving me there wondering what I was supposed to sign.

"Seen you over to Gert's 'bout lunch time." He nodded his head in the direction of the Public Beach, squinted one eye at me, "turnin' in collected bottles with a little girl probably your sister. Ain't that right?"

Inside my head a voice was yelling 'run away, run run run', but my feet stayed planted in the hot sand, the blue raft in Fred's hand still seemed possible.

"Well, no matter," he said as he handed me the raft. He put a piece of paper on the shelf.

I looked at the paper.

"What your name?"

"Kurt."

"Just sign it 'Kurt'. Be all right."

I took the raft in one hand and the pencil he offered in the other and signed 'Kurt'. It was easy!

We fooled around with the rafts for another forty minutes and when they got out, I got out. When they went to sit in the beach chairs under the umbrellas, I did too. When they ordered cokes and signed for them, I watched how they did it, and I did it too.

But best of all, after we returned the rafts, when they went to the clubhouse shower-room, so did I. The four of us walked on the duck-boards across the hot sand to the stairs, joking and talking about riding the waves, and went up the stairs and through the door. Inside, everywhere I looked, were white octagonal tiles, bordered and accented with blue ones. On the floor, on the walls, in the shower stalls and around the sinks and toilets. The place was so clean I stopped cold, afraid to walk on the floor with my sandy feet. Eric and his two friends stepped into a recess in the floor to the right of the door. It was sunken about four inches lower than the surrounding floor and it had six little shower heads spaced along its length about two feet high. They each pressed a button on the wall in front of them and the shower heads sprayed water at their feet. They took off their swim suits right there, rinsed them a little and wrung them out. I copied them. They went to another black man behind a counter and handed him their swim suits. He gave them numbered tags on elastic bands that they put around their wrists. He dropped the swim suits down a chute, and they were gone. Then they signed chits and got thick white towels in exchange and found empty shower stalls. I did as they did, worried about getting my suit back, but more worried about doing something wrong and being tossed out. The shower was wonderfully hot and the stream of water thick and strong and embracing. There was a chrome doohickey and when I pushed it a gel-like stuff came out. I smelled it and it was soap! What a place! This was heaven! The other boys were singing and yelling and throwing soap globs at each other over the walls separating their stalls and some old guys told them to pipe down, and they did. I followed them to a locker room where we all dried off. There was a wooden box with wooden slats on top that rocked back and forth when Eric stood on it. A fine white powder poofed up onto his feet.

"Stops athlete's foot," he told me when he saw me looking. "You should do it too."

I did. We returned to the counter and gave the attendant our numbered wrist bands. He gave us back our swim suits, washed, dried, and smelling sweet.

"Wanna come to the game room?" Eric asked me.

"Maybe next time."

"We come almost every day."

"We do too," I told him. "See you tomorrow, maybe."
"I hope so. Bye."

"Man, where've you been!?" Marty said as I returned. "We thought
you drowned. Mom's gonna kill you!"
    "Where is she?"
    "She took Sara and Nick over to the main lifeguard station to make a
report." He noticed how clean I was and dry. And I smelled good too.
"Where were you?" He smiled at me conspiratorially. "Were you at
The Beach Club?"
    "Yes! It's unbelievable! You just sign for everything! Huge towels
and hot water and a thing to keep athletes off your feet! And they wash
and dry your trunks for you. Feel!"
    He touched my dry swim trunks. "Pretty cool. But Mom's still gonna
kill you."

    That summer and the next three until we moved, I became such a
regular at the Club that everyone except Fred assumed we were members. Pretty often I played with Eric and his friends and signed for rubber rafts, but mostly we still played and swam at Will Rogers. But every
day before we left, I'd take Nick by the hand and run the two of us through
the shower-room and we'd be fresh as daisies on the trip home. Sara
learned the ropes too and used the women's shower room.
    From the time he was thirteen or fourteen Marty always had a job,
but he spent most of his days off at the beach with us or with some of his
friends. He and his beach friends were great body surfers and he spent a
lot of time teaching me. He loved the beach, the water, the sun, the
peacefulness and sense of abandon of it as much as we little kids did. I
wanted him to come with me to the Club, but he was afraid he'd be seen
by someone he knew from school who knew we didn't belong. He was
torn between being embarrassed that I was sneaking in, that we didn't
belong, and pleased that I was getting away with it. But more embarrassed than pleased.
    On the other hand my mother thought it was great. It gave her a
peaceful forty minutes or so, alone, to get ready to go, and three kids,
clean, dry, and smelling good, who didn't fight in the car on the ride
home.

    Why did he have to kill himself, I thought? The ugly little clock
click-clacked its way back into my consciousness. It epitomized the es-
sential wrongness here. A wave of pain and loss rose up and tightened
my throat and my eyes started to tear. I couldn't take my eyes off that
clock. I hated it. I just fucking hated it. I grabbed it and went to the

sliding glass door and opened it, thinking I'd throw it off the balcony. I looked to see where I could throw it and not have it land on someone. But while I was looking, the gentle sound of the surf washing up on the sand filtered into my consciousness. It washed over what had seemed like the jack-hammer sounds from the clock in my hand and became the only thing I heard. I had the feeling that whatever it was that had pushed Marty to kill himself, it could have been washed away by that sound. No matter how insurmountable his problems had seemed to him, he had only to open this door and listen. Maybe leave the office, take the elevator down and walk across Ocean Avenue to the steps that descend to the Pacific Coast Highway and cross it to the sand. Take his shoes and socks off and walk down to the water and let the coldness sting his toes and then just stand there and listen to the sound of it. Let it soothe and restore him. Throw that fucking clock in the water and listen to nothing but the waves washing it, whatever it was, clean. It would have worked. I knew it. I tried to make myself stop crying.

I looked south along the balcony. John Wolf's office was more brightly lit than the others. I went back into the office, closed the sliding door and then closed the curtains across the whole glass wall. I checked the time as I put the clock back on the desk. It was 9:50. I turned on a group of lights over the desk and file cabinets and computer. I went through Marty's keys until I found the right one for the file cabinet drawers. I figured I had about twenty-five minutes before I'd have to leave to meet Tina Cox, so I ran through as many of the files as I could to get a sense of what was there.

I started with the drawer labeled GMW. Inside it was further divided into GMW/Partner Shares; /Partners; /Staff; /Office Improvements; and /Office Management. From the first file I found that Marty owned 25% of the firm, Wolf 20%, Marshall 15%, Cox, Woodman, Davidson, Weiselman, McCord and Hamilton each 6 2/3%. There was a Staff Incentive Program that provided that 15% of the Net Partnership Profits would be divided among all of the secretaries and support staff, before the partners took their cuts. The Partnership called for weekly draws against each partner's percentage of the firm's net profits, and was to be adjusted up or down based on actual receipts at quarterly intervals. I scanned the printouts at the back of the general information section. They covered every week from the inception of the firm eighteen months before, up until about two weeks before Marty's death. In one column were the weekly draws for each partner, and in an adjacent column an adjustment figure reflecting over or under-draws against the quarterly postings. Jesus! These guys make the big bucks, I thought. Marty was drawing $10,000 a week before taxes and other deductions, John Wolf struggled to make ends meet with a meager $8000, Marshall $6000, and the lesser lights practically starved to death on about $2700 a week. Maybe

I should have listened to Marty and my mother and gone to law school after all. I flipped through a couple of pages more and noticed that after the first six months or so they were still drawing the same amounts, but there were negative numbers in the adjustment column for all of them. I looked more carefully. It had taken Marty just four weeks to begin adjusting his draw down, first to $8000, then $7000, and finally to $6500 where he kept it for the remainder of the year. By the end of the ninth month, when the third quarterly report of receipts had been posted, he was drawing enough less than his percentage of the profits entitled him to so that he would probably balance out by the end of the year. I skipped forward to the year-end postings. He was in the red to the tune of $4500 and change.

Cox, Woodman, Davidson and Weiselman had been slower to respond, but by the end of the year Cox had a slight surplus and the others were overdrawn in the $1500 range. But Wolf hadn't adjusted at all, and by the end of the first year, he'd posted a deficit of nearly $155,000. Marshall had waited until the third quarter report to cut his draw and had ended the year overdrawn a little under $48,000. McCord and Hamilton had been quicker to adjust and each of them finished the year about $8500 overdrawn. I skipped ahead to the most recent quarterly report. Marty, Cox, Woodman, Davidson, McCord and Hamilton were all caught up and even posting slight surpluses. Marshall had cut his overdraw almost in half to $28,000. Weiselman's overdraw had gotten worse, to $4500, but the killer was Wolf. He had apparently done nothing to ease the flow, and by the end of six quarters he was overdrawn nearly $300,000 worth. I put the file back in the drawer and took the next one.

It contained Financial Statements and four years' worth of summaries of tax filings for each of the partners, including Marty. The dates on the cover sheets were all the same, about a year before the Partnership papers had been signed. They must have submitted this information to each other when they were first considering the partnership. I felt guilty looking through Marty's stuff. I knew he was, had always been, incredibly private when it came to money matters. Generous, but private. The Financial Statement put his net worth at $2.5 million dollars, which surprised me. With the kind of money he had been making for as long as he had been making it, I would have guessed more like $5 or even $7 million. Make a lot, spend a lot, I thought. But Marty had never been like that. He had valued his house at only $400 thousand. I thought $600 thousand was more like it. There were some limited partnership investments, and I figured he probably undervalued them as well. That's what I would have expected from him. Very conservative, very low key and safe. Keep it solid and real. My mother's influence. But when I looked closer, what really amazed me was his debt level. It was practically nonexistent. For a guy that had been making between $350 and $500 thousand a year for a long time, he had a mortgage under $125 thousand, mortgage payments under $1000 a month, lease payments on his car and child support payments for the girls. And that was it. Together, that only came to $2500 a month. He also showed expenses for the gardener, the pool service, and Maria, the maid, along with utilities, which brought his total overhead at home to under $6000 a month. Even on his reduced draw, he made more than that in a week! I thought of my mother again, and smiled, betting with myself that the toilets in his house were unimaginably clean.

John Wolf's numbers told another story. He put his net worth at $3.75 million, but I suspected it was grossly inflated. He'd purchased his home less than a year before the date on the Financial Statement, and unless he put about 65% down, there was no way the numbers worked. His payments were $8600 a month, which meant a mortgage somewhere around $900 thousand. If he'd put 20% down, which seemed a lot more likely from everything else I could see here, it would have meant a house worth about $1.125 million, but he showed it at $2.25 million. From the address of it, I thought, no way. He had a cabin at Arrowhead that he listed as worth $600 thousand, and payments for it of $3000 a month. No stocks, no bond, no limited partnerships, and no cash to speak of. The rest of what he called his net worth was made up of cars and boats, but he had payments on all of them too, so it looked to me that the values were pumped up to give his net worth a boost. What was astounding were the incidental expenses he listed. He must have been a much more entertaining fellow than I found him, because he listed monthly expenses of $8000 for that. And they must never have had a moment's peace over at the Wolf spread with the coming and goings of maids, cooks, gardeners, and the limousine service that together were setting him back $6000 a month. He belonged to a golf club, a beach club, and a health club around town. With all of it, I figured he was running in the red even at the $8000 a week figure. The fact that he was overdrawing against the partnership profits just made it worse. It gave me a suffocating feeling just to read about it. My mother would not have been pleased either.

Marshall listed assets of $2.5 million and liabilities of $1.5 million. He had payments and expenses that totaled $18 thousand a month. The numbers looked realistic to me. He had a house, some stocks and some cash savings. He had three kids in private schools, and his wife was apparently suffering from a medical problem that kept an RN on duty pretty often. He had some wiggle room, but not much, and I liked him for having been able to cut his overdraw as well as he had.

Weiselman was a mystery. Even at $2700 a week, he should have had plenty of leeway. He had a modest house, a wife, one kid in private school and one pre-schooler, no gardeners or maids or cooks, and no regular or on-going large expenses that I could see. With $1200 a month mortgage payments, and some ordinary household expenses, and payments for only one of his two cars, and some part-time child care, it looked like he was spending no more than $3200 a month. Even after taxes, he should be taking home nearly $6000. He should have been able to at least reduce his overdraw, if not eliminate it like the others. Maybe ol' Gary has some bad habits, I thought.

Davidson was where Weiselman should have been. One house, one wife, two cars, two kids, some payments, some savings, some old law school loans not paid off yet. But he was in good shape, and had adjusted to the lowered draw easily.

The others were foot-loose and fancy free. Cox, Woodman, McCord and Hamilton were all single, had a little savings and spent money because they were earning it, probably for the first time in their lives. Cox was buying a small house in Santa Monica. Woodman, McCord and Hamilton lived in expensive apartments, but all of them could cut their expenses to next to nothing without much hardship.

The last file was for one Robert C. Thorne. What was he doing here? Along with his financial statement and tax returns there was a resume. A supplicant, I thought, and from the look of things, an also ran. He had been a Marine during the Korean War, stationed the whole time near San Diego as a military policeman when he was eighteen, nineteen and twenty, then college on a GI Bill, and law school at the University of Wyoming at Laramie. Not exactly the hallowed halls of Harvard. He'd worked for just one firm since law school, doing Personal Injury cases in the LA area, and listed himself as Negotiator / Impasse Resolution Specialist. Marty had drawn a line through that and had written, Nazi Headbasher, instead. Attached with a paper-clip at the top of the page there was a copy of a memo that read, "From the desk of Marty H. Goldman to: John Wolf. Absolutely not. Sorry, John. Marty." Considering his income, it surprised me that Thorne lived in a house in Brentwood, only a few blocks from Marty's place on Seascape. But further down, I saw title to it was in a woman's name, probably his wife. She went by her maiden name, which was Greenwell, the same name as the firm Thorne had worked for at the time he applied for a place in the embryonic GMW. I looked at the card he'd shoved into my shirt pocket. He still worked there. He made about $85 thousand a year working for his wife's old man. Considering the rookies at GMW, working with the gliteratti of Hollywood, had been making more like $140 grand a year before they had to cut their draws, it was no wonder the forty-eight year old Thorne had had figurative and literal stars in his eyes. I pictured him a knuckle-dragging, thick-browed goon like Rudolph Hess to Wolf's Club Med Hitler.

I put the file back and took out the one marked, GMW: Office Improvements. I scanned the first page. It allocated $675,000 for Reception area, Conference Rooms, Library and support staff room improvements and equipment, and $25 thousand for each of the lesser partners, and $35,000 for Marty, Wolf and Marshall to decorate their offices. It provided for a 5% contingency. Monies saved could be kept. I thought of Weiselman. There was also an allocation for an Opening Party in the amount of $15 thousand. So I figured with the contingency money the whole shooting match came to $987,000.

I put the file aside and called Marty's house. Sara answered.

"Hi, how's it going?"

"Kurt!! Where are you?" She shifted her voice to low and quiet, and said, "That guy Bob Thorne came back and has been here with Roberta all evening. The phone rings all the time, some of it condolences, but mostly John Wolf and Gary Weiselman for Thorne. What's going on?"

"I'll tell you later. I called to ask if you would contact that guy Rabbi Krasznik. This is getting complicated and I'm going to be busy all morning, maybe all day tomorrow."

"What do you want me to do?"

"Ask him if he can do the service. Find out how he wants to go about it. Tell him I'll be in touch with you by early afternoon to find out what he needs. I'll take care of the money. Could you do that?"

"Of course."

"Thanks. That'll be a big help."

"What day?"

"Let's plan on Sunday afternoon. See if he's available then."

"What about..."

I could feel her composure slipping away. She was taking a few calming breaths.

"...an autopsy. That's all Roberta and Bob Thorne talk about. Won't that delay a funeral?"

"Let's plan the service for Sunday, okay? We'll see about the rest"

"Okay."

"Thanks. I'll call you tomorrow."

"Kurt? Be careful."

"What do you mean?"

"Just be careful. The tone here is kinda mean."

We hung up. I would have said sleazy. Mean gave me pause.

I took up the Office Improvements file again. I'd forgotten that Roberta had had pretensions of Interior Decorating. Marty had let her do his office. I looked around, and smiled. The things people do for love. She'd gone over-budget by $4000. There were six drafts from a GMW Improvements Fund that totaled the $35 thousand, and a photocopy of a check Marty had written for the $4000.

Weiselman had spent $6500 and pocketed the rest.

The others had stayed under-budget by amounts ranging from a thousand or fifteen hundred to $3500 for Hamilton.

Wolf, of course, was something else. On top, under one of those prong and clasp things that hold files together, there were drafts that

totaled $48 thousand from the fund. There were copies of memos from
Marty to Wolf and answering memos from Wolf to Marty that started
out friendly enough, but became terse and impatient on Marty's part,
and at first cavalier and dismissing from Wolf, but then nasty. Maybe
even mean, I thought. I browsed through the sheaf of photocopied bills
for Wolf's office. It was far too thick, and there were far too many expensive ones for $48 thousand to cover it. I wondered how Wolf had
gotten drafts in excess of the $35 thousand in the first place. Who in the
hell had administered the Improvements Fund?

I got the file marked Office Management and flipped through it. There
were copies of computer print-outs for salaried staff disbursements, dis-
ability insurance payments, federal and state withholding payments, and
payments of rent and parking to the Pyramid Group that managed the
building. There were printouts for the Office Improvements Fund. All
of the printouts listed, Warner Warner and Carpenter, An Accountancy
Corporation, at the top. A first batch of disbursements came to $48,790.
Then a single one for $4800 that said, 'Demo', in the lower left hand
corner. Then another string of disbursements that totaled $58,000. What
the hell was going on? I flipped back and forth trying to see if what I
suspected were true. Then I found the memo from Marty I was looking
for.

"From the desk of Marty H. Goldman to: John Wolf. John, this is
outrageous. It's come to my attention that not only have you gone over
your capital improvement allocation as we've previously discussed, but
you've torn out what you've had done and are re-doing it! I'm instruct-
ing WWC to re-pay the Fund everything over $35,000 from your part-
nership profit allocations over a sixth month period. Marty."

I looked, but couldn't find a response from Wolf.

There was a letter from Marty to a Jeff Larson at Warner Warner and
Carpenter telling him that Wolf's draws should be reduced by $3,200 a
week for the next twenty-four weeks beginning immediately.

There was an evasive reply from Larson, outlining how long the firm
had worked for Wolf and Marshall before being invited to do the accounting for GMW, and how excited they were about this new relationship, but cutting through the bullshit, they were telling Marty that any
reduction in Wolf's draws would have to be approved by Wolf himself.

There was a memo from "The desk of John Wolf to: Marty -Take it
easy, everything's under control. John."

The dates on these letters put them before both the first and second
quarterly profit report and the onset of the negative numbers. Even if
Marty couldn't force Wolf or WWC to reduce the draws, there should've
been negative numbers reflecting his decorating and re-decorating she-
nanigans by the first report. I already knew there weren't. So, along
with the $300 thousand Wolf owed in over-draws, there should have
been another $75,000.

The printout for the opening party was dated 3/31/81 and showed bills for $31,200 had been received and paid, $16,200 over the allocation that had been agreed on in the partnership papers. Marty's first memo asking WWC for an expense report on the party was dated 4/5/81, a month and a half after it had taken place in February. There were copies of half a dozen memos and phone pad notes throughout April from Marty to his secretary, Ronnie, reminding her to call WWC about the report.

By the second Friday in May, he'd written memos to Ronnie and John Wolf, "If I don't have the expense report from the office party by next Monday, WWC will cease to be the accountants for GMW. Marty." The printout had a memo from Wolf attached, dated May 21, "Sorry, this has been in Miriam's desk. WWC sent it to me weeks ago. I didn't realize you wanted a copy. We ran over, but it was a Grand Opening! Everybody was impressed! John." The printout was accompanied by photocopies of the invoices with Wolf's signature and approved for payment scrawled across all of them.

Marty had placed check marks next to the amounts in one column and on the invoices themselves, reconciling them. At the bottom he had written, "$21,200. Where's the other $10,000?" There was a copy of a memo Marty had sent to WWC on June 3 asking for an explanation.

There was a letter from Larson at WWC dated June 30 saying they were investigating and would send him all the details when they had them.

At the bottom Marty had written, "Victor", and underscored it heavily. Below that there was a memo to Ronnie, "No more hard copies to file on any GMW matters! Do not save anything RE: GMW on your hard disk. Save on floppy and I'll copy to my computer. NO ACCESS TO ANYONE!"

The second quarterly report showing the negative numbers must have arrived within a day one way or the other of the WWC letter and this memo. Some fun.

I wondered when Marty had time to do legal work for his clients.

I checked my watch. It was 10:10. I had to get going to meet Tina Cox, but not before I checked Marty's computer. I swivelled the chair around and turned it on. At the C prompt I typed in DIR and got a list of everything on the hard disk. Clients Directory, Projects Directory, GMW Directory, DBS/Studio Sheets, probably the files I'd been looking through, and, alphabetically, a directory labeled CODED.

I tried cd\Marty and got INVALID PASSWORD for my efforts. I tried MHG, M. Goldman, and M.H.Goldman, but came up empty. I figured I would ask Ronnie when I met her, but I suspected she wouldn't know either. I went through the names of his girls, combinations of initials, my mom and dad, me, Sara, Nick, birthdays that I could remember and his anniversaries. Nothing.

I shut it off and took a quick look through the remaining file drawers. In each there was file after file on clients and projects. In the bottom drawer on the far right were phone books and a small flat briefcase. I locked up the file drawers and turned off the lights over the desk and re-opened the curtains. I went out on the balcony and saw that the light was still brighter in Wolf's office.

I went quietly to the elevators and pushed the button. When it arrived and announced itself with the telltale bong, I got in and quickly pushed the door close button. I heard an office door open, and what I thought was Wolf's voice saying, "Is someone there?" as the doors closed.

In the lobby only Ron Lawton remained. He looked up as I approached.

"You need me to sign out?" I asked.

"Yes, thanks." He offered me the clip board.

I looked at the signature below mine. It had been John Wolf.

Lawton watched me and said, "I signed in for him to save him the trouble." His look held mine.

"Thanks. I'll probably see you tomorrow," I said.

"Anything I can do, you got it. Anything," he said.

I got to the lobby door and turned back to him. "Do you know a place in Venice called Sandy's?"

"Sure, it's on Main, somewhere near Marine or Rose. Go out Ocean and look to your left for Main. That help?"

"Yeah, thanks. I'll find it."

Chapter 7

I made a U turn on Ocean Avenue and headed south. Just past the pier, Ocean becomes Neilson and a few blocks later becomes Pacific Avenue at the city line between Santa Monica and Venice. Like Ron had said, I could see Main running parallel to Pacific one block to the east. It was only a couple of blocks to Marine. I turned left, then right on Main, still heading south. The stores and shops got hipper and the restaurants less café. I remembered Venice fondly as bohemian and grunge and slightly unsavory. Gentrification respects no boundaries, let alone memories. I knew I must be close. The parking spaces on both sides of the street were filled. Sandy's was on the west side. I turned right on Rose expecting to go around the block, but found a public parking lot behind the storefronts, meters and all. The sign read, Meter Hours 10am to 4pm. Definitely not Berkeley. I parked as far to the north as I could and walked back on Marine to Main.

Sandy's couldn't make up its mind between being something like the old Ratskeller at Larry Blake's with a decent jazz trio, sawdust on the wooden floors to absorb spilled beer, booths, and a bar complete with brass foot-rail, or some swankier fraternity hang-out like Henry's in Berkeley, or just about any college town, with a good measure of fern-bar thrown in. They'd covered it all, and judging by the clientele, it worked. There was a small blue collar crowd as well as a smattering of college kids, and a lot of the young professionals like Tina Cox; some left-overs from Venice's happy hippy and Beat days, and the nice quiet well mannered types good jazz usually brings out. I was taking all this in and not really looking for Tina when I noticed her in the front corner at a small table under a few hanging ferns.

She was lost in thought as I approached her table. She looked up at me and then at her watch.

"10:30. Right on time. I would have bet on it."

"Same mother. Can I get you anything?"

"Another chardonnay."

I returned with her wine and a Dos Equis and shot of vodka.

"I thought you didn't drink."

"It's been a long ugly day."

"I'll bet."

"I met John Goodman. I've got a good feeling about him. Thank you."

She smiled for the first time. She was really very good looking. She was wearing Levi's and a man's white T-shirt. I glanced under the table. Sandals. She was one of those people who looked right no matter what they wore or where they wore it. She watched me while I looked.

"Everything okay?" she said with a raised brow.

"Just checking." I took a sip of the vodka and a sip of the beer.

"An interesting approach." She put aside her first glass and took up the one I'd brought. She was more than good looking, beautiful actually, but wounded and drained. "John's the best. So is Bob Winters. Winters is the one you're going to need."

"Have you been to their offices?"

"No, not since they moved."

"They're in the Bradbury Building. Do you know it?"

"No, but I've heard about it"

"You should go see it - they've kept it exactly like it was, but modernized it at the same time - it's gorgeous!"

"You know it? From before going to see John?"

"My dad had his office and factory there in the fifties. Nick and I used to clean up on Saturdays and play there."

"Marty?"

"He was already working at after-school jobs by then. He was eight years older than I am. He probably worked for my dad when he was younger, but I don't remember it."

I took another sip of the vodka and beer. "Do you want to begin, or should I just ask questions?"

"Do you know enough to ask questions?"

"How about, why'd he do it?"

Her hands tightened around the wine glass and she looked at me with hardened eyes. She couldn't hold it and her eyes began to water. "I don't think this is a good idea. I can't do this." She started to get up but I grabbed her wrist.

"Goddammit, sit down. Please."

She did. She looked at me both hurt and surprised, but also with some amusement. "That was very un-Marty like."

"Different fathers."

"Really?"

"No, not that I know of, anyway. But there's been talk."

She smiled.

"You said you'd help me. I can see I'm going to get nothing but grief from everyone else, so I know now how much I need your help. What was going on that you think was serious enough to cause this?"

Her eyes softened. I wished for Marty's sake he had slept with her. It was unlikely. My intuition told me she not only admired him, but had a crush, maybe even loved him. I have this great, infallible intuition. Once in a while, I'm even right. But with Marty, it would have been out of the question. I'd like a shot at it. My brother's dead one day and I'm thinking about getting into the pants of a woman that had a crush on him. Some guy. I smiled at my enjoyment of the procession of my thinking, like seeing your reflection in opposing mirrors.

"What's funny?" she asked.

I just shook my head, like, it's nothing, or never mind.

"What?" she pressed.

"You don't want to know."

"I want to know." She was serious. At least she thought she was serious.

"I was just thinking that I wished Marty had slept with you." I left out the part about me.

"What?! Where do you...what makes you think..."

"Intuition. I meant it as a compliment. I think you're trustworthy and bright, and there's no pretending you're not good looking. I think you cared for Marty. I think Marty would have known those things and they would have helped him. Even if it had been only once. I think he needed a friend. Someone close. I don't think he had that. But I don't think he would have let himself."

She had began by looking at me as though from some amused distance, but now sat rigid, stricken with renewed grief. Her eyes overflowed with tears. At first she made an attempt to brush them away, then gave in to it. She bit her lip to stop its trembling.

"You're right," she said finally. "And we didn't. We never got personal in any overt way. Never touched, never hugged or even kissed like brother and sister. But the feelings were there. I know they were. Dammed up." I sipped at the vodka and beer and let her take her time. She calmed herself. "We worked well when we worked together. Which wasn't that often. He worked more closely with Gary. A lot with Woodman and Davidson, but mostly with Gary. Those three had specialties and Marty brought them in to hammer out and refine deals he'd worked out for his clients. He had me develop deals of my own, clients of my own. Marty recruited the four of us when he was at DBS. From the very beginning he moved some of his clients over to me, women to begin with, but some of the older men, who were less active. He gave me a chance to work difficult deals where the clients were no longer hot. At first I thought it was the same old game, you know, where I wasn't going to be taken seriously because I'm a woman. I confronted him about that and he was shocked. He said of the four of us, he thought I had the best chance of being a deal maker. A rain maker. And he wanted to train me for the day he left DBS to build his own firm. Was I interested? You can't imagine how excited I was. Marty is...was...not only the best, but the most creative, and best of all, honorable, truly decent in a business where honor no longer exists and decency is unheard of."

She sipped her wine. She smiled at me. "I love to talk about him. I've never had anyone I could talk to about this."

I'm pretty fucking honorable too, I wanted to tell her. And creative?! You should see what I do! She looked so warm and lonely. Maybe in another lifetime. I smiled and she went on.

"Everybody at the office assumes it's about the Danny Sutton deal. Do you know anything about it?"

"No," I said.

She took a deep breath. "It goes like this. Sutton is a long-time client of Marty's. He's a producer who's done some good work, or at least work that made everybody a lot of money. He was in the right place at the right time if you ask me. And I don't think Marty liked him. I don't know how or why they got together in the first place, but I know it goes way back at DBS. He hadn't done anything for a few years and was complaining about it. Then he was offered a movie at Millennium. Just one. He wanted to grab it, but Marty told him to hold back. For some reason Millennium really wanted him and Marty was able to put to-gether an incredible eight picture development package with a money guarantee whether any pictures got made or not. Then Millennium was bought by Garvin Perry. Do you know who he is?"

"I've heard the name."

"He's an oil tycoon from Houston. Unbelievably rich. Pictures him-self a modern-day Howard Hughes. Decided he wants to rub shoulders with the movie crowd instead of the Arabs. So he bought Millennium. There have been rumors that follow him around about mob connec-tions, but I've never seen them confirmed. But he's used to getting his own way. Millennium had had a string of expensive flops and they've been in financial trouble for some time, one of the reasons Perry got the deal he wanted for the studio. When he and his boys took over they started looking for ways to cut expenses, deals like the one your brother had made for Sutton jumped out at them. They tried to break the deal, tried to intimidate Sutton, went so far as to threaten to blackball Marty and his clients from all Millennium projects if they wouldn't renegotiate. Sutton was scared and wavered. Marty was outraged at both the reneg-ing and the threats of blackballing his other clients. If he caved in, it would put him in a terrible position around town. Marty's reputation was at stake. Perry acts and thinks like some union-busting thug from the thirties. Maybe he is connected, or just likes to act like it. But what-ever it was, Sutton got the message and wanted Marty to get him what he could, but get him out of the line of fire. His caving-in left Marty in an awful position. He had to do what his client wanted, but it looked as if Marty was caving in to Perry's intimidation. It was supposed to be a one-time cash buy-out of the Sutton deal, but it was a lot of cash, and that meant huge tax considerations. That's Gary's specialty. Marty and

Gary and Mel worked over the deal with a man named Lyle Faustini, a leftover from before Perry bought Millennium. It was Faustini who'd cut the deal in the first place, and had it all on the line with Perry if he couldn't get it renegotiated. It got nastier and nastier, but they finally had it structured so that everyone was satisfied. Millennium would save $2 million. Sutton would get this huge buy-out. Marty and Faustini reviewed and approved a draft copy and Millennium prepared the final contracts. They were sent to GMW, directly to Gary, for review, since the tax considerations were crucial. Gary approved them and sent them directly to Sutton for his signature. Marty should have reviewed them first, but for some reason Gary sent them on directly. By that time Sutton was so scared and anxious to get Perry off his back he signed them and sent them directly to Millennium."

She got up and stretched. Nice body. "Want anything? I'm going to get another."

"Another beer and another shot." I reached for some money, but she waved it off.

When she came back she had a basket of warm sourdough. "Want any?"

"Thanks, I'm starved."

"When Marty learned that the contract had gone to Sutton without his review and that Sutton had signed and sent it to Millennium, he was angrier than I've ever seen him. I'd never heard him yell at anybody about anything, but he was furious with Gary, furious with Ronnie Hook, his secretary, and furious with Faustini at Millennium. He was worried, and even though he didn't say so, I knew he smelled trouble. When he talked to Sutton, Sutton was too relieved to be concerned. When Millennium sent GMW copies for our files, Marty's worst fears were confirmed. The signed contract had left out provisions that had been in the drafts. And they had immense repercussions for Sutton. The tax treatment would save Millennium another $800,000 and cost Sutton almost as much. When Marty told Sutton he went nuts. He called Marty at the office a couple of times the first week to find out if Marty had gotten Millennium to restore the missing tax provisions, but then when there'd been no progress in the talks with Faustini, he got frantic and was calling eight or ten times a day at GMW, and god only knows how often at Marty's house. This went on for weeks, always abusive, drunk or sober, while Marty tried to get Faustini to re-draw the contracts as they'd approved the drafts. Faustini and Perry sat tight. Sutton got another attorney and is suing GMW for three million dollars."

This and Wolf. Some fun. I must have looked skeptical.

"What?"

"Tell me about John Wolf."

"What about him?" she said cautiously.

Her guarded reaction worried me but I decided I had to trust her. I supposed I did anyway. "His overdraws, his office improvements, the grand party. All of it. And Marty."

She sat back re-appraising me.

"You have been busy, haven't you?"

"Not as busy as I plan to be."

"What do you mean?"

"This whole thing smells. Something's wrong here. I don't know what, but I can feel it."

"Intuition?" she asked with an innocent smile.

"Absolutely," I said.

We both reached for the sourdough and our hands touched. It sent a small electric jolt through me. She didn't seem to notice. More's the pity, I thought. My head was spinning ever so slightly. My resistance to alcohol was non-existent.

"Wanna walk on the beach?" I asked her. "I gotta get some air."

"Sure." She didn't laugh out loud but had a smirky smile that was just as bad. "Bottoms up," she said and tossed down the last of her wine.

"Right," I said. Most of my second round was untouched. I dumped the vodka into the beer glass and drank it down. Stupid, stupid, stupid, I thought, knowing I'd regret it.

We walked along Main to Rose and then three blocks down to the beach. Neither of us talked. The moon still shone brightly on the calm water. Other than Marty being dead, it was a pretty nice night, I thought. I could say something like that to Nick and we'd both find it funny and sad and heartbreaking in the same way. I wondered about Marty. I hadn't been around him enough to know if underneath the warm but seriously adult exterior he shared the same skewed sense of humor. Then I wondered about Tina.

"Except for Marty's being dead, it's a pretty nice night," I offered.

She stopped walking and I got a couple of steps ahead. I turned to look at her. Her hands came up as though to ward off a blow and her face went in a second from shock to outrage to a gasping laugh. She started to laugh but it got caught up and confused with crying and she sat down with her face in her hands and wept. She looked up at me and shook her head. I took it as a good sign that she had a small smile on her face.

"Sometimes it's hard to believe you're his brother."

"That's what I was afraid of."

"What do you mean?" She got up slowly and wiped tears from her face and drew in a deep breath and sighed it out. We walked again.

"Everything's too serious. I can't believe Marty was that different from me and Nick. That he buried the silliness and playfulness."

She smiled, "Not always."

I turned to her, "What?"

"Five or six years ago, when I'd first come to DBS, his daughters were in the reception area, meeting him for lunch I think, and when they came out of the office to the elevators, I was waiting for the elevator too, he was just being silly with them. It seemed so natural and so out of character at the same time. I think the nicest part was that when he saw me he didn't seem embarrassed. And he didn't stop, either."

I could feel tears well in my eyes. What a waste, I thought, as another wave of pain and anger gripped me. I was on the water side of the path and looked away from her.

We'd been walking along the concrete bike and rollerskating path that runs parallel to the water, close to the parking lots, from Venice Beach right up to the Santa Monica line. After Sandy's, even the slight hint of a cooling sea breeze felt good. I stopped and took off my sandals and stepped off the path. The sand was cool and soothing. She took off her sandals too, and we headed down to the water. She took hold of my hand.

"John Wolf," I said.

She let go of my hand. I have a way with women.

"John Wolf. Before you can understand Wolf and GMW, you have to know about Marty at DBS. Do you?"

"Not much, just that he'd been with them right out of law school and had a lot of famous clients and he made a shit-load of money."

"All true," she smiled, "but the important thing was that Marty had carried the firm for some time. The name partners, Diamond, Bernstein and Silver were all retired or semi-retired, and the younger guys like Barry Malovitch and Larry Klein and George Zeffaro were really just coasting. They all had clients, and money came in from their deals, but without Marty's work, they would have been just another LA firm doing okay. It was more and more obvious to everyone, all around town, and everyone expected Marty would bolt. But he had this loyalty, maybe even an unreasonable gratitude towards Silver, and knew that if he left the firm would sputter and maybe die. Silver had recruited Marty, and had gotten him started. Year after year they gave Marty a larger percentage of the partnership profits, but it wasn't the money he was after. He wanted the recognition. He really wanted his name on the door. A visible sign that the reason the clients and the money came through it was his presence. It had become his firm, and everyone knew it. He wanted it to be Diamond Bernstein Silver and Goldman. They turned him down and upped his ownership percentage again. Marty later told me they'd adjusted the numbers so that Diamond, Bernstein and Silver each held an 18% stake in the firm, Marty 16%, and Malovitch, Klein and George Zeffaro had 10% each."

"What about the rest of you?" I asked. "Weiselman, Davidson, you and Woodman?"

She smiled. "We were salaried. A good salary, but no percentage.

Not really. Besides working with Marty, getting a percentage was a great incentive for us to come with him to GMW. The outrageous thing was that Marty accounted for at least forty or forty-five percent of the billings. Anyway, Marty stewed about their decision for a couple of weeks. He was hurt. Especially when he found out that Silver had voted against it. That's where John Wolf comes in."

We'd walked under the Santa Monica Pier.

"Want to keep going?" I suggested. "I'd like to see something."

"Sure. As far as movie deals, movie directors and producers, actors and the studio people were concerned, Marty was the best. The most reliable, the guy that could get it done. If he were involved, it would happen. His influence was enormous. Did you know that he'd been offered the top slot at two different studios in the past five years?"

"I heard about one. Two years ago, in the fall; he was coming up north on Fridays to teach an entertainment law course at Stanford and we had dinner and he told me. Actually, he sounded interested."

"Really?"

"Yeah, it was the only time I'd ever heard him sound tired or bored with his work."

"What did he say?"

"That the deals were always pretty much the same. That the names and faces changed, but the fun had gone out of it because the scramble for the money was overshadowing the desire to do the work, even among the most creative and talented people. Something like that. He said it's a sewer now, a fancy expensive one, but a sewer just the same. Time for a change."

"But the studios are just the other side of the same deals."

"Maybe. Maybe he had something else in mind. It was the creative aspect of things that got him excited when we were talking. The offers from the studios interested him he said because he'd be in a position to decide what projects got done. He must've decided it wasn't there at the studios after all, and that's why he turned them down. I wish he'd made the change."

We were even with 81436 Ocean Avenue. I noticed Wolf's office was no longer brightly lit, but Marty's was. I didn't think she noticed anything unusual about the lights, but she definitely caught me looking.

"What?"

"Back to John Wolf."

She looked at the Penthouse Floor, then at me. "There're always lights on at night," she assured me.

"Hmmm...." I raised my eyebrows to say, that so?.

"Wolf. John Wolf is to music, musicians, recording producers and recording companies what Marty was to movies. All the biggest names were in his stable. All the biggest recording deals, all the biggest tours, everything happened through his office. The difference was that with Marty, you couldn't have found a soul who could honestly say he treated them unfairly or dishonestly or say he'd made promises he didn't keep. It just never happened. Marty was skilled and tough and demanding and unbelievably thorough, but never the slightest bit underhanded."

"Like a good chess player."

"Exactly."

"And Wolf?"

"He takes no prisoners. Slash and burn all the way."

"So what ever possessed Marty to get involved with him?"

"I think it was because he was stymied by Diamond Bernstein and Silver, and with what you say about him taking the offer from Paramount seriously, I'd have to say his desire to get the recognition he deserved overshadowed any misgivings he might have had about John. It must have overshadowed the excitement he might have felt about the creative possibilities heading a studio offered."

"But why Wolf? Marty must have been aware of his reputation. Wolf sounds like the worst possible example of Marty's complaints."

"He is. But with two rain makers like Marty and Wolf, in different but complimentary areas of entertainment law, GMW seemed guaranteed to not only succeed, but to dominate. To be the only real game in town. To..."

"To what? Punish Diamond Bernstein and Silver?"

"Maybe. Probably." She looked unhappy and slightly ashamed, like she'd been the first to tell me there's no Santa Claus. Or maybe it bothered her he wasn't a saint.

"Who sought out the other?" I asked.

"I don't know. Why?"

"Just curious. Did they get along in the beginning?"

"If you asked Gary or Joe Woodman, they'd probably say yes."

"But not you."

"No. It seemed forced and antagonistic."

"For instance?"

"For instance the beach."

"What about it?"

"Marty said he was going to move to the beach. No one thought he was serious. Particularly Wolf."

"Why?"

"It's twenty minutes away from town and the center of things. Forty or forty-five minutes if traffic is bad. And it usually is. And worse if you're coming from Pasadena or La Cañada or, god forbid, the Valley. The people we deal with are a pampered bunch and don't like to be inconvenienced. They don't like anything except to be pampered. Marty wasn't suggesting it. He made it clear he was going to set up shop here. If that was a deal breaker for Wolf, so be it. He'd open up alone. Well, with me and Gary and Joe and Mel. I loved the idea. Marty was the only guy in town that could get away with it, and for some reason it was important to him. So it was non-negotiable. I found a little house nearby, so commuting's not a problem for me."

We were in front of The Beach Club now. It hadn't changed a bit. Same bright white building and blue canvas awnings. Same paddle-ball and tennis courts. Even the stairs to the shower room, and the duckboards were unchanged. The sand was clean and well groomed. They used to drag a big wire mesh thing behind an old army jeep to screen the sand clean. From the look of it I supposed they still did. The water was probably more polluted now, but it looked the same. Same ocean, the same water, I thought as we came to the tall green fence that separated The Beach Club from Will Rogers State Beach. The Merry-Go-Round was still the slightly tilted metal one of thirty years ago. I walked across the sand and sat on it. Tina sat next to me.

"We used to sneak in here."

"Who did?"

"Me mostly, but Nick and Sara too."

I told her about our being broke and about going to the beach and my adventures with the rich and privileged, about signing the chits and never knowing what happened with them, about all the hot showers and clean towels and going home in freshly laundered trunks. She savored the story, thought it was great. Then the thought hit her.

"Not Marty!?"

"No," I laughed, "he was too embarrassed to. He was embarrassed by my doing it. Tell me about Wolf's office improvements and the office party and his overdraws."

"What do you know about that, and how? That's confidential."

"I'm a partner now, technically the senior partner. As far as GMW is concerned, I'm Marty."

She looked at me, trying to decide if I were serious or not.

"I was in Marty's office before I met you tonight."

She mulled it over for a minute, came to a decision, and told me, "Wolf wanted Marty more than Marty wanted him, so he gave in about the beach. In fact, started acting like it had been his idea. Marty found the building, wanted the penthouse and his corner office, but after that let Wolf take charge of the improvements. Those kind of details were not things Marty would care about or want to spend time on, although I heard Roberta had wanted Marty to insist that she be the decorator. Wolf loves the glitz and was thrilled Marty had no time or interest in it. Wolf's wife, Bettina, also thinks she's a decorator. Marty knew it was a big thing for Wolf, so he told Roberta no and left it to Wolf and his wife. She ended up doing all the common spaces and Wolf's office."

"Twice?"

She looked at me and laughed. "Pretty thorough for a couple of hours."

"Same mother, remember?"

"Maybe," she smiled. "Anyway, yes, twice. She wanted to surprise John, so she had the work done behind closed doors and he worked in one of the un-assigned associate's offices. We have two. When she finished, he just didn't like it. Told her not to worry, that they'd start over. Apparently that's how they did their house. Trial and error. Mostly error.

The partnership agreement specified the dollar amounts for various aspects of the office improvements and we allowed for a 5% cushion. Marty was busy with four very large deals for clients and the separation agreement with DBS for himself, me, Joe, Mel and Gary. Roberta did get to do Marty's office. Anyway, Wolf had been using an accountancy firm..."

"Warner Warner and Carpenter..."

"Yes, and wanted them to handle everything at GMW. Marty had no objections, because as it was turning out, the firm he was familiar with handles everything for DBS, and would've had a conflict of interest."

"Why?"

"The separation agreement isn't complete, but when it is, there will be money that comes to GMW from various deals each of us did while we worked there. It's better if someone independent of DBS examines the studio receipt sheets."

"No honor among thieves?"

She didn't laugh.

"So Warner Warner and Carpenter didn't exactly hold Wolf to the spending limits everyone agreed to," I said.

"Right."

"Same with the party and the overdraws?"

"Basically."

"How did Marty become aware of Wolf's overspending?"

"I don't know."

"I saw a lot of memos back and forth between Marty and Wolf. Did you ever see them talk about it face to face? Maybe in some kind of partnership meeting?"

"Never in partnership meetings. They tried to put on a friendly face in front of the rest of us, but they did at least once. John just brushed Marty off. Marty found out about the improvements before the first quarter sheets came out. By the second quarter's sheets John's money habits began to look like a pattern and Marty got worried, then upset, and frustrated. But I know Marty considered the worst part to be that Warner Warner and Carpenter appeared to be fudging the numbers. None of it showed up on the first or second quarter sheets and it should have. The one time I know about, he cornered John in the library and it became a shouting match. It was amazing because Marty never shouts! He normally just burns inside, and gets hotter and more intense in a funny patient way, figuring his next move. But he lost his temper about the overspending and Warner and Warner. These are two guys used to having it their own way. Marty didn't get very far with him. John is smooth on the surface, but underneath, basically, very nasty, and wasn't going to be intimidated."

"How could the accountant guys hope to hide the overspending?"

"We borrowed $2 million from First American Bank to set this up. $1 million was for improvements. The other $1 million was to be a reserve, to augment receipts if necessary until we were really up and running. Do you know our rent is $50,000 a month? And the parking is another $12,000! And the interest on the first million is almost $10,000 a month!"

I smiled shaking my head. Mom would not have approved.

"It was a line of credit, so the more we used the more interest we paid. If we could keep out of it, we didn't. They pushed the overdraws and overspending into that account. So we've all been paying interest on John's office overspending and the party. It was supposed to be used only for the basic monthly expenses and staff salaries, but not partnership draws. We've all been adjusting since the second quarterlies came out. Marty came down on WWC and they reduced Wolf's draw. It should be paid back by now. I haven't seen the last quarter's sheets yet, but I think things have gotten a little better."

"Guess again."

"What do you mean?!"

"Don't you keep tabs on it weekly?"

"God no! I look at my sheets quarterly and adjust. I think I've actually been in the black since the fourth quarterly." She was pleased with herself.

"Don't you keep tabs on the others?"

She looked at me like I were crazy. "No! It's none of my business. I wouldn't pry! The reserve fund comes into play if someone goes over, but WWC corrects so that they balance out in a maximum of four quarters. They're supposed to include any interest paid out if fund money is used to cover draws. That I will check on. I'm not going to subsidize Wolf!"

"I hate to repeat myself, but guess again."

"What?" She was apprehensive and suspicious. She wanted to hear and knew from the look on my face that she didn't.

"Wolf is overdrawn $300,000 give or take. If you include his office and the party, it's more like $375,000."

Even in the moonlight I could see her face change color from healthy tan to ghostly white.

She said nothing on the walk back to her car and neither did I. I figured it was at least 12:30. A lot of sensible types who knew they had to get up early for work were leaving Sandy's and getting into cars up and down the street. Everyone was happy, everyone animated. High on drink if not on life. Which made me notice the two door looking guys, definitely not young professionals, and not blue-collar or jazz types either. Sandy's drew from an even wider spectrum than I'd noticed before.

Both were big and bulked-up, both dressed up, like thugs with a generous clothing allowance. They stood on the sidewalk, not high on drink
or life that I could tell. More like they'd come too late and missed a
parade and were unsure what to do next, not really looking at anything
or doing anything, but not exactly just aimlessly passing the time either.
We approached Tina's Alfa and she took keys from her purse.

"Nice wheels," I said. "What year?"

She turned to me very pleased. "'67. My high school graduation
present from my dad. Do you like it?"

"I love it. This is one of my two all time favorites. I got to drive a red
one just like it one night when I was hitch-hiking from Barcelona to
Rome."

This was a woman whose sudden smile sent a warm rush right through
me, like brandy on a cold night. On an empty stomach.

"I'd like to hear about that some time," she said.

I had this wild urge to kiss her. I felt like my idle was running too
high. I tried to consciously slow it down. The way we were standing by
her car reminded me of her and Gary Weiselman that afternoon.

"What did Weiselman want from you this afternoon?...at your car,
when you were leaving?"

Her eyes dropped to the street, "To pitch you about the autopsy."

"And?" I thought I tossed it off casually, with a slightly musical lilt to
my voice, but the tightening sensation in my throat, and the serious look
in her eyes told me otherwise. I was really thinking, Et tu Brutus?, and
she knew it. I wondered how long I'd be prisoner to these waves of pain
and grief and anger. They came out of nowhere, held me in their grip,
then as suddenly left, leaving me feeling drained and staggered.

She put her hand on my arm gently, looked me in the eye, smiled and
said, "Not a chance."

My kinda girl.

As I was walking down Main and turned on Rose, I admitted to myself that I was tired and emotionally drained, but even allowing for that,
it surprised me how much the mention of an autopsy bothered me. Maybe
it made his death real in a way that just being told he was dead or that he
shot himself didn't. I let myself dwell on it as I walked back to the rental
car. I tried to allow for the fact that I'd always been petrified by the idea
of dying. The more I thought about it, even putting aside Thorne and
the money considerations, and the possibility of them finding some hook
to hang a plausible counter argument to suicide on, it was a desecration.
I tried to defuse it in my mind, tried to picture his spirit leaving his body,
the body becoming just a shell. No longer significant. Like a coat he'd
taken off and left behind. It didn't work. Cutting him up for an autopsy
was a violation of some kind that I couldn't exactly explain to myself. It
demeaned him. Like it was the beginning of a scorched earth policy

meant to undo him, to erase his existence. Make some Cuisinart puree of him to satisfy these vultures. It scared me. Life is such a wisp of smoke as it is, how could I let them drag his body through the streets behind the golden chariot of an insurance pay-off? Dice him and slice him and leave him beside the road? I supposed I feared that if someone could do it to him, someone could do it to me. This was the body of my brother; his flesh and mine were joined. I smiled, because I had to admit to myself, there was a large element of avoidance in my refusal to sign the autopsy request. As if I could keep death further away from me by keeping some of its ugliness from him. If I couldn't defend him in life, couldn't save his life, I'd sure as hell defend what I could of him in death. I thought about identifying his body. About the Coroner's Office. I looked at my watch. It was 12:45. What the hell, it wasn't going to get any easier.

There were only three cars still parked in the lot behind Sandy's. Another man approached from the Marine Street side. I stood next to the nearest car, a BMW, fishing the keys from my pocket. I looked at all three, mentally looking for my car, my own car, then remembered the rental. It took a moment for me to focus. I knew it wasn't the Beamer. It was the one farthest from me. The Mustang. I heard a car accelerate and tires squeal and headlights shine low, then bounce high as a car sped through the dip between the street and the lot. The guy approaching me was alternately illuminated by the lights behind me and darkened by the shadow I cast.

"Look out! Look out!" he yelled.

I instinctively turned to look but simultaneously hurled myself onto the trunk in front of me just as a speeding car behind crashed into the driver's door. It sounded like an explosion and glass flew from the BMW as steam hissed from what looked like an Olds or Buick below me. The car I was on lurched sideways but I managed to keep my balance enough to stay on. The other car backed about a car length and surged forward again, coming right for the trunk area. I jumped far enough off to stay clear of a second lurch just as it hit. A man and woman came from the Rose Street side and he immediately began yelling.

"Hey! Hey! That's my car!"

The man ran forward, leaving the woman behind. With witnesses in front and behind, the battering car decided to withdraw and suddenly reversed with acrid rubber smoke billowing up from the spinning back tires. The car weaved recklessly side to side and narrowly missed the owner of the smashed BMW. The woman huddled against the building as the car reached the street and roared off to Main and from the sound of it went south.

The guy from the Marine Street side rushed to me.

"Are you okay? My God! I've never seen anything like that!"

I stood on rubber legs and I felt light-headed.

"I think so," I said.

I took a couple of breaths while he held my arm firmly and supported me. The other man and woman arrived.

"Holy fucking shit!" he said. "Look at this! What the hell is going on?"

The guy holding me said, "A couple of gang-bangers out for a joy ride, I bet."

"Jesus! Jesus! Jesus! What a fucking mess! Did you get a look at them?" the BMW guy asked me.

I hadn't thought about it while it was happening, but as soon as he asked, I realized I had a picture in my mind of the general shape and outline of the two dour looking guys from in front of Sandy's behind the windshield of the Olds or Buick. I wasn't sure. I've seen too many movies, I thought. But then again, maybe the parade hadn't passed them by after all.

"Not really," I told him.

The woman felt safe enough to leave her place against the brick wall. She came up to her boyfriend or husband and put her arm around his slumping shoulders.

"I think I got the license plate number."

An hour later we'd given two of the West LA Police Department's finest as much information as we could. The tow truck had come and had the BMW up in the air. The cops thanked the woman for the plate numbers and told her they were amazed she'd been able to get them under the circumstances. I borrowed a pen and a scrap of paper from the little notebook of one of the cops and jotted down the number, then put it into my wallet. The cops said the car was probably stolen, but they'd check on it. I didn't say anything about the guys from in front of Sandy's. What would have been the point? Not only wasn't I sure, but I'd sound like some paranoid lunatic, and there wouldn't have been anything more they could or would do about it. But I remembered what Sara had said.

Chapter 8

I checked the time. It was 1:45. I drove to the address on the card Kaplan had given me. I found myself checking the rear-view mirror a lot more often than I usually would. I felt foolish doing it, almost as though the movie town mentality had seeped in and I were playing a part. That's how everyone down here seemed to do it. No one could just live and go about their business, it was all done as though on stage or up on the big screen, being viewed by an appreciative audience. What a load of shit, I thought, but then I flashed on the Beamer, and checked the mirror again.

The Coroner's Suite was really the whole basement level of the building, approached from the back of the Santa Monica City Hall and City Offices Buildings on Main Street. There were a dozen empty parking places to choose from.

There was a Coroner's ambulance backed up to a loading dock. Handy, but I thought it sort of took the dignity and romance right out of death. I had to count myself lucky to be walking in here. It could have been the loading dock for me too. Like Kaplan had said, the place was open 24 hours a day. I went in.

A tired, disinterested looking rent-a-cop sat at a desk reading. I stood in front of his desk and waited a moment for him to acknowledge me. He didn't.

"Excuse me."

He didn't respond and he didn't look up. I waited a couple of seconds and knocked on the desk as if it were a door. He looked up at me with a don't-do-that look and back to whatever he was reading. It was late and I was tired. I closed my eyes and breathed slowly in and let it out in a controlled blow through my lips. Either he was a colossal asshole or he was just tired too. I gave him the benefit of the doubt. I waited patiently for about half a minute. When he made no move to respond, I knocked again.

"Where do I go to identify someone?"

"Dead or alive?" he asked without risking loosing his place.

"Dead."

He looked up and smiled, "You've come to the right place," he said, and went back to his book.

Asshole. "Where?"

He jerked his thumb over his shoulder. There were two identical doors, neither of them marked.

"Which one?"

He jerked his thumb more to the left than to the right so I assumed that was the one he meant.

"Do they pay you for this, or you just don't have anything better to do?"

He didn't move a muscle or blink an eye, but he didn't like it.

I went through the door on the left. There was a hallway beyond it with every other light along its length out. There were closed office doors on both sides, but about five doors down on the left, one was open and lit up, sending a fan of light into the semi-dark hall. Inside a guy was eating a sandwich, drinking a Coke and reading a paperback. I stood in the doorway and knocked. Through a mouthful he said to come in. Three's the charm, I thought.

"I'm here to identify someone."

"Name?"

"Mine or his?"

"Both."

"His is Marty Goldman. Mine is Kurt Goldman."

"Yeah, I got a note here someplace, from Kaplan at Groman."

He sifted through the mess on his desk and found a pink telephone pad message.

"You're the brother? The executor?"

"Yes."

"Shot himself, right?" he said without thinking.

"Right."

He looked up at me. "Sorry. Come on this way. We can make this quick."

I followed a pace or so behind him as we walked to double swinging doors at the end of the hall. I thought about bailing out. Just saying I'd remembered I had to do something else or tell him flat out I'd changed my mind and would come back later. In fact, I was rehearsing different ways of phrasing it when I ran out of hallway and we came to the doors. He paused with his hand on the right-side door and turned to me.

"Ready?"

"Yes," someone said. I felt a little light-headed again.

He went in ahead of me and turned on a ceiling full of bright flores-cent lights. It was cold in there, but not like a refrigerator. Just chilly. I wondered how long they could keep people, bodies, here like this. There were six or seven gurneys side by side with sheet-covered bodies lined up like race cars with nowhere to go. Name tags on bluish white toes. The movies got that right, I thought.

"Here," he said. He pulled back the sheet and revealed Marty from his head to mid-section. "That him?"

Another of those inconvenient and debilitating waves grabbed at me and got hold of my throat. Tears welled up and spilled out and my breath came in short choked gasps. I nodded. It was the best I could do.

"We can go then."

I stood transfixed. Both unable and unwilling to move. "This is my body, this is my blood," ran through my mind.

"Ready?" he said.

I shook my head no.

"Just meet me back in my office. You'll have to sign something."

He left. I wanted to go nearer and I wanted to run away. I wanted both so desperately I started to tremble. I tried to force back moans I could feel welling up in my throat, like waves waiting their turn to wash ashore. I wanted to breathe life into him somehow. I wanted to scream at him to get up. To stop fooling around. If it had been Nick, I would have. Both because he might, and because he would appreciate the humor in it. But with Marty it wasn't funny. He wasn't going to get up. This was real. I looked at his sweet kind good face and saw where the bullet entered his right temple and lodged near his left eye creating a large but surprisingly confined bruise that went up through his eyebrow and back to his left ear, and down across his cheek and stopped about an inch above his mouth. It didn't seem to have brought him peace if that's what he was looking for. Just death. Another wave passed through me and the tears were hot on my face.

The next thing I knew, words started tumbling out. "YOU STUPID FUCKING ASSHOLE!" I shouted, "YOU COULD HAVE DONE THAT ANYTIME!!" Tears streamed down my face and I took a step forward. I wanted to pull him off the gurney and punch him in the mouth, slap his fucking face silly. It took me a long time to calm down.

His expression wasn't sad or glad, not pained or relieved, but annoyed. It was an odd expression, I thought. I wiped the tears away with the palms of my hands. There was a sink in the room. I splashed cold water in my face and dried it with a paper towel. I looked at Marty again and I wondered how long he'd had a gun and where he got it. And why? For this? It seemed important to get answers about the gun. I also had a desire to see it. To touch it and hold it in my hand. To feel the weight of the thing that had ended his life so easily.

I went back to the guy's office and signed the paper. If he'd heard me yelling at Marty, he wasn't planning to comment on it.

On my way out, as I passed the Security Guard sitting at his desk, he flipped me off without looking up from his book. Without thinking, I back-handed him with a closed right as hard as I could across his nose and mouth. He grabbed for his face with both hands, blood oozing between his fingers as he and his chair tipped over backwards. There's a limit to my patience, I reminded myself.

The air outside had cooled off some and I felt a little better.

It was 1:40 and I was hungry. I drove along Ocean Avenue and passed 81436. The Café De La Mer was closed now. I was checking the mirror regularly, like a pimply teenager before a date, fearing the worst.

I half expected to see the Olds or Buick or whatever it had been, parked in front. More movie thinking. It was infectious. I had a key and could let myself in at Megan Dunphy's in Laurel Canyon, and I knew she kept more food in that house than an all-night truck stop, but by the time I got over there it would be quarter after two or worse and I had to be back over this way to Century City to meet with Victor and John Goodman at 6:45. I had to think about it, but I decided I was more tired than hungry.

On the way to Sandy's I'd passed something called the Pacific Hotel. It had had the look of a one time fine place, only that one time had been back in the twenties and now it looked like it served a transient and social security crowd. I drove there. It filled a long but narrow city block, and the backside faced the Santa Monica Bay. I parked in the public lot behind the building. They must have had a hundred rooms, and there were only six spaces designated for the hotel. I didn't think I'd need a reservation. I took my one smallish suitcase from the trunk and walked around to the front.

The desk clerk looked up as I crossed the shabby lobby. Not related to the Security Guard at the Coroner's, I thought. The rug and chairs and couches had probably been there when the Hotel had been young and gay, but were threadbare and worn now. Everything was surprisingly clean though. Just old and worn out.

"Good evening, or rather good morning," he said.

"I'd like a room, please."

"Certainly. How long will you be staying?"

He was about forty-six or seven but looked twenty years older. He was too thin and too pale, but he had a genuine dignity that I liked. I guessed he'd been a drinker for a long time but was dry now.

"Three days," I said, surprising myself.

"And how will you be paying?"

"How much a night?"

"Twenty dollars a night. Fifteen for cash in advance."

I started to reach for a credit card but changed my mind and pulled out two twenties and a five. More movie paranoia, but it seemed like a better idea at the time.

"And what name will you be using?"

The way he said it was such an invitation I couldn't resist.

"Mike Hammer," I said with a straight face.

"Just so," he said as he printed the name in a registration book. He spun it around for me to sign, and pointed to the line below his printing. "How often do you change the sheets around here?" I asked before I thought about how it would sound.

He saw me catch myself, and smiled, "Only when they really need it."

He chuckled and I laughed with him, but I wasn't as confident about a good night's sleep, not even for the three and half hours I could at best hope for. I could picture myself laying there trying to imagine who else had enjoyed the same sheets since the last time they'd been washed. I thought of the old Marx Brothers gag about changing sheets, Groucho changes with Harpo and Harpo changes with Zeppo and so on. Oh well, I wouldn't be on them long tonight anyway. He gave me a key and told me two floors up. Room 211.

The stairway was wide and grand and curved gracefully to the next landing. The handrail and balusters and newel post had been done with pride and craftsmanship maybe sixty years before, and now someone was keeping it as clean as it had likely been back then. From the landing, the next flight of stairs were ordinary. I found 211 and opened the door. The room faced the ocean and the windows were wide open. The bright moon still shone on the water, and the breeze ambled across it and the sand and joined me in the surprisingly large room. There was an easy chair, a small desk with a lamp and chair, and a dresser on the adjacent wall left of the door. Across the room under the windows, the bed was an old Full, smaller than a Queen but bigger than a Single. There was a night table next to it. I turned on the light switch. An old brass and glass ceiling fixture lit the room romantically, or maybe dimly, depending on your mood. The bed was made tight as a gnats-ass, military style, and the sheets, god bless them, were crisp and white and smelled of bleach. A favorite smell, thanks to my mother. Nothing was clean until the smell of bleach jumped off it and successfully outraced any other smells in the room to you. Through a door on the wall to the right I could see there was a claw-footed tub with brass tubing and a big handsome shower-head. The shower curtain was clear plastic and clean as a whistle. Everything was. I'd sleep like a baby, I thought. I set a bedside travel clock I'd brought with me for 5:45, got undressed and crawled in. I didn't think about Marty or the partners or Victor or John Goodman at all.

Clean clean clean was the last thing I was thinking.

Chapter 9

THURSDAY

———❦———

By 6:15 I was sitting in Il Fornaio in Beverly Hills. They opened at 6. I liked that about the place. In Beverly Hills the only people I expected to see out and about this early were the gardeners and non-live-in household help on their way to work, and I hadn't expected to find any place interesting, or for that matter, English-speaking, open. I also liked the few people who were up at that hour and here. There were seven of us. These five guys, and one woman, looked like the Beverly Hills I remembered. Rich, wealthy, whatever, but comfortable with it. They'd done something to make a lot of money and they lived well, but they didn't have to flash it or talk about it or find a way to let everyone know about it. Whatever it had been that they'd done, they were proud of. It was the work. When we were kids, the Marx brothers' kids were our age, from Marty on down to me, and we knew them and their fathers through cub scouts and PTA. And Danny Thomas and George Burns and Milton Berle and Danny Kaye, all those guys had kids in Hawthorne Elementary or Beverly Hills High School. They loved what they did. Beverly Hills was their town, the place where they lived and shopped and ate and worked and raised their families. It was just a good place. And since they were all famous, they could go about their business without being gawked at or intruded upon. For the current crop, it was an idea. A prestigious zip code. A place to flash the Rolls, the big titted, but too-young girl friend, the oversized diamond rings and watches. All the gold chains. But the guys who were up at six were different. I'd look at one or another and think, Marty should have been partnered with him. They looked like people who lived their lives rather than staged them. I could picture Marty here early. He'd fit. I kept wishing he'd walk in. I tried to see it. Will it. I felt too much like a tourist, but this was his town in the old sense of it, and mine, by extension. I wanted to meet these early morning guys and find out who they were and what they did. I wanted them to tell me they knew Marty, or knew of him. I wanted them to tell me what a rarity he was these days. I knew it. But I wished I could hear it from one of them.

The waiters and waitresses reminded me of the help at The Beach Club. White shirts, black bow ties and black pants. They were pleasant without being overly friendly or intrusive. I had a Cheddar cheese omelet, bread baked in the back, jam I thought they must have made here too, and good, good coffee. It was 6:35 when I paid and left.

I found 101 Stargate Avenue and parked in the underground garage. It cost $6 for each 20 minutes! I hoped Victor's office validated, or this was going to be a short meeting. Gravettz and March Accountancy was on the 6th floor. Big double walnut doors with brass lettering. Marty's paying for this, I thought. Inside though, it was nicely mundane. Lots of utilitarian offices for the grunts, two bigger nicer furnished offices for Herman Gravettz and Victor. Nothing fancy, just comfortable enough to keep clients from looking around, wondering if they should find higher-flyers. It was 6:45 on the nose. I heard voices down a hall and followed them to a meeting room. Victor and John Goodman and Bob Winters were drinking coffee. Winters was tapping his fingers furiously on the arm of his chair. John and Victor greeted me.

Winters grunted and said, "Let's get started."

John said with compassion and unfeigned interest, "How are you today?"

"Fine."

Victor offered me coffee. I told him I'd just had some. Victor reviewed a yellow legal tablet for a moment. "Let me run down this list first, then we can focus on one area at a time afterwards. First, the autopsy."

I didn't say anything but my expression must have darkened, and he waved off anything I might have been about to say.

"Wolf is livid. He wants the autopsy done today. Roberta wants it. Bob Thorne insists you have a fiduciary duty to sign the request. It's crucial. Without that insurance money GMW will fold. The income stream has not been good. It has not kept pace with expenses during the first eighteen months of operations. Without Marty, it will slow to a trickle."

Bob Winters shot Goodman a look.

"Second: Barry Malovitch is anxious for Kurt to meet with him and sign what he says is an agreement to resolve all outstanding issues between Marty and DBS. I don't know exactly what Marty had in mind, but I do know he expected it would be a considerable amount of money. It would be helpful if Kurt could find any notes or settlement proposal drafts Marty might have done in preparation for his meeting with Malovitch. You might also talk to Woodman, Davidson, Weiselman and Cox to see if Marty brought any of them into the process. My guess is not, but you should check.

"Third: I don't have a copy of his will. Do you?" he asked me.

"No. I've never seen it."

"That's the first order of business," Goodman said. "We've got to find the original, and get the court to confirm Kurt as executor. Victor, have you any idea where it might be?"

Victor told us, "My guess would be in his office at home. Probably not at his GMW Office, but you never know. He has two safe deposit boxes that I know of. One in this building, in the bank on the first floor, one at the bank on the ground floor of the building DBS occupies. I think you'll find it in one of those places, if not at the house, unless he has another box that I don't know about."

"We've got to get ahold of that, Kurt, or we're stuck. We can't begin without it. I know how difficult this must be, with funeral arrangements and all, but can you take some time and try to locate the will?" John asked.

"Yes."

"Fourth," Victor continued, "I've prepared a list of Marty's personal assets and liabilities, and all of his bank accounts that I know of. I don't think there will be any others. These are his personal accounts, and ones for Marty H. Goldman, A Professional Corporation."

He handed each of us a copy.

Goodman scanned the list. "I see he just bought a car through his Professional Corporation. $50 thousand. Do you know where it is?"

"At his house, I suppose," Victor offered.

"Kurt," John said, "would you please ask your sister-in-law not to drive it? It belongs to the PC, and she may not be insured on it. We'll want to sell it as soon as possible."

"The GMW Partnership is really a collection of PC's," Victor continued.

Goodman broke in, "Excuse me Victor, but as soon as the court confirms you, Kurt, and issues letters testamentary, you'll close down the personal accounts and open an estate account. Every bit of money your brother had, or has coming will pass through that. Bob, what do you think about the Professional Corporation?"

"I don't think we have a choice. I think we have to keep it open. I don't know if it's legal to have Kurt serve in his brother's place there, but he'll have to. Until all issues between the partners are resolved, and the old partnership settlement agreement is reached, we have no choice."

"I agree. If any one challenges..."

"I don't understand? What's the problem?"

"Your brother's professional corporation is registered with the Secretary of State as a particular kind of corporation. It assumes the person guiding it is qualified to do work of that nature, in this case, legal work. You should be a lawyer if you're going to head a PC set up for that purpose. I don't know who would challenge you, but they could. What I'd like to know is, what's the situation at GMW?"

Victor looked uncomfortable. "Here are the sheets for the last quarter." He handed us each copies of the Warner Warner and Carpenter report I'd seen last night. I didn't mention it.

"Jesus!" Winters said, "Look at the goddamm rent!"

He and Goodman exchanged a look.

I wanted to jump in and suggest they look at the overdraws, the office improvements and the party spending, see what an asshole Wolf is. But I didn't say a word.

Victor pointed them out. In fact he was very thorough, showing us who had responded to the overdraws quickly and who had not. He flipped back and forth through the quarterly reports. "Marty was very worried about Wolf. Look at his overdraws. Everyone else corrected when it became obvious they were in the red. Not Wolf. These sheets don't show it, but Marty was also aware of problems in the office improvement allocations." Victor took a few minutes to enlighten us. He had a pretty clear picture of the improvements and party expenses that I'd seen last night. Victor let it sink in.

Winters looked at Goodman and rolled his eyes in dismay, then gave Victor a withering look. "How in god's name could you let him get away with this? Didn't the partnership agreement have a balancing mechanism? Ours sure as hell does!"

Victor was indignant. "We had nothing to do with it! If you'll look here," he pointed to the WWC masthead, "another firm has been handling the GMW account."

"And why is that?" Winters said accusingly.

"Because Wolf insisted. He'd used WWC for years. Marty had no objections and besides, he didn't want to involve the firm he was familiar with at DBS because of potential conflicts of interest when they reached a settlement."

"Why didn't he use you?" Bob persisted.

"We've done Marty's personal and PC bookkeeping and tax returns for years. We weren't set up for the kind of things taking on GMW would involve."

"Like what?" I asked.

"The most obvious, and from our point of view, the deciding factor would have been the monitoring of studio and recording company project receipts. It's a huge task, particularly when you know who's on Marty's client list. And Wolf's. Just enormous."

"Had you been asked?" Bob asked.

"From the outset Wolf wanted WWC," Victor bristled.

It was clear Victor had wanted the GMW account. Probably was disappointed Marty hadn't insisted on it.

"Victor, thank you," John Goodman's baritone calmed the waters, warmed the air. "I think we've all gotten a picture of what's involved. Before we go into details, we must find the will and get Kurt confirmed by the court." He stood, ready to go. "Bob, I'd like you to accompany

Kurt to GMW this afternoon."

Bob grunted assent. He gathered up his briefcase and said, "Let's swear him in as President and Secretary of the PC right now. If we're going to GMW, let's go in full blast."

"Good idea," Goodman agreed. "Kurt, raise your right hand."

I did. Goodman had me convene a corporation meeting, and in less than a minute I was sworn in as President and Secretary of "Marty H. Goldman, a Professional Corporation." Victor had his secretary type up minutes of our meeting and my election to office and I signed and everyone else witnessed it.

"There's something else." Victor was anxious to get it out. Goodman and Winters turned towards him. "I think...Marty thought there was something wrong with the WWC sheets."

"We've seen that. You showed us. We'll look into it," Winters said irritably stuffing notes he'd taken into his briefcase and buckling it shut.

I was thinking about what fun I was going to have at GMW with him in my corner.

"Not those sheets," Victor said.

Everybody was looking at him, waiting. He seemed to wish someone else would take over now. He couldn't seem to get started.

When a few seconds had passed in silence, Winters said in exasperation, "Are you going to tell us or should one of us guess?"

"I think he meant the studio sheets."

"What do you mean you think?" Winters demanded.

"Marty called me and said he thought there was something wrong with the sheets. He said 'fishy'. He wanted us to reconcile them."

"Well, did he say 'the studio sheets' or not?" Winters coaxed him.

"He had to take another call. When he came back on the line he said he'd been trying to get copies from WWC for a couple of weeks, but they were stalling him. Since he already had the GMW quarterly sheets and he knew I had them, I don't know what else he could have meant."

"So you not only don't know what he thought was wrong, you're not even sure he was talking about the studio sheets, right?"

"What else?" Victor began, but Winters cut him off.

"How should I know! But I know we can't just go in there and ask to see things without a reason, can we now? Great!" Winters said gnashing his teeth and looking at Goodman with barely controlled anger and frustration. "Just great!" He looked at me like I'd just rear-ended his Rolls. If he'd had one. In his case, I thought, it would have been a perfectly restored '50 Ford Coupe. "Let's meet somewhere private near GMW at one for a little pow-wow. I'll set up a meeting with the partners for 1:30." He looked at his watch. "I've gotta get outta here. I've got an appearance at 9:30 downtown. I'll never make it." Without looking up he asked, "Where are they?"

I didn't have the heart to tell him. Fortunately Victor jumped in.

"At the beach. Santa Monica. 81436 Ocean Avenue."

"At the what! What did you say?"

No way Victor was going to repeat it. Bob's thick neck, already red from a too-tight shirt collar and the mornings deliberations, went closer to purple. I fought back a smile. If ever a guy was a candidate for a heart attack, I thought.

"Maybe you should accompany Kurt for a day at the beach, bring a little pail and shovel," he challenged Goodman.

John smiled tolerantly. It served only to further enrage Winters.

"I just knew it!" he muttered. Then he pointed to me, "One p.m. Be there. If I'm late, wait for me. And for godsakes, don't talk to any of the partners until I get there!"

"There's a coffee shop on the ground floor. Let's meet there, outside," I suggested.

"Fine," he said, waving his hand as he walked out of the meeting room, "whatever."

John shook hands with me, then Victor. "We'll be in touch. Kurt, find that will." He left.

Victor looked shaken but relieved. I checked the clock on the wall. It was 8:45. I reached in my pocket.

"I hope you validate."

I stopped at the receptionist's desk to get the parking validation stickers. I asked to use the phone. She handed back the ticket with only one sticker good for twenty minutes. I stared at it, doing the calculations in my head, then at her. She shrugged.

"You gotta be kidding," I said.

She gave me a pained expression, but when it looked like I was going to use up the first one just waiting her out, she relented and plastered on five more, crowding them wherever she could, front and back. She said I could use the phone in the first office behind her. Sara answered on the second ring.

"It's me," I said.

"Where are you? Megan said you never showed up last night."

"It got too late, so I stayed in Venice. I'll try to call Megan, but if you talk to her first, thank her, and tell her I'm going to stay where I am for now. Did you talk to Krasznik?"

"Yes. He'd like to talk to you and Nick and probably Roberta and the girls." She gave me a phone number to arrange a meeting.

"Can he do the service on Sunday?"

"Yes, 2p.m."

"Where?"

"At Hillside Memorial, where Morgan's buried." One of my mother's brothers. "Have you been to Groman's?"

"Yes."

"Eli and Maia say Marty wanted to be cremated."

"I'll call Groman's and let them know. What about Roberta? Does she agree?"

"I think so. She's preoccupied with the autopsy business. What's going on?"

I gave her the short version. She was silent and I knew it bothered her in much the same way it did me. I told her about problems at GMW. No details.

"How's Roberta been acting?"

"What do you mean?" Sara always had a higher tolerance for Roberta and her hysterical dramatics.

"Generally."

"How do you think? Her husband just killed himself! Give her a break, Kurt."

"Specifically, then. Has she been on the phone much?"

"She's had condolence calls. I've been answering the phone. Dozens of condolence calls."

"Has she been taking the calls?"

"No. She's too upset. She asked that I take messages and thank the callers and tell them she'll be in touch when she's up to it."

"What about Bob Thorne?"

"What about him?"

"Calls?"

"No, he's been here most of the morning."

Great, I thought.

"Not in the office?" I didn't intend the alarm in my voice.

"No, why?"

Assuming Roberta had keys to his desk and file cabinet, I couldn't think of a way to keep them out if they intended to go through his things before I could get there. But I knew I didn't want Thorne in there. Or Roberta. I had to tell Sara enough about the problems at GMW so she'd understand why they were so intent on the autopsy.

"I know you can't keep them out, but try to hang around if they go in. I don't want them to take anything. Okay? Nothing."

I knew it put her in an awkward position, and she was hesitant.

"It's important."

"Okay," she said. Then, "You wouldn't believe the sweaters and lingerie."

"The what? What are you talking about?"

"Nothing. It's just odd."

"Odd how?"

"Dozens of sweaters in the closets. I helped Maria straighten up last night and every time we'd open a closet there'd be half a dozen new sweaters still in their packages ready to tumble out. And drawers full of new lingerie still in the packages. Maria sort of rolled her eyes, like 'this goes on all the time'."

"So? She likes sweaters and underwear."

"It's like she goes shopping to pass the time."

"She's a spoiled rich person. She should learn to window shop. I've got to get going. If they look like they're taking anything from the office challenge them about it."

"When are you coming back here?"

"Around four."

Chapter 10

I drove down the ramp into the underground lot at 81436 Ocean Avenue and used the magnetic gate card to raise the barrier, then drove around until I found a slot marked GMW:MHG and pulled the Mustang into it. I walked back up the ramp to the sidewalk and around the building to enter from the front rather than take the elevator from the garage to the lobby. I took a parting look at the ocean and sky and tried to hear the surf through the traffic noise. I could, or at least imagined that I could. That was nice. It brought a smile to my face. The muscular security guy, Lawton, was there in the lobby. He had been watching me enjoying myself. I felt a little self-conscious. Maybe a little guilty too. But he brightened when I came through the lobby doors. He offered me the sign-in sheet.

"Wolf's in, Marshall's in, and Ms. Cox. None of the other partners yet. No one asked for last night's sheet," he said matter-of-factly.

I handed it back.

"Thanks."

He nodded.

I went to the Penthouse and got off the elevator at GMW. It was a bee-hive of subdued and melancholy activity. No workplace smiles or exchanged comments or greetings, just people coming and going doing their jobs under the cloud of Marty's death. It occurred to me part of the mood of the place was likely the doubt about its future, and with it, theirs. The telephone operator sat behind the granite reception desk busy with dozens of lights flashing and a boop-boop sound with each new incoming call. She answered and directed calls with amazing skill and calm. The receptionist behind the side marked Music was away from her desk. The woman seated behind the side marked Film had her head turned from me talking with another woman. I walked past without pausing. As I neared Marty's office, someone behind me was calling.

"Excuse me! Excuse me sir! Can I help you? Do you have an appointment?"

I turned. It was the woman who'd been standing talking with the Film receptionist. I waited for her, and she caught up to me and went just past me.

"May I help you?"

She'd managed to slip herself between me and Marty's office. It was a nice move, I thought. She was small and slender, kind of skinny really, with mousey red-brown hair. No make up. Her eyes were red-rimmed. She looked as though she hadn't slept well.

"I'm Marty's brother," I said.

"Oh! Oh, I'm...I can't tell you..." her eyes began to tear and she covered her mouth.

"I'm Kurt," I said, and offered a handshake.

"Ronnie Hook," she said, taking my hand, "Marty's secretary."

"Would you come into his office with me, please?"

"Of course."

I was about to take out my keys, Marty's keys, but she got to the door first. It was unlocked now. She pushed it open and went in ahead of me. There were full cardboard boxes stacked on the floor near the desk, and the surface was cluttered with file folders, a second desk calendar and appointment book, and some personal photographs in small frames, face down. There were empty cardboard boxes in front of Marty's file drawers.

"What's this?" I said.

"What?" she said plaintively.

"This!" I pointed, "What the hell is all this crap!"

Her eyes met mine only briefly and she put a hand to her forehead; the other hand was turned backwards resting on her hip as though to keep her from crumpling into a heap on the floor. Before she could answer another woman came through the door with a box in her arms. When she saw me and Ronnie Hook, she didn't stop, but slowed, appraising the situation. She looked back and forth between us and then stooped to set the box down on top of one of the others.

"Get that out of here," I said.

"What?"

"Get that out of here."

"Who do you think you are?" she demanded.

"Miriam, this is Marty's brother," Ronnie Hook informed her.

"Well, he has no business in here. Mr. Wolf is moving into this office." She gave me a look of untroubled annoyance, and told me, "you'll be able to retrieve Mr. Goldman's things on Monday. Ronnie should have them boxed up by then."

"Is Wolf here now?" I asked her. I could feel it coming.

"He stepped out."

"Do you know when he'll return?"

"I'm afraid I couldn't say."

She started for the door. I could see Ronnie Hook relax a little.
"Would you please get this stuff out of here?" I asked.

She looked over her shoulder at me and smiled, continuing out the door. I grabbed the box she'd just left. It wasn't very heavy. I followed her out to the hallway. She wasn't quite to the reception area when I threw it down the hall towards her. When it hit, she turned and let out a little yelp of surprise.

"If you don't get those fucking boxes outta there they're going off the balcony!" I shouted.

She ran towards Wolf's office. Marshall poked his head out of his door. Cox too. I glared at both of them. Rotten fuckers, I thought, Marty's not even in the ground and they're sitting on their asses while Wolf makes his move. I went back into Marty's office and grabbed one of the empty boxes and swept all of Wolf's crap off the desk into it. I stepped into the hall again and pitched it about as far as the first one. It scattered his junk here and there because I hadn't closed or sealed the top. I went back into the office and got two more and threw them to about the same place in the hallway. When I came back with two more there was quite a crowd gathered. It was the Olympics of box throwing. The elevator bonged and Wolf came around the corner from the reception area. He had to push his way through the spectators.

"What's going on? What's going on here?"

When he'd pushed through on the way to his new office, he saw what was going on. He charged about two steps towards me and stopped. I must've had a quart of adrenalin flowing by then because I felt like superman, like anything I thought or willed was going to happen and no one could stop me. I pointed at him. Bad dog. Stay. Sit! I threw one box, then the other towards him. They landed at his feet. Miriam came up behind him.

"I told him it was your office now."

"Call security! Call them right now!" he bellowed.

Marshall came through the on-lookers behind Miriam and Wolf. Cox just behind him. The elevator bonged again and Weiselman and Woodman came towards their offices and the pile of boxes and crowd of people. Miriam turned to go call security, but Marshall stopped her.

"Wait, Miriam. Just wait right here. John, let me talk to him."

"There's nothing to talk about! He's trespassing! I want him out of here!"

I went back into the office. I slid the huge glass door to the balcony open. The crowd was curious about my prolonged absence from the hallway and had stepped past the pile of boxes and now crowded into the open doorway. I checked to see if anyone were at risk below and then threw the first box off the balcony. There was a collective gasp from the assembled GMWers. I went back for another.

"Stop it! God dammit, stop it!" Wolf screamed at me.

"Then get your fucking shit out of here! And keep it out! This is

Marty's office, you cocksucking sack of shit! I'm going to use this office! I'll let you know when I'm done with it! Got it!?"

Marshall gently placed one of his big arms over Wolf's shoulder, like an elephant would his trunk, and eased Wolf behind him.

"I'll handle this, John. Just go back to your office. I'll be there in a little while."

"If you need any help finding it, just ask, asshole!" I was on a roll now.

"Don't think this is over! You're in WAY over your head now!"

"Take it easy. Calm down, now," Marshall told me. He approached cautiously, like a lion tamer with an unruly newcomer.

"Get Miriam or whoever the fuck she is to..." I motioned to the remaining boxes.

Marshall went back into the hall and organized a safari, lined up the bearers, and shepherded them into and out of Marty's office. The boxes were gone before you could say hocus-pocus. Marshall closed the door behind the last of the box-bearers. The adrenalin was still pumping. Marshall sat on the couch at the south end of the room. He put his feet up on Roberta's glass coffee table. His big sloppy frame seemed to overwhelm the furniture.

"May I?" he asked with a smile.

"Sure, why not?" I said. I sat behind Marty's desk.

"John just doesn't think sometimes. It was terribly insensitive of him to move in here so soon after. There's nothing I can say," he said.

"Just keep him out," I said.

"Have you had an opportunity to secure counsel?"

"Goodman, Winters Callan and Street. Bob Winters or his secretary should be calling this morning to arrange a meeting for 1:30 this afternoon."

"Good, good. Great. I can imagine how awful all of this is for you. But if you can, imagine what turmoil it's placed all of us in."

He stood.

"If you need anything, come see me. I'm just down the hall. Ronnie Hook can assist you if you need it."

He poked his head out the door. He looked back to me.

"Back to normal now," he said and smiled as he left.

Not hardly, I thought. I sat at the desk letting my system slow back down, trying to remember what it was that I wanted to do here this morning.

There was a knock at the door.

"Come in."

Tina Cox opened the door and peeked through the crack.

"Is it safe?"

"That depends."

"On what?"

"Whether you're trying to move in or just visit."

She smiled, came in and closed the door and sat in the huge indentation Sandy Marshall had left in the couch.

"You have a way with people."

"As Lyndon Johnson used to say, 'Come, let us reason together'."

"Exactly." She thought for a moment and said, "John's an ass. I'm sorry he put you through that."

"I needed the exercise."

"Kurt," she hesitated, "be careful. John won't let it lie. None of it."

"Thanks."

"Sandy says we're going to meet at 1:30. Will John Goodman be here with you?"

"No. Bob Winters." I was about to tell her he wasn't too happy about it either. Tell her he was Grumpy of the Seven Dwarfs, make her laugh, both for her sake and mine. It was so easy to assume I could trust her. That we were friends. Or that I could at least rely on her loyalty to Marty. I'm such a sucker for a good looking blond. Or brunette. Or whatever. But I kept it to myself. We looked at each other for a moment. I'd like to say we looked at each other with some expectation, but that would be stretching even my optimism.

"I better get to work," I said.

She looked a little hurt, then forced a smiled as she got off the couch and headed for the door.

"Me too," then added, "will you be around for lunch?"

"Probably."

"I'm buying," she said.

"I was really planning on just working here."

She frowned. I'm such a sucker, I thought. "Why don't you stop by when you're ready to go?" I suggested.

She brightened and said, "Okay," as she went out the door.

Chapter 11

I swivelled around and turned on Marty's computer, typed in DIR at the C prompt and hit enter. I realized there was a computer file for DBS Sheets, but last night I hadn't seen a corresponding paper file in the file drawer. I looked again. Not there. What I really needed was access to the CODED Directory. I knew I could probably fool around forever and not hit on Marty's password. I looked at the phone on the desk, but didn't immediately see what button would summon Ronnie so I went to the door and poked my head out. She was sitting motionless at her desk staring disconsolately at her computer.

"Excuse me, Ronnie, would you come in here please?"

She turned, her face lit up and then just as suddenly fell, and her lip quivered.

"What's the matter? What'd I do?" I asked.

She struggled to compose herself. "For a moment...you sounded just like him."

She got up and followed me into Marty's office. I sat behind the desk and motioned her into the chair in front of it. She seemed reluctant to sit or stay in here with me. I think she wanted to be left alone. To do whatever she had to do and not talk to anyone. She seemed to be trying to will me to tell her never mind, and dismiss her. She noticed the computer behind me was on.

"I need your help," I started.

If I could read her mind and the expression on her face, it was saying good luck. She didn't respond. Didn't move a muscle. This quiet little mouse was going to wait me out until hell froze over. It struck me that she was made from tougher stuff than met the eye. I decided to try another tack.

"I know about some of the problems Marty was having with Wolf. I know about the Party, the Office Improvements and the overdraws."

A hint of a smile played at her lips. She was poised on the edge of her seat, as though either ready to take dictation, or run like hell if I started throwing boxes again. But the little smile was encouraging.

"I was here last night."

I thought I saw the slightest arching movement in an eyebrow.

"I went through files to try and familiarize myself with what might have...with what was going on."

She was paying attention, but she wasn't giving away a thing. She crossed her legs. You'll have to do better than this, her posture suggested.

"I know Marty recently asked you not to keep any GMW matters on your computer. Why?"

"He decided some matters were too confidential."

"From whom?"

"From anyone other than himself and me."

"Was he afraid someone would tamper with your computer?"

"I couldn't say."

She was beginning to annoy me.

"How long have you been his secretary?"

Her chin began to tremble and her eyes overflowed and she whispered words through the hand that had gone to her mouth.

"Fifteen years."

She couldn't be more than thirty-five or thirty-six now so Marty had probably been her one and only boss. Her whole working life had been with him, I thought. She was fighting for control.

"Did you like working with him? Did you like him?"

She looked at me like I'd just twisted the knife his death had stuck in her heart. I noticed she wore no wedding rings. She started to cry in earnest. She covered her face.

"I need your help," I repeated.

You do it your way, I'll do it mine, I told my conscience.

"What do you want?" She looked exhausted but maybe ready to help.

"First, why didn't he want any GMW matters on your computer?"

"All of the secretaries' computers are on one network so we can assist each other when it's necessary. They're also all tied into the same system for printing as well."

"Okay; next: do you know the password to his CODED Directory?"

"No."

"Shit!" I thought for a moment, "Okay. Do you have a copy of the files that might be stored there? Did you save the information on the floppies you used to transfer stuff to Marty's computer?"

She hesitated before she answered. "No."

I had the feeling "no" wasn't the final word on the subject. I thought she wasn't sure enough of me yet.

"Can you tell me if Marty ever got the studio sheets he'd asked Warner Warner and Carpenter for?"

"No."

"No you can't tell me, or no you're sure he didn't get them?"

She hesitated again, but seemed to be thawing out. Maybe even enjoying this in spite of herself. She smiled ever so slightly.

"No, he had not got them."

"Shit! Do you have anything on your computer or on floppies about any proposed settlement agreement with DBS?"

"No."

"But he was working on it?"

"Yes, of course."

"And they'd be on his computer?"

"Yes."

"But in the coded file?"

"Certainly."

"What about the DBS/Studio Sheets? I see a directory for them on the computer, but no file in the drawer."

"Mr. Davidson may have it. Just after the first of the month when the sheets come in from DBS, he reconciles them for monies owed to our clients and to calculate the totals from which the GMW share will be figured. He's an accountant you know. As well as an attorney. Then Marty would review them and when he was satisfied, I use the disk DBS sends over to enter the information into our computer records."

"Does he usually hang onto them this far into the month?"

"Yes, he does it as a back-up to DBS's accountants, so there's no question about the dollar amounts going to clients. Since the client's check would have already gone out directly from DBS and their accountants just after the first, there's no great urgency. It's just a precaution; a double check, and of course, to keep track of the totals."

"What happens after an agreement between DBS and Marty?"

"What do you mean?"

"Would DBS and their accountants still get the sheets on clients or projects from the studios, or would GMW get them directly?"

"With a few exceptions, very close client-friends of Marty's, if a project or client deal was worked out at DBS, the sheets go to their accountants; if the deal was done through GMW we get them, or in our case, Warner Warner and Carpenter. The agreement will determine percentages of the monies still flowing from deals done at DBS by Marty, Tina Cox, Mr. Woodman, Davidson and Weiselman that should come to GMW, or in some cases, directly to the individual partner."

That seemed strange. It must have shown on my face.

"In a few cases the partner took on something special, put in time in an unusual way, or for some reason decided not to use partnership draws to cover the time spent on a special project."

"Like what?"

"The most important one is International Distributors. Marty got involved because a friend from college asked him to. The DBS partners weren't interested in it for the firm. So Marty began it on his own. Not drawing DBS partnership funds against the hours he logged on the project. After about ten months it got more involved, and it became clear that much more money was at stake than was at first apparent, the time burden on Marty had gotten to be too much. Mr. Diamond and Mr. Malovitch suggested Marty bring it into the firm."

"They smelled money," I interrupted.

She smiled and went on, "They worked out an agreement as to cost sharing and benefits if Marty won. He did. His friend, Mr. Jacobs, was awarded more than $12.5 million dollars. The total legal fees awarded were over $5 million. International Distributors appealed the decision, but was ordered to pay 10% interest on the judgement to an escrow account while the appeals were pending."

"How long has it been going on?"

"Four years."

"So?"

She smiled again. "It's grown to over $16.5 million. Over $7 million in fees."

"And that goes to Marty?"

"Not all of it. I believe the figure was around 26%."

"Why should DBS get 74% of something they turned away in the first place?"

"The case dragged on for three years before trial, and was two months at trial. It was an immense amount of work. DBS funded most of the costs. Marty could never have funded those outlays of time or money by himself. He was glad to have the firm come in on it with him."

"Where does it stand now?"

"It's over. International Distributors lost. The judgement stands. The money is to be released from escrow in a month."

"Is there a record of the agreement Marty had with DBS for the 26%?"

"It wasn't like that at DBS. They liked each other. It was more like a family there."

"No agreement?" I was incredulous.

"Not a contract in writing. They sat down and discussed it and agreed and shook hands on it."

"Who was at the meeting? Were you there?" A little hope flickered.

"Mr. Malovitch, Mr. Diamond, Mr. Bernstein, Marty, and Elaine, Mr. Malovitch's secretary."

"Did Elaine take notes?"

"Yes, of course. She took notes and they each initialled the page when they had agreed and then she photocopied it and gave each of them a copy."

"Do you know where Marty's copy is?"

"No."

"Any ideas?"

"He's..." she stumbled again, finding it as difficult to think of him in the past tense as I did, "...was very organized and neat."

Mom rules, I thought.

"I'm sure it would be in with the DBS file."

"The one Davidson probably has?"

"Possibly, but I believe he was keeping another file for DBS separation matters. I know that's the way he has...had it logged in his CODED directory."

"Did you work on those files?"

"Yes, but only after Marty had accessed them for me himself."

"He must have kept back-ups of his computer's files, right?"

"I never thought about it," but by the slight glint in her eyes she was thinking about it now.

"But you don't know where he'd keep them if he did?"

"No, I don't."

Another dead end. All avenues led to his computer's CODED directory and all were futile without the password. Time to move on, I thought, before she clams up.

"Marty had sent memos to you and Wolf about the Office Party expenses."

"That's right."

"And he finally he got them. Wolf said they'd been sent to him and Miriam had had them in her desk?"

"That's right."

"Did Marty ever get anything from the Warner guys identifying what the undocumented $10 thousand was for?"

"You must have been here a long time last night," she said matter-of-factly.

I shrugged.

"Or you're as thorough as he was."

"Same mother," I said.

The little smile had returned to her lips. "No, nothing from Warner and Warner."

She looked at me, now either willing me or challenging me to ask the right question. I let my mind drift for a moment. She was waiting impassively. A little light went on.

"From someone else?"

"Yes," she said, as pleased with me and herself as any teacher who'd coaxed the answer out of a lackluster pupil.

"Who?"

She was making up her mind now, no longer the mouse in this cat-and-mouse game.

"Me," she said with evident pride.

"How?"

"I told you, the secretaries' computers are linked." Another smile escaped her before she could reign it in. "Marty had so much on his mind and Mr. Wolf was not being helpful."

"So you accessed Miriam's computer?"

"Yes."

"And?"

"Mr. Wolf had paid Mrs. Wolf ten thousand dollars for professional services as his party consultant."

"WHAT! He paid his wife ten thousand dollars?!"

"Yes."

"That rotten thieving scummy....!"

"Yes," she said under her breath.

"Did you give Marty the information?"

"I left a memo on his desk," her lips began to quiver, "late Tuesday evening so he'd find it first thing Wednesday morning," she managed to say as her dammed-up crying spilled out.

Marty was busy killing himself about then.

"So he never saw it."

"No."

"I didn't see it last night or this morning. Did you retrieve it?"

Her crying slowed, then stopped, "No," she said shaking her head.

"Did you see anyone Tuesday night who might have stayed after you left? Or does anyone routinely get here earlier than you in the morning?"

"There were a lot of people still here Tuesday afternoon and evening. I was only back in the office a short time before I left again for a dentist's appointment at 3:45. It doesn't usually start clearing out around here until 5:30 or 6. Wednesday morning I think I was the first one in. I usually am."

"Would anyone feel free to just come in here if you or Marty weren't around?"

"They shouldn't."

I remembered Marty's calendar entry for Tuesday.

"You were out of the office on Tuesday?"

"Yes."

"With Marty? At Millennium?"

"Yes." She shifted uncomfortably.

"Would you tell me about that, please?"

"I really can't. It's confidential. A client's confidential business." She was shaking her head no.

"Ronnie, for now, I am Marty. I'm supposed to have access to things as he'd have access to them. I need to know what's been going on. What happened on Tuesday at Millennium?"

She was still shaking her head no, but now she was looking at her lap and wringing her hands, and I didn't think the no was for me. Tears began to run down her gaunt cheeks and she tried to brush them aside. Her body jerked in small spasms as she tried to hold in the sobs that wanted out.

"Please, Ronnie, tell me," I said.

When she looked up she startled me. Beneath the controlled surface, her anger seemed raw and outraged. She ignored a stream of tears.

"We met here at 8:30 to get the files. We went in separate cars so if it got late, I could go on to my dentist's appointment. We met Mr. Sutton at Millennium at 9:30. Marty and he prepared for their meeting with Mr. Faustini which was scheduled for 10."

"You were there with Marty and Sutton?"

"Yes."

"I know roughly what it's about, Ronnie. Were Marty and Sutton in basic agreement about how to proceed?"

"No. Sutton wanted it to just go away. Take what Millennium was offering and just leave it alone."

"And sue GMW for the rest, and then some?"

She looked at me with what I thought was suspicion, but her anger carried her past it. I realized I should shut up. If she figured I had another source of information, why should she supply me with any?

"Yes. Mr. Sutton is an unpleasant man. Very demanding and very vocal, very abusive with people he thinks have to take it, but underneath, he seems to me to be a timid and weak person. Very unsure of himself."

"What was Marty suggesting?"

"Marty had met with a lawyer representing his malpractice insurance company on Monday. They discussed the validity of the claim by Mr. Sutton against GMW."

"And?"

"He would have a very good case. But Marty was more interested that they discuss a case against Millennium."

I pulled back a little. Really? I was thinking, that's more like the Marty I know.

"Marty had convinced Mr. Besser from Prudential, the insurance carrier, that there was a strong case to be made against Millennium, Mr. Faustini and even Mr. Perry for negotiating in bad faith, for conspiring to breach a valid contract, and perpetrating a fraud. Marty had convinced Mr. Besser that given the circumstances, it was in the best interests of the insurance company to assist in the costs and prosecution of the suit against Millennium and the others rather than run the very real risk of having to pay Mr. Sutton what might amount to several million dollars. Mr. Besser agreed and his secretary and I exchanged information Monday afternoon. By Monday evening we'd prepared a complaint. Marty tried to convince Mr. Sutton that he should drop his suit against GMW and together they should go after Millennium. Not cave in to them. Mr. Sutton did not want to fight with Millennium or Mr. Faustini, and especially not Mr. Perry. Mr. Perry has a very nasty reputation.

"At 10 we met with Mr. Faustini, Mr. Salio, and Mr. Perry's personal assistant, a Mr. Cooper. I don't know who Mr. Salio is, and he didn't enter the discussions. Actually, he never said a word. Mr. Faustini and Mr. Cooper waved copies of the signed contracts around like they were showing off newly printed Bibles. Mr. Faustini is a large man, not tall, but thick and heavy-set. He's completely bald, I think he even shaves his head around the sides. He looks like a retired football player. He pounded the table and yelled about the original contract that Marty had negotiated with Millennium before Mr. Perry had bought it. Mr. Sutton actually agreed with Mr. Faustini and Mr. Cooper that the whole problem could be laid at Marty's feet for having created such an outrageous deal. Of course it was Mr. Faustini that had negotiated the contract with Marty for Millennium in the first place. Mr. Sutton did everything he could to distance himself from Marty except go sit on the other side of the table with Mr. Faustini and Mr. Cooper. It was humiliating for Marty.

"It was clear to me, and I'm sure to Marty, even though we didn't have a chance to discuss it, that Mr. Faustini and Mr. Cooper had previously talked to Mr. Sutton. They had gotten his compliance, and were relying on his suing GMW and not pursuing any claims against Millennium over the changes in the contracts. When it was clear Mr. Sutton was not going to be any help at all, and was acting in concert with Millennium, Marty gave Mr. Faustini and Mr. Cooper copies of the complaint we had prepared. Marty reviewed it while they read through it. Mr. Cooper whispered something to Mr. Faustini, then Mr. Cooper excused himself and left.

"Mr. Faustini jumped from his seat and bellowed and carried on and waved the complaint in Marty's face. He accused Mr. Sutton of selling them out. So it was completely clear that they'd had dealings behind Marty's back. It was beginning to look like Mr. Sutton had been involved in Millennium's attempt to break the contract from the outset.

"Mr. Cooper returned and Mr. Perry was with him. He's a huge man. Six feet five or six, and he must weigh more than three hundred pounds. Not so much fat, but huge and scary looking. He looked like a mountain that was going to fall and crush us. Mr. Sutton took one look at him and just fell apart. He protested his innocence. Said he had nothing to do with the complaint and would not be a party to it.

"Mr. Perry and Mr. Faustini hovered over Marty like they were gestapo police, shouting at him and waving the complaint around and pounding the table. Marty didn't look well. He was edgy and not quick to respond as he normally would. Even in the office when we were gathering up the files I noticed it. He seemed off. Preoccupied. I don't know what word to use, but he wasn't himself. Mr. Perry and Mr. Faustini were all over him, and he was just unable to respond.

"He looked dazed. He stood up, I think to remove the physical advantage Mr. Perry and Faustini were using by hovering over him, harassing him from above. But when he stood, his legs seemed weak and I could see he was dizzy."

I couldn't tell if Ronnie Hook's anger at the recollection of this scene would propel her through the telling of it, or if the recollection would suck the wind from her and prevent her from finishing. She took a few breaths.

"Marty put his hands on the table to steady himself, and he looked right at Mr. Perry and then Mr. Faustini and then Mr. Cooper and he said, 'if this contract isn't voided and copies with all the relevant tax provisions restored, readied for my review and Mr. Sutton's signature by noon tomorrow, my office will file this complaint by close of business tomorrow.

"Mr. Perry surged towards him as if to tackle him, but Marty collapsed to the floor."

Poor, poor Marty, I kept thinking. I felt drained as wave after wave of grief and anger washed over me. Ronnie's anger was giving way to her feelings and she began to weep.

"I could see Mr. Faustini and Mr. Perry exchange looks like they'd won. Mr. Perry said, 'the Kike fainted!', that's what he said, then he said to Mr. Cooper, 'get him outta here. This meeting is over.' Mr. Cooper and I helped Marty to a couch and got him some water and he seemed to revive, but he was so pale and his skin was clammy. He muttered 'pills', but I didn't know of any pills or prescriptions he used so...and then Mr. Sutton and Mr. Faustini were leaving together and Mr. Cooper asked me if he were okay and I said I thought so, and they left us. In a minute Marty sat up and his head seemed to clear and his color returned, and he realized that everyone was gone.

"He didn't say anything for a minute, but I could tell by the way he clenched his teeth and compressed his lips he was embarrassed and humiliated and livid. 'I've got to see Rick Rosen. Would you go back to the office and type up any notes you've taken and call Mr. Besser's office and tell him or leave word for him that we should keep our scheduled meeting for tomorrow? Do you have enough time before your dentist's appointment?' I told him I did. We walked out to the parking lot together and I had the feeling he wanted to explain or say something, but he didn't. I would have been surprised if he had, but he didn't."

"Who's Rick Rosen?"

"His physician."

I felt worn out and beaten up. Ronnie looked relieved to have been able to tell someone, anyone about this. My headache was returning. I looked at the ugly loud-ticking clock on the desk. It was 11:30.

Something else dawned on me.

"When you were in Miriam's computer, could you tell if Wolf's computer is tied into it?"

She smiled that little smile again.

"Did you happen to see any listings for the studio sheets?"

She was fighting an ear to ear grin and losing.

"Did you retrieve them?"

"No. There wasn't time."

"But they should still be there?"

"I should think so."

"The files weren't coded?"

"They were."

I was puzzled. "So how did you get in?"

"I took a wild guess as to the code."

The mouse that roared, I thought. I waited for her to tell me. She smiled again.

"GOD," she said. "Wolf's password for his coded files is GOD."

Chapter 12

Before Ronnie left Marty's office I had her show me how to use the phone system without the help of the reception area operator. She showed me how to reach each partner without going through their secretaries, how to get an outside line, and how to connect to her. When she left, I fiddled around until I got what I thought should be Davidson's office. Someone picked up the phone but didn't respond. I remembered Ronnie had told me that when the phone system was used inter-office like this, the office doing the calling was identified by a light blinking on the receiving phone. Maybe Davidson was spooked getting a call from Marty's office.

"Mel?" I said, only half convinced I'd done it right and gotten his office. The line was silent for an eight count and I was just about to hang up and try again when he spoke.

"Who is this?" he asked uncertainly.

"It's Kurt. I'm in Marty's office. Would you come down here please, and would you bring the DBS file with you?"

The line was quiet again. At first I thought that he didn't like being summoned by me. Then I thought he was deciding whether or not he should show me the file. I even had time to wonder if he was busy shredding it before I could get my prying eyes on it, but just about then, I heard sniffling and the unmistakable drawing in of breath that trying to stifle crying creates.

"Mel?"

"Yes, yes, I'll come. I'll be there in a minute."

"Thanks."

I was out on the balcony looking at the water, listening to the muted sounds of the surf washing up on the sand. I was trying not to think at all, trying to let the sunlight sparkling on the water hypnotize me. I was trying to let the beach sounds lull me into some pleasant reverie of our shared past, Marty's and mine, at the beach. We were broke, and we knew it. Poor in one of the richest towns on the face of the earth. We were going to school with the kids of the rich and famous, but it was okay. At least it was for us younger kids. It didn't really seem to matter all that much. Those were pretty good days. I remembered going home with Jimmy Marx and exploring the secret passageways that ran everywhere in his father's house. We would lift the hinged seat of a cushioned bench near the fireplace in their den and climb in. It was ostensibly for firewood, but Jimmy showed me how the back was false, and pushed aside, opened onto a series of hallways and stairs that paralleled every room in the house. He was a rich kid and I wasn't, but we had fun together. We were in the Cub Scouts together too, and Carrol Rosenbloom still owned the Rams then and one of his kids was in our troop and we got to go to some games and have our picture taken with Crazy Legs Hirsch and Y.A. Tittle and some other guys I couldn't remember. The world was tighter then, more cohesive. The parts fit better, connected in a seamless well-ordered way. I knew that it wasn't the same for Marty. He was old enough to know he didn't fit, old enough to be embarrassed by being someone's guest at the places where his friends could sign for the bill on their father's accounts. He knew it was because we weren't rich or famous. He wouldn't sneak into The Beach Club or any of the other places his classmates hung out. He was determined to walk through the front door and take satisfaction and pride from knowing that he belonged and was welcome. That his kids would be able to sign for the check on his account. There was a knock at the door. I took a last look and sucked in a long breath of the cool fresh air coming in on a light breeze off the water and went back into the office.

"Come in," I said.

Mel Davidson cautiously opened the door, stuck his head in and asked, "Are you ready to see me?"

I fought off a laugh. I tried to turn it into a welcoming smile.

"Of course."

I motioned him to the couch. He sat there and put the file on the glass coffee table. He looked uneasy. I was standing and had a picture flash through my mind of Marty at Millennium. I sat in the arm-chair.

"Thanks for coming," I started.

He looked at me as though he could hear the words but couldn't make sense of them. He seemed lost. He seemed genuinely hurt by the loss of Marty, but I had a sense that more than anything else, he was adrift. Rudderless.

"First, were you or any of the other former DBS partners involved with Marty's negotiations of the settlement agreement with Barry Malovitch?"

"No, not me anyway. I don't think Marty had given any of us any of the details."

"But he'd discussed it with you?"

"Yes, of course. He kept us posted in a general way."

"Have you talked with the others? Have they said anything about it?"

"I work closely with Joe Woodman. We talk about it. Marty hadn't consulted with him either if that's what you mean."

"And Weiselman and Tina Cox?"

"I don't think so. Tina if anyone. She had more independence at DBS, and had made more deals on her own. Her stake in the settlement would be greater."

I took a moment to look at the file. There was a summary sheet that listed clients or projects by name and the studio that held the rights. There were dollar totals. I recognized most of the names. Marty's client list was truly a Who's Who of the movers and shakers. The rest of the pages were supporting printouts for the summary. I saw Sutton's name and Millennium's name but there was a goose egg in the dollar column. Davidson noticed my noticing. I looked at him and raised my eyebrows. He shrugged uncomfortably.

"Their idea of hardball?" I suggested.

"I suppose," he said, his posture and expression aimed at distancing himself from the topic.

"Did everything reconcile the way it should?"

"Except for Sutton, yes, it usually does. The firm that works for DBS is reliable."

"How long has Millennium been withholding on Sutton?"

"This is the second quarter, the second time."

"So Marty was aware of it from the last quarter?"

"Yes."

If Sutton threw money around like some of these other bozos, he couldn't afford to be stiffed for anything like two quarters. I was thinking the poor bastard's panic was due to more than just Garvin Perry's reputation. I wondered if Marty had included Breach of Contract in this context as part of the complaint against Millennium and Perry and Faustini. Probably. Maybe that's why they thought Sutton had broken some agreement they thought they had with him. I'd have to ask Ronnie. There were no notes attached to the file. Nothing about the settlement agreement. There had to be another file.

"Where's the other file?"

"What file?"

"Where's the second file on DBS? On Settlement Issues?"

He was flustered. "Tina might have it. I don't know. Marty never let it circulate."

"Did he keep it here in the file drawers?"

"Maybe Gary," he offered.

I looked at him curiously. "But it should be here, right?"

"I think so. Nobody would take it without asking. I mean unless maybe Marty took it home to work on. But I'm sure it would be on his or Ronnie's computer if you can't find the physical file itself," he said helpfully, "probably both."

He waited. He seemed to be holding his breath, then taking little gulps of air. I didn't think he had a lot more to contribute.

Even though I hadn't pressed it with Tina Cox, I'd thought about asking her, then Ronnie, flat out why they thought Marty did it. I still wanted to, but for a couple of reasons, maybe the same reasons with each of them, it didn't happen. The simplest reason was talking about it confirmed it. Made it real. Not talking about it kept it at a safer more abstract distance. Part of it, I knew, was I wanted information from them, and if I upset or offended them it would stop the flow. It almost had with Tina. And asking the question would undoubtedly release a flood of pain and grief because of their strong emotional connection to him. After seeing Tina's response to even the suggestion of it, I knew I wasn't ready to put them through it. I wasn't ready to put myself through it. And I knew I needed to get a better feel for what was going on before posing the question to the people I felt were closest to him and could best answer. I needed a better grasp of the context of his life and death and how these people figured in it before I could assess the value of their insight. But here was hapless Mel Davidson, a little too far down the food chain to have any great insight, I thought, but I felt like the reasons for not asking just weren't there. With him, I thought I could at least get the words out. I needed to learn how to ask the question and sift through the answer. It would be good practice. Lucky Mel, I thought.

He looked anxious and ready to go. Fidgeting like it's 3:09 and he's watching the second hand on the clock of his third-grade classroom wall.

"What made him do it?" I asked, "What do you think?"

Suddenly it was 2:09 instead, and the second hand had stopped moving. A range of emotions crossed his face, dread, pain, maybe shock at my asking, but then he surprised me, and seemed to calm himself from the inside out. He looked at me steadily and spoke slowly, thoughtfully.

"I've thought about nothing else since I heard the news. No one wants to talk about it. Well, I don't think that's really true. I think everyone wants to talk about it but it's too soon or they're embarrassed or afraid of seeming to be insensitive. I don't know, something like that. I tried to talk to Joe, but he's so emotional, you know? Especially about Marty. But I told my wife it didn't make sense. Marty was tough. Very sure of himself and his abilities. I just can't imagine the business with Sutton and Millennium or the problems here at GMW with Wolf pushing him to do something like this. It's just not believable."

He looked at me and his eyes were wet. "What made Marty so special wasn't just how good he was at this, or how much he cared about things working out well for his clients. He had a feel for film as art. He loved it. If he could free the most talented people to do their best work, he knew he was a part of it. Do you understand?"

"I think so."

"I went to film school at UCLA, before law school. I thought I could make films." He smiled. "I wasn't any good. I loved it, but it just wasn't something I could do well. But I still wanted to be a part of it, contribute something to film. Working with Marty showed me how. It's not believable," he repeated, crying.

I mentally moved him way up the food chain.

He looked at me and shrugged, like, that's the best I can do. Not bad. Class dismissed.

I sat there for a while after Davidson left. I had my hands folded across my stomach, my feet up on the glass desk, my eyes fixed on the indistinct line where the pale sky met the only slightly darker water. I had to concentrate to see it. I let the concentration act like a filter. Whatever got through got through. Out of the mouths of babes, I thought. I still didn't know enough and felt I wasn't ready to focus on why Marty did it, even if it was the first and most natural question, but Davidson's dismissal of Sutton and Millennium and Wolf brought me up short. It rang true. Frustrated or not, the Marty I knew would have dealt with Wolf and GMW and Millennium and Sutton like a chess player, one move at a time, but looking for openings and planning as far ahead as he could. Marty's attempts to get the studio sheets from Warner and Warner suggested he was doing what he could about whatever he suspected there. The meeting on Monday with his malpractice insurer, and planning to meet with him again on Wednesday afternoon to get the complaint ready to file, confirmed he wasn't rolling over for Millennium. None of it pointed to his having felt helpless or checkmated or ready to give up. What was so hopeless? Where was the despair? I felt another of those waves about to engulf me. There was a knock at the door. I took a deep breath and tried to shrug it off.

"Come in," I said.

Tina Cox put her face then neck then shoulders through the door. Testing the waters.

"Wanna get outta here?"

Her smile hit me like sunshine at the end of a long tunnel.

"Yeah," I smiled back at her, "let's go."

I looked at the ugly chrome clock on the desk. It was 12:15.

On the way through the lobby Ron Lawton looked up from whatever he was doing and gave me a little thumbs up gesture. Hang-in, take care, do well, something like that. Whatever he had in mind, it was welcome. I wondered if anyone had told him about the disturbance at GMW this morning.

Chapter 13

We found a table outside at the Café De La Mer. The air had heated up some, but there was the usual light breeze coming off the water. The sky was cloudless. Tina had gotten a salad and an elaborate chicken entree and lemonade. I got lemonade and a fresh brioche. True to her word, she paid.

"You're a pretty cheap date," she said.

Our trays fit into indentations in the table, I supposed so that you'd use the tray and they'd have less mess on the table to clean when you were done. One or two small birds hopped from the ground to the table and approached the food heedless of our existence. I looked around. It was the same everywhere. They were not going to be denied or shooed away. The only successful strategy seemed to be to submit to the extortion. Tina threw little bits of this or that on the ground and the birds would leave the table to eat it. There seemed to be an established rule that they would stay away long enough for you to eat something and exchange a few words before they returned to demand more.

"Are you in training?" she asked me.

"What?"

"The bread and water." She took a mouthful of her salad and nodded to my brioche and lemonade. "Maybe in training for jail food?" she said around a mouthful of salad. She held her hand in front of her mouth as she chewed and spoke.

"Wolf," she offered in return for my blank look. "If you give him half a chance, he'll find something to file a complaint with the police about."

I shrugged. "He will or he won't."

"Believe me, he will if he can," she warned. "He's fuming. He's on a rampage. We've been meeting on and off all morning preparing for a partnership meeting with you and Bob Winters. John could hardly sit still. It's all he can think about, and with all the problems facing us, that's saying something. You wounded his pride and embarrassed him. He's nasty enough without giving him a revenge motive."

I thought she was reprimanding me. I was about to tell her to fuck off. I thought she was about to tell me if Wolf wants Marty's office, he should get it. She read the look on my face like it was written in ballpoint on my forehead. She reached out and touched my hand.

"No no!" she said, "I'm not suggesting...I know John had it coming. Moving into Marty's office was outrageous." She smiled, "You put on quite a show. It was wonderful, really, but go easy, okay?"

She gave my hand what I regarded as an affectionate squeeze and I felt better. I can be bought cheap, I thought. But not completely.

"Do you have the DBS settlement file?"

She stopped chewing and regarded me, no doubt mulling over my talent for seizing the moment at the expense of sustaining the mood.

"No," she replied flatly. "Why?"

"It's not around. Davidson only had the DBS studio sheet file. He said other than Marty, you had the most at stake in the settlement. That maybe you might have it."

"No. Marty didn't pass it around."

"Did you discuss the settlement with him?"

"Of course."

"Do you know where things stood? Like what had been resolved or what hadn't? Percentages? Dollar amounts. Buy-outs of partnership equity?"

"No. Marty said it was going well, that they'd agreed on almost all of the issues and I trusted his judgement. What DBS owed him dwarfed the rest of us, so we left it to him."

"Did you know about an initialled copy of notes from their meeting about International Distributors?"

"Marty mentioned it."

"But you never saw it?"

"No. Where does Ronnie say it is?"

"In the missing file."

"Hmmm..."

"So, where do you think the file is?"

I immediately regretted asking the question almost as much as I did the tone that had crept into my voice. So did she.

"What the hell is that supposed to mean!"

She looked poised to get up and leave. I motioned her back to her seat.

"I'm sorry, that sounded bad. Really, Tina, I'm sorry."

She was only partially mollified.

"The file's not in the office," I told her, "and I'm pretty sure it's not at his house, and Ronnie and Mel Davidson have no idea where it is."

"Well, I have no idea where it is either," she said, still annoyed.

"Okay, okay! Jeez!"

"Well, 'Jeez' yourself. That's insulting!"

Our eyes met and she eased off and smiled. "Have Ronnie get you what you need off her computer," she said as she returned to her lunch.

"Right," I said stupidly.

I had the sinking feeling I'd just painted myself into a corner and would have to decide right now that I either trusted her enough to tell her it wasn't on Ronnie's computer, and then probably have to also reveal I couldn't get into Marty's computer, or not tell her, and have it be obvious I was withholding something and that I didn't trust her and lose what? A source of information? A semi-confident? Whatever, it would be lost. Nice work, I thought.

"What?" she probed.

I found myself looking at the sunlight sparkling on her long blond hair twisted up in a bun, held in place at the back of her head by a gold gizmo with a thick gold pin. She had tanned arms with little downy blond hair here and there on her forearms, shining like little trustworthy beacons along an unfamiliar shore. I thought about getting familiar. I also decided I needed to trust her.

"This goes nowhere else, okay?"

She gave me a withering look, but I persisted.

"No one, okay?"

"Of course," she promised, her annoyance returned.

"It's not there."

She looked as though the words were in some other language.

"Of course it's there."

"Ronnie says she never worked on it, just Marty."

"Then it's on his computer."

"It's in a CODED directory."

"And you don't have the code."

"Right."

"Well, you can get the information from Barry Malovitch."

Yeah, his version. I involuntarily made a face. Poker's not my game.

"It's not like that at DBS," she insisted.

I raised my eyebrows and my mouth drew back a little. Yeah, sure.

"I'm supposed to meet with Malovitch sometime soon. I'd like to have Marty's copy of Elaine's notes, and I'd like to have that file. I want to know what Marty's expectations were and where they stood according to him."

"Maybe Gary."

"What?"

"It's not very likely, but Marty could have given Gary the file to look over tax aspects of a proposed settlement. Would you like me to ask him?"

"No thanks, I will. It makes sense though. Thanks."

"It might be better if I asked him."

"What? Old Gary doesn't like me?"

"It's not just you," she said, suggesting it was at least in part me, "he's been kinda weird lately. For months, really. But he's gotten it into his head that you're going to be a problem. You know, the..."

"Autopsy." I finished for her.

"Yes."

She was waiting for me to confirm or deny. I shrugged.

"What's that supposed to mean?"

"Gary shouldn't sharpen his scalpel just yet. He and Wolf may have to postpone their little slice and dice-fest."

She stopped eating, her fork in mid-air, and looked at me like I'd just confirmed some nagging suspicion about a fundamental character flaw.

"What's the matter with you? You think that's funny? That's sick!"

Where's Nick when I need him, I was thinking. She gave me a horrified look and shook her head, like I'm hopeless, or what's the use, probably thinking that not only were Gary and Wolf right, but they didn't know the half of it. She looked as though she were going to stand and remove herself from my vile company but was waiting for me to stop her by apologizing again. Sorry, sister, only one to a customer. I raised my eyebrows up and down, Groucho style, to tell her that.

"Different fathers," she said contemptuously and stood to huff off.

As she turned to take a step away from our table, she bumped into a hard charging Bob Winters. He held his brief case in his right hand and I noticed he was gripping the handle so tightly his knuckles were white. I had the feeling he'd have liked to club me with it. I didn't know if it were because he just failed to notice Tina, or if he were so intent on getting to me while his irons were hot, but he smacked into her like Dick Butkus into some rookie tailback, knocking her back a couple of stumbling steps. She caught herself on the chair she'd just left.

"Are you outta your goddam mind?" he shouted for openers as he slammed his briefcase onto the table. The indentations in the table held the trays firmly in place, which was impressive considering how hard he'd slammed it. I reconsidered their purpose, what with all the lawyers in this building.

"My thought exactly," Tina agreed.

"Bob Winters, Tina Cox," I said.

Bob looked at her like she'd materialized out of thin air. I could see it dawn on him that not only was there a person there with us, but she was one of the partners. He fumed more, if possible, and from the part of his neck bulging over his shirt collar all the way up to his crew cut hair, he turned that attractive shade of red-purple. He summoned up all his patience and tact, and was able to momentarily calm himself and forget me and he shook hands with her.

"Nice to meet you Miss. Cox. Would you excuse us, please? We need to talk before the meeting."

"Gladly," Tina said, and resumed her huffy exit.

Bob Winters and I watched her go. If it had been under other circumstances or just another person there with me, it would have been one of those nice moments when two men watch an attractive blond take her long shapely legs for a walk. When she'd gone from sight, one might say to the other, my oh my oh my!

"You're the goddamm limit, mister!" Winters said instead.

My oh my oh my, I said to myself. If Winters wouldn't cooperate, I'd have to do it myself. I smiled, thinking, I have to do everything myself, as I've frequently complained to my helpers.

He wiped his hand through the bristle on his head. It came away wet. He found Tina's napkin and dried it. It was sunny and comfortably warm with that gentle sea-breeze, but he was agitated and sweating like it were ninety. "I gotta get a cold drink. What's that?" He pointed to my lemonade.

"Lemonade," I said.

"Don't move! I'll be right back."

He returned with three large glasses of lemonade and tossed down the first one before he sat. He started working on the second as he got comfortable in the chair. I sort of hoped he'd gotten the third one for me, but when he saw me eyeing it, he just glared while drinking, to warn me off. He watched me over the rim of his glass like he didn't know where to begin or if it would make any difference. He closed his eyes and drank more slowly, purposely trying to calm himself. His color returned to what passed for normal on him and he opened his eyes and looked at me. He was fighting to keep his voice under control and his blood pressure down.

"I told you not to talk to any of the partners until after we'd met with them today. I told you! We have to get along with these guys. It's going to be a long haul. It will be longer and harder if we have to fight them every inch of the way. If we have to fight them, we will. But If we don't, or if an issue is not an issue, let's not make it one. Understand?"

"Like what?"

"Like what!!?" He rolled his eyes around wildly, maybe inviting God to witness this idiocy, "Let me think a minute." He pinched the bridge of his nose between first finger and thumb as though trying desperately to think of something, then as though it had come to him in a flash, he threw his arms wide and exclaimed cheerily, "Oh, I know, I know," he smiled at me, then just as suddenly stopped smiling and yelled, arms waving , "like throwing Wolf's stuff off the goddam balcony, that's like what! Like telling him to move out of ...."

"Out of Marty's office!" I shot back. "If that little cocksucker can't wait a day or a week or a month or a year if that's what I choose, fuck him. Right now it's my office. I'll let him know when I'm through with it."

He looked at me in disbelief. "What on earth makes you think it's yours?"

"I'm Marty's executor. According to John, I act in his place in everything he was involved in. Including GMW. So, I figure as long as the

GMW partnership exists, and Marty H. Goldman, A Professional Corporation is still a partner in it, that office is still Marty's, and therefore mine. Wolf's an asshole and he's out of line and if you can't see it that's too fucking bad, but I'm not going to start rolling over for him on this or anything else just because he's used to getting his way."

He was shaking his head like even if I were right, I was choosing the wrong battle in the wrong place at the wrong time. Like I didn't have a clue. Maybe he was right. I really didn't care. Fuck him and fuck Wolf. As I watched him, he avoided my eyes, and I had the feeling he was searching for some way out, for some escape or reprieve. I could see his eyes suddenly fix on the peaceful blue water as though he'd never seen it before, like he were surprised it was even there. A measure of tranquility came over him.

"Wishing you'd brought a bucket and shovel?" I asked.

He smiled thinly and sighed. "Maybe your brother had a pretty good idea, after all."

I had the feeling he wanted to tell me he couldn't work with me. That he was going to tell John Goodman to handle it himself or just drop me. I think he'd decided to tell me something along those lines until I suggested it to him first.

"If you want out Bob, get out. No hard feelings. If Goodman doesn't do this part of the work himself, I'll find another firm. But as for kissing Wolf's ass or any of the others' at GMW in order to get along with them to resolve the problems, it's not going to happen. Besides, things are beginning to look even messier and uglier than you predicted. Now would be a good time to bail out."

He looked annoyed and intrigued. I didn't think he was the kind of guy that would ever allow himself to bail out of anything he'd undertaken, even if it had been forced on him. He raised a inquisitive brow.

"Enlighten me."

"I'm not sure enough to talk about it yet.

"Swell. Any idea when you might be?"

"Early next week. Wednesday at the latest. The funeral's arranged for Sunday afternoon, and I'll have to focus on that this weekend." Along with breaking into Wolf's GOD file, I thought.

He looked skeptical, still teetering between wanting to get as far away from me as fast as possible and sticking around because his sense of duty wouldn't let him bail out. "Give me a taste. Give me something," he growled.

"How about we meet with the GMW guys first and have coffee afterwards? Maybe I take you across the street to the beach, get you to take off your shoes and socks and that hangman's noose around your neck and we can decide where we are and where we're going or if you're just plain gone."

He finished off the third glass of lemonade in one long swallow.

"Okay. But I gotta have your word you won't bait Wolf."

He waited for a reply.

"Your word. Right?"

I thought about Wolf, and his moving into Marty's office, and I could feel a switch click on, or maybe a flood gate start to open. I closed it. What the hell, I thought, it would only be for an hour or two, and I knew I needed Winters. I could restrain myself for that long.

"Right."

"Good. Now some business. The first thing they're going to want is the autopsy request signed."

I clenched my teeth and said nothing. He looked at me without a hint of emotion or interest in any emotion I might have about it.

"It's very simple. You have a fiduciary duty to make decisions in the best interest of the estate. If GMW can show it wasn't legally suicide and gets the two and a quarter million from the Key Man policy, the value of GMW and therefore your brother's estate goes up. If they don't, it doesn't. If they don't, it's likely GMW will fold, and First American Bank will call the loan, and the estate will be hurt immeasurably. Maybe be insolvent. Any questions?"

I shook my head no. Winters eyed me for a moment.

"If you don't agree to sign, they can, and according to Bob Thorne, probably will go after you personally. Do you understand?"

I had a sinking feeling in the pit of my stomach, a slight case of light-headedness and I felt like the sunlight had become brighter and much more yellow. In fact my whole field of vision was bright yellow. I could feel the blood drain from my face. I think it ended up in my shoe.

"No," I managed to squeeze out.

Winters looked at me curiously. "You okay?"

"Explain," I said.

"You have a duty to the estate. If you breach that duty your sister-in-law could sue you personally for losses to the estate your actions, or your failure to act, cause. As far as the partners go, they have no standing to sue you, but they can sue the estate, and those suits could certainly injure the estate, or cripple it and give your sister-in-law added grounds to hold you personally accountable. Whatever money or property you have could be taken to satisfy a judgement against you. Got it?"

My head was spinning. The picture he was painting was becoming all too clear. Thanks, Marty, thanks a lot. I nodded that I understood.

"Good," his tone closing the lid on the need for any further discussion of the issue.

"They faxed my office an agenda of issues they want to discuss this afternoon. The autopsy was first. Their lease is number two. The First American Bank loan is number three. The Sutton suit is number four. The status of the DBS settlement Agreement is number five."

He was looking at me to determine whether I could or would fill him in if I knew anything about any of them, or tell him I didn't. When I said nothing, he just grunted.

"Not ready to talk yet?" he said sarcastically.

"Let's let them do the talking. Let them get us informed."

"Good," he said. "And when we have our little outing at the beach afterwards, you'll be so kind as to fill me in?"

"As much as I can, but by Wednesday at the latest."

He grunted assent. "Let's go."

In the lobby we signed in. It was 1:25. Ron Lawton handed Winters the clipboard first, then me. Bob had stepped into the elevator and was waiting for me to sign and join him. Lawton positioned himself so his back was to Winters and hovered over me while I signed.

"Could I talk with you sometime soon?" he whispered.

I signed the sheet and looked up at him. His face was troubled, and he had an expectant look like I could help.

"Sure," I said, "when?"

"Tonight?"

I thought for a moment about where I had to go and what I had to do. "How about Sandy's, tonight at ten or ten-thirty?"

"Yes, thanks." He forced a smile.

"I'll try to be on time, but things are pretty hectic. Wait for me. I won't forget. I'll be there."

"No problem. Thanks again."

The elevator bonged as we stepped out into the reception area of GMW. I could feel Winters assessing the digs, thinking too much, as in too lavish, not too much as in far out. Winters was not a far out kind of guy. The huge granite reception desk, the huge brass Goldman Marshall & Wolf letters above it, the thick carpet and white couches around the huge glass and chrome coffee table, the paintings, all of it just too much. He seemed to be appalled, mentally shaking his head. He strode purposefully to the receptionist in the center.

"Bob Winters and Kurt Goldman. We're expected for a 1:30 meeting."

The woman seated to the right behind the Music side of the desk looked up, smiled at Winters and took over. A look of distaste crossed her face as her eyes met mine, but her forced smile came back when she stood to lead us to the meeting. A witness to the box throwing event, and not a sports fan, I thought.

"Right this way Mr. Winters."

I had the feeling that as far as she was concerned I wasn't invited, but I came along anyway. We walked down the hallway towards Marty's office. At the end of the hallway were the glass doors to the large Conference Room. Ronnie was at her work station outside Marty's office.

"Ronnie, would you accompany us please."

She looked up startled. She wasn't the only one.

"Excuse me?" she and Bob Winters said simultaneously.

"I'd like you to take some notes. Bob Winters, Ronnie Hook, Marty's secretary."

Winters nodded to her, "Miss Hook," but glared at me.

Ronnie looked at Winters and the other woman for guidance.

"The partnership meetings are for partners only," the guide dog stressed, "and invited guests," she smiled at Winters.

I could see Wolf's secretary, Miriam, seated next to him. The guide dog's eyes followed mine.

"She got promoted?" I asked, then to Ronnie, "I'm inviting you."

The guide dog rolled her eyes in exasperation and pushed one of the doors open and held it for us. Ronnie took up a pencil and pad and followed us into the conference room. Winters was grinding his teeth, but he didn't say anything. I knew he thought I'd already reneged on my word not to bait Wolf, but I didn't think so. I had the feeling Ronnie didn't like Wolf, despised him in fact. I also had the feeling that she'd not had that much direct contact with him. That she dealt with him on the inter-office phone or through Miriam, but primarily had formed a picture of him through the effects his dealings had on Marty. I was hoping that seeing him in action for herself might coax her into telling me things I was sure she was holding back on. I was also hoping she might see or hear something that she knew to be untrue, and let me know. It was worth a try and Winters' displeasure.

Wolf sat at the head of the table, his back to the ocean, Miriam to his right, on the side of the table closest to the doors. Seated next to her along that side were Marshall, Bob Throne and who I guessed to be McCord and Hamilton. Across the table were Gary Weiselman on Wolf's left, then Woodman, Davidson, and Tina Cox. That left three empty chairs on that side of the table and the chair at the end opposite Wolf. Winters left the chair next to Tina Cox empty, probably for me, and sat in the next one down. Ronnie sat in the last chair on that side. As I came around the end of the table, Wolf sort of nodded his head in the direction of the chair next to Tina. It was a silent impatient order. I took the seat opposite him, at the end of the long length of the table, instead. He looked at Ronnie like she'd been headed for the ladies room and wandered in here by mistake. The well trained Miriam read her boss's thoughts and saved him the effort on an inquiry.

"Is there something, Ronnie?"

Ronnie looked from me to Miriam and then to Bob Winters and John Wolf, uncertainly.

"I'd like her to take notes. If *you* don't mind, of course," I smiled pleasantly at Miriam and ignored Wolf.

Miriam started to politely protest, but Wolf cut in.

"Fine, whatever, let's get started. Miriam, pass those out." Miriam went around the table giving each of us an agenda. She hesitated a moment at Ronnie, but gave her one. "Mr. Winters, I'm John Wolf; this is Bob Thorne, Sandy Marshall, Mathew McCord, Bruce Hamilton, Gary Weiselman, Joe Woodman, Mel Davidson, and Tina Cox." He nodded to Thorne, "Bob."

Apparently secretaries didn't get introduced. Miriam didn't seem to notice. Ronnie's lips were pressed tightly into a thin line.

Bob Thorne pivoted a few times back and forth between Wolf and Winters and finally to me, like he was the test pilot for the company that made the swivel mechanism for these chairs. He fixed me with his best impasse/resolution specialist look. His eyes bore into me, with no hint of a flicker or waver, like heartless lasers whose sole purpose was to cut me to shreds. I had to admit to myself, a shiver went through me. He was pretty good at this. I met his look, and I'm sure he knew immediately he was going to win the eye-ball contest. High up on my stomach, at the bottom of my breast bone, I could feel a thumping, not so much my heart pounding, but the surging of blood in some artery or vein. No doubt about it, this guy could rattle me, if I let him. So I purposely focused on his resume, his wife's father's firm, his scratching and aching to get into the big leagues and I settled down inside. I smiled a little bit.

"Roberta wants the autopsy request signed now." He held me in the grip of his unblinking glare. Wolf started to chime in with something but Thorne held up a hand without taking his eyes off of me. He was the man. He was in charge. He'd handle me. Wolf could sit back and watch a master at work. His tone was strong, his posture determined and unyielding. I imagined him waiting for everyone at the table to score him, raise the little placards with numbers on them and post his score. I'd have given him a 9.25 myself. I was that impressed.

I didn't say anything. After several moments of silence, it troubled the assemblage. Bob Winters jumped in, assuming it was a non-issue after having informed me of my lack of options.

"I've explained the situation to Kurt. I've relayed your position on the matter. He's aware he has a fiduciary duty here."

Thorne smiled at Wolf. Mission accomplished. He was still lobbying for the job Marty had refused him. He passed the form down to me by way of McCord and Hamilton. A flicker of sympathetic regret crossed Hamilton's face as he slid the form to me. He looked at me and our eyes met. I must have had the unhappy beseeching look of an early Christian to his Roman guard when he was told it was his turn to train the lions. He slid his pen to me. Go get 'em, pal, and may your god be with you, as it's lunch time. I could feel the blood first creep towards my face, then rush. I felt paralyzed. Everyone was looking at me. I had the sinking feeling of being called on in class when you had no idea what they were talking about or what they wanted from you, except in this case, I knew what they wanted. I was in danger of retreating so far into myself they'd have to do an autopsy on me just to find where I'd gone. I was at the wrong end of the telescope and they were getting further and further away. Wolf took my inaction as a challenge. I looked to Tina for help. Actually, I would have settled for a little smile of sympathy or understanding. Anything. I didn't really expect help. Her eyes briefly met mine then shifted away. I guessed I'd sliced and diced myself right out of her good graces.

"Sign the godamm form and let's move on!" Wolf hissed at me.

I looked at Wolf's angry face, then at the others around the table. From their looks, Bob Thorne and a disheveled Gary Weiselman were competing with Wolf for most annoyed with me. My heart was pounding and I had a sudden flash of a Sheriff nailing foreclosure signs to the Canyon House and my new project, the Canyon Creek House. I wondered if Jane, my ex-wife, would let me stay in her garage awhile. But that might get too complicated. My mind wandered around the familiar territory of the Panoramic Hill, my projects there, and before that, the long summer days working with Zak. It gave me back a sense of place, of a larger brighter world outside this room and its problems. I snapped out of my interior free-fall. Bob Winters was impatient, like I was in line in front of him boarding a plane, and stopped for no reason, and no one could get around me and I wasn't moving and didn't look likely to. When my eyes met those of Sandy Marshall, there was warmth and compassion there. I thought of his wife, and wondered what her situation was. I tried to muster a little smile at him. There was a hint of one in return.

I looked at Thorne, then Wolf and said, "I suggest we move on."

Bob Winters rolled his eyes and muttered, "Oh Christ!"

Wolf and Thorne exploded together. Thorne got to his feet and stormed down to my end of the table and hovered over me. He picked up the pen and thumped it down on the form and growled through clenched teeth.

"If you don't sign this now, and I mean right now, I'm going to file a motion in Superior Court asking the court to overrule you. And they will. I will demand a restraining order against any cremation or burial until this is decided. And then Roberta will file a damage claim against you personally. Do you understand? I'll also file to have you discharged as executor. Now sign it!"

Wolf had stood at the same time and was shouting down the length of the table at me, but I couldn't hear the words. I'd slipped further back into myself and felt like someone had turned off the sound. But the picture was clear. Too clear. The tops of my ears felt hot. The lack of sound coming through to me was a strange phenomenon, but it had the interesting side effect of drawing my attention to visual idosyncracies I might not have otherwise noticed. Gary Weiselman was the only one of the lesser partners that was greatly agitated, and he was pointing his finger at me and intermittently muttering or yelling something, but what was interesting was that it was intermittent. He kept stopping to play with his nose. Pinching it between his thumb and first finger, rubbing it, then wiggling it like a rabbit testing the air for danger. He also ran his hand through his thick black hair. Not once or twice, but repeatedly. As soon as his hand was done with his nose, it went to his hair. Then back again. His words, whatever they were, seemed incidental to his fidgeting. I could feel myself falling farther back into the free-fall until what Weiselman was saying started to filter through. It was like a mantra he was repeating, looking at me, then at the table in front of him, then back to me. Coming from him like an incantation over and over again.

"Fucking stubborn!...fucking Marty!...fucking brother!...fucking stupid! fucking stubborn!...fucking stupid!...fucking..." he kept muttering.

I wondered what stubbornness he had in mind about Marty? I thought about it a moment and decided Marty was never stubborn. Determined and focused and thorough I'd say, but not stubborn. I might have to plead guilty to it, but not Marty. I thought no one else noticed, but then Tina put her hand on his to calm him down. A sort of there, there gesture. He shook it off angrily and yelled down the table to me.

"We've got lives! We've got our own problems! You can't come in here and fuck us around! You don't know what's going on! It doesn't matter! Marty's dead! He won't care if there's an autopsy! Goddamm you! We need that insurance money!!"

He looked like a bad night-after, and I remembered his inability to lower his overdraw. I'm the last one to see what's obvious to everyone else about whether or not someone's using drugs, but even to me it seemed clear Weiselman was a drug induced mess.

"He killed himself," I shouted back. "If the insurance company won't pay for suicide, you're all shit-out-of-luck! I'm not going to help you cut Marty up into little pieces hoping to find something to defraud them with."

"You have a duty to Roberta and the estate!" Thorne yelled in my ear.

"And to us!" Weiselman snivelled.

Wolf banged his fist on the table, then pointed a well-manicured finger at me, "Goddammit, you're making the biggest mistake of your life. No one gets in my way and walks off into the sunset. I'll have you taken apart."

"He was my brother! I'm not going to help you cut him up for money looking for some pot of gold."

"You'll do as you're told!" Thorne yelled again at my ear.

He was too close, and his position above me was unsettling. I looked at Ronnie Hook and knew she was thinking the same thing I was. Marty at Millennium. As a tactic it was very effective. I felt the physical intimidation. I felt light-headed. I didn't like it. Any of it.

"Would you step back, please?" I said without looking up at him.

He brought his face down closer to mine and sneered, "Just as soon as you sign this."

His face was no more than three or four inches from mine. I tried to ignore him. I looked down the length of the table at Wolf. It was a choice between trying to grab his lip or ear, something that would prevent him from any immediate response while he had the advantage of being above me, and being cool. Chilling out, as they say. Winters had the look of someone who'd been forced to dog-sit for a friend, and now, too late, was finding out the animal wasn't housebroken. I also thought of my promise to him.

"If you want to discuss the other items on the agenda would you ask this foul breathed Impasse/Resolution Expert to get his face out of mine. Please."

Thorne's posture changed immediately. He stood straight up like someone had caught him bending over in the shower at the county jail. He looked at Wolf for help. Hearing the words Impasse/Resolution Expert coming from me unsettled him. No one moved or said anything. I pushed my chair back and stood. From the look on Wolf's face, I had the feeling he'd have liked Thorne to put a hand on my shoulder and push me back down. But if there was a moment when he seriously thought about it, it passed, and I had the feeling with it was the end of his second unsuccessful interview with the firm. Assuming it continued in existence, I was pretty sure it was going to be without the services of Bob Thorne.

It was amazing how a little change of perspective can alter a situation. I felt much better. I walked around the table on what was the Film side to the glass door and slid it open enough to go out. No one said a word. I put my hands on the rail and took a couple of deep breaths. There were a dozen sail-boats clustered around the end of the Santa Monica Pier, and a few more scattered here and there around the bay. I wondered who the people on the boats were that could take off in the middle of a Friday afternoon to go sailing. I thought of my mostly successful attempt at building a sail boat with some college friends, and of our day trips across the bay to Sausalito. We called ourselves Buen Amigos. Those were some good days. I wondered where they were and what they were doing now. The gentle breeze had picked up a little, and it felt good. I felt good. They could do what they wanted. I wouldn't help. Qué sera´, sera´, I could almost hear Doris Day sing.

When I turned and re-entered the room the first thing I saw was Ronnie Hook. There she was with her patented hint of a smile, and she discreetly winked at me.

"I think your second agenda item was the lease," I said.

Bob Winters was breathing easier and his eyes met mine without his usual look of exasperation, but I was betting he hadn't mentally put away his pooper-scooper. I returned to my seat. Thorne was left standing there with his dick in his hands. So to speak.

"Sit down, Bob!" Wolf ordered.

There was a pitiful abject compliance about him now as he sat, but underneath, he was seething. If he hadn't done himself any good with Goldman Marshall & Wolf, particularly Wolf, and he knew he hadn't, he would at least ream me as soon as he could on Roberta's behalf. He seemed to be comforting himself with the thought, while he played with Hamilton's pen. I was betting Hamilton wouldn't ask for it back. Thorne suddenly stood and went to Wolf's shoulder and whispered something to him. Wolf nodded. They both looked at me and Thorne smiled venomously.

"You'll have to excuse me." he said looking at me, then Bob Winters. "I need to file a request for a restraining order." He took obvious pleasure in telling me.

"Where's the body?" he added for good measure.

That hit me hard. My good feeling evaporated and I could feel one of those involuntary waves start to rise up. Tina Cox, Ronnie, Joe Woodman, Mel Davidson, Sandy Marshall, and even McCord and Hamilton looked embarrassed. Miriam seemed fascinated by her nails. Wolf couldn't care less. Bob Winters seemed pretty unfazed himself. Tina gave me the first warm look since before the slice and dice comment. It stemmed the rising tide. I even managed a little smile of thanks.

"You mean, sort of like, 'where'd I park the car?'"

Winters groaned, impatient with me. "He needs to know where your brother's body is so that if the court decides to issue a restraining order, they can name the proper mortuary."

"Thank you," Thorne said to Winters. "I expect to have that restraining order before the end of the day."

"Groman Brothers on Washington." I said.

Thorne bent to whisper something else to Wolf and then left.

Wolf liked to delegate. He introduced Miriam to Bob Winters and turned her loose. She shuffled through some notes and began to fill us in on Wolf's behalf. She ignored me and spoke to Winters.

"The lease payments are $50,000 per month. The parking is an additional $12,000. The firm has been running negative overall. We've been dipping into the second First American Bank Loan funds to supplement. The interest on the first First American Bank Loan, the Capital Improvements Loan, is now running at a fixed amount since all of those funds have been expended. $10,000 a month. The interest on the second loan, has been climbing. It's now at $3000 a month. With the basic office expenses and staff salaries and withholding and insurance, we're coming up short about $20,000 a month."

While she was speaking, the change that came over the room was amazing. It would ultimately come back to Marty, his death, the autopsy and the insurance money, but right now there was an awakening taking place. Even the Music side guys were shocked. McCord and Hamilton were shocked but subdued, not about to challenge Wolf. Sandy Marshall seemed resigned as though he could see where this were going, and where it had come from. Cox already knew, but Woodman and Davidson were shocked and disbelieving. Weiselman seemed frightened.

"How can that be?!" Woodman moaned. "We've cut back on our draws. What's going on?"

Wolf held up his hand, taking charge, "The point is, this is where we are," he said, deflecting them. "It will get worse."

"Worse! Why? What do you mean?" Weiselman protested, only one or two steps away from hysteria.

I had to admit, I was enjoying it.

"Miriam..." Wolf delegating again, maybe hoping they'd shoot the messenger.

"It depends on where Mr. Goldman's clients go. The portion of the money that DBS has been holding pending a settlement with him that would have come monthly to GMW would have easily wiped out our deficit. Now however, whatever the outcome of the settlement agreement with DBS, the monies that would have come here from old DBS client-deals will likely be a one time payment covering the period from when Mr. Goldman left DBS up until his death, unless the clients stay with one of you at GMW. If Mr. Goldman's clients go elsewhere, half of the income of those client's deals made here at GMW will go elsewhere. Since Mr. Goldman accounted for more than one third of all GMW income even without the money that was projected to come from the DBS deals, the loss will be huge."

Weiselman was tapping his fingers, then running them through his hair, then pinching at his nose, sitting still impossible for him. He looked like he wanted to get up and do twenty or thirty laps around the table. I wished he would, if it would settle him down. He abruptly got to his feet.

"Gotta use the head," he said as he left the conference room.

Tina watched me watch him. No one else took note. Miriam looked at Wolf. That was enough. She sat down. It occurred to me that she was particularly well informed. Which made me wonder if: a) she and Wolf were having a little pillow talk, or b) if it were common for a personal secretary to know all of the details of her boss' business. Or c), both? If (b), I thought it even more likely than I'd thought before that Ronnie knew more than she'd told me.

"I've got a meeting with Brent Scoma from the Pyramid Group at four. I'm going to tell him we have every expectation that the insurance will pay off and that we will be in a position to conduct business as usual. But I'm going to insist on a rent reduction for the next six months. It will take the pressure off. By then we'll know more about the insurance. Once the insurance money has been received, we will re-imburse them for the reduction."

I was thinking, you're dreaming. If I could read minds, so was Winters. Tina looked skeptical, but the others seemed buoyed and willing to grasp at this straw.

"How much of a reduction are you going to insist on?" Winters asked, not very successfully keeping the skepticism out of his voice.

"Twenty thousand a month," Wolf said as though it were a done deal.

"What makes you think they'll go for it?" Winters persisted.

"What choice do they have? They can spend money suing, but if we don't get the insurance money, there won't be anything for them once First American Bank comes in."

Ronnie's face hardened. When she saw me looking at her, she shook her head no almost imperceptibly. I didn't know what she meant, but it was exactly what I'd hoped for by insisting she sit in.

"Have you spoken with the bank yet?" Winters asked.

"Yes."

"And?"

"We have a meeting scheduled here for 5:30 this evening. After the Pyramid Group. If the rent can be reduced I'm confident we can get the bank to suspend payments on the loans. Temporarily, of course. You're welcome to attend," he said to Winters. I guessed that I wasn't.

"And if they don't?"

"Then we have a problem."

"The loans were made to you jointly and severally?" Winters prompted.

"Yes, of course," Wolf responded irritably.

"So if the bank won't suspend the payments, and decides to call the loans if you can't or don't make the payments, the..."

"Not going to happen!" Wolf insisted angrily. "If we move ahead on the insurance angle."

"Have you explored other options to trim..." Winters began, but Wolf cut him off.

"We've explored everything. Let's move on. Miriam."

Tina was becoming more and more agitated. She looked at me and I did my Groucho eye-brow thing and smiled a little. Go get him honey, I was thinking.

"Wait a minute!" she demanded. "If we're running short $20,000 a month, I'd like to talk about partnership draws, capital improvements, and the party."

Ah, yes.

"We're not here to go into elaborate detail. We're here to bring Mr. Winters up to speed. To let him know where we stand and what we need to do."

Tina started to interrupt, but Wolf held up his hand and cut her off.

"We can get into those details at our next partnership meeting," Wolf offered.

If the firm lasts that long, I thought.

"John," Tina persisted, "it's come to my attention that you've continued to overdraw and that you've overspent on both your office and the Party. I want to know..."

"I don't give a good god damn what you want!" Wolf yelled. "Not now! Miriam! Move on!"

Tina was fuming and I thought she was going to get up and leave, but she didn't. She glared at Wolf. And at me! I gave her a what-did-I-do shrug. She wasn't amused.

Miriam let things calm down while she took an unnecessarily long time with the agenda and her notes. Weiselman returned and sat down. His hair was combed and his face washed and he looked more in control. Better living through chemistry, I thought.

"Mr. Sutton's attorney has indicated they intend to proceed with their suit," Miriam began, Weiselman groaned and started to protest but Wolf held up a hand to quiet him, "unless GMW is willing to pay him the amount the lost tax treatment will result in, and..."

Weiselman winced and looked ready to jump in again, but didn't. Miriam eyed him, then continued. He sat silent.

"...and provided GMW does NOT file against Millennium, Mr. Perry, Mr. Faustini or Mr. Cooper."

"File what?" Tina and Joe Woodman asked simultaneously.

"According to Mr. Sutton's attorney, Mr. Goldman had some wild notion that Millennium and Mr. Perry and Mr. Faustini had acted improperly. Apparently he had threatened them with a suit at their meeting on Tuesday morning."

Wolf glared at Ronnie as though it were her fault. "What about it?" he demanded.

Ronnie looked around not knowing what confidences to protect or from whom. She hesitated too long for Wolf.

"Goddammit, I want to know and I want to know right now! Had Marty prepared a suit against Millennium and Perry and...."

" Mr. Faustini and Cooper, " Miriam offered helpfully.

"Whoever. Did he or didn't he?"

When she hesitated again it was too much for Wolf. He slapped his open hand down loudly on the table, startling everyone.

"Speak, dammit!"

Bob Winters was fighting to restrain himself. I think if he hadn't wanted to let this thing play itself out, he would have loved to teach Wolf some manners.

"John," Sandy Marshall said, " stop it. You're scaring her. Give her a moment."

"You keep out of it, Sandy." He focused on Ronnie again. "I'm waiting!"

Ronnie's mouth tightened and when she looked at him there were tears in her eyes, but I didn't think she was afraid of him. I thought they were from confusion and uncertainly about where her duty lay. She looked to me for help. I smiled and nodded. Tell him. Wolf didn't like her looking to me for anything.

"He's got no say," he said to her. "You work for me now."

"No, she works for me. As long as GMW is still in business and Marty's Professional Corporation is the senior partner in it, and as long as she wants to."

"This is getting us nowhere," Winters injected, exasperated. He looked at Ronnie. "Would you please tell Mr. Wolf, was Marty preparing to file a suit against Millennium?"

Ronnie looked at me and smiled. "Yes."

"On what grounds?"

"That Millennium and Mr. Perry and Mr. Faustini orchestrated the whole thing. That they were intentionally breaching the contract with Mr. Sutton, withholding payments, in order to coerce him to renegotiate it. That they were therefore negotiating in bad faith, that they were perpetrating a fraud insofar as Mr. Sutton would have a case against Marty's malpractice insurance."

Winters let some air whistle out through his teeth. His brows raised up and there was a little smile on his lips. He liked it. It was what he'd do.

"Thank you," Winters said, as though having pried an answer out of a reluctant witness.

"That's outrageous!" Weiselman protested, "He's out of his fucking mind, screwing with them!"

"If Marty believed they'd orchestrated the whole thing," Tina said, "we should file and fight them!"

"Stay out of it Tina! You don't know anything about it!" Weiselman challenged her.

"And you do?" she shot back.

"I know we don't want to fuck around with Perry!" he said. "I know that much for sure!"

"What makes you such an expert? Have you even met him?" Tina challenged.

"No! Of course not! What would make you think I had? That's ridiculous!"

I had the feeling he'd have gone on forever, protesting too much, as they say, if Wolf hadn't slammed his hand down on the table again. Winters was getting increasingly irritated with him.

"Enough!" Wolf yelled at them. "Tina, what do you know about the status of the DBS settlement negotiations?"

"Not much," she said ignoring Wolf and speaking to the rest of us. "Just that Marty said he and Barry Malovitch were close to a resolution on all issues." She looked at me, then Ronnie. "Can you add anything, Ronnie?"

Ronnie looked at me briefly. I put on a stone face. Don't give them a thing, I was trying to tell her.

"No, no, I can't."

Wolf glared at her. "Or won't," he grumbled. "I'll contact Malovitch myself. We'll get this resolved."

I was hoping Winters would jump in, but he didn't.

"Don't," I said.

"How's that! What the hell!" Wolf was outraged. "Goddammit, Mr. Winters, would you be so kind as to tell your client to butt out!"

Winters was looking at me now for the third time with that look in his eyes like I'd broken my promise. I raised my eyebrows at him and shook my head no.

I looked down the table at Wolf. I found myself pointing a finger at him, which is not a usual gesture for me. Not that finger. "The issues are between Marty H. Goldman, a Professional Corporation, and Diamond Bernstein and Silver. They are not between you or GMW and DBS. If Tina and Joe and Mel Davidson and ol' Gary here want to negotiate separately from any settlement Marty was working on, or any that I might conclude with DBS, they're free to do that. But, as far as I can see, you're not a party to it. So, I'm telling you here and now, please do not contact Barry Malovitch or anyone else at DBS.

"The money DBS owes is to THIS firm! To GMW! We have every right to conduct the negotiations! We need that money! If your brother hadn't been dragging his feet on a settlement and holding out for more for himself, we'd have it by now! I have no intention of standing by while you make the same mistake! I'm sick of your interference! I want you the hell out of here right now!" he bellowed, pointing at me. First finger.

He stood, like maybe he planned to come down the length of the table and throw me out himself. He took a step or two in my direction, but Sandy Marshall stood and blocked him, taking hold of his arm. I didn't think he was prepared to do anything more than make a little show of it, but you never know. I was thinking about the open door to the balcony and assisting him in the retrieval of the box I'd thrown off this morning. Showing him the short-cut.

Finally Winters came to life. "He's right," he said to Wolf. "We'll handle all of the issues between Marty H. Goldman and DBS. If any of you others would rather handle your own separation agreements, please let me or Kurt know. I believe we're scheduled to meet with DBS soon." He stood and started to pack up his brief case. "I think we've covered everything on your agenda. I'd like to return and sit in on your meeting with First American Bank."

Wolf was purple with rage, but allowed Marshall to speak for him and GMW.

"You're welcome to. Thank you for coming today." He let go of Wolf's arm and Wolf charged out of the conference room like it were on fire, calling behind him, "Miriam! In my office!"

Marshall came up to me and shook hands, then said, "I hope you won't take offense, but it might be better if you let Mr. Winters come alone this evening."

Without looking up from packing his briefcase, Winters said, "My sentiments exactly!"

"Is it something I said?!"

For the first time, Ronnie smiled freely. Tina, who had been clustered with the remaining GMW partners, came up and patted my arm. "Not bad, buster, not too bad at all. Could we have dinner? I'd like to talk about DBS with you."

Winters gave me a funny look, but cut it short. "I'm outta here. Ms. Cox, Mr. Weiselman, Mr. Woodman, Mr. Davidson, Mr. Hamilton, Mr. McCord, a real pleasure," he said. Like a root canal, I was thinking. "Kurt, we have a date I believe."

"I'll meet you downstairs on the patio in five minutes."

He gave me another of his impatient exasperated looks, and rolled his eyes, but I thought it was more for show than anything else. He seemed pleased, actually.

"Terrific. I'll wait with baited breath."

"Which is, no doubt, better than Thorne's," I said.

Winters threw back his head and bellowed with laughter. "I give up," he said pleasantly, "I'll see you downstairs in five." He held up his hand with five fingers spread wide to confirm the time limit as he left the conference room.

Ronnie was lost in thought and had remained seated as though trying to regain some energy.

"Would you come with me to Marty's office, Ronnie?"

"Now?"

"Yes."

Ronnie got up and started for the door. I reached behind her and pushed it open and she went out. Before I could, Tina put a hand on my arm.

"Would you wait for a minute," she asked me.

Ronnie was waiting. I told her I'd catch up to her. She went into Marty's office. When I turned back, Davidson, Woodman, McCord and Hamilton and Gary Weiselman were waiting.

"We've discussed it and have decided not to pursue a DBS settlement separately from Marty, well, from you and the estate. If Bob Winters wants something in writing from each of us to settle on our behalf, have his office call us. In any case, we'll each call Barry and tell him that's what we've decided to do."

"Fine," I said. I took it as a vote of confidence from everyone except Weiselman. He was looking a little ragged again and sullen and wouldn't look at me directly. I decided to prod him. "Et tu, Gary?"

He looked daggers at me and said, "Just don't fuck us up!" He stalked out.

"Nice talk," I said good naturedly to his back.

"Definitely different fathers," Tina said, then, "I'd like to talk with these guys about Millennium and John's overdraw position and his office and the party. Do you mind?"

"Do I mind what? Do you want me to go? I'm going," I said with mock injury.

"No, no. Do you mind if I discuss what you told me?"

"I'm kidding Tina. Of course not. I'm amazed you guys don't already know about it."

"We were hoping you could stay," she said. They all seemed to want some support in even discussing John. A timid revolution in the making.

"I can't. But you guys kick it around and I'll meet you someplace for dinner and we can talk about it then. Tina can fill the rest of you in if she and I come up with anything interesting. Okay?"

They all nodded in agreement.

"Where should we meet and when?" I asked Tina.

She wrote an address on the back of another one of her business cards and said, "How about eight or eight fifteen?"

"Fine. I'll see you then. Gentlemen."

In Marty's office Ronnie sat in the easy chair at the coffee table. Somehow I had the feeling it was a first. When I came in, she started to jump up like I'd caught her sleeping on the job, but I motioned her back.

"Relax. It was a rough meeting."

She looked at me with that little hint of a smile I was coming to like. Then, from fatigue and the need to release pent up tension, she laughed out loud, shaking her head.

"What?" I said.

"It's just funny to think of you and Marty as brothers. He would never act like that. Never."

"He didn't need to. He was smarter than I am, and could get things to fall into place with very little fuss. Someone once described me as an upstream swimmer. I think it's not only true, but I don't think I'd know what to do if I ever found myself going downstream. Not that it's happened, or's likely to." I sat in the couch and put my feet up on the glass coffee table. She looked at me like a school teacher, and for a minute I thought she was going to tell me to get my feet off it. Instead, she laughed again and put her head back on the cushions with her hands over her eyes.

"What?" I said again.

"That," she pointed to my feet on the table.

"What about it?"

"Every time Marty was in here and Roberta was around, they'd sit here and if he started to put his feet up, she'd wrinkle her nose at him." Ronnie gave me a look, "She decorated the place, and, well," she shrugged. We were silent a while.

Then I asked her, "What was it that Wolf said that had you shaking your head?"

"Everything. He's such an ass. But in particular, the lease agreement is also signed jointly and severally." She looked at me to make sure I knew what it meant. I was pretty sure, but she clarified it to be sure. "It means each of them is responsible individually as well as jointly through GMW. So when Mr. Wolf says the Pyramid Group has no option, that's nonsense. They have the same option the bank does. If there's a default, the Pyramid Group can sue the Partnership and the individual partners, or in Marty's case, his estate. That means houses, bank accounts, stocks, cars, anything. They're all on the hook and Wolf knows it. I can't imagine that the others are unaware of it. It's not unusual for a clause like that to be on a bank loan, but in my experience, it's rare on a lease. The Pyramid Group has a large stake in this space, more than sixty thousand dollars a month, so they wanted all the protection they could get. On the other hand, it's possible the others didn't think about it much when they signed. Everyone was so excited about the new firm, I could see how they might have overlooked it, or just mentally pushed it into some corner of their minds."

We sat in silence again.

"Thank you, Ronnie."

"Thank you," she said earnestly. We'd crossed over a barrier and she seemed at ease with me now. She looked directly into my eyes and her hint of a smile reappeared. "I take it you have Marty's keys?"

"Yes."

She held out her hand. I dug them out of my pocket.

She took them from me and went through them. Past the 'Off' key and the 'Master' key and past Marty's house key and the key with the Mercedes logo, to his new car I thought, and past what looked like another car key, maybe to Roberta's car, and then she stopped at another, a brass one that had something stamped on it.

"Do you know what this one is for?" she asked as she held the keys out to me.

I took the keys and looked at the one she'd singled out. It had TBC stamped on it, and below that, #26. "No," I said.

"It's for a garage space at The Beach Club. Here in Santa Monica. Do you know it?" I found myself being pulled into my thoughts and memories, experiencing a kind of mental undertow. I was still listening to her, but my mind was racing backwards and forwards in time. "It's next to Will Rogers State Beach," she was saying, "Marty has a membership there. It was very private for him. I don't think Roberta even knows. He had the club bills come here to the office. The Gravettz firm handles all of Marty and Roberta's bill paying, except this."

I felt a stab in my heart and wasn't sure if it were more from pleasure or pain. I was engulfed by such a mixed wave of love and sympathy and admiration for Marty and his determined, front door return to The Beach Club. And the success that had made it possible. At the same time, heartache for what I thought must have been his sense of foolishness in wanting or needing to complete the circle, and from it, his need to keep it secret. No one would have known or cared why he chose that Club. He was rich and belonging to beach clubs must have been common in his set.

Ronnie had all but disappeared and I was drifting contentedly on a raft just out past the small rolling waves, half-way between The Beach Club and Will Rogers, along with some of the Beach Club kids, waiting for a big one. The sun was bright and hot, the water cool and clean. It might have been any one of a dozen times, and I could see Marty and his friends in the water, even further out, north of The Beach Club, on the public side, hoping for the big one too. I waved to him and he hesitated, afraid of giving me away, so I waved again, and finally he smiled and waved back. The recollection now painted a picture that I couldn't shake: I wanted to not only get away with sneaking into the Beach Club, I wanted to press my luck to some undefined limit by calling attention to myself getting away with it. Marty's instinct, on the other hand, was to stifle himself to protect me. It occurred to me just how much he'd protected us all. If it weren't instinct, it was learned from disappointed experience, but either way, he took it upon himself to do what wasn't going to get done without him. He was the parent, the one we could rely on. He was our rock. He didn't hover or interfere, but he kept tabs on me and Nick and Sara, even my mom and dad. He made sure we were all okay, and if he thought we weren't, with a word here, or a suggestion or an off-hand offer there, he'd let us know we had a place to turn if we needed it.

"Do you know it?" Ronnie repeated.

I came back from my thoughts, and told her I did. "Thank you." I reached over to her and shook hands. I got up to go and motioned her to stay. "Recharge your batteries," I suggested. "Think about what you want to do. I'd like to have you stay as long as possible, but I can see hanging around here might not suit you. Let me know."

"Thank you, I will," she said.

Winters was waiting for me at the same table we'd occupied before the meeting. He was drinking more lemonade and he looked at his watch as I approached.

"Right on time!" he said cheerily, then groused, "you said five minutes! It's been fifteen!"

"Time flies, as they say. Let's go across the street."

"You really want to go to the beach?" he said in disbelief. "I thought we were joking. I don't have time to go to the beach! I have to get back to L.A. and then come all the way back out here by five-thirty." He looked at his watch again. "It's almost four now."

"So make a call. Don't go back to L.A."

He looked at me like I'd goosed a nun.

"What's the worst that could happen," I said. "You fail to do this or that and someone sues you for incompetence. You prove you're not by beating them and the whole thing goes away and everybody's happy! Simplicity itself."

"Alright! Alright, for Christsakes! Let me call the office. Stay put. Try not to get into any trouble while I'm gone."

Chapter 14

⟞⟩⟨⟜⟞⟨⟜⟩⟞

We walked across Ocean Avenue and north on the meandering path that runs through the strip of park along the edge of the cliffs. About a quarter mile up, where Wilshire all but dead-ends against Ocean, it becomes the California Incline traversing the cliffs in a long slow descent to the Pacific Coast Highway. Once there we walked up a spiral path to a foot bridge that crossed over the PCH, and then spiraled back down on the beach side. The breeze came and went. Winters was content not to talk, but he walked with the determined purposefulness of a teenaged boy expecting to get laid. I'd suggested to him that he leave his briefcase in his car in the Pyramid, but he wouldn't consider it. He held onto it like it contained the codes for launching nuclear weapons. When we crossed through one of the parking lots to the sand, his shiny black Brogues seemed to hesitate of their own accord. I sat on a telephone pole sized wooden log that defined the end of the lot and took off the shoes and socks I'd worn especially for the occasion.

Winters looked at me when I looked at him, and his look said something like, not on your life. I shrugged and said, "suit yourself" and walked into the sand. It was cooling off, but still warm, and as I walked I forced my feet into it in a wiggling motion to dry the sweat from them. He followed for half a dozen steps in that clumsy way big shoes impose on you when you're in sand, and muttered, "Oh for Christsakes! Wait a minute!"

He put the briefcase down and attempted to balance on one foot and take off the shoe on the other, wiggling and contorting his stocky body to keep from falling. Going back to the wooden log seemed to be out of the question. Sitting in the sand was a less likely prospect. He struggled with one, then the other until he had them both off and his socks tucked neatly into them and held in one hand. His pants were long and the neatly tailored cuffs began to puff and swell with collected sand as he walked to catch up to me. When we'd walked about thirty yards across the sand towards the water, we came to the concrete pathway that the bicyclists and roller-skaters use. When he saw it, he looked at me like I'd purposely duped him.

"Oh for Christsakes!" he said again.

I thought he was going to repeat the whole process in reverse and put
his shoes and socks back on, but he fooled me and stopped to empty the
sand from his cuffs and then he rolled them up to mid-calf, a very white
mid-calf, and dumbfounded me by taking off his jacket and tie. He folded
them up carefully and managed to get them into the top of his brief case.
This has to be a first, I thought. Some of his perpetual redness of face
got several shades lighter without the tie. The sound of the waves
whooshing up on the wet sand had a soothing effect on both of us. We
walked along near the pathway, but stayed in the sand.

"If John Goodman could see you now," I suggested.

Winters laughed and said, "Don't you dare tell him! I've cultivated
my workaholic persona since he and I were in law school. If he found
out about this, he'd try to get me on one of his goddamm European
vacations, or worse yet, some goddamm Cruise!"

"Heaven forbid!"

He unbuttoned his shirt and gray curly chest hairs that hadn't seen
the light of day in a long time fought each other for a taste of the ocean
air. A little ways up there were benches on each side of the pathway.

"Let's sit," he nodded to them.

The sun was no longer high, but had peaked, and its angle made the
glare off the water blindingly strong. I closed my eyes and let it bathe
me. We could have sat on the other bench with our backs to the water
and no glare, but after that meeting I sought it out with the same hungry
need and longing of a struggling plant rising through a blanket of scattered trash on an abandoned lot.

"Tell me something I don't know," he said, "now, before Wednesday."

I thought for a moment. "For starters, the lease is signed jointly and
severally as well as the bank loans."

"Oh, swell! Are you sure?"

I opened one eye and squinted it at him, then closed it again and let
the sun continue to warm my face. I was sure, I told him with my silence. I followed one of those little black things that float in and out of
your vision as it crossed the white-yellow backlit screen of the inside of
my eyelid. By moving my head just slightly I could make it jump to the
top or the left or right, and then watch it drift to wherever the currents
took it.

"About the autopsy," he said conversationally, figuring there was no
need to get excited or beat a dead horse, "I want you to be clear on this:
I think you should've signed the goddamm thing. The chances are the
court will grant the restraining order and overrule you and allow the
autopsy. So what did you accomplish except to piss them off?"

I started to say something but he held up a hand to cut me off.

"Save it. I don't want to hear it. I'm just telling you, as your lawyer,
what I think. I expect Thorne will have the restraining order by the time
I get back there, and by Monday afternoon, unless you try to obstruct
them, they'll have the court order for the autopsy. Get used to it."

"What do you mean, obstruct?"

He shot me a look like I were truly demented.

"I'm just asking," I said.

He looked at me suspiciously. "You could insist we go to court and oppose any motion overruling you. You'd lose. I guarantee it. It would drag things out one or two days, three at the most."

"And if I insisted?" I smiled.

"You won't," he assured me.

"What makes you think so?"

"I believe you want me and John Goodman in on this with you. And I think you're a lot more reasonable than you let on. Maybe not a lot," he corrected himself, "but some."

"Don't count on that."

"Oh, believe me, I don't, but your instincts are pretty good from what I've seen. You may not use very good judgement at times, but I think there's more method than madness. I think you made your point with them. Just go a little easy. What else can you tell me?"

"Does that mean you're in?"

"Oh for Christsakes! Do you think I'd come out here on the beach and get my shoes full of sand and miss an appointment in town if I weren't?" I squinted my eye open and saw he was looking at me. He smiled and held out his hand, and we shook on it. "Besides John's twisting my arm on this, I'm curious enough myself now to see it through. I did some calling around this morning, and your brother has a remarkable reputation. I wish I'd known him. But it makes this whole thing all the more bizarre. What else can you tell me?" he repeated.

"There are issues at GMW and at DBS that Marty felt uncomfortable having on Ronnie's computer because it's tied in to a central network. Anyone at GMW could have accessed it. He was working on some GMW issues..."

"That you're not prepared to name?" he interrupted me.

"Right, not yet. Anyway, to keep it private, he worked on them and the DBS settlement on his own computer. If he had Ronnie do anything, it was on a floppy disk, and then Marty transferred it to his computer when she was done. I've seen one file folder on DBS, but it's only client lists and projects and studio sheets of their earnings. Nothing about what Marty thought were his legitimate claims. I've determined that there's another DBS file where Marty has settlement issues laid out. I also believe there's a copy of notes taken by Malovitch's secretary, and initialled by Malovitch and Diamond and Marty, laying out an agreement concerning ownership in the proceeds of litigation against something called International Distributors."

"And you can't find it?" he asked.

"No, but I think Weiselman may have it."

"Have you asked him?"

"Not yet, but I will."

"What's the problem? Malovitch will have a copy of the notes on…"

"International Distributors," I reminded him.

"Whatever."

"He should," I said unenthusiastically.

"Besides, if you can't find it, the physical file, it'll be on your brother's computer, right?"

"It should be - in fact I'm certain it's there - I took a look at the directory listings. I think everything of any importance is there."

"Good, then get Ronnie to help you. Go through the directory and print out anything you think is important to us. Do it soon. I have a feeling your welcome there is just about used up." He sat back and began to enjoy the sun on his face.

I ignored the part about my welcome and didn't repeat my contention about it being my office. I told him, "I'd love to but it's CODED."

He lifted his head off the top of the back rest and gave me a look I imagined he'd use on jay-walkers blocking his path when he had the light.

"And?" he said, knowing what was coming, but not wanting to utter the words himself, leaving open the slim possibility he was wrong.

"And, I don't know the code and Ronnie doesn't know it either. I've tried a dozen combinations of names and birth dates and anniversaries, but nada."

"Oh for Christsakes!" he said.

"I want to set up a meeting with Malovitch, but I don't want to go in there without Marty's take on the various issues. And if they initialled a memo on International Distributors, I want it."

"You don't think you can trust Malovitch to produce his copy?"

"Would you want to rely on that? From what I've seen so far, the DBS settlement breaks down into several major issues. First, the amount of money, or the percentage of money from deals done by Marty and Cox and the others for clients while they were at DBS. Second, there are the partnership equity issues, the remaining partners buying out the departing ones, in this case, just Marty."

"What about the others?"

"They were salaried. It would be nice to know what Marty thought his equity was worth. I have reason to believe his percentage of ownership was 16%, but I can't prove that, and I don't know what it's 16% of. By the way, Cox and the others want us, you and your firm to complete the settlement negotiations with DBS for them. She said she'd call Malovitch and tell him we're authorized to deal on their behalf. If you need something from her and the others, call them or have your office prepare something for them to sign." He took that with a shrug. "And lastly, International Distributors."

"What is that?"

"It's a lawsuit that Marty took on for an old college friend. He began it on his own, outside DBS. At first the other partners weren't interested. After it became clear it was potentially very lucrative, they wanted in. Also, as it progressed, it was taking more time and money than Marty could handle alone. So they worked out a percentage deal. DBS paid all of the costs and Marty could bill hours against the percentage they'd agreed on, which was 26% for Marty, 74% for DBS. That's what the memo or notes they initialled is supposed to have spelled out."

"And you think Malovitch would deny it?" he was incredulous. Some one must have told him how much like a family they were over at DBS.

"You tell me. The fees amount to more than $5 million. They've been collecting interest while appeals have played themselves out. International Distributors lost and the money is about to be released from an escrow account. It's grown to $7 million. Marty's 26% would be a million eight-hundred and twenty thousand."

"My god!" Winters whistled.

"So, let me ask you again, would you want to rely on Malovitch's...what? Honesty? His integrity? His memory?"

"He's gotta believe you have the note. So he couldn't act as though it didn't exist."

"Maybe."

"What do you mean, maybe?" he asked suspiciously.

"Nothing. For now, at least."

"More for the Wednesday afternoon edition?" he said sarcastically.

"Something like that."

"Have you found the will yet?" he asked.

"No, I haven't had a chance to look. But I will tonight or tomorrow. I think it must be in his office at home. I'll just have to go through everything one page at a time."

"John gets very nervous when we're working on something without court approval. Technically, you're not the executor until the court says so."

"I'm surprised Thorne didn't jump on that."

"Very good. Maybe you should have gone to law school. He should have. He could have made a case that Roberta, as next of kin, can decide those matters until you're approved by the probate court. He's not the brightest light around."

"That's what Marty thought too."

"What d'ya mean?"

"Thorne wanted a job at GMW. Wolf wanted him but Marty nixed it. Thought he was a Nazi. Didn't want any part of him."

"Where did you get all the information? Or don't I want to know?"

"You don't want to know." Especially on Wednesday, I was thinking.

"Well, on that note of understanding and mutual trust, I've got to end this little outing." He looked at his watch. "It's quarter after four. I'd like to see Wolf in action with the Pyramid Group, particularly if what you say about the lease is true."

He dusted off sand from his feet and shook out his socks and got them and his shoes on and rolled down his cuffs. He buttoned his shirt and put his tie on and carefully brushed off his jacket and folded it neatly across his arm. He grabbed his brief case and was ready to tackle the world.

"Why don't you stay here and enjoy yourself? Maybe for a month or two? Keep you outta trouble." He threw back his head and laughed, enjoying himself immensely, and walked back along the concrete pathway. I watched him chug along, glad to have brought him so much joy. I closed my eyes and let the sun make love to my face.

I thought about going to The Beach Club.

I couldn't remember ever having gone into The Beach Club through the front door. All those days with the kids from the Club, we'd always approached from the water side. When I got close, I left the sand and walked through the public parking lot just south of the Club and used the narrow sidewalk that ran along the west side of the Pacific Coast Highway. The front of the Club was screened from the street by a ten foot high ivy covered chain-link fence that ran the two-hundred and fifty or three hundred foot length of the Club along the Highway. There was a sixty-foot wide opening with a rolling gate that could be closed and locked. It was open now, and at its north end, just inside the fence, there was a little booth with a stool for the guy sitting there to check i.d.'s or passes or whatever gained one entry into their world.

Inside the fence there was a large courtyard of dark cobblestones. Lighter colored ones defined a circular drive that passed under a blue canvas awning that sheltered guests from sun or rain. They could leave or enter their cars under its protection to the large white double doors with blue script letters proclaiming The Beach Club. There were huge brass door pulls below the lettering. Parking attendants in black trousers and white waist jackets were on hand to take cars to a parking area at the south end of the property nearest the fence along the Highway. Just west of it were a line of fifteen garages. The cobbled drive continued between the end of them and the south fence of the property. It seemed likely that there was a second wing west of the first since Marty's was #26. The guy at the booth was unprepared for anyone approaching on foot. When I spoke, he jumped.

"Excuse me," I said.

He grabbed dramatically at his chest with both hands, like Red Fox on Sanford and Son, experiencing the big one.

"God! Don't do that! Ya wanna kill me? I gotta weak heart! What you want?"

Probably not the standard greeting for arriving Club members, but he seemed confident I wasn't one.

"I...my brother's a member here. I'd like to talk to someone about his membership and his garage space."

He seemed pleased to have correctly pegged me as not a member. He was a fine judge of character.

"Well, let me think, " he said unhurriedly, "it's Friday and it's about," he looked at his watch, "oh my! nearly four-thirty, just about time for me to quit." His pace quickened as he tidied things up in the little booth.

"Before you go," I said, "who should I ask for?"

"Eric, ask for Eric. Tell him I'm waitin' to go. Tell him to send someone out here now. Can you do that?"

"Sure."

There was a doorman in the same black trousers and white jacket as the parking attendants. He smiled as I neared.

"Good afternoon, sir. Do you have your Club Card handy?"

I didn't remember seeing one in Marty's wallet and wondered where he kept it.

"I'd like to speak with Eric. Can I go in, or do you have to go get him?"

"Oh no, feel free to go in. Eric should be in the office behind the front desk." He pulled open one of the doors for me.

I'd never gotten to this entry area in my days of sneaking in. It was attractive. Large and airy. The white walls and blue trim motif throughout had a convincing feel, privacy, exclusivity without ostentation, as though there were never any doubt. All of the door knobs and escutcheons were old and worn but wonderfully polished solid brass. I had a reassured feeling, a feeling I figured the decor was supposed to evoke, that hundreds or maybe thousands of well manicured and well-heeled hands had confidently pushed and pulled them. I marvelled at what I thought were the certainties of the rich. I had the feeling that they never had doubts. I wondered if Marty had gotten over that sense of being an outsider. I knew he'd been confident in his abilities, and probably had confidence in his standing and reputation. But all that was different from belonging. One look around this place, and I knew if I had all the money in the world, I'd never belong. Maybe that's not such a bad thing, I was thinking. There's a complacency that's part and parcel of belonging that makes it suspect to me. Maybe I was just making excuses.

There was a long mahogany reception desk that looked like a saloon bar. Behind it to the left were fifty or sixty square cubby holes for notes or mail like you'd see in a hotel. To the right was a glassed in office. The guy behind the desk looked up and smiled as I approached.

"Can I help you?"

"I'd like to see Eric."

He turned and rapped gently on the glass. A man at a desk looked up and rose when the desk clerk nodded his head towards me.

"Can I help you?" he said.

"You're Eric?"

"Yes."

"For starters, the guy in the booth by the gate asked me to remind you to send someone to relieve him."

Eric looked at his watch and signalled the desk clerk to do something about it. He looked back to me, as though to say, anything else?.

I wasn't quite sure how I wanted to begin. He waited patiently. He seemed like a nice man. Fifty, slight build, bright very direct eyes, a tanned bald head with a neatly trimmed skirt of hair around the sides. I found myself phrasing it in various ways in my head, but none of them seemed right. I knew I was making it unnecessarily difficult. He looked as though he'd like to help.

"My brother is a member here. Was...he's dead." I could feel dark clouds gathering and the involuntary tightening of my throat begin.

"I'm so sorry," he said genuinely, "was his death recent?"

"Wednesday," came out of me.

"His name?"

I had to wait for a moment to make my throat loosen. "Marty Goldman," I said finally.

"I am so sorry. I read about it yesterday. I liked him very much. What can I do for you?"

"I'm his executor. The executor of his estate. I just learned that he had a membership here and that he had a garage space." I fished the keys from my pocket and showed him the TBC #26 key.

He nodded, "Yes, I know. That key is also for his closet."

"Closet?"

"In the executive-locker room. The executive members have a larger, more private dressing area and instead of lockers, they have walk-in closets. It allows them to keep a few changes of clothes here so if they come during the week...."

"I'd like to take a look at both, if I may."

"Certainly." He hesitated a moment, then said, "I'm sorry to have to ask, but I need to see some identification. You understand. I'm sorry."

"No need to apologize." I showed him my driver's license.

"Thank you. Follow me."

He came around the counter and we walked down a hallway to a door. Outside we were between the first and second garage wings. Numbers 16 to 30. He stopped at #26.

"This is your brother's." He smiled a sly friendly smile. "Go on, open it."

The key fit in the handle in the center of the door and I turned it and the door rolled up. For a long second or two I didn't know what I was looking at. The headlights were like large bug-eyes sitting on top of sensuously curved fenders. The hood was long and vented on the sides and ended at the square windshield with its sturdy shiny chrome frame standing almost, but not quite, upright. The white top was down and folded in its place behind the back seat. The paint job was what they now call Hunter Green, or what used to be called British Racing Green. It was a perfectly restored '37 Packard convertible. Marty Marty Marty.

I turned to look at Eric.

"He's kept it something of a secret," he smiled at me. "He's had it here for two years. Comes to the Club two or three times a month, takes it for a drive, then washes her and locks her back up. Never brought anyone with him." He winked at me, "I think it was like a mistress to him."

I turned back to the car. More like the lost love of his life, found, I thought. Like all that was taken away restored. I wondered when I'd ever run out of tears for a brother I was getting to know better in death than I did in life. Eric watched a slight shudder run through me.

"I should get back to the office. If you want me to show you to his closet, come get me." A kind and sensitive man.

"I will. Thank you."

When he'd gone I approached the car. The seats were tan glove leather. The dash, some kind of burl wood. The steering wheel too. There was a tall four-speed floor shift. I opened the driver's door and sat behind the wheel. It was perfect. Not a scratch or blemish that I could see anywhere. A good thing my dad doesn't know about it, I thought to myself. I looked in the glove box. There was a thick manila envelope. I took it out and opened it. It had the registration and some warranties and receipts from the restoration work. There was a bill of sale as well, dated three years ago. Before GMW. The dates on the receipts all came quickly after the bill of sale, so it looked like he'd lined it up in advance and got the work done in about a three month period.

I noticed a photo that'd been under the manila envelope. Marty had had it laminated in clear plastic to protect it. It was one I was familiar with even though I hadn't seen it or a copy of it for probably twenty-five years, but I remembered it immediately. Marty, tall and handsomely gangly at about thirteen or fourteen, me at five or six, Nick at three or four, Sara at eight or nine and my mom and dad, both young, both laughing. Jeez, my dad was so handsome and well-built then. All of us dressed up. There was such an easy joy in our faces. I'd forgotten that. That there'd ever been a time when we had that. It was just before my dad began to work with his brother and father. Before they screwed him. He was working for a guy named Gerber, who thought the world of him and his talents, and paid him accordingly. I guess by most standards, for sure by any standard of comparison that came later, we were in great shape financially. Emotionally, we were sound too. The crippling betrayals my dad was to suffer hadn't come yet and it showed. On all of us. I'm looking up and sharing a laugh with my mother. Marty's standing behind me, hands on my shoulders, my dad next to him, close, warm, both smiling at whatever set me and my mom off. Sara and Nick to the right in front of my mother. A dour look on Nick's face, uncertain about having had to get dressed up for the photographer we had come once a year in those days to take professional pictures. For Marty the crash must have been all the more painful because he was old enough to remember the family in this picture. I didn't. Not really. I just remembered the picture, and some of the others like it.

I fished around at the back of the box but there was nothing else. I started to slide the paper work back into the envelope but something blocked it. I pulled the papers out again and dumped the envelope into my lap. A floppy disk dropped out. It had a label marked '37Pack which seemed entirely reasonable. I started to put it back, but it occurred to me, what would he have on a disk about the car? Maybe restoration parts houses. Maybe a list of mechanics that could work on it. Maybe correspondence with potential sellers when he was first looking to buy. I started to put it back again. I changed my mind and decided to take it with me. I locked up the garage and went back into the Club and found Eric. He took me to the Executive locker room and showed me Marty's closet. He left me alone. No mistresses here, I supposed.

There were two suits and two white shirts, still in the plastic coverings that come from the cleaners, a pair of what I'd call dress shoes and a pair of canvas deck shoes below them on the floor. There were built in dresser drawers with a few pair of underwear, swim trunks, Bermuda shorts, and some white cotton athletic socks. It was a large walk-in, but Marty didn't make much use of it. I closed it up and found Eric again.

"Thank you for your help," I said.

"You're most welcome. It's such a shame. Unbelievable, really."

I looked at him for an explanation.

"I'm sorry, it's none of my business."

"No, I'd like to hear. What makes you say that?"

"It's just that he was always pretty upbeat, not outgoing, but upbeat and assured. I always took pleasure in seeing him. We didn't talk much, but it was good to see him, if you know what I mean?"

"Yes, I think I do," I said.

"He just didn't seem like," he looked at me apologetically, "the type to end his own life."

I raised my eyebrows. Words weren't going to come.

"Well, we never know what's in someone's heart, do we?"

I shook my head, no.

"His membership is paid through the end of the year. I'd be pleased if you'd use it. You're most welcome to."

He'd made up a laminated membership card in my own name and handed it to me.

"Thank you," I said, "is the garage paid up too?"

"Yes. If you need to keep the car here beyond the end of the year, just let me know. I'd be glad to arrange it. If," he hesitated again, "if you decide to sell the car, let me know. There are some Club members who'd love to have it. I, myself, would be interested."

"I'll remember. Thank you again."

Chapter 15

I'd dropped the floppy disk down the neck into my shirt since it wouldn't fit in my pocket. I could feel it against my skin and see its outline. It took me almost an hour to get back to GMW. I skipped rocks into the surf and watched a volleyball game for awhile, eyed a few well-built girls in string bikinis try to catch the last of the day's sun. I wished I had access to a computer somewhere other than at GMW or in Marty's home office. I didn't want to go back to GMW. I was sick of it. Let Winters deal with them for awhile. And there'd be Roberta and probably Bob Thorne at Marty's house. In the end, without having decided to, I found myself back at 81436 Ocean Avenue. What the hell, I thought, it was there and so was I. It was 6:40

Ron Lawton was in the lobby when I came in. I signed in and he reminded me about our meeting at 10:30.

When the elevator bonged and the doors opened, the reception area was deserted. I headed for Marty's office. At the end of the hallway, in the conference room, I could see the back of the heads of McCord, Hamilton and Gary Weiselman, and across the table from them, Tina Cox, Joe Woodman, Mel Davidson, Bob Winters and two guys that were undoubtedly from First American Bank. I assumed Wolf and Miriam were at the head of the table, but I couldn't see them from where I was. Winters' eyes briefly met mine and if there were a message there, it was a silent don't come in here, but his glance shifted back to Wolf, who I assumed was the source of the muffled words I could hear. If body posture and facial expressions were any indication, I thought, Wolf wasn't making much head-way with the bankers. They had the look of poker players holding all the good cards. The others sat slump-shouldered and sullen faced.

I tried the knob to Marty's office door. It was locked. I hoped it had been Ronnie, but was having what I thought were only slightly paranoid thoughts that Wolf or one of his lackeys might have had the locks changed on me. I tried the 'Off' key and was relieved when the knob turned. Inside, I went to Marty's computer and turned it on before I'd even sat down. I took the floppy out of my shirt and while I was waiting for the thing to boot up wondered what secrets were waiting on it to be revealed. Hope was springing, if not eternal, momentarily. At the C prompt I put the floppy into the slot, closed the latch and typed A: and got the A prompt. Please please please, I was thinking, hearing James Brown or whoever it is that sings that, please let me in! I typed in DIR and got back coded: (1) Directory (18) files, and the date when it had been first created, about the same time Marty'd had Ronnie clear her computer of any files he thought were sensitive. Shit shit shit! I thought. Blocked again! What the hell would he have used for the code? I sat there thinking about everything and nothing, hoping something would magically float to mind. Some intuitive gem that I could regale Nick or Sara with later. How I'd cracked the code. I was absently fiddling with the little locking latch mechanism that closes over the opening of the floppy slot to keep the disk in, when the edge of the gummed label caught my eye. I removed the floppy and looked at it. If the disk had only one directory on it and the disk itself were labeled '37Pack, and the file was about the Packard, why the hell would it be Coded? On the other hand, if this disk were Marty's back up for his Coded files, why was it labeled '37Pack? In a flash of what I just knew was going to be intuitive, deductive oh-so-creative-code-cracking, I put the floppy back and typed cd\coded. I was prompted with Enter Password: and with eyes closed in prayer and teeth clenched, typed '37Pack, and hit enter. I opened my eyes to find Invalid Password. Just to be sure, I removed the floppy and got back to the C prompt and performed the same operation. With the same Invalid result. So much for my infallible intuition.

I shut off the computer and put the floppy back into my shirt. Behind me in the middle of the glass desk there was a pink phone memo from Ronnie to me. Malovitch had called and suggested a meeting at 8:30 tomorrow morning to resolve all outstanding issues. Saturday. Marty was resting uneasily on a cold steel table at Groman Brothers waiting for Thorne's court order and a likely appointment with some dismantlers and Malovitch's wetting his pants to get things resolved. They were a family over there at DBS alright, a little bit like the Manson family, I thought. Ronnie's note said Malovitch would expect me at 8:30 unless I called to tell him otherwise. Nice of him to help me plan the day. There were two phone numbers, marked home and office, for my convenience. I could call anytime up to 11pm. I folded it and put it in my wallet.

I had to try Weiselman on the other DBS file. If that failed, there was really no point in delaying. Getting into Marty's Coded file was looking less and less likely. I left Marty's office testing the door to make sure the knob was still locked. I sat on the large white sofa against the wall in the reception area. I felt slightly narcoleptic, nodding off, or almost nodding off as I waited for the break-up of the meeting with the bank guys.

At 7:15 the two guys I'd assumed were the bankers came down the hallway to the reception area and headed for the elevators like a lynch mob was in hot pursuit. I must have been invisible, because while they waited for the elevator they spoke without so much as a lowering of voice or a casual hand over the mouth to keep what they had to say from my invisible ears.

"Get the notice papers drawn first thing on Monday morning. Send a copy to Wolf. I want them to know we're not fucking around. If they're late on the first, we file. End of story," the first guy said.

"Right," the second guy agreed.

He looked my way, but through me like I were a fly on the wall, and then the elevator arrived with its telltale bong and they got on and the doors closed. Winters came down the hall with Tina Cox and Woodman and Davidson. Wolf and Miriam and Marshall, then McCord and Hamilton walked down the hallway past the reception area headed in the direction of their offices, but I had the feeling there was going to be a little Music Side caucus in Wolf's office. They were all pretty grim faced, but Wolf managed a sneered recognition of my presence as they passed the reception area. Cox, Woodman and Davidson were equally grim-faced, but looked more or less resigned and just plain tired. Winters looked surprisingly upbeat, as though he'd heard some good news. If he had, it'd apparently escaped the notice of the others.

"Mr. Goldman," he greeted me, "how good to see you. I'd like a word with you before I go. If I may. Could we step into...." he looked around for comedic effect, "...your office?"

I smiled, accepting the sarcasm, "Of course."

The elevator bonged and Tina and Davidson and Woodman got on.

"Eight-thirty?" Tina asked.

"Right," I said as the doors started to close, then added quickly, "where's Weiselman?"

"Still in the conference room, I guess," she said as the doors closed.

Winters and I walked back to Marty's office and I let him in.

"I'll be with you in a second. I want to see Weiselman before he goes."

Winters looked at his watch and said, "I'd like to get outta here before breakfast."

I went into the conference room. Weiselman was sitting with his back to me. He looked like he'd been playing mother-may-I and forgot to say the magic words and now had to stay. I walked to the far side of the table and sat opposite him. He seemed simultaneously immobilized, without the energy to get up, and in the grip of an oncoming manic surge like I'd seen at the earlier meeting. He looked at me when I sat, his eyes furtive and agitated. He looked like he was getting ready to do the marathon around the table he should have done earlier, except now was shackled to the floor. He had a trapped, cornered animal look that had nothing to do with me, but seeing me made me the focus of it.

"Whada you want?" he snarled.

"I want the second DBS file, Gary."

He laughed a shrill nutsy laugh and ran his hand through his hair and from the look on his face I thought he might've as well been dancing around a flaming waste basket, yelling, "Too late! Too late!" I pictured him skipping around the room pulling the ashes from the waste basket and spreading them into the air above his head like flower petals.

"What file?" he challenged me.

"Marty's file on the DBS settlement. His calculations and appraisal of the situation. The memo initialled by Malovitch and Diamond and Marty. The file he gave to you to assess tax issues," I bluffed.

His eyes were wild and panicky, but he called me.

"Never heard of it," he smirked.

I hated that. I wanted to grab him by the throat and punch his face to putty, but I didn't. We just glared at each other.

"When I find it, I'm going to shove it up your ass," I said just for something to say to him, and rose. "I hope you've put aside a little something for a rainy day. I have the feeling stormy weather's headed your way. I think you're gonna get wetter than the others." I got up and started for Marty's office and Winters.

His face was sweaty and oily at the same time and what I was now assuming was a drug call was ringing loud enough for the neighbors to complain. He was twisting and folding his hands and wringing them at a furious pace.

"What the hell does that mean?" he asked. "What's that supposed to mean?" he called after me, his voice high and shrill.

If I could have done it convincingly, I would have liked to exit singing or at least whistling Stormy Weather. I had to content myself with it playing in my head.

"Thorne got the restraining order," Winters said as soon as the door closed behind me.

"Swell."

"I have to appear at a hearing Monday morning when the court hears his motion to order the autopsy. You could save us all a lot of trouble by signing the damn thing."

He looked at me like he already knew the answer but felt obliged to ask. He shrugged.

"I want you to object," I said.

"You want what!?" he said, getting to his feet from the couch, looking as though he were going to charge me, grab me by the shoulders and shake some sense into me.

"For the record," I said holding up a hand to calm him. "You don't have to file a motion or turn it into some pissing match with Thorne, just state for the record that Marty took his own life for his own reasons and I object to an autopsy conducted for the sole purpose of trying to skirt the suicide clause in his insurance policy."

Winters groaned, then spoke to me in the sarcastically measured tones I'm sure he reserved for his more obdurate clients and obstinate children. "What good do you imagine that will do? He didn't leave a note. We don't know why he did it. That makes a difference. It leaves open to question what his motives were, and if he were proceeding with an understanding of the consequences of his act. That's the whole point. Was it legally suicide? The judge will have to grant them the order to proceed. You're wasting their time and mine by not signing the autopsy request and making this hearing necessary in the first place! I've got more important things to do. I'm not going to..."

"Then I will!" I shouted at him. "Tell me where the fucking courthouse is and I'll go!"

He gave me that you're demented look while shaking his head.

"I mean it! I'll go! You take care of your more important matters. They're not going to find anything and I want to object to them cutting him to ribbons looking. It's obscene! He's my brother!" I was shouting at him, my voice coming from some other time, some other place where there was still a chance I could protect Marty, somehow save him. It didn't make sense, but there it was.

"Calm down...calm down..." he said soothingly. Soothingly for him, at least. He thought for a moment and then said, "Okay, listen: if you can reach his personal physician before nine on Monday morning, and if you can get word to me before nine-thirty, and if he can tell you categorically that there was no physical reason, no diagnosis of illness, or disease or possible condition your brother was aware of, or any medication that he knew about that might have had an adverse influence or prompted your brother to end his life, I'll raise the objection on that limited ground." He looked at me like a parent doing something he'd probably regret later to keep an upset child from spinning out of control. "Deal?" he said.

"Yeah. Fine," I answered.

"But if you don't succeed in getting that information, or if the doctor has some light to shed on this, we don't object. Right?"

"Right," I agreed.

"Good," he said, "but I gotta warn you, you're almost guaranteeing that Thorne and Roberta will sue you personally and the partners will sue the estate. By objecting, you're just waving a battle flag in their faces." We just looked at each other. I knew he was right, and he knew I knew it. He shrugged, have it your own way, but didn't say it.

"What happened with the Pyramid Group? And First American Bank?" I asked.

"Ah! That!" he said, trying to keep it strictly business, but relishing it, struggling not to let it show. "Wolf succeeded with the Pyramid Group in reducing the rent. He asked for a reduction of $20 thousand. They agreed to $5000, and only for three months. After that, if they can't resume full rent, they'll be considered to be in breach of the lease agreement. First American Bank was not so kind." A smile was slipping out from between his lips. He swallowed it.

"I heard the bank guys discussing it at the elevator; they were going to prepare notice papers Monday morning and send a copy to Wolf. What notice?" I asked.

"That's interesting," he said to himself, then answered me, " a Notice of Default - a preliminary step in the process - what it really means is that the bank isn't going to waste any time. They're going to come after the assets of the partners as fast as they can, before anyone else does."

"Like who?"

"Like the Pyramid Group. Like mortgage holders of the notes on their homes. Any creditors of the partners are going to get in line pretty fast if payments aren't made on time once they get wind of a problem."

"What about the estate?"

"The process is slower. They'll have to file Creditor's Claims. You'll reject them. Ultimately the probate court would decide, but it'll never get that far."

"Why not?"

"Trust me, I have a plan!" he said.

"Like what?"

He looked at his watch. "Not now. How 'bout I save it for Wednesday at the latest!" he laughed.

"I got a note from Ronnie that Malovitch called. He wants to meet tomorrow morning."

"I can't."

"I can," I said. "And there's no reason to postpone it. I can't get into Marty's coded files and Weiselman denies there's another DBS file."

"What makes you think he's lying?"

"Trust me, he is."

"I should be with you at DBS. Postpone it."

"I want to go. Not to resolve anything necessarily, but to get him to lay out their position. I'd like him to commit."

Winters was waiting for the why, but I wasn't going to say, and I think he had an inkling anyway. "Okay, but make a point of telling him that I couldn't be there and that without representation, your discussion with him can only be exploratory. He's a lawyer, he'll understand. You'll be putting him on notice. It ties his hands. There's only so far he can go. Just don't sign anything!!"

"Right. Why spoil my record now?"

"Exactly," he said, "and find that will!" He grabbed his trusty briefcase and strode to the door. "I'm outta here," he announced as he opened it and left.

It was 7:20 and I had a little more than an hour to kill. I thought about fooling around with Marty's computer some more but what was the point? Using '37Pack had seemed inspired, but its failure had made getting in appear hopeless. What I needed was a thousand monkeys on a thousand typewriters and I was 999 short. I went to the couch with the idea in mind of just sitting down and putting my feet up on the coffee table and watching the rising moon work its magic on the darkening water. I had to turn my head uncomfortably to the left to see it so I decided to sit in the easy chair instead. When I got up to move I decided to slide open the door to the balcony so I could hear the sound of the surf. When I sat back down and got my feet up and put my head back another wave of narcolepsy engulfed me. I had the feeling that if I let my eyes close for more than a blink, I'd be asleep. I went to the balcony and breathed in the cool salty air. I thought about going to Wolf's office to take a shower to both freshen and wake up. Maybe a cold shower, I thought, as various pictures of Tina Cox floated across my mind. I was tired. That was my excuse, and I was sticking to it. Visions of Tina Cox were replaced by thoughts of Wolf. I was that tired. It started with his office bathroom and the shower, weighing the thought of the soothing water against the certain hassle if or when he found out, then the palace itself, and somehow ended with a vision of Wolf as a sham figure like the Wizard of Oz, only a truly malevolent one, pulling the strings and levers from his throne, god-like. "God-like" I said out loud, "God". Wolf's code. I'd almost forgotten about it. I went to Marty's desk and checked the clock. I still had an hour. The address Tina had given me was in Venice so if I left myself fifteen minutes to get there I'd have forty-five minutes to attempt my little B&E.

I turned on the computer and typed DIR at the C prompt. I scanned the list of partner names and office administration directories and spotted one labeled Wolf. I tried cd\Wolf and hit enter. I was in. I typed F5, hit enter, and got a long list of what were certainly his clients and projects, and right where it should be alphabetically, the tell-tale Coded listing. I scrolled down to highlight it and entered #1 to retrieve it. It prompted me for the Password. I typed GOD and hit enter.

God bless Ronnie Hook! Across the top of the screen it read Wolf\CODED*.* and when I pressed F5 again I got a long list of files. I felt like a kid in a candy store where the owner had stepped out for a minute. I didn't know what to steal first. I wanted to read and explore, but from the length of the list, it would take all night. It might take half the night just to print them. I went out to Ronnie's desk and rummaged around her computer station until I found a box of floppy disks. Before I could close the drawer they'd come from, the elevator bonged. I had the urge to run or hide. Do something. Anything, except be seen. But before I could unfreeze my mind or feet from the foreboding that seized them, Sandy Marshall was looking down the hallway from the reception area. He smiled and waved and turned to go the other way to his office, took a few of his elephant-man's heavy, measured steps, but just as I was breathing easier, he turned back to me and approached. I tried to hide the motion as I eased the box of disks back into the drawer and closed it with my hip by stepping forward. Ronnie's computer was between me and Marshall, so I was confident he didn't see it. I'd left Marty's office door ajar and the hum of the computer and the light of it were unmistakable.

"I'm really very sorry for all of this," he said. "I wish there were something I could do or say to make it easier for you."

He shrugged his oversize frame in his oversize clothes in a gesture of helplessness. If he weren't so genuine, the effect of him would have been comical. I almost asked him how he'd gotten mixed up with an asshole like Wolf. And stayed mixed up with him for so long. But I didn't. He noticed the door, the hum of the computer, but didn't say anything.

"Thank you," I said. "It helps that I believe you mean it."

He smiled, then informed me, "I'm meeting John here in thirty or forty minutes."

He let it hang, neither suggesting that I should steer clear of Wolf, or that I might prefer not to be seen by him.

"Well, good night then," he said.

"Good night."

He started back towards his office and I returned to Marty's. I closed the door only part way, listening for Marshall's office door to open and close, and when it did, I returned to Ronnie's computer station and got the disks.

When I was safely back in Marty's office with the door closed and locked, I loaded disk after disk, repeating the #8, Copy to: instruction, adding A and waiting for the disk full and the instruction to supply another. It took six of the ten disks in the box, but I had it all. I exited the files, the directory and turned off the computer. I debated what to do with them. The box wouldn't go unnoticed in my shirt and the disks loose in it wouldn't work either. I looked around for something to put them in. I was looking for an empty manila envelope in the file drawers and in the bottom one found the small-ish flat leather briefcase with Marty's initials in gold set off nicely by its dark rich color. There were three sections for files or papers, the one in the middle zippered. They were all empty. It looked like it had been used for a while, then retired in favor of the larger locking one I'd seen at Marty's office at home. I put the disks into the zippered section and added the '37Pack disk from my shirt. It was 8:10 by the obnoxious clock on the desk. I looked around to see if I'd forgotten anything. I closed the balcony door, turned out the lights and made sure the door was locked as I left.

In the reception area I pushed the button for the elevator. It must have been already on its way up, because it bonged almost immediately, and as the doors opened, the realization that Wolf would be on it hit me. I had one of those fight or flight surges of adrenalin, but there was no where to run, and no real reason to. I didn't want to be seen by him, but there was no point in going to ridiculous lengths to avoid it. It was my office too. So what if I were here breaking into his files? Nobody's perfect.

The doors opened and two men with their backs to me were talking to Wolf. He looked between them at me, his face registering surprise, and I could see him shoot them a look to kill the conversation.

"What are you doing here?" he challenged me.

"Research," I smiled at him as I let them pass out of the elevator before getting in.

They headed towards Wolf's office without exchanging another word. I assumed that was for my benefit. They looked familiar, but I didn't place them.

The address Tina Cox had given me was 87 Millwood Court. In the lobby I asked Ron Lawton if he knew where it was. He did. The man was a fountain of information, but he had something else on his mind.

"You see those guys with Mr. Wolf?" he asked me.

"Yeah..."

He looked at the sign-in sheet and sneered, "Mr. Smith and Mr. Jones?"

"What about them?"

"They look like they're in the Entertainment Business to you?"

"No, I suppose not. Do you know them?"

"No, but they were around here a month ago for a coupla days, then again last week. Always hanging around the Café or across the street in the park. That's one of the things I wanted to talk to you about. To-night. They weren't the only ones. They look like hoods. Tough guys. Now they show up with Mr. Wolf. What's Wolf doing with some tough guys?"

I thought I remembered where I'd seen them now. Them or their twins. I tried to shrug it off with Ron.

"I've got to get going Ron, but I'll see you at 10:30. We can talk about it then, okay?"

He smiled more warmly. "Okay. You just take care." He looked at the sign-in sheet again. "I don't like it."

Neither do I, I thought.

Chapter 16

I went out through the lobby and around to the ramp to the underground garage. I retrieved the car from Marty's parking place and took myself to Lincoln Boulevard. "Oh no!" I'd told Sara I'd get back there by 4. I considered stopping at a pay phone to call her but decided I'd better spend the time trying to find the address Tina had given me so I wouldn't be late. Maybe I could call from there. I winced at the thought of Sara trying to hold off Thorne and Roberta all day if he'd shown up to ransack Marty's office at home. It was too late to worry about it now, but that didn't stop me. I was having mental conversations with Thorne, noisy confrontations, as I watched for California and turned right, then left on Shell and right again on Millwood following Ron's directions. I thought he must have been mistaken. There were no restaurants here. Not only was it a residential neighborhood, but a sign was warning me there was No Outlet since Millwood ran only one block in this direction and then dead-ended. I checked the address Tina had given me. No mistake there. I drove slowly looking for number 87. I found it in the middle of the block on the right hand side. I saw Tina's Alfa parked in the driveway and then confirmed the house number.

The house was a one story Victorian cottage, what they'd call a workman's bungalow in Berkeley. There was a little dormer in the portion of the roof that faced the street with a window that let soft warm light glow through it. It must have been built in the 'teens or early twenties, but had been well maintained. That or Tina had put money into it. There wasn't much light left, but from what there was, it looked to be pale blue. There were a few gingerbread touches around the eaves and along the rail of the porch that ran the width of the front of the house. Those were painted white to contrast. There was a patch of neatly trimmed grass divided in equal halves by a stepping-stone path to the front door, and on each side an orderly eighteen inch wide flower bed with pansies and snapdragons and maidenhair ferns covering the ground between. On the porch wall next to the front door was a mail box. It said Cox on it.

She answered the door in a breathless hurry.

"Hi. Come in quick. I've got something on the stove."

She left me to close the door as she retreated to the kitchen. She was barefoot and wearing Levi's and a white T-shirt. Jeez, what a nice athletic body, I thought. Her long blond hair was piled haphazardly on top of her head in a knot held by one of those elastic doohickies. She was stirring what smelled like spaghetti sauce. There was a warm homey feel to the place, and the smells from her cooking permeated the little house, making me realize how hungry I was. It smelled delicious.

She'd had a few walls removed so that the whole downstairs was basically one huge room. There was a door off the kitchen that I guessed was a laundry room or back porch, or both, or maybe a bathroom. To my right were steps going up to the dormer I'd seen from outside. The floors were wide handsome clear fir planks, old sub-flooring sanded and sealed and varnished, with colorful area rugs and a couch and coffee table defining the living room area. A claw-legged oak table and four chairs created the dining area, and a desk with a computer and a chair and file cabinet served as her home office. There was a counter with bar-stools that separated the living room from the modern but country kitchen with its hanging copper pots and pans and Wolf Stove. There were a few framed prints, one by Degas, another by Matisse, but what was most interesting was an original oil, hanging in the place of honor over the fireplace, impressionist, but recent, I thought, of a woman standing on a high outcropping of rock overlooking a stream where it widened to a pond in a glade, her head bent and arms hanging at her sides. Tina looked up from her stirring and tasting.

"Nice, isn't it?" she said.

"It's much better than that; it's powerful and hopeful and heartbreaking at the same time. Where'd you get it?"

"It was a gift," she said with a hint of a smile. "I'm pleased that you like it. I love it. I'd stop eating if I had to before I'd give it up."

I looked but couldn't make anything of the signature. "Who did it?"

"A local. He's lived here in Venice for fifty some odd years. He's pretty well known in some circles. People have been collecting his stuff for the last five or six years. He's seventy or maybe a little older now. Ric Clausen. Ever heard of him?"

"No, but I'd love to see more of his work. Is his stuff at a gallery?"

"No, just his studio."

"Does he let people come see him?"

"Not any more, but if he knows you, you're welcome." She smiled at me, "I'd be glad to take you if you're serious."

"I am. I doubt if I could afford one, but I'd love to see more."

"Good. We'll do it. I think you'll like him."

I was looking around at the place. "Did you make the changes. Open it up like this?"

"Yes."

"You did a good job of it. It's a great space...has a good feel."

"Thanks. Go upstairs if you like. Here." She poured and offered me a glass of red wine. I hesitated, remembering how easily I'd gotten woozy the night before. Jeez, I thought, it seemed like a month ago. What the hell. Why put a damper on it?

"Thanks," I said as I took it from her. There was a salad in a large wooden bowl on the counter near the wine bottle. It had a fine strong vinegar smell that was making me salivate. I reached in and took a pinch with my fingers.

"You must be starved if all you've had to eat today was your bread and water."

"I am and it is."

"This'll be ready in five minutes."

I sipped at the wine while she stirred the sauce. I wanted to put the wine glass down and ease up behind her, slip my arms around her and nuzzle her neck. Maybe cup her breasts in my hungry little hands. Nice thought. Nice guy. While I was thinking it she turned to see what I was doing. Our eyes met and held. She smiled and said, "Go see the upstairs," before she turned back to the stove.

I went up the steep uncarpeted stairs and to my delight found that what had been an attic space with the dormer window had been opened up so that the size of the little house was doubled. The whole upstairs was a huge bedroom and elegant bath. The flooring was the same wood plank. Between the roof rafters the depth had been lessened with what I guessed was insulation and covered and then plastered, so that between the exposed rafters, panels of off-white plaster made the area seem lighter and larger and higher. There was a blond wooden-framed futon bed close to the dormer window not much more than a foot from the floor to the sleeping level. There was a thick down comforter on it. I was thinking how easily I get hot at night and how a comforter like that would just about suffocate me. I wondered if she had a lighter one. At the other end of the space was a glassed off area with a toilet, separately glassed-in shower and a deep Japanese style soaking tub. The glass surrounding the bathroom was etched with a bamboo pattern that made for a kind of peek-a-boo privacy. There was an opening skylight over it. I tried but couldn't recall how much of a mortgage she had on this place, but I remembered that it'd been pretty low. She must have sunk a good chunk of cash into remodeling the house to its present state and still end up with a modest mortgage. I went back down stairs.

The couch and coffee table were perpendicular to the wall across the room from the stairs and centered on a small fireplace with a semi-circular opening outlined with pale yellow brick, the same brick that the little hearth was made from. She had a fire going. It might be innocent as all get-out, but I was thinking I'd better be careful. I hate to be suspicious or distrustful, but a little warning bell was ringing and a little light was flashing. Tina turned around and tossed one of those smiles of hers that reached down into my innards and said hello.

I turned off the bell and put out the light.

"Dinner's ready," she announced.

We helped ourselves to the spaghetti with one of those wooden spoons with pegs on it from a colander in the sink where it was draining, and heaped on sauce from the gurgling pan on the stove with an attractive copper thing somewhere between a huge serving spoon and a ladle. She took a loaf of sourdough wrapped in foil out of the oven and opened it onto a serving plate. It was already sliced with garlic butter warmed into it. She asked me to bring the salad bowl to the table and she brought the bread and wine. When we sat, I closed my eyes for a moment, not in prayer, but with the conscious notion of drawing a line between where I'd been today and where I was now. Between everything else and this. I started clowning with alternatives. Between the good and the bad. Between the honest and dishonest. Between the ugly and the beautiful, I was telling myself, when I opened my eyes on Tina. I thought if I could shut it all out and just smell the smells and taste the tastes, I could keep the boogey-man away for awhile. I wondered how it was that she was unmarried. I was too tired to pretend not to notice how appealing she was or go to any effort to hide it.

"A penny for your thoughts," she said.

"They're worth more," I told her.

"Is my credit any good? I may be out of work soon."

We both started to eat. She ate, I wolfed.

"I'll take a second on your house," I suggested.

She smiled. We ate in silence for a little while, but I could tell she was waiting for an opening or trying to figure a way to take the conversation to a prearranged destination. You get on the bus, you go where it takes you, I was thinking.

"Can we talk about the firm and DBS for a little while and then put it away?" she asked.

"Sure," I said, disappointed. So much for a line between this and that.

"I'm sorry. I know how sick of all this you must be but we, me and Joe and Mel, and even Gary, we're relying on you and Bob Winters. None of us realized how bad it was, or how much John was still overdrawn. It's just overwhelming."

"I don't think Marty's too wild about the situation, either," I said.

She pulled back like I'd reached across the table and slapped her. We stared at each other. I was trying to decide if I regretted saying it. I was so hungry and everything smelled and tasted so good, that if I got myself thrown out before I ate, I surely would. I thought about apologizing. It had been almost seven hours since the last one and she was on the brink of being entitled to another. I tried to keep them at least eight hours apart, otherwise no one thinks they're sincere. Her eyes welled up. This could go either way, I was thinking. Either she's going to throw me out or maybe I should just push it all the way and take the opportunity to ask about a lighter-weight comforter. Just kidding, I told myself. But I had to admit the thought was there. I laughed and it broke the spell.

"You're right," she said, shaking her head like she couldn't believe how insensitive she'd been.

What the hell, I could accept that. Besides, I was still hungry. So I said with exaggerated surprise, "I am?! Does that mean I can finish dinner?"

"Are you ever serious?" she laughed.

"I'm completely serious. I'm far too serious. And I'm hungry. Far too hungry. Not to mention sick of the whole mess. So how about we eat first and talk about it over coffee or wine afterwards. Okay? The food is good, the setting is good, the company, with minor lapses is," I paused both for effect and time to reconsider, but plunged ahead in heedless fashion, "beautiful."

She blushed. Either I was totally clueless and I was easily taken in, which I was willing to consider, or she was both pleased and surprised and flustered. It took several seconds before she could raise her eyes to mine and accept the compliment with a little nod and agree to talk later. The thought crossed my mind that she may just be a pretty good actress and I was working on a sucker-of-the-month award.

"Agreed," she finally said.

We ate in silence again. I didn't know about her, but for me it wasn't an uncomfortable one. I was content. The food was good and the room was cozy. Not too hot. Most rooms were too hot for me. She had several windows opened part way so that the air in the room was fresh and at the same time, warmed by the fire. I had the added advantage of having her to look at, which I did, often. She radiated warmth and beauty without the slightest effort. I was even beginning to feel a little bad about my crack about Marty. Hell, he'd chosen it, hadn't he? I reminded myself none of them had. I should keep that in mind, not come down so hard on these guys. They were just learning to swim when the ship went down. Funny and sad if they were looking to me to be some kind of a life-raft.

I tried to smile. I was being buttered up royally with the dinner and the cozy little fire, but I didn't really care. Why should I? What difference did it make? Better here with her than in the conference room at GMW.

"How did you meet the painter, what's his name? Ric?"

"Clausen," she filled in for me. "Marty. One of Marty's old clients, Lew Sykes. Do you know him? He was in a lot of films in the forties and fifties and into the sixties."

"I know the name. It sounds familiar to me, but I couldn't name anything he's been in." I said.

"He was one of Silver's clients. When Marty first started at DBS, he was given a few clients whose careers were winding down. It was a way of introducing him to the whole process of dealing with projects and the studios and the different kinds of deals that had been carved out until he was ready to pull in clients of his own and make the deals himself. Sort of a hand-me-down training system; it's like that at all the firms when you're fresh out of law school. Anyway, Lew Sykes and Ric Clausen have been friends since they were in grammar school. Lew and Marty got to be very close, more than just client and lawyer. That was usually the case with Marty. Very few of his clients were just clients. He socialized with them privately as friends would, but not publicly, in the limelight. He was too private for that." She laughed at herself, "I digress. Lew took Marty under his wing and Marty met a lot of people through him. Ric was one of them."

I was looking at the painting again. It was one of those works that pulled you in and held on and then stuck with you for a long time after.

"Marty gave it to me," she said, as though confessing.

I looked at her, wondering again if they'd slept together. She must've read my mind.

"It hung in his office at DBS. He loved it, but Roberta never liked it. She thought it was depressing. When she decorated his new office at GMW she made a big stink about it not fitting in. Marty knew how much I liked it and he gave it to me," she said a little defiantly. "That's all."

I wondered why Marty hadn't just hung it in his office at home. I wondered why Tina hadn't hung it in her office at GMW. I thought of several possibilities. That Roberta would've probably objected to it being in their house, even if it were in his office, and Marty didn't think it was worth the hassle, and objected even more if she saw it in Tina's office. Or that it might've started talk in the office, or that Tina might just prefer to have it be a part of her own world here at home. I also thought it may have been to share something with Marty in an intimate but private way. In the end it didn't matter. It'd found a good home, and I could picture Marty with a pleased expression knowing it. Probably getting as much pleasure from knowing how much she liked it as he'd gotten from it himself.

"It looks at home here. I'm sure he was pleased."

"He never saw it here," she quickly and unnecessarily insisted.

I wasn't sure if I believed her at first, but from the expression on her face I knew I was supposed to. I guess I did, at that.

"He didn't have to. He would have known."

Her eyes welled up with tears, going wider, and she bit at her lip and nodded agreement. What a waste, I thought for the millionth or billionth time. We'd both pretty much finished eating.

"Let's talk DBS," I said cheerily, rubbing my hands together like I couldn't wait.

She smiled and wiped away the tears. She refilled our wine glasses and stood, taking the bottle with her.

"Let's sit over there." She led the way to the couch.

"Could I use your phone before we start?"

"Sure, it's on the back side of that post," she said, indicating one in the kitchen. There was another sitting before her on the coffee table. I imagined she was granting me some privacy, but in the little house, it was six of one, half a dozen of the other.

"This one's fine," I said as I sat next to her on the couch and pulled the phone closer to me. "I told my sister I'd get back to Marty's house by 4." I looked at my watch. It was 9:15. I grimaced. "Didn't exactly make it, did I?"

"Not even close."

I dialed Marty's. It rang about six or seven times and I almost hung up. Sara picked it up out of breath.

"It's me," I told her.

"Where are you?! Where have you been? You said you'd be here by four!"

"Calm down, Sara. I'm sorry. It's been pretty hectic."

"Where are you?" she repeated.

"At Tina Cox's." She was silent and I thought it was because she couldn't place or didn't know the name. "One of Marty's partners at GMW."

"I know who she is. What are you doing there?"

Once an older sister, always an older sister.

"We just ate. We're going to now talk about important matters." I smiled at Tina. "Is everything okay there?"

"Yeah, great. Just great," she fumed.

"Has Thorne been around?"

"Of course he's been around! He's been here since early this evening. He's been gloating about his restraining order. What's going on? I can't keep him at bay indefinitely."

"What do you mean?"

"He got here around six-thirty and he and Roberta went out to dinner shortly after and they're not back yet. He wanted to go through things in Marty's office with Roberta. I told him you'd asked that nothing be disturbed. Roberta shrieked at me about it being her house. He huffed and puffed and complained that it was you that needed watching, but when they come back, I expect he'll insist. What do you expect me to do?" Her voice was tired and exasperated and plaintive.

"Don't let him."

"And just how am I supposed to stop him?" She was close to the end of her rope.

"Get a blanket and go to sleep on the couch in there. Make sure you're in pajamas or something, so you can make it seem more like they'd be intruding on your privacy by coming in. If they come in tell them you're sleeping. No no," I revised, "better yet, leave a note on the office door that you've decided to sleep in there tonight. That way, they'll have to disturb you to come in, and you can sort of hide behind the door and let them see you're in your pajamas and tell them tomorrow. I'll get there by eight at the latest and go through things myself."

"And where are you going to be sleeping?" she said with the edge in her voice that must get taught to them in older sister school.

"Venice," I said, "unless I get lucky."

I could picture her lips compressed in a silent reprimand.

"Just kidding," I added after a pause. "If Thorne gives you a bad time, tell him I'll be there at 9. Tell him he can come or send someone and if I take anything with me, he can catalogue it. That oughta satisfy him, or at least put him off 'til tomorrow."

"What's the restraining order about."

I explained.

"Then how can we bury him?" She was about to lose it. She's pretty tough underneath it all, and I could feel her reaching down for something to get her through her sense of desecration and outrage.

"We can't."

She started to cry.

"Listen," I tried to comfort her, "we'll have the service." I didn't tell her that it was a near certainty the judge would allow the autopsy. "We'll do what we can do. Right?"

"Right," she said without much heart.

"I'll see you at eight," I said and we said goodbye and hung up.

I remembered I was supposed to see Malovitch at 8:30. I took the phone message with the numbers for Malovitch Ronnie had left me from my wallet and called his house.

"Hellooo." his voice sang out in a New York nasal.

"Barry Malovitch, please."

"Speaking. Who am I talking to?"

"Kurt Goldman."

"Oh, I'm so glad to hear from you. I hope this doesn't mean you can't meet me tomorrow?"

"I can, but not at 8:30."

"Anytime," he said happily.

I could see him waving his hand expansively.

"How 'bout 7:00 in your office?"

"In the morning?!"

"Yes. I'm sorry it has to be so early but I don't think I'll have any time the rest of the day."

"Oh that's fine. Just fine." His voice was less enthusiastic than the words.

"See you then."

We hung up.

Tina was quiet, subdued like she'd been caught eavesdropping. I pushed the phone away from me and took a sip of the wine. I had the beginnings of a headache or maybe just a buzz from the wine. I decided I'd better not drink any more.

"Do you have any Cranberry juice?" I asked.

She gave me one of those looks I'd become accustomed to, like I'd turned down caviar for a Snickers Bar.

"Sure." She brought me back a large glass filled with ice and what I'd come to think of as the nectar of the gods. I pressed the cold side of the glass against my forehead and eyes. It helped.

"DBS," I said.

"Millennium," she countered.

That surprised me.

"Getting John to re-pay his overdraws and the overspending on the party and especially on his office is going to be difficult, but Joe and Mel and I at least are in agreement about it, John has to make good on it."

"What about 'ol Gary?" I asked her.

Her eyes avoided mine and she seemed evasive.

"He makes a show of being angry, but he doesn't really respond."

"For instance?"

"For instance when we discussed John. Mel and Joe and I intend to ask Warner and Warner for a To Date statement through next Friday on where we stand, sit down with John next weekend and just iron it out. If we don't get the Key Man insurance money, and I don't think for a minute that we will no matter what John or Bob Thorne say to the contrary, and the firm is going to fold, his overdraws and the other monies have to be accounted for before the rest of us start assuming liabilities."

"And Gary?" I reminded her.

"I'm getting to him. That seemed straight-forward enough, a first step, the second being DBS, and settling with them so we know what money we have coming, so if we do face liabilities from GMW we'll have an idea what resources each of us has."

She looked to me for confirmation. I nodded, said, "Makes sense, so?"

"So Gary is nervous and agitated all the time, but he won't focus on things. We asked him to sit down with us and confront John when we have the To Date statement and he said no. We asked him why and he shrugs it off like it's not important, at least to him. We talked about what we might expect from DBS and he rails about you and the autopsy and not trusting you to deal with DBS, but he shows no sign of wanting to negotiate with them for himself or outline any proposal which Joe and Mel and I thought we'd do if you think it would be helpful. You know, if you don't find Marty's file."

"We'll see," I said noncommittally. "What about Millennium?"

She took a deep breath. "For whatever reason, Gary seems to want to steer clear of DBS and he's scared to death of Lyle Faustini and Garvin Perry at Millennium. But the really strange thing is, as combative as John usually is, he won't talk about Marty's plan to file against Millennium. Not only won't talk about it, he won't hear of it if one of us, me, primarily, brings it up. I think it's exactly the right thing to do. Even if you, representing Marty's share of GMW and Mel and I and Joe voted together, we'd still only have 45% to Wolf, Marshall, McCord and Hamilton."

"And Gary?" I asked, guessing what was coming.

"There's no way he'll vote with us to file against Millennium. Whatever's going on with him, there's no chance he'll join us."

"You discussed it with him?"

"Joe and Mel and I sat down with him after the first meeting. While you were out with Winters. The three of us agreed it was a good idea, if you'd go for it."

"And Gary?"

"He went nuts! 'Absolutely not' he screamed. He's really out of control."

I tapped my nose and raised my eyebrows.

She shrugged, "Probably. I don't like to think so, but it's getting pretty obvious."

"So if he voted with them, it would be 55% to 45%, and without him, Marty and you guys 45%, the others 48% plus?"

"Right," she said.

"So you can't do it without him."

"There's another way." She smiled at me and turned to put her back into the corner of the couch and drew her legs and knees up so she could rest her chin on them and face me directly. She tucked her feet into the crevice between the two couch cushions we were sitting on.

This was her little brainstorm coming and she was both proud of it and hesitant to ask. Or a good enough actress to make me feel she was hesitant. I'd been leaning in the direction of accepting her at face value because if she were acting, I wasn't discerning enough to tell for sure, so I might as well give her the benefit of my doubts.

"You file against Millennium in the name of Marty's Professional Corporation. If you can get Marty's malpractice insurer to join you in the suit, assuming Sutton files against you, so much the better. That was the direction Marty was going. It still makes sense. You'd have standing because it's Marty's PC that would be the first target of any action that Sutton takes, then GMW second. And whether Sutton files against Marty's PC and/or GMW or not, Millennium is still guilty of conspiring to breach a valid contract and a host of other things. So if we can't do it through GMW, you can. It makes no sense to roll over to the tune of $800,000 for this little scam Millennium and Sutton appear to have cooked up!"

She was right. Even if it were a neat way of putting me and the estate out front in the line of fire, keeping her and everyone else's hands at GMW clean, if GMW ducked the fight and agreed to pay Sutton the money, Marty's share would add $200,000 to Marty's PC's liabilities and therefore to the estate. Without a shot being fired. Even if it got more complicated by filing against Millennium, Sutton turning around and suing GMW for the $3 million for instance, the value of the suit against Millennium could far outweigh either the $800,000 or even the $3 million. The only real problem would be Winters. Would he be willing to drag his firm into something like this? There might not be a pay-off, and the cost of litigating against something like Millennium and Garvin Perry, with almost unlimited resources, made very little sense on the face of it for them. Even if he saw it in the best interests of his client, The Estate of Marty H. Goldman, before Winters would even consider it, I had the feeling he'd want to know exactly what was making Wolf so willing to fork over $800,000 that he clearly didn't have, rather than go to court against Millennium. I wanted to know. Weren't people always suing movie studios all the time anyway? Why the fuss?

"Why do you think a guy like Wolf would shy away from a suit with Millennium? He seems pretty contentious to me. Why would he agree to roll over for $800,000 that he doesn't have? That GMW doesn't have?" I asked her.

"I don't know. Maybe the fear of being black-balled by Millennium," she shrugged.

"If GMW folds, Wolf and Marshall probably go back to a strictly music clientele, so what would it matter if a movie studio black-balls him or his clients? They operate in two different worlds."

"Not really," she pointed out, "things are changing. Music people cross-over into movies all the time now. Also, there've been mergers and take-overs and rumors of mergers and take-overs. It's not very clear who owns what or who controls what any more. Or for how long. It's all money now, the specific product is just something that happens while all these people make lots and lots of money. Wolf just may have his finger on the pulse of where things are going and not want to risk running afoul of someone like Perry, who has money and connections that reach god-only-knows-where."

"I'll talk to Bob Winters about it."

"But what do you think?" she implored me in an exaggerated joking tone, but only half joking.

If I weren't such a trusting soul and hadn't already decided to take her at face value, warning signs or lights or bells would have been going off again. I was lost in the warmth of her face, and took the warmth for integrity. Her toes had crept out from under the cushion and were wiggling against my thigh, prompting me to reply.

"I think I'll talk to Winters and then talk to you about it."

She pouted and shrugged, but didn't give up entirely. "But basically, you agree, right? You see the sense of it? For Marty's estate as well as for us, right?" On came the electric smile.

"I suppose Joe and Mel were all for it?"

"Of course."

"And Gary?"

"No."

"Why not? He's got nothing to lose if the estate sticks its neck...my neck out."

"I told you, he's scared to death of Faustini and Garvin Perry. He was out there with Marty on at least one occasion, and even if he didn't actually meet Perry," she smiled grimly, "it had a profound effect on him."

I hadn't heard that. I'd have to ask Ronnie when that was.

Her foot nudged me again, and she prompted me with a smile, waiting for her answer. I patted her foot and tried to joke my way out of it. "Of course. How could I disagree? Your logic is irrefutable. Inescapable." I gave her a wide-eyed guileless smile. End of subject. "What about DBS? You got any inescapable or irrefutable notions there?"

She frowned but gave in on any more discussion of Millennium.

"I think you can trust Barry to be fair," she said flatly. "Even if you don't have Marty's file, I think he'll be forthright about what Marty had coming, and where they'd gotten in their settlement talks. And I can give you a pretty good idea of what I think my stake there is. The same for Joe and Mel and Gary. There's no great mystery in what we should have coming. We were salaried, but had profit percentages tied to Marty's overall contribution to DBS."

"How was that supposed to work?"

"Marty was grooming us. I told you he gave us some of his clients; we worked for them and any new deals they were involved in. They didn't show up as Marty's clients so he didn't get his 16% partnership profits against them, and since we didn't have any vested partnership percentages, Marty and Barry worked out an arrangement. The three of us got a bonus of 5% of those deals. The settlement should include something along those lines. Barry'll fill you in on it."

I put my head back to rest, planning on closing my eyes for a minute, but found myself looking at the ceiling instead. The joists supporting the floor above were exposed rough-sawn fir 2x10's with the bottom side of the fir floor planking from above exposed over them. Nice effect, I thought.

"Regardless of Thorne's restraining order, we're planning on a service for Marty at Hillside Memorial Cemetery Sunday at 2." I was still staring at the ceiling. The words came out pretty matter-of-factly, I thought. If I'd had to look at her face it would have been another story. "If you're going to be there, maybe you could bring me some notes on that?"

She didn't answer for a few seconds, and I abandoned the safety of the ceiling to see if she'd heard me. When I looked at her she was biting the knuckle of the first finger on her right hand. She nodded yes to me. We looked at each other and I had the feeling that if either one of us said anything we'd both start to cry. Just looking at her was an unbearable confirmation that Marty was dead and even if we couldn't bury his body on Sunday, we were going to be burying something that we could never have back again. I closed my eyes and tried to stop the tears from leaking out.

"Would you hold me? Please," she said. Before I could say anything she'd slid across the couch and curled against my chest, the knot of hair on the top of her head just below my jaw, her left arm gently on my chest, her warm fingers resting on the bare skin of my neck and shoulder. I could feel little shudders of suppressed sobs ripple through her. I stroked the top of her head and let my fingers play with the piled-up hair with my free hand. When it started to feel too good, and my thoughts turned away from Marty and back to the heavy-weight comforter, I began to nuzzle her head with my lips. She sighed, and held onto me a little tighter. I was thinking about a lighter comforter, about not wanting to break the spell or the mood when I remembered Ron Lawton. As best I could without dislodging her, I reached into my pocket for my watch. It was 10:10. I toyed with the idea of standing Ron up. Her breathing became more regular and she seemed to let go, melting into me. I tried to count the number of hours Marty had been dead. To put the situation in perspective. I was getting cozy with a woman that'd had at the very least a crush on my brother now dead all of sixty hours. What a guy! Maybe they'd had something more going. If there was an attraction between us, for her part, I reluctantly reminded myself, it was probably a need to feel close to something or someone connected to him. And here I was. That was a plausible excuse for her, but was it the same for me?

"I've got to go," I said, answering and not answering myself.

She stirred, dreamy, sleepy, clinging to me in silent protest.

I patted her shoulder and stroked the top of her head in a perfunctory way.

"I gotta go."

She pulled back from me and gave me a cool tight-lipped appraising look.

"You're serious."

"'Fraid so. I said I'd meet someone at 10:30."

The merest hint of a smile crossed her face, and for a moment I thought she was going to suggest that I skip it. That I stay there with her. That we could negotiate about the comforter. Sixty hours or not, I wanted to. But because I let it, as quickly as the moment came it went, and instead of the smile, a look of having been deceived replaced it. Promises made, promises broken. She turned herself around and put her feet on the floor, pausing to look at them, as though there were a lesson there to be learned. We both stood. Strangers who'd shared a cab and let the talk get too personal, and now the ride was over. It was awkward. I felt bad for both of us. It would have made it simpler if I'd had a coat or a jacket or something to busy myself with to cover the retreat, but I never wore them, and the trip to her door was like walking barefoot on broken glass.

I wanted to go easy and take care with each step, and at the same time, run like hell and get it over with.

I got to the door convinced that we were both wondering what she'd do if I kissed her. Or tried to. She smiled. I smiled. What a guy! Sixty hours crossed my mind. Maybe another time, I thought. A real prince either way. Her smile faded and she closed the door with a firm and what I thought sounded like a final thud. "Ask not for whom the door thuds," I mumbled to myself as I walked away from her house.

Chapter 17

—————◦◦◦◦———————

I walked back to the Mustang and got in. I started it and let the engine warm up. This had been the only time in my life I'd actually gotten the car I'd asked for and reserved over the phone. I listened to the pleasant rumble of the 5 liter engine, turned on the lights and shifted the four speed to first. I checked the rearview and side mirrors and hung a U turn. Near the corner of Shell I passed what looked like the same Buick or Olds that had rammed the Beamer in the lot behind Sandy's. Except it couldn't be because as I passed it I could see there was no damage to its front end, and that little episode had been only twenty-two hours or so before. Besides, the cops seemed pretty sure the car was stolen. I was laughing at myself as I turned left on Shell, but out of the corner of my eye caught sight of its lights come on just as it went out of view. I sped up. I was having an adrenalin rush. I was spooked and couldn't shake a feeling of trouble. There was nothing in the rear-view, but when I neared the corner of Shell and California I slowed only a little, then ran the stop sign as I turned right. I punched it and the Mustang's 5 liters dug in and hurled me to the corner of California and Lincoln, where I sailed through the red light and squealed through a left turn. I was doing over sixty. Explanations for the cop that I was sure would be pulling me over soon were running through my mind. None of them sounded remotely plausible. I checked the mirror. Nothing. I slowed down and started to relax.

I drove for a couple of blocks trying to recall the cross streets on each end of the block of Main where Sandy's was. Rose and Marine, I remembered. I was looking for whichever of them I'd pass first going in this direction when out of nowhere headlights flooded through my rear window. I had the fleeting thought that it was a cop, but there were no red lights, no sirens, only the sound of an engine working hard to catch me. Whoever it was, they were closing in. I jammed the accelerator to the floor and began to outrun them. When I got to Rose I had the light and waited 'til the last second, slid through a left turn, steered into the skid, punched it and flew west towards Main. I checked the rear-view again. The big sedan was skidding, breaking, trying to slow down enough to make the turn onto Rose but was suddenly cut off from doing it by another car that stopped next to it. Between me and them. I had to stop when I came to Main. There was too much cross traffic to ignore. I could see that when the sedan backed to turn behind the second car, it backed too, again blocking it. If I hadn't been so scared, I would have liked to go back and watch the cat-and-mouse game and thank the fool driving what I could clearly see was an old but perfectly kept or restored black '65 Plymouth Fury two door Coupe. I had the funny fleeting feeling that my old friend, Steve Alder from the Buen Amigos sailboat days, had come from the twilight zone to save me. He'd had an exact duplicate of that car fifteen years before. And much as I'd have liked to see the outcome, I wasn't about to stick around. I raced across Main, turned into the lot behind Sandy's and parked. They say lightening never strikes twice in the same place. I was counting on it. I wasn't about to get caught walking through the lot to either Rose or Marine and then be exposed on Main, so I found the back door into Sandy's. I had to force it, first wiggling a credit card at the latch, then kicking it hard and it popped open. It took me through a storage room with aluminum beer kegs and boxes of imported beers and hard liquor. The door on the other side of the room took me to the hallway where the bathrooms and a couple of pay phones were. I came into the big front room from back there. The place was crowded and noisy. The bar was to my right and Ron Lawton was sitting there nursing a beer. I checked my watch. 10:30 on the button. I'd made pretty good time. Not surprising considering the incentive.

"Hi," I said as I sat down next to him.

He looked around surprised. "I was watching for you. I didn't see you come in." His look a question.

"I parked in back. I came through the back door."

"They don't have one for customers."

"They do now."

He looked more closely at me. "You okay?"

"Tired," I shrugged.

The bartender passed by and I asked him for a Dos Equis. He put it on the bar in front of me and held up a glass. I waved it off and sipped at it from the ice-cold bottle. It had a welcome, calming effect. I was trying to decide if I were completely paranoid and nuts, or if there were really a chance that some fools meant me harm. My fear was real. I was thinking I could start from that and try to sort out the possibilities. Ron looked over my shoulder towards the hallway. The look on his face made me turn and look. A big, long-haired, dark-skinned man in an army jacket and Levis and worn cowboy boots came from the bathroom or telephones and sat at a small table with his back to a section of wall. His

hands were in his coat pockets and he left them there when he sat. He
stretched out long legs and crossed them at the ankles. He surveyed the
place without much interest, but I noticed he was positioned to watch
both the front door and anyone who might enter the way I had. Ron
watched him sit, then looked back to me.

"Sure you're okay?"

"What's on your mind?" I asked him. It was his meeting.

"Well, first, let me tell you again how sorry I am about your brother."

I nodded, accepting his condolences again.

"See, he helped me."

His tone suggested something more than a ride to a bus stop on a cold
night.

"I worked as a janitor at the Wells Fargo Building on Wilshire."

He answered my blank look. "Where Diamond Bernstein and Silver
have their offices."

I nodded.

"One night your brother was working late. I was runnin' the floor
polisher in the lobby and he said goodnight and I said goodnight and he
went through the lobby around to the underground garage. He always
went around. Never down the elevator to the parking garage. Know
what I mean? Outside and down?"

I nodded again.

"Like you been doin' at Ocean Avenue. I notice things like that. Your
brother comes back and asks me if I got a car. 'Yeah', I says, 'I do'. Could
I give him a jump, he asks me. 'Sure', I say. See, his Jag won't start. Tells
me what an unreliable piece o' shit it is, but he loves it anyway. So we go
outside and down to the garage and we fool around for twenty minutes
or so but it ain't gonna start, that much is clear. He thanks me and says
he'll call a cab. I'm just about finished for the evening and say I can give
him a ride. He says 'no', I insist and so he accepts."

I was beginning to wish I'd stood him up.

"On the ride home we start to talk. He'd always been nice, say hello
and all, but we don't exactly travel in the same circles, you know, so we'd
never said much more than hello or goodbye. He asked me how long I
been janitorin', what I'd do before that, you know, small talk. Only I can
tell he's not just askin', he's listenin'. I been in 'Nam. Been into some
mean shit. He told me about you. Tryin' to keep you out, you fucking
up with the draft board an' all. We talked personal like."

He paused, either thinking about what he wanted to say, or maybe, I
was wishing, not having much more to say. I waited, thinking about the
protracted battle with my draft board, about Marty finding and paying
for the doctor that certified my ruptured disc and un-soldier like lower
back, about the three times the board had ordered additional physicals,
unwilling to give up on me, pushing me three times to the brink of having to say no and go to jail instead of VietNam. For the millionth time I
examined my belief that I was prepared to go to prison rather than into

the army. I was scared to the bone, but thought I would have said no anyway. Marty rescued me. He was furious a year before when I'd given up my student deferment, guilty at having it to hide behind, rather than just my opposition to the war. My draft board immediately reclassified me 1A, prime meat. Marty told me it was the stupidest, most cavalier thing he'd heard of. What good did it do? But he understood. I knew he did. And he lined up the doctor and the tests and after the third try to put me in an unflattering shade of green, the board re-classified me 1Y, which meant if the commies were marching up Telegraph Avenue in Berkeley, they'd call on me for the defense of the motherland.

I thought about Tina and the heavy comforter. About Marty and Tina. About who was in the big sedan and if it really had anything to do with me or was a figment of an over-active and over-tired imagination.

"He asked me 'what'd you like to be doing?' Just like that. I said I had plenty experience with intelligence and special operations in 'Nam. Thought I'd like to have a security business of my own. Me and a few of my buddies from over there could do a better job then the stiffs we see at the Wells Fargo Building, that's for sure, or for that matter any of the places 'round town. 'What would it take?' he asked me. I tell him I been saving some money. Got so much. Need so much more. But I need someone will hire me. Give us a chance. Your brother loaned me what I needed and helped get me started. Helped us get bonded and licensed. I got twenty guys, really good reliable guys now, and we have six big buildings right here in Beverly Hills, California. He got me the first two. The others came in time. But he got me going. Let me figure out how much to pay him back and how fast. I paid him every nickel. But I owe him. I'll always owe him."

I sipped at the beer, that all too familiar ache returned to my heart, in some ways stunned, but at the same time not very surprised. I was glad for Ron to have had Marty as a friend and patron. Glad to hear more about Marty's sweetness and generosity. But I was tired and wanted to go home to my clean old hotel room and sleep.

"He put in a good word for us with the Pyramid people. We already had a pretty good reputation by then, but I know it helped."

He looked at me like there was no way for him to tell me how much Marty meant to him. I felt the same way. We could finish our beers and go our separate ways connected to Marty like step-brothers to a common father they each loved.

"I should have seen it," he said. "There were signs I just plain ignored."

I remembered Marty and Maia in Berkeley and how little I'd noticed. I thought about my call to him on his birthday, just three days before he blew his brains out and how I'd heard nothing in his voice to alarm me. Or thought I hadn't. Or now wanted to believe I hadn't. What signs did Ron Lawton, security guard extradinaire, expect he should have seen?

"Like what?" I asked without much interest.

"Like the cars parked out on Ocean with guys sitting in them. Guys like the guys with Wolf tonight. And other guys like them from time to time sitting in the park acrost the street. I never connected it to your brother, but now it seems obvious. Like it was there callin' to me, but I'm in these big offices now in Beverly Hills and Santa Monica and I sort of lose my edge, get used to lawyers and expensive suits and clean rides like all these guys drivin', and I just don't see what's right there in front of me."

I was interested now. Alarmed. What he'd been saying was starting to come through in a new way. Like it'd been out of focus and had been foggy and blurry, but what he saying was becoming all too clear.

"What are you saying!? Are you out of your mind!?"

"I think guys had been following your brother for at least two months, maybe three or four before he died. I think they followed and watched him. I think those two baboons with Wolf were in the park at least four or five times hanging out. I think they or some other guys like them came 'bout the same time your brother came in the mornin' and hung 'round and left when he did. Shadowed him. I don't know why and I don't know if they meant him any harm, but they were around too long and too often. They weren't there for the ocean air."

I was picturing it, a retroactive sense of impending harm, a sense of panic in my stomach rising to my throat while I was sitting there and I wanted to yell to Marty, look out! They're closing in on you! The help-lessness gripped me like one of those dreams where someone's in danger, and your voice won't work, or your legs are bound and you can't run to their aid.

"Did you ever mention it to him? Ask him about it?"

He shook his head no. Some security guy. No wonder we lost in 'Nam.

"Why the hell not if you were suspicious? What the fuck were you doing?" My voice had risen.

Ron didn't look at me but across the bar into the mirror. His lips were pressed in a tight line. I'd been looking at him but he wouldn't meet my eyes. I looked at him in the mirror. His eyes were wet. I noticed the long-haired guy was watching us. Not casually.

"I fucked up. But I wasn't his body guard!" He'd turned to look at me directly. "I was the fucking security for the building!" he voice pleaded with me, but the words were falling on deaf ears. His own as well as mine. He was anguished at his failure to see what he now believed was there to be seen. To protect Marty from some unknown but very real threat that he believed had been within his reach to thwart. "I fucked up," he said again, quietly, the tone no longer expecting or hoping for absolution. "I fucked up."

I couldn't meet his eyes. His pain would only serve to unleash mine and I was already drained. And I couldn't and wouldn't absolve him. I resented his failure. And knew at the same time I was hiding behind it to avoid thinking about my own. How could I have not heard anything in Marty's voice if all this were going on around him? I knew Ron wasn't the only one who'd fucked up.

I was looking in the mirror when I noticed the big guy in the army coat get up from his table and come up behind me and Ron. He nodded a curt expressionless greeting to me into the mirror and leaned over and whispered something to Ron. He looked at me, whispered something else and returned to his table. Ron looked at me like I'd pissed on his shoes or stolen his good luck charm.

"Why didn't you tell me about the chase over here!?" he demanded.

"I wasn't sure it was a chase," I said defensively, "I wasn't sure what it was. What makes you think..."

He interrupted me impatiently, "Because those guys have been hanging around all day since we saw them with Wolf. When you left, they left. I had Tate follow them following you." He motioned towards the guy at the table.

"He's one of your guys?" I asked.

"More like three of them." he said. "Tate is a problem solver. He solved yours tonight."

"Was he the guy in the Fury?"

Ron nodded.

"If I hadn't been so scared, I thought about going back to thank whoever it was. What happened?" I watched Tate watching people come and go through the front door, then occasionally shift his glace towards the back. "Is he expecting those guys here?" my voice skipped up a notch before I could reign it back down. "Do those guys know Tate was protecting me?" I was worried it might complicate the situation. Maybe make Wolf, if Wolf were really behind them, more reckless. That's all I needed.

"Not likely. Tate challenged them, made it a traffic dispute that got too personal." Ron smiled. "They've clocked out for the night," he said matter-of-factly and sipped at his beer and thought about where things stood. "I've had Tate keepin' an eye on you since you threw Wolf's stuff off the balcony this morning. "Not much like your brother, are you?" He didn't wait for an answer. "You got his attention with that one. Only problem is, now you got those guys' attention too."

"I think I had it before that," I said.

"What d'ya mean?"

I told him about the guys hanging around Sandy's the night before and about the Beamer. I took the scrap of paper with the plate number out of my wallet. I told him what the cops'd said about the car probably being stolen. He took it from me and put it in his shirt pocket. He was thinking about it.

"If it was the same guys, I'd expect them to show up here looking for you in spite of Tate. Since you were heading in this direction and been here last night, even a couple of apes like that'd figure you were coming here and give it a try. The guys tonight are with Wolf, we know that. But I'm worried about last night."

Swell. Starters backed by pinch-hitters. I wondered what the odds were that they were unconnected.

He was scaring me, whether he intended to or not. I was suddenly swamped with the feeling that LA wasn't nearly big enough, that there was nowhere to run. I wondered if Marty'd felt that way? If he'd even been aware that someone was shadowing him? If they were. From where I was sitting now it seemed likely. How mean was Wolf willing to get? And why? I was beginning to wonder if Thorne had intended only on being coy with Roberta about Marty's death possibly being murder, but had unintentionally let more information slip than he'd intended. Or if he were even privy to Wolf's darker plans. I thought about my room at the Pacific Hotel and wondered if they knew I was there. Ron was thinking along the same lines.

"Where you stayin'?" he asked.

I hesitated for a minute, considering my options. He frowned at my evident lack of trust or confidence in him. My options seemed limited at best.

"The Pacific Hotel. Up the street."

"I know it. When did you check in?"

"A little before two last night. This morning," I corrected myself.

"What room?"

"211."

"Did you use your own name?"

The question caught me off guard and for a moment I almost answered yes, when I remembered I hadn't.

"No."

"What name?" he asked.

I was embarrassed to say.

"What name?" he repeated, maybe giving me the benefit and assuming I hadn't heard him.

"Mike Hammer," I said.

He rolled his white eyes in his dark brown face and nearly choked on a mouthful of beer.

"I didn't think I'd get away with Shaft."

"I think you're probably okay there, but I'll have Tate stay on you all night."

I started to protest.

"Don't worry, you won't know he's there unless he wants you to. Where're you going in the morning?"

Suddenly he was my daddy and my travel agent, but I had to admit I was relieved as I caught a glimpse of Tate in the mirror in front of me.

"I'll probably go into Beverly Hills to Il Fornaio for coffee, then to DBS then out to Marty's house - 1830 Seascape Drive, Brentwood - by 8."

"Tate'll be too conspicuous there. I'll have someone else on you when you leave Il Fornaio."

"You really think this's...."

I was going to say necessary but before I could get the words out, he said, "Yes". End of subject. He got no argument from me. "Stay put. Please." He went over to Tate and filled him in. Tate kept up his watch without indicating he was even aware of Ron's presence. Ron seemed satisfied. I was thinking about Tina Cox, Tate having followed me there, when Ron came back and sat next to me at the bar.

"If Wolf wanted to have you popped, you'd have been popped by now." If that was supposed to have made me feel better or safer, it hadn't.

"The question is, then why go to so much trouble? And look at the risk he's running if he got tied to those guys? What's he want from you?"

Good question. I toyed with the idea that he'd had his heart set on that corner office. Really wanted it! For my own sake, I figured I'd better give it more serious thought. Wolf didn't know I'd invaded his files. Not yet, anyway. At least I thought he didn't. And since I'd only invaded them tonight, what did they expect to gain by following me around last night? Was it possible they believed Marty'd had some information that I might've found? Everywhere I'd been looking, I came up blank. What would make them think I had something they didn't want me to have? Or hadn't wanted Marty to have? They may not have known that I was locked out of Marty's coded files. No, assuming they didn't know about the coded files, even if they thought I had access to everything of Marty's, what did he have that would hurt them? If there were something, it was safe to assume they would've tried to access his computer to get it. They'd come up empty. They would have seen the coded files in his directory, so they'd know it existed. They could have looked for hard copies in his office or at his house, or they could keep following me to see if it appeared I'd found something or gotten into the coded files. In fact, they'd probably assume I had access to the coded files. That must be it! If they assumed it, they'd have to follow me around to see if I went anywhere or did anything that would indicate I was acting on the information they didn't want public. I thought about the disks with Wolf's GOD files in the little briefcase in the trunk of the Mustang. Then I flashed on Marty's new briefcase at the house. It had been empty. I hadn't examined the papers on the trestle table. Some of them could have come from his briefcase. He might have spread them out there for an overview of something, intending to put them back when he was ready to return to Santa Monica. Or someone might have emptied it for him. Looking for hard copies of something he wasn't supposed to have. Something they might have been willing to kill him for. But if they were following me around, it was clear they hadn't gotten whatever it was from him. And if they hadn't gotten it, or it wasn't there in the first place, why kill him? Why not just burglarize his office at home or break into his car and steal his briefcase? Unless they knew he knew. Even if they couldn't find the papers or computer files to keep someone else from getting the information, they could keep him from acting on it. I suddenly realized I'd accepted the idea that he'd been killed. Just like that. What in the hell for? These guys weren't dealing in national security secrets. It was insane to buy into this. I was definitely over-reacting.

"Good question," I said to Ron, "I don't have a clue. I'm tired. I'm going to head home. So to speak."

He smiled at me. "Take care," he said.

"Right."

I went out through the front door. I could see Tate stir as I left.

Chapter 18

SATURDAY

———◦◦◦◦◦———

Ron was right. I hadn't seen Tate. Not a sign. I hoped that was good. I'd gotten up at 5, taken a long hot shower, dressed and gone out to the parking lot facing the ocean. I watched the water and listened to the surf for a few minutes. The air was fresh and crisp. I had the little briefcase with me, no longer believing it was safe in the trunk of the car. I warmed up the trusty Mustang and took a leisurely ride on the 10 as far as National. I checked the rearview often but saw no sign of the '65 Fury or Tate. I meandered up Castle Heights Avenue through the jacaranda lined neighborhood to Beverwil and north to where it becomes Beverly Drive at Pico. Il Fornaio was just up the street half a dozen blocks at Dayton. It was 6:02. I parked headed north on Beverly and crossed the street. If Ron had someone on me, I couldn't see who or where. There were only two other cars on Beverly. Maybe another two or three on Dayton. No one in any of them.

When I entered and found a table along the wall on the Dayton Way side, I spent a few minutes looking at the few of people there, all at separate tables. I was pretty sure the old heavy-set guy with black rimmed half-sized reading glasses and sweat clothes and the dolled up middle-aged woman in a business suit and the early thirties guy in a crisply starched shirt with his suit jacket neatly hanging over the chair across the table from him were not any of Ron's operatives. I wondered why the woman and the young guy were so dressed up on a Saturday morning. The waitress came to my table. A good looking brunette that had nice eyes and a nice body but seemed smile-challenged. It was early and Saturday so I forgave her. I ordered a decaf latte and the seven grain toast. I went outside to get a paper from the box on the corner. There was a car on the same side of the street as the Mustang about eight spaces ahead of it. A guy was sitting in it. Ron's guy, I thought. I considered getting him a cup of coffee and a bagel or something, thought better of it and returned to my table with the LA Times.

As I got comfortable the waitress brought my coffee and toast. Still no smile, no good morning. She left the check with the food. Like I shouldn't consider lingering over a second cup. She'd brought some apricot jam that was delicious. I scanned the front page, took a sip of coffee and flipped it over to scan the bottom half below the fold. I saw it in the right hand corner: DA To Investigate Death of Movie Lawyer. Below that, Possible Foul Play in Death of Attorney Marty H. Goldman. My head began a slow spin, and my stomach joined in shortly after. I read further. The Assistant DA was someone named Brian Browning. I found what I was looking for when I turned to page A12 where the story was continued. "According to attorney Robert C. Thorne, acting on behalf of Mr. Goldman's widow, Roberta Goldman, the District Attorney's Office is investigating several leads in what was at first believed to be a suicide." It continued in that vein as though Thorne had written it himself, suggesting a connection to a rash of burglaries in the well-to-do area. The last line mentioned the 2pm service at Hillside Memorial Park Cemetery on Sunday. I wondered if the DA really had any interest in an investigation, or if Thorne and Wolf had orchestrated some pressure on the DA's Office to at least look into the possibility of foul play. And from that had secured the services of an over-eager reporter. I turned back to the front page and read the byline. Someone named Gerban Nadir, and under that, Freelance Contributor. It looked like the work of Thorne and Wolf, alright.

Wolf and Thorne would push the foul play notion just as far as they could to muddy the waters and cast further doubt on suicide to increase their chances with the insurance company.

I finished the coffee and toast, paid and left. The waitress' name, Vann, was in the upper right hand corner of the check in a box marked Server. Nice name, I was thinking as I paid the cashier. As I headed for the door Vann found her smile. It seemed to say more than have a nice day.

I was about to cross to the Mustang when I noticed the car I'd seen before was gone. I was alone on the empty street. I felt vulnerable. Like a possible foul play waiting to happen. Where the hell was Ron's guy? I didn't know which I hated more, feeling threatened, or being afraid. They both made me mad. The DBS office was only two or three blocks away. I checked the time. It was 6:50. Fuck them all. I changed my mind about the Mustang and decided to walk.

The air was beginning to heat up. What crispness there'd been was gone and the day promised to be hot. I wondered if Beverly Hills still had the local village feel for the kids that lived here, the way it had had for us, or if the inflated money and frantic pace and constant turnover of the entertainment establishment made that impossible. The stores I passed had more impressive facades than before, and the familiar names of Giorgio, Armani, St. Laurent, Tiffany and dozens of others suggested the village was gone.

The lobby at the Wells Fargo Building was too small and too tall, which made it oddly claustrophobic. The floor was an unpleasant mix of almost-black and dirty-gray marble tiles. Marty had come here five or six days a week for fifteen years. I wondered if it'd bothered him the way it did me. The pattern continued two and a half or three feet up the walls. It wasn't any better there. DBS was on the sixteenth floor. It was the sixteenth floor. When the elevator doors opened there was another lobby that served the two elevators that came up this far, but there was nowhere else to go, no other offices to choose from, only one set of huge Rosewood doors with Diamond Bernstein and Silver in six inch brass letters. Below that in smaller letters were the names of the other partners, in order of importance, not alphabetically, since Malovitch was first among them, then George Zeffaro, Larry Klein and a dozen more. The door was unlocked and I let myself in. It was quiet and calm and richly decorated in a subdued wood-wall and tapestried way. Comfortable looking couches and easy chairs were clustered around coffee tables and there were writing desks here and there. It took me a minute to pick out the location of the receptionist's desk. The place was more like a men's club. No hurry here, the decor said, no quick buck guys, just good sound lawyers representing their clients, taking care of them the way a well-heeled uncle might look after a favorite nephew. Or maybe a young bright nephew taking care of a favorite old uncle. Nothing about the place suggested anything as crass as business took place here. There was no receptionist. I went through another set of large doors at the back of the reception area and wandered past several large offices, nothing like the size of Wolf's, but inviting and chummy. I called out.

"Hello?"

"I'm down here," a voice called from a few offices away.

Malovitch's office was on the south-west end of the floor and the view was terrific. Terrific, if you wanted to look at parts of LA and Beverly Hills and Westwood. And that through a medium-thick layer of brown smog threatening to get worse if the heat kept up for another day or two. When I stepped into it he stood to greet me. There was the smell of cheap perfume in the air. It was probably an expensive men's cologne, but he'd used too much, and he and the room smelled like the cosmetics counter at a five-and-dime. He seemed undecided about whether to greet me effusively, like a long lost brother, or at least the brother of a spiritual brother, or use the somber tones of condolence. He tried for a little of both. I could see in the direction of the ocean, but even on a clear day it was too far to be visible.

"Sit down. I'm glad you could come."

He followed my eyes to the view and smiled with pleasure, obviously used to people appreciating it, commenting on it, but making a show of modesty about the talent and accomplishments that presumably brought him here.

"This used to be Marty's office before he left. Did you know that?"

"No."

He shook his head sadly.

"Such a waste. Such a waste," he said.

I had the feeling that if he could have squeezed out a few tears for effect he would have. I knew I was being unfair. He looked at me with such sad eyes. Why should I think his tears would be any less real or sincere than my own?

"How's Roberta doing?" he asked.

I shrugged. "So so."

"She's taking it very hard. Very hard. Dotty, my wife, you met her, they're very close. She says Roberta is having a terrible time."

Marty's not in very good shape, himself, I wanted to say. I had to remind myself yet another time, Marty did this. He chose this! Well, probably. In any case, these people are entitled to their reactions. Lay off.

He smiled, "Did you know that Dotty introduced Marty and Roberta?"

"No," I said. I'd never thought much about how they'd met.

"Roberta was very determined. Very determined," he laughed. "She knew who Marty was, a big-shot movie lawyer, famous clients and all that, and had heard he and Ellen had just divorced, probably from Dotty! She didn't want to take any chances that Marty might meet someone else, you know, get involved or anything, so she and Dotty planned a party. I forget what the pretext was, but it was a big party, thirty or forty people. I remember now! It was just after we'd finished remodelling our house and were dying to show it off, so we made it a sort of second house warming party! Roberta got Marty in her sights that night and bam!" He punched a fist into the other palm. "She nailed him! Very deter-mined." He looked at me. "You never knew how they met, eh?"

"No."

He sat reflecting a few moments. "He had to have his name on the door! That was the whole problem."

He looked to see if I understood. Of course, his eyes said, his thoughts on the matter came only from love. I could tell he was dying to explain. He wanted me to know how the whole thing could have been avoided.

"He wanted Diamond and Bernstein and Silver to add Goldman to the firm's name. It wasn't enough that he was making over half a million a year. He wanted his name on the door up there with theirs. I told him, 'Marty, everyone knows how much you bring to the firm. Why make a fuss? It's their firm. They started it. Let them have their names on the door! What do you care? You're making more money than any of them!'

I told him that! None of the rest of us made close to what he made. And he had the best office in the building."

I raised my eyebrows, as if in sympathy, to confirm the message he was trying to impart, to say: what more could you do? You were the voice of reason. Why didn't he listen? If only he'd listened to you, he'd be alive today! He smiled contentedly because I understood.

"And the beach?" he sneered, now that I understood, "why should clients, and I'm talking big clients, shlep out to nowhere? It didn't make any sense! I tried to tell him, but would he listen? No! He was such a *big macher*! He'd have his own firm and his name on the door and the ocean breeze and fuck the rest of us!" There was anger in his voice. Malice.

I saw what I took to be a small satisfied look come over him, as if his unspoken thoughts were, and look where it got him! Look at him now! I'm alive and he's dead! He caught himself. He realized what he'd said and that he'd said too much. He looked at me first for sympathy and support, and failing that, for a sense of my understanding that it all came from love of Marty. Distress over this preventable death. Right.

"Bob Winters suggested that I remind you I'm here unrepresented; that as a lawyer, that would have some significance for you."

"Of course, of course. And Bob Winters is?" he said with a wary half smile.

"The lawyer representing the estate. From Goodman Callan Winters and Street," I said. "And that Tina Cox, Joe Woodman, Mel Davidson and Gary Weiselman want us to represent them in their settlements with Diamond Bernstein and Silver."

"Of course," he repeated, but his disappointment was clear, "of course. That goes without saying!" His voice had a false cheeriness. Then, "Yes, Tina called yesterday."

"I'm supposed to meet my sister at Marty's house at 8. I thought you could familiarize me with the current status of the settlement agreement, and the elements involved in it. I'll go over it with Bob Winters, and we can meet with you again."

"Good, good. That's fine. But the reality is...is that it's pretty much a done deal." He seemed almost certain he could make it stick. "We'd pretty much agreed on all the terms of it and Marty had done everything but sign it. Let me just call George Zeffaro in." He held up a hand to put me on imaginary hold. He pushed a button on his intercom phone and said, "George, could you come in now please?" There was a silence while we were waiting for George. Malovitch seemed uncomfortable. "George is a lawyer here, but he's primarily the firm's comptroller. He keeps track of partnership matters. Things like that."

A very nervous, short, balding man that looked like Dom Deluise on not quite enough Valium came in and nodded to Malovitch and shook hands with me. He had to juggle an armful of file folders to do it. "I'm very sorry about your brother," he said distractedly. He sat to my left in a second arm chair before Malovitch's desk. He put the file folders on the floor in front of his feet. He took a five page summary agreement and handed me a copy and one to Malovitch and kept one for himself. "This represents the separation agreement between Marty H. Goldman, A Professional Corporation, and Diamond Bernstein and Silver."

I glanced at the first page, flipped through and turned to the last. They hadn't wasted any time. It was signed by Malovitch on behalf of DBS and had a place for my signature as both President of Marty H. Goldman, a Professional Corporation, and Executor of the Estate of Marty H. Goldman. The last phrase was a blanket "releases all interests in, or claims to, known and unknown, etc.". When I looked up and smiled at George Zeffaro then Malovitch, Malovitch took it for acceptance.

"It's really very straight forward," Malovitch began.

"Let me call your attention to a few numbers," George Zeffaro offered. "First, your brother's percentage as a partner here was 12%. The firm has an appraised residual net value of $10 million. Marty's share would be $1,200,000. There are suits outstanding against the firm from two former partners. There have been judgements in their favor which total $4 million, which we are appealing, and in which we expect to prevail. And when we do, Marty's estate would receive the money we're deducting here. Marty's share of that liability is $480,000. That leaves $720,000. Our Partnership Agreement calls for contributions to Special Litigation Funds. If those are not made, and the partnership has to fund them for any reason, the partnership can assess the delinquent partner fees in triplicate. Marty disagreed with our positions in the two litigations, and failed to make contributions. Assessed in triplicate, he owes the firm $138,000. That leaves $582,000."

He seemed more nervous than when he began, his eyes waking from the Valium, or whatever. He looked to Malovitch for support. Malovitch was sitting tipped back in his swivel chair tapping a pencil against his teeth, taking it all in. He ran one hand through his wiry steel-gray hair in contemplation. His look confirmed that it sounded just about right to him. He gave Zeffaro a confirming nod to go on.

"The Partnership Agreement calls for a division of monies from deals made while at DBS between DBS and the departing partner's new firm. It's a 60/40 split, except in certain cases that don't apply here, based on the partnership percentage, in Marty's case, 12%, like I said. That means GMW through Marty is entitled to 12% of 40% of the monies that come to us, DBS, from client deals Marty worked while here. Cox, Woodman, Davidson, and Weiselman were salaried, so they're not entitled to separation money."

That was going to come as a surprise to them. This slick sonofabitch had it pretty neatly packaged.

"In any case," he continued, "the current stream puts that figure at $16,500, give or take. We've been placing that amount monthly in an escrow account for Marty pending resolution of all separation issues. That amounts to $297,000. It can be released to GMW as soon as you sign this."

He looked at Malovitch to see if he thought he'd left out anything. Malovitch pursed his lips. He seemed satisfied. George Zeffaro sat back. Mission accomplished. Malovitch tipped forward and placed his hands on the desk.

"I understand Mr. Wolf is very anxious to have it," he said with a satisfied smile. "Any questions?"

I didn't say anything right away, and he took it as concurrence.

"Well good, then. You go over the agreement with Mr...."

"Winters," I said.

"...Winters. Perhaps we could conclude this by Monday afternoon?"

George Zeffaro, relieved now, had stood and begun to gather his files. Malovitch also stood. They both smiled. They both thought the meeting had gone well and was over. They were both prepared to shake hands with me and say good-bye, although I hadn't made a move to get up. Malovitch repeated his invitation to end the meeting.

"So, until Monday?"

"I have a few questions," I said.

When I still hadn't moved, Malovitch's smile faded, and he reluctantly sat back down. George Zeffaro wasn't sure whether he should go or stay and he stood there unhappily.

"Like?" Malovitch said.

There was a hint of irritation in his voice that I thought was intentional. To send a message to me.

"First, I believe Marty's percentage of the partnership was 16% not 12%."

Zeffaro started to say something but Malovitch jumped in to shut him up. He had a stern look now. He wasn't about to argue point by point. He wanted to hear it all. He had his hands folded in front of him. The areas around his knuckles were white.

"Anything else?"

"International Distributors."

Zeffaro sat down heavily, clutching his files to his chest.

"It's very complicated," he began, but Malovitch barked a command at him.

"George! I'd like to hear what he has to say." Malovitch turned back to me like he'd saved me from the interruption of a rude child.

"What about it?"

"It's my understanding that Marty had a 26% interest in the proceeds worth about $1,800,000."

"Ohhh my god," Zeffaro moaned.

"Shut up George!" Malovitch said to him.

For me he had a sneer.

"Anything else?"

"Two more," I smiled back at him, then at George Zeffaro. I asked George, "First, what are the 'certain cases that don't apply here' when you determined the 60/40 split?"

George Zeffaro was pale, a furtive, worried look in his eyes, in his gestures. He kept pushing his glasses back up his nose even though they didn't appear to have slipped down, and repeatedly wiped his forehead with the heel of his hand and then wiped whatever came away onto the side of his arm chair. He fidgeted, appeared to want to answer, to explain, but Malovitch was in charge and shut him up again, this time with a look.

"And?" Malovitch said through nearly clenched teeth.

"Where is it written or how was it determined that Cox, Woodman, Davidson, and Weiselman are entitled to nothing?"

"Anything else?" he said, as though he'd already answered the other questions.

"That's it," I said, then added with a smile between old friends, "for now. Except I'd like a copy of the DBS Partnership Agreement Marty signed here. And any amendments or updates to it. Before I leave. If possible."

"We're being very generous," Malovitch said, shaking his head sadly at my lack of appreciation. "Very generous."

He turned to Zeffaro. "George, go get copies of the Partnership Agreement for Kurt."

George Zeffaro seemed so glad to get out of there, I wondered if he'd return.

"And the amendments? Updates?" he asked on his way out.

There was a long silence. Malovitch gave him a pretty good what-are-you-talking-about look.

"There's been nothing since '76 in Marty's case. Go get him a copy of the original agreement and the '76, George." George did as he was told. "I think someone may have confused you. Marty was given bonus percentage points to calculate his draw since '76. Don Diamond and Moe Bernstein and Alan Silver were very generous with him, but those points were never given as an increase in his Partnership standing. No no no," he shook his head, "nothing since '76."

He smiled at my folly. My silliness. He shrugged. I could be forgiven, he seemed to suggest, if I'd listen to reason.

"As to International Distributors, that's already been factored into the firm's net worth; it's already been accounted for. You might dispute the figure for the firms net worth, but you, or rather Marty's estate, should be prepared to spend forty of fifty thousand for an appraisal if you do. No, I think you'll find we've been very fair."

He wet his thumb and first finger and turned to the second page of his copy of the Settlement Agreement they'd prepared and pointed to it. He spun the page around to face me. He sat back in his chair with a smarmy smile and locked his fingers together behind his head. All there in black and white. George Zeffaro returned and handed me a thick sheaf of copied papers. Cold. Not warm, not copied for me now, but previously prepared, and I thought probably edited. The title page said it was the Partnership Agreement, 1976. The one under it was for 1965.

"And the memo you and Marty and Diamond initialled?" I tried.

He gave me a what-are-you-talking-about innocent look. He turned his hands to show me he'd come up empty. I'd come up empty.

"What? What memo?" he said to me. Then to George, "Do you know about any memo, George? Did I miss out on some meeting?"

George could bring himself only to shake his head no. I thought words failed him because he feared his voice would fail him. Or betray him. This was going somewhere he was not prepared to go. He continued to shake his head. I wanted him to blurt out the truth. To come clean. He looked like he wanted to. But he didn't.

"I think we have a problem," I said, surprising myself, because it was without anger.

But I could feel it rising. I could feel this guy sitting on all the cards and holding the keys to the money Marty had coming. If he denied the memo it was because he had Marty's copy or knew that Weiselman did. Or at least was sure I didn't. He was sure I had nothing. He was betting on it, and was confident it was a sure thing. That had to mean Weiselman had cut a deal here for himself by dealing them the memo and the information that I couldn't get into Marty's files. And only Tina and Ronnie knew that for sure. No way Ronnie would say a thing to Weiselman. Tina. Swell.

He smiled tolerantly. "No, we don't. You don't. We're being very generous under the circumstances. Go over this Agreement with your attorney. I'd like it signed by Monday. It won't get any better, I can promise you that. As far as Tina Cox and Woodman and Davidson are concerned, they were Marty's proteges. If you think they're entitled to something, give it to them from this."

He tapped the agreement with his index finger. He smiled at me, then at George Zeffaro, as if to say, see, that wasn't so bad. It occurred to me he hadn't mentioned Weiselman. He got up. So did George Zeffaro. I sat for a moment considering my options. Once again, they were few. I couldn't get into Marty's CODED files and I didn't have the memo. If the positions they'd already staked out were any indication, the Partnership Agreements they'd given me were almost certainly edited to support their views on the 60/40 split. And, more, I had nothing to support 16% versus 12%. I was stymied and he knew it. In that context, I supposed he was right; they were being generous. I wanted to pound his slimy smug face. I had the feeling if I got up now, it was an admission of defeat. I hated that. So, I didn't get up. I had this picture come to mind, me as Burt Lahr doing the Cowardly Lion in the Wizard of Oz: Come on come on, I'll tear ya apart! I'll tear ya apart! At the same time, I remembered Weiselman and having wanted to say something, anything, as a parting shot. I looked at Malovitch. I managed a smile. "Ever heard of a workman's lien?" I said. "Marty worked here for you and you're stiffing him money. I'm Marty H. Goldman for now, and I don't like being stiffed."

His smugness slipped a notch. I didn't know for sure if it'd work or would apply, but if it did, I knew from builders who'd used them, the court would act on it quickly and it could tie up any account of theirs I could identify. And a lot of money.

"He can't do that, can he!?" Malovitch turned and demanded of George Zeffaro.

One of those funny quirks of the law, I was learning, was that lawyers in one field rarely knew anything about any other. They looked at each other uncertainly. I stood. I felt better. I was on a roll. A mini-roll, but a roll.

"You bet your fucking ass I can! I'll talk to Winters Monday morning, and by Monday afternoon you won't be able to get milk money out of any DBS account. And as far as the escrow account for the International Distributors money is concerned," I gave him a big stage wink, "don't start spending it just yet. It might as well be in Fort Knox for all you're going to see of it!"

He went white, shaking with rage, pointing at me and shaking his finger in my direction.

"You think you're gonna twist me around?" he yelled, suddenly losing control, "you think you can come in here and dictate to me?! You're gonna fuck with me?! You and Marty, you think you can have it all your way and fuck the rest of us!? Leaves us to fend... calls and dares to demand I release the funds to GMW or he won't...!"

George Zeffaro broke in. "Barry! Barry! Take it easy. Calm down. It's okay." He gave me a look somewhere between an apology for this outburst and an accusation for having caused it. "Maybe you'd better go."

Malovitch was panting, trying to reign it back in. I looked at him in disbelief. Get a grip, buster. Let's remember who's been jerking who around here. He managed a grim smile.

"Marty was too damn stubborn for his own good," he said, regaining some calm, a nasty smile on his face. "Now you too?" he scoffed. "Get out."

Just one big happy family at DBS, I was thinking on the walk back to the car. But I was wondering about the call Marty had made to him.

Chapter 19

———◦◦◦◦———

It was 7:55 when I pulled up in front of Marty's house on Seascape. I hadn't seen anything that looked like someone following me. Not Ron's guy. Not the bad guys. Maybe their union got them Saturdays off. I hung a U turn so I'd be headed back toward Sunset, parked, locked up the car taking the little briefcase with me and crossed the street, then the lawn on the pathway to the front door. Halfway up I saw the home delivered copy of the morning's LA Times. Sara doesn't need that, I thought, so I picked it up and dropped it between the thick bushes and the house. I'd tell her about Thorne and Wolf's conspiracy with the DA's office later.

Just before I could knock, Maria opened the door. She looked tired and drained but expectant, as though more than just having heard my car or seen me coming up the walk, she'd been waiting for me. There was a momentary light in her eyes as I said hello and stepped inside, and I thought she was about to speak when Sara came up behind her. The light flickered, dimmed, then went out.

"Jeez," Sara hissed in a whisper, "where have you been?" She motioned me to follow her as Maria closed the door very quietly. "Let's go to the kitchen."

When she'd closed the kitchen door behind us, I took my watch from my pocket and showed it to her.

"I'm early! It's not even 8 yet!" I protested.

"Yeah, well, that's fine for you, but I expect Bob Thorne will be here any minute!"

"Did you have a problem with him last night?"

"What would make you think that?" she said sarcastically.

"Just a guess."

"It's not funny Kurt! That guy could have been Hitler's right hand man! He banged on the door and said they needed to get started sorting things out. I told them I wasn't dressed and that it was late and it would be better if they waited until the morning when you'd be here."

"And?"

"And Roberta went nuts, and Thorne did more of his huffing and puffing. I'm getting out of here. I'm going to stay at Megan's. I can't be here any more. Roberta's hysterical and helpless one minute and like some demon-possessed witch the next. I can't..."

"Okay, okay, settle down. You've done fine keeping them out 'til now."

She was in uncharted territory, a tangled thicket of grief and exhaustion and anger with no compass to guide her. Megan Dunphy's seemed like a good idea since I wasn't going to be staying there. A way station.

"Why don't you get packed and I can take you to Megan's when I'm done here. What time did Thorne say he was coming?"

"He just said 'first thing in the morning'."

"That could mean anything. I'd better get started. Keep Roberta away..."

"How! It's her house! How do you expect..."

"Take it easy. Just try to keep her busy with planning the service for tomorrow flowers, who speaks and when stuff like that. Just don't mention that I'm here. If she comes into the office, she comes in. So be it. But otherwise, I'd prefer to work in there alone until Thorne gets here. Okay?"

"Fine. But Roberta and I are supposed to see Rabbi Krasznik at 10:30. Will you be able to see him?"

"If not, I'll call him."

She frowned, disapproving. "He specifically said he wanted to talk to you."

"I'll try. But if I can't, tell him I'll call."

"When?"

"Tell him I'll call by noon. I'll either make an appointment with him then for later, or talk to him on the phone for as long as he wants."

"Okay. I'm going to take a shower and get dressed." She hesitated and then hugged me tightly. We've never been much on hugging, so it surprised me, but I could feel the good of it for myself as well as her. She stood back and looked me over like she hadn't seen me in some time.

"Do you know what Roberta told me last night. After Thorne left?"

"What?"

"I was in the kitchen for a drink of water and she came in and started babbling and said her shrink agreed it wasn't fair of Marty."

"What? The suicide?"

I could see a shrink saying something like that. There was some truth in it. It hurts a lot of people.

"No," she shook her head. Her composure was beginning to slip. From the look on her face I had the feeling I didn't want to hear this. "It was unfair of him to bother her late at night with his problems. When he couldn't sleep. He tried to talk to her. She said he couldn't sleep and he wanted to talk and she and her shrink agreed that it wasn't fair of him to interrupt her sleep."

Tears ran down her face and she looked at me, then came into my

arms. I knew we were both seeing the same dismal picture of a dis-
traught Marty, besieged on all sides as I was beginning to see so much
more clearly, trying to find either comfort, or more likely, have a sounding board to try and make sense of all that was happening. And who did
he have to turn to? Sleeping beauty. And her trusty shrink that he was
no doubt paying for.

   I went into the office and closed the door behind me. The first thing
I did was investigate the papers on the trestle table. There were eight
separate piles. Each was a project comprised of a script, files on an actor
and director client of Marty's, their history of previous work and a list
outlining possible associate directors, producers and studios that might
be interested in distribution. Marty's usual work was confined to negotiating contracts for clients on a project they'd been offered. Creating
projects was something new. Here he was acting as a packager or executive producer. It occurred to me that this was a production company in
the making. I wondered if he already had rights to these scripts. Or if
they were written by clients of his. I made a list of the principal names
for all of the projects, planning to check them against his client list when
I had a chance. In any case, it didn't look like the kind of thing that
would've been in his briefcase to be lugged back and forth to work every
day. It looked more like something with long range implications that he
was keeping here to develop in privacy. This wasn't the reason for the
empty briefcase.
   I started in the top drawer of the file cabinet and leafed through each
page of each file. I was looking for his will. Since there was no separate
folder for it, I was hoping it would be stuck between the pages of something else. I went through the escrow papers on the purchase of the
house, the file on the purchase of the new Mercedes 450SL. Another of
those huge sedans, I thought. Lawyer cars. What a waste. A ton of
money and no fun. For all the headaches his old Jag XJS V-12 had caused
him, I knew he'd had fun with it. I went through the file on the copy-
right he'd gotten for me on a screenplay about Zak. There were copies
of the letters I'd gotten from a couple of producers and one director
who'd been interested in it. He took an option, but nothing happened. I
put it back. The DBS folder was empty except for the reference to the
office computer. The coded file. The fat GMW file had copies of the
things I'd seen at the office, but no will tucked in there. I went through
the client lists from DBS, the Brad Merlon file, and a fat one on International Distributors, notes, motions, and original findings, but didn't find
it. I almost missed the divorce file. I flipped through it, purposely avoiding
reading it. It seemed too much an invasion of his privacy. What differences he and his first wife had had were none of my business. Nor were
the terms of their divorce. Until the will fell out of the file.
   The signature was signed in the ink of a blue ballpoint pen so I as-

sumed this was the original. John Goodman would breathe easier when I told him I'd found it. I read it. It seemed fine to me, but what did I know? It left the house to Roberta so she and Lucy would have a roof over their heads. It left some limited partnerships and a lot of cash to his girls. It mentioned insurance policies and referred to the terms of his divorce. It anticipated the value of the house would be less than the combined value of the remaining assets going to the girls, and the executor was to adjust so that the final division would be equal. Fair enough. I was given broad authority to sell property, withdraw from limited partnerships and make prudent investments as I saw fit to enhance and protect the assets of the estate. A bunch of other legal jargon I figured Goodman could sort out. I put the will into the little flat briefcase with the computer disks. I decided I'd better look through the divorce file after all.

He'd been generous. No more than I would have expected for support and schooling and medical costs for the girls, but surprisingly generous to Ellen. What had he said? She'd found a dentist that was filling more than her teeth. He tried to laugh it off, like Nick or I might have done with each other, but it cut deep. Looking at the divorce papers and his generosity, I had the feeling he'd ultimately felt guilty that ignoring her while pursuing his budding career had pushed her to it and some of his contempt had spilled back on himself. I went through the remaining files, but my attention was wandering now that I had the will. What a relief!

There was a second Brad Merlon file. The single page in it was a note in Marty's handwriting referring again to the office computer and no doubt the coded files, but what caught my eye was $50K gift. Gift was underscored heavily. Next to it a phone number circled repeatedly. There were doodles, notes, question marks alternating with double P's turned into fat pouty-lipped Kilroy faces looking over fences. I didn't think Marty was one to doodle, but I had the instinctive feeling he'd been on the phone with Merlon and they'd been interrupted, maybe more than once, giving Marty time to think about the $50K in a variety of ways and to doodle some of his thoughts. It was odd, but what about all this wasn't? I copied the phone number down and put it with the others in my wallet. I put the file back. I placed sheets of blank paper sideways between the groups of papers on the trestle table to keep them separate as I stacked them. I began to empty out the file cabinet drawers and stack the files on the desk. Then I took all the old rubber-banded DBS stuff from the bottom drawer and stacked it on the desk too. After Malovitch this morning, I decided I should take a look through it. It was going to take at least five or six boxes for the whole mess, I thought, and before it got boxed up, I'd better go through it. You never know.

Roberta and Bob Thorne barged through the door.

"Thanks for knocking," I said.

"Don't give me any of your crap, mister. I want to know what you think you're going to take?"

He was dressed like it was any other day at the office, dark blue suit, snappy white shirt and pale blue silk tie. These guys really know how to maintain an image, I thought, taking a quick inventory of my faded Levis and white T-shirt and sandals.

I looked over my handiwork. "Everything but the furniture," I said evenly.

"He can't do that, can he? Tell him he can't do that Bob!" Roberta shrieked.

Sara was standing at the doorway, clearly relieved that her duties in this arena were finished, but troubled nevertheless.

"Just what do you mean?" Thorne demanded.

"I mean that just about everything here relates to Marty H. Goldman, a Professional Corporation, or to Marty's estate. I'll probably need it, so I plan to take it."

He was edging close to me, hovering again, hands on hips, jaw jutting out. Everybody in this town's an actor, I was thinking, putting on a show. "Step back, Bob, your breath's no better today."

"Are you going to let him talk to you like that!?" Roberta demanded.

"No!" he turned his head to her, then back to me, " You've gone to far, bub. Step outside!" Thorne poked me in the chest for emphasis.

I looked down at his finger where it lingered unromantically on my chest. "Take it away or it won't come back whole," I hissed in my best tough guy voice. Life's but a stage.

"Please," I added.

It didn't work. He left it there. It was going to be a defining moment in our relationship. I could tell. He had this little smirk on his face that had fuck you written all over it. I hated that. Before he could counter I grabbed his left ear with my right hand and his upper lip with my left. I wiggled my hands like a basketball player getting himself ready for a free-throw. He howled in pain and when his hands instinctively came up - and off my chest, I was pleased to see - I randomly grabbed a single finger on each hand, suddenly pulled him towards me, then simultaneously twisted them and reversed direction, bending them abruptly back to him as his hands were still advancing to me. There were cracking sounds. His first howl was nothing compared to the one that came now. He sagged to his knees trying to cradle one hand in the other against what must have been terrible pain. But since both hands were hurting, neither was in much condition to comfort the other. His face went white and wet with the kind of perspiration I thought came from shock. Roberta was screaming in either sympathetic pain, or her more general and usual hysteria. I stepped back from Thorne. When he could speak, his words came in choked wheezy gasps, as though his lungs had holes in them and the air wasn't travelling as it should.

"You're dead. You are dead! Roberta, call the police! You're under arrest! I'm making a citizens arrest!!"

"Is that a death threat? I'm not a lawyer, but I think that's against the law, isn't it? I asked you to take your hands off me. I think Sara saw enough to verify..."

"Put the phone down, Roberta." She hesitated. "Put it down!" he yelled.

Roberta looked more angrily at Thorne than me. Thank god for little favors, I was thinking, I've only got a few thugs to deal with. Thorne's got her on his back. Sara had gone into the kitchen and I could hear her dump trays of ice and some water into a bucket and bring it to Thorne. It was a champagne bucket. Ya gotta love LA.

"Put your fingers in here," she said. "It'll ease the pain and slow the swelling."

Thorne stood slowly on rubbery legs, his fingers eager for the ice in the bucket on the desk. He was pale and the crispness was gone from his suit. What the hell, it was Saturday.

"Call my office, Roberta ask for Connie. Tell her I need her here."

Roberta dialed and asked for Connie and was connected. She held the phone out to Thorne. Roberta was in no mood to pamper him and play secretary when, in her eyes, he'd failed her. He begged her with a look of helplessness, but she ignored it and shook the receiver a couple of times in his direction for emphasis, an impatient reminder that she had no intention of standing there all day. Thorne carefully took his hands from the safety and comfort of the ice-water and tried to find a combination of fingers that would let him hold the thing. He took it from Roberta and held it gingerly and spoke curtly. Water dripped from his hands to the desk.

"Get over here. I need you to catalogue whatever," he looked venomously at me, "the executor takes."

He hung it up, or tried to, but it was more of a drop and landed askew. I put it back into the cradle. Roberta stormed out of the room. Thorne followed her. I could hear her screaming at him somewhere in the direction of the living room. About his manhood. About his parents' marital status. It quickly became a blur, like an air-raid siren gone on too long. He began to yell back. Good for you, I thought, don't take that shit from her. The door slammed and it got quiet. Roberta re-appeared in the doorway to the office.

"I want you out of my house. Don't you ever come here again!"

"That might not be possible, Roberta. But if it is, I'll be glad to honor your wishes."

"If you ever come around here I'll have the sheriff arrest you for trespassing. Do you understand!?"

What could I say? She was working herself into a frenzy. Anything I said she'd react to and it would just get worse. So I didn't say anything. Sometimes that's best.

"Do you UNDERSTAND!!" she demanded again.

I ignored her and spoke to Sara. "If Thorne's person Connie gets here before I get back, tell her I'll be right back. I'm going to get some boxes to pack this stuff in."

Roberta turned on her heel and stormed from the room, slamming the office door behind her.

"Don't let Roberta back in here alone. And don't let this Connie person in here at all."

She gave me another of those, I'm not your vassal, and I don't want any part of this looks.

"Try?"

She rolled her eyes and said, "Just don't get side-tracked. Get right back here."

"Me? Side-tracked?"

Going and returning from Brentwood's Westgate shopping district I hadn't seen anyone that might have been from Ron. Then again, I hadn't seen anyone from Rent-a-Thug either, so I guessed it all evened out. But I was worried by the absence of Ron's guy. Whatever was going on, it had been reassuring to think I had some help not too far away.

Connie was twenty-seven or twenty-eight, a long legged, good look-ing slender blond with short hair and an attitude. I don't know what Thorne or Roberta might have told her, but whatever it was I thought she was counting herself lucky I hadn't attacked her yet. She watched me continuously with darting, suspicious eyes while she made a list, file by file and paper by paper as I filled the file boxes I'd gotten at the Brentwood Stationary store. They allowed me to hang those green file holder things just the way they'd hung in the drawers, so I had a sort of travelling file cabinet, readily accessible if needed. At 10 Sara came in to tell me she and Roberta were going to see Rabbi Krasznik. She reminded me to call him before noon and gave me his number on a slip of paper. I already had the number and the slips of paper and business cards were beginning to mount up. I let it pass and took the slip and thanked her. At this point she was in no mood for me to crack wise about it.

At 11:40 Connie and I were done. I'd cleaned out Marty's desk, file cabinet and the trestle table and she'd catalogued everything down to an already opened box of Uniball pens I'd taken. There'd been twelve origi-nally and there were ten left, which she dutifully recorded. I had the feeling she suspected me of pocketing the other two. I loaded the five boxes into the Mustang, three in the trunk and two in the back seat. I came back into the office and prepared to call the number Sara'd given me for Krasznik. Connie seemed unwilling, or had been instructed not to leave me alone in the room.

"This is private," I told her as I dialed the number.

She was flustered and uncertain about what to do.

"Why don't you go into the kitchen. I promise I won't steal anything. You can frisk me before I leave." I gave her a little smile, and she actually smiled back. She went into the kitchen, but she didn't completely close the door behind her. I pictured her just on the other side of it, trying to listen. What the hell, there wasn't going to be anything very secret about my conversation with Krasznik, but it just wasn't any of her business, or more to the point, Thorne's.

Krasznik's deep voice, familiar even after seven years, came on the line when his secretary put my call through. Sara and Roberta had just left, he told me.

"I'm very troubled," he began.

Tell me about it, I almost said.

"I remember your brother very well. He was a good man. What's all this turmoil? Isn't a death in this manner enough tragedy? It's a sin to leave him unburied like this! An outrage!"

I could tell he was warming up now. He'd always had the presence, even over the phone, of someone very close to God. If not actually His right-hand man. He may not have been Orthodox, but I wouldn't have been the one to quibble about his credentials.

"You are the oldest son now! It is your responsibility! The law requires that his body be returned to the ground no more than a week after his death. From what your sister tells me, that may not happen?"

"It doesn't seem likely," I admitted.

"The LAW requires it!" he boomed.

I had the feeling a second citizens arrest was imminent. "Rabbi, I'm doing what I can," I said lamely. Some brother's keeper.

"I want to see you face to face," he said. "Can you come here? Soon?" It wasn't really meant as a question.

Besides, how do you politely turn down an audience with God?

"Sure. Where are you?"

"I have an office here at Hillside. Do you know it?"

"I'll find it. When?"

"Now! We haven't much time! This whole business is an outrage!"

I couldn't have agreed more, but for now, in his eyes, I was part of it.

"I'll be there in twenty minutes. Maybe twenty five."

The line went dead. He'd hung up. God moves in mysterious and sometimes abrupt ways, I thought.

I took up the little briefcase and headed for the door. When I pulled it open I almost bumped into Connie. We both had a start.

"I'm outta here. It's been a pleasure," I said. "Wanna frisk me?"

Her smile was friendly. Now that the task at hand had been com-
pleted, some of her juices seemed to be flowing. Her smile had maybe
coyly stitched to it. She saw the little briefcase and was all business again.
"What's that?"
I looked at it, then her, innocently.
"My briefcase," I lied.
Her smile twisted into a sneer of disbelief.
"With MHG on it? I don't think so. Your name is Kurt, isn't it?"
"It was a present - from Marty - when he got his new one."
I walked back into the office and she followed me. I showed her the
bigger briefcase with his initials. She was dubious, but didn't press it. I
was just glad she hadn't looked and seen his was empty. She would have
assumed I'd emptied it into the little one. Maybe demanded a look. I
definitely didn't want her reporting to Thorne or Wolf that I was running around with a bunch of computer disks in a briefcase with Marty's
initials on it. I decided to take a chance. I pulled the little briefcase open
so that only the divided section with the will in it showed.
"By the way, I found the original of Marty's will," I told her as though
I'd just remembered.
She peered in. I could feel her hand preparing to reach in and snatch
it. I closed it.
"I'll have someone from Bob Winters' office send a copy to Thorne."
End of subject. I remembered Marty's new car was in the garage. I
wanted to go through it too before I left. I wished I'd given myself more
time to get to Krasznik. I headed out of the office through the sliding
glass door to the back yard. Connie followed me uncertainly, not sure
where we were going, not sure she wanted to go, but certain she shouldn't
let me out of her sight unless I was headed off the property.
There was a flagstone path through neatly trimmed grass to a wrought-
iron fence with two gates. The one to the left went to the swimming
pool and a pool house. The one to the right went to the driveway and
garage. Connie and her long legs and high heels were struggling with
the rough, uneven stones but gamely trying to keep up. Before I'd gone
far enough along the path to make it clear which way I was going, I
stopped and turned to her, gave her a friendly, slightly leering smile.
"Thought I'd go for a swim. I don't have a suit, though; wanna join
me?"
She was flustered again and blushed, thoughts of no swim suit, skinny
dipping, having Roberta come back and find her swimming naked with
me, or even just standing there watching me seemed to be running
through her mind. Through my mind at least. I stood there like I were
really waiting for an answer.
"How 'bout it?"
She stammered and recovered enough to realize all she had to do was
to insist she couldn't allow me in the pool. I thought she was about to
when I said, "Just kidding," and headed towards the gate to the garage. I

took a peek over my shoulder at her and smiled at her combined discomfort and relief. With one hand on her hip, she wagged a finger at me for my naughtiness. Money in the bank.

Marty's car was a Mercedes 450SL okay, but I'd been wrong about it being one of those huge sedans. It was a baby blue two door coupe, the Mercedes version of a sports car for rich guys. It gave me one of those all too familiar pangs of combined pleasure and grief, like his having moved his office to the beach, seeing he'd done something other than what would have been expected of him, something for fun, or just because he'd wanted to. The car was locked up. I found the key and opened the trunk first. There was a set of golf clubs. I hadn't known he played. It looked like a good set. They also looked brand new and unused. Other than the spare, and some golf shoes that also looked new and unused, there was nothing. I noticed a piece of paper stuffed into one of the golf shoes. It was a receipt from the Hillcrest Country Club Pro Shop and the customer's copy of the credit card slip for $1248. Marty's signature. And the date was only a week before he died. I had a feeling it had been a birthday present to himself. Inside the car were a carton of Winston Filters and several packs of Wrigley's Doublemint on the passenger seat. The glove box had a California map, an LA County map and a leather folder with the Mercedes logo on it. It contained the Owner's Manual, the Service Contract, and a photocopy of his insurance policy. The car was registered to the PC. I shoved it back into the glove box but something was obstructing it.

I felt around at the back and found a pill bottle. It was a prescription that had been filled for Marty at the Brentwood Pharmacy two days before he died, 100 pills of Desyrel, prescribed by a Dr. Richard Rosen. "Take one (1) every four hours as needed" and "TAKE WITH FOOD or WATER" was printed below. Jeez, I'd forgotten all about getting information from him for Winters. I'd leave a message with his service. Tell him it was important I talk to him before Monday morning. I'd leave him my dad's number for a return call.

There were no file folders, nothing that might have been in the empty briefcase. It occured to me that I could drive his car and let Sara use the Mustang if she were going to Megan Dunphy's. Free her to come and go independently. I liked the Mustang better, the power and the stickshift, but besides the convenience of it, driving his car seemed like a nice idea.

"I'm going to switch the boxes to this car and take it. It's registered to my brother's Professional Corporation," I told Connie.

Her brow furrowed and the corners of her mouth turned down but she kept her doubts to herself. I had the feeling she couldn't wait to give her list and make her report to Thorne and be done with this. When I walked to the street, she accompanied me. She might as well have been my parole officer. Whatever her feelings, she took her job seriously, or at least wanted to keep it. As we neared the street I saw a cream colored

'62 Porsche Super with chrome baby moons, looking like it'd just been driven off the showroom floor.

"Yours?" I asked her.

She smiled, pleased with herself. "Mmm hmmm."

"It's a beauty. Had it long?"

"A year and a half."

"Was it that clean when you got it, or did you have it restored?"

"It was my ex-boyfriend's. He restored it," she said.

"And he gave it to you?" I asked incredulously.

"Not exactly."

Her smile had all the warmth and compassion of a shark circling a bloodied swimmer. So much for money in the bank, I thought. I wished I hadn't asked.

She watched and followed me on foot as I pulled the Mustang into the driveway close to the Mercedes and switched the boxes. I took Marty's address/appointment book from where I'd tossed it on the back seat and slipped it into the briefcase. I parked the Mustang back on the street and returned for the Mercedes. I bid Connie adieu and backed the car to within a length or two of the street, just as Roberta wheeled a big dark gray Mercedes sedan, Marty's old car, I guessed, in behind me. She honked the horn furiously, like she were trying to scatter sheep on a country road. I thought she wanted to get past me to put her car in the garage. Silly me. I motioned for her to back up. I thought if she'd pull back into the street, I could back the rest of the way out and she could pull in with an unobstructed path to dock her boat. Oh, silly me. Her car lurched and rocked into the driveway behind me as she slammed it into park and came flying out of the driver's door.

"Where do you think you're going with that?!! Get out of that car!?" she shrieked. "That's mine!"

She was closing in on me like a linebacker on a skinny punter. I had visions of saliva flying from her mouth in long gooey strands, heavy breathing coming in the angry over-spaced gasps and the exaggerated physical gestures of a slow-motion replay. Sara was getting out of the passenger's side. I was taking a wild guess here, but figured she hadn't told Roberta about not driving the new Mercedes. I had no desire to get out but sitting in the little car looking up at her was not much of a choice either. Connie was coming up the driveway, the suppressed smirk on her face an indication of how thoroughly she was enjoying my discomfort. Turnabout being fair play and all, I had to smile to myself. Roberta's mouth was going a mile a minute and it all seemed to come down to the little car was hers and she intended to drive it. I had a fleeting sense of a scene in which Roberta presses Marty to get a new car and give her his Mercedes sedan so she can get rid of her old Chevy station wagon and is rankled no end when he gets not another sedan, but this cute little car and leaves her to drive the big, not so cute, old Mercedes. Such were the trials of the matrons of Brentwood.

Whatever she'd been saying, it ended with, "Get out!!"

Connie and Sara were standing next to her, not too close, and not in support of her, but in muted fascination with the rising intensity of it all. Sara put a hand on Roberta's arm and tried to calm her.

"I'm sorry Roberta, it's my fault. I forgot to tell you. Kurt asked me to tell you..."

Roberta spun towards her and screamed, "Tell me what!!??"

"That the lawyers for the Estate...that the car belongs to Marty's Professional Corporation....that it can't be used."

"Then what the FUCK is he doing in it?!" she demanded.

Sara raised a brow and shot me a look like, good question, but didn't say it.

"I thought you could use the Mustang. So you wouldn't be tied to where I am or where I have to go. I am the PC for now, so the insurance covers me on this," I said to Sara.

"You are NOTHING! You can't take MY car!" Roberta yelled in frustration.

Since Sara wasn't going to be any help, she looked to Connie. Connie was caught somewhere between her previous fascination and what I thought looked like horror. She was shaking her head slowly from side to side, but it wasn't clear to me what she was referring to.

Roberta looked from Sara to Connie. The grieving widow was without help. She had to do this alone.

"Get out of that car right now!" she ordered.

I was getting fed up with this.

"Roberta," I said reasonably, "move your car so I can get out. Call Bob Thorne. Have him call Winters. They can discuss it."

"There's NOTHING TO DISCUSS!! I want that car!" she yelled.

I was starting to get mad. I took a deep breath in an attempt to control it. "If you don't move your car, I'm gonna go over the grass and outta here."

"You COCKSUCKER!!" she screamed at me.

"FUCK YOURSELF, YOU ROTTEN FUCKING WHORE!!" I bellowed at her.

The silence, as they say, was deafening. Sara and Connie seemed to wince in anticipation. Roberta glared at me and spoke through clenched teeth.

"Marty would NEVER talk to me that way!!" she hissed.

"Yeah? And look where it got HIM!!" I shot back.

She allowed herself a moment of stunned silence. Her hand came to her forehead as though faint. She leaned on Connie.

"Help me into the house," she gasped.

Connie helped the stricken Roberta across the grass to the pathway. She struggled to balance as they went to the front door.

I backed the car as close to the big Mercedes as I could to give myself room to make the turn from the driveway to the grass. Before I shifted into drive, Sara came up to the window, her lips pressed tightly together in what I thought was an immanent reproach.

"Don't say it. I don't want to hear it. Here, take this." I gave her the keys to the Mustang. "I've got to get outta here. I told Krasznik I'd be there. I'm gonna be late."

I could see Maria down the driveway where she'd come out the back door from the kitchen. She was saying something to me like nada or la nada, but I couldn't make it out. I think it was in Spanish, but with her accent, I wasn't really sure. But I saw that Roberta was suddenly no longer in need of assistance. She pulled away from Connie and yelled through the front door.

"Maria!! Come here this instant! Instante!!"

"You know what she asked me when we left Krasznik's office?" Sara was saying.

I was trying to see what Roberta was up to and get the car onto the grass and knew I was going to be late for Krasznik.

"What, what are you talking about?" I asked irritably.

"Roberta. Do you know what she said when we were leaving Krasznik's office?"

"I have no idea. I give up. Tell me." Still curt.

Her eyes began to tear. "She said, 'How did I do?' Like it was an audition or something." She bit her lip and took a breath against any more tears. "Poor Marty," she sighed. Grief being replaced by dismay being replaced by a rising sense of anger and futility, "poor, poor Marty." She played with the keys in her hand.

"Thanks for the car, Kurt. I've got to get out of here. Call me at Megan's after you've talked to Krasznik. Nick and I are going to see dad this afternoon. Can you stop by?"

"I think so. I'll try."

She reached into the window and gave my shoulder an affectionate squeeze. Connie stood on the porch watching us, unsure of what to do next. Run like the wind, I was thinking, and get as far away as fast as you can. I drove onto the grass and across it to the street. I headed towards Sunset and the relative tranquility of my interview with God.

Chapter 20

The little Mercedes didn't have the punch of the Mustang, but it was unbelievably quiet and smooth, fun to drive in its own way. It had a lot of road sense, hanging tight at 55 or 60 as I zipped through the curves along Sunset heading to the 405 South. On the freeway, after getting settled in the fast lane I began to inspect the car's interior. Everything smelled new and rich, especially the leather seats. I began to fool around with the radio looking for a station when I looked up and saw the sign for the Mesmer Avenue off-ramp to Hillside Memorial Park Cemetery. I took a quick look, figured I could make it, and abruptly cut across three lanes of sparse traffic and just made the off-ramp. I heard honking and tires squealing and thought there'd been a car I hadn't seen and had cut off, but when I looked in the rearview, cars were honking not at me, but at a big dark-windowed sedan that had tried to cut across the traffic after I did. It had been too late, and after skidding and blocking traffic, it was forced to continue south on the 405. It leapt forward under full power once the driver realized he couldn't make the off-ramp, speeding to the next one, I guessed. Too much to be a coincidence. Where the hell was Ron's guy? I looked at the clock on the dash. 12:30. Christ, I thought. Even giving myself the benefit of every doubt, I was going to be at least twenty minutes later than I'd told Krasznik. Next to that, any problems with Wolf's goons seemed like a harmless playground scuffle.

I turned left on Bristol and right on Doverwood into Hillside. Signs directed me to the Chapel Office. I parked the car and locked it. I took the little briefcase with me. A prim no-nonsense secretary led me down a short hallway to Krasznik's office. Down the hall and across from it was the open door to the Family Anteroom, which was curtained off from the general seating of the Chapel itself, to the side of the raised stage-like platform for the casket and flowers and a speaker's podium. She had the air about her of an indignant teacher taking a troublesome student to the Principal's office. I've warned you, her compressed lips seemed to say. Now you're going to get it! She opened the door and ushered me in and sealed it behind me.

Krasznik sat in a well worn leather high backed chair behind a huge carved Rosewood desk from some other century. He stood to greet me and shake hands across it. I'd forgotten how big he was. How imposing. Nothing one wouldn't expect from God or His right-hand man, or should forget, but I had. He must've been six-five or six-six and weighed more than three hundred pounds. His hands were thick and huge and strong when we shook, making mine feel like that of a child.

"Sit!" he ordered as he returned to his chair.

I sat.

Krasznik wore the black robes of an Oxford Don. I could see at the open neck below his flowing beard that he had a dark suit and tie beneath it. He wore a headdress of some kind. Not a yarmulke, but something more turban-like and colorful, festive, that brought to mind the Greek Orthodoxy. Sara had told me he was a Talmudic scholar and taught at both UCLA and a Yeshiva in the Fairfax District, LA's Little Israel. God help those kids, I thought.

"It's a sin," he reminded me, "a sin and an outrage!"

I nodded. I figured I was here for a caning and might as well take it as best I could and get it over with.

"Suicide is an affront to GOD!" he intoned, his eyes boring into mine from over his half-sized reading glasses. His fingers tugged and played with the thick coarse-haired gray beard, with streaks of black, that flowed across the top of his chest like an unruly bib. The agenda apparently would start with Marty's sins first. Mine would come soon enough.

He looked across the table studying me. If this man was not God, I had the feeling it was going to be as close as I'd ever come.

"There is a purpose to life," he said firmly but more kindly, "to savor the struggle; to appreciate the gift God has given us in the opportunity to struggle, and take pleasure in the struggle. We are here to please God," he said.

I couldn't have agreed more. But that put Marty's suicide as an issue squarely between himself and God. Maybe Krasznik felt qualified to make judgements about it, but I didn't. Assuming it was suicide. I didn't think this was the time to raise other possibilities with Krasznik in defense of Marty.

"It is an outrage that his body is to be desecrated!" he thundered suddenly.

He'd get no argument from me on that score, either. But his look sent a shiver through me, his eyes telling me it was my responsibility to stop it. My failure. I felt weak and stupid and helpless before him. Completely lacking. I had a sense of what he must put his students through when questioning them, except this wasn't some oral exam, but a life test I was failing. He moved on, not out of pity or mercy, but having made his point, ready to deal with the reality of the situation, now that we both understood it better. Understood my failure to deal with it appropriately.

"I want you to tell me about your brother. I remember him well enough, from his wedding to his first wife; from your sister's wedding held at his house; from your mother's funeral. A good man, a mensch-you know that word?" I nodded I did. "This is just," he threw his hands up, at a loss, "inexplicable. But I want to hear from you; what this man meant to you; what did his life mean to you? From this I will construct my remarks for the service tomorrow. I've seen your father and younger brother-they were here yesterday; right on time-" he added over his glasses, "and your sister this morning." He closed his eyes as though seeking strength to go on. "And his widow." Roberta must have put on quite a show, I was thinking. Krasznik had thought he'd seen it all, being the Rabbi to the rich and famous as well as the UCLA and Yeshiva students, but I was betting Roberta was a whole new species to him. It might have been my imagination, but I thought he shuddered before he continued. "Tell me what he meant to you."

It was a good question. I didn't know if I'd ever asked it of myself about anyone in my family. Or friends. I thought about them a lot. The kind of people they were and about the way they conducted their lives, but I hadn't thought about what they really meant to me. I had with my son, Jason. He meant the world to me. He was my connection to it. He gave meaning to the phrase, "God so loved the world, that he gave his only begotten Son," because before he was born those had been only words to me, and after, I thought the world could go to Hell before I'd see a hair on his head harmed, much less trade his life for it. It gave those words such a sweet and painful poignance, a heartbreaking, overwhelming reality. I had the feeling that I knew why we were here and what God wanted from us. He wanted not to be alone in consciousness and intelligence, but to share the exhilaration and profound beauty of it. And be loved for sharing it. I thought that the existence of God was now entrusted to and scattered throughout every atom of creation. That his existense had been consciously made dependent on the success of the process. The parallel between parents and children brought that home to me. You gave them life, yet it was the only way you could extend your own existence. You might be afraid of death, or selfish and petty, but the needs of your child would draw something better from you, make you put their life and their well-being above your own. It didn't always work. All you had to do was read the paper and see the horrors parents all too often inflicted on their children. But on the whole, it did work. It made the world work. It wasn't a static and fixed universe, renewal and regeneration was the pattern after which all of it was made and everything hinged on its success. I thought in those terms what a crushing blow Marty's death must be to my father. I thought about Jason dying before me and felt an unspeakable dread, a helplessness and futility that was so complete it always made me lightheaded and heartsick, just sweeping away everthing else.

In college I'd written a poem about a large flat rock in the middle of a fast rushing river. A solid safe place where weary swimmers trying to cross could rest. That was Marty, I told Krasznik. He was our rock. He was the safe place in the rushing waters where we could rest when we were weary and couldn't go on. In the poem, the rock had held and held, until finally it could hold no more, reluctantly giving in and giving way to the rushing waters.

Krasznik leaned forward, his palms flattened against the surface of his desk and looked over his little half-glasses at me and asked, "And who was Marty's rock?" I sat mute. He shook his head slowly and sat back, his hands now folded in front of him.

I sat in the little Mercedes outside the Chapel Office and cried for almost half an hour.

It was 2:10 when I stopped. I didn't have a plan or a clue about what to do next. I felt rudderless and adrift. I decided to go to my dad's place. Maybe I could catch up to Nick and Sara away from everyone else. Maybe I could hold someone's hand. Maybe someone would hold mine. I got back on the 405 North and took the 10 East. I got off at Robertson and headed north. When I got to Monte Mar Drive the familiarity of the neighborhood seeped into my consciousness and I thought of stopping to see Carla Feldman.

Carla and my mother were pregnant at the same time with me and her son Robby. I was born six weeks before him. He and I were close until I was ten and we moved out of Beverly Hills. But I never had a birthday that Carla forgot. No matter where I was or what I was doing, she always managed to find me by phone or by mail. She was a constant, a kind of Obi-Wan Kenobi guiding star. I turned left on Monte Mar then right on Lark Ellen Circle and pulled up in front of her wonderfully Ozzie and Harriet house. I sat in the car not knowing what to do. I didn't want seeing her to become an excuse to wallow in grief or have it spill over onto her. I would have liked to see her, but not now, I decided. I'd reached for the keys in the ignition to start the car when she startled me by knocking on the roof of the car.

"You weren't going to stop by?" her voice a little injured. "I've been expecting you," she said, "I hoped you'd come by. I'm so sorry. I read about Marty yesterday. Can you come in?"

"No, I should get over to my dad's. I wanted to see you though." I wanted to go in her house and have her tell me stories about our trips to Catalina when I was nine and ten and eleven and was her guest on the Island for half of those three summers. She civilized me a little. She told great funny stories about my introduction to island life and sneaking into the Avalon Country Club, where they were members and sneaking in was unnecessary. I wanted to let her transport me there. She leaned in the window.

"You okay?"

"No."

"No reason for you to be," she said and kissed me on top of my head. "If you want to talk, if I'm not at the races, I'm here." She laughed her infectious laugh.

"You still going to the races?"

"Every day. I lose a bundle on those nags, but I have a ball!" She giggled again. "Take care of yourself. Tell your dad how sorry I am."

"I will," I said as I started the car.

She stood in the street, short, round, full of life at 65 or so, waving as I drove off. Just seeing her gave me a lift.

Chapter 21

I parked behind my dad's place on the corner of Doheny and Beverly Boulevard. There were a dozen or so spaces back there. I saw the Mustang and Nick's Mercedes sedan. I decided it would be a good thing, and safer, to leave the boxes of Marty's stuff with my dad rather than haul them around with me in the car. I took one up with me and Nick helped with the others, so we made it in just two more trips. We put them on the top shelf in my dad's bedroom closet. He was incoherent and seemed drugged. He wore an old maroon velveteen robe and slippers with the backs crushed down, his thin pale legs looking as though they were without blood. Sara said he hadn't taken anything, but he seemed unable to focus his thoughts or even his eyes. He looked as though he were asleep with his eyes open. He didn't have his choppers in, so his mouth was small and collapsed. His face fleshy and grizzled with two days worth of whiskers. The heavy curtains were drawn, so the apartment was dark and especially depressing. Under the best of circumstances, I hated to be in it. I usually insisted on taking him somewhere, or going on a walk when I came to visit, just to escape the dinginess of it. With the curtains open it wasn't bad. But he favored a cave-like feel and complained when I opened the curtains and windows for fresh air. I feel a draft! was a refrain I'd heard from him my whole life. It could be ninety out, and he felt a draft.

"We need to talk," Nick said.

Sara seconded the motion with a nod, indicating we should go outside. Not talk in front of my dad. I was all for that. Nick wanted a smoke anyway. He'd had an unlit cigarette in his mouth since I'd first knocked on my dad's door.

"What in the Holy hell do you think you're doing?" Nick demanded as he lit up. He inhaled the smoke the way the rest of us breathe air, as if his life depended on it. He was irritated with me for some reason, but he made a point of blowing the exhaled smoke to the side, away from me and Sara, as a courtesy, whether I deserved it or not, his look implied.

"What'd I do?" I asked in genuine innocence.

He rolled his eyes in disbelief. Sara jumped in.

"I told him about Thorne."

"Oh, that." I said.

"Yeah! That! Are you out of your fucking mind? You broke his fingers three hours ago and you ask 'What'd I do'? I got clients looking at three years for less. Not county time either."

"I asked him to take his hands away."

"Yeah, well maybe you better explain that to Detective Phillips."

He handed me a business card that read, Los Angeles Police Department, West LA Division, Detective Dave Phillips, 1663 Butler Avenue, Los Angeles, Ca. I looked at the back out of what was now becoming a habit. Sure enough, Phillips had written: Call me soon! Don't make me find you. There was a phone and extension number. Nick was calm now, as though just taking pleasure in having an after dinner smoke. I made a sort of shrug gesture with my face.

"Where'd you get this?"

Nick didn't speak. He nodded towards Sara.

"He showed up just after you left. Thorne filed a complaint after all. He wanted you arrested. I told the Detective that Thorne was abusive and put his hands on you and you asked him to take them away and he didn't. I told him that he pushed you a second time before you responded."

"And?" I asked.

"And he said he'd like to talk to you about Thorne. But also about an incident at the Coroner's Office? And he said your name came up in a hit and run in Venice. Kurt, what's going on?"

Nick was taking it all in. He'd evidently already heard this from Sara. He shifted into his Criminal Defense Lawyer mode, listening, absorbing, but not saying much, letting the DA's guys have their say. He lit another cigarette. He looked at me as he coolly blew the smoke up and away. He raised his brows a notch, as if to say, Any comment?

"It's getting uglier and more complicated," I said.

"That's it?" Nick asked incredulously.

I thought about it for a moment.

"For now, that's it," I said. "When I know more, and I know for sure, we can talk about it. Okay?"

"Don't wait too long. You don't have to be in this alone, okay?"

"Okay," I said, then gave him a playful smile, "can I call you if I get arrested?"

He smiled back. "Can you afford me?"

"Probably not."

"We'll work out a payment plan. Just don't do anything stupid."

"You don't think it sounds as if he already hasn't?" Sara chimed in.

Sara was going to stay with my dad until he was ready for bed before going to Megan Dunphy's house. Nick wanted to get to his office. We agreed to meet at 10 the next morning at the Bronx Deli, across the

street from Il Fornaio. Nick would pick up my dad. After, we'd go to
Hillside together for the service.

"Call the cop," Nick said. "Talk to him. You might be surprised. He
might be able to help - whatever's going on."

In the car I checked the LA County map again. Butler crossed Santa
Monica Boulevard near Sepulveda. It was 4:10 when I turned right out
of the lot behind my dad's place and took Beverly Drive to Santa Monica
where I turned left heading west. On my right, I was driving past the
twenty block stretch of grass and trees and flowers with cinder-rock path-
ways for walkers and joggers known as Beverly Gardens Park. It was
only eighty or ninety feet deep from the road to a line of trees that
boundaried the park on the north side, separating it from houses on each
block I passed, but it was a beautiful concession to public open-space at
an incalculable loss of land use for profit. When we were kids we came
through one or another section of this park on our way to Hawthorne
Elementary School. I passed the section of park at Santa Monica and
Rexford. It was gone now, but there'd been a bamboo patch there about
forty feet square. In the middle of it I'd removed enough bamboo to
create a ten-foot by ten-foot hideout. It had been one of half a dozen
places I'd created for myself around town to have somewhere to go to be
alone. Beverly Hills was a safe quiet village then, where parents could let
their kids wander to and from school without much supervision, and
without any fear at all. In our house, the rule was to be home before
dark, or to call and let someone know where you'd be if you weren't.
Marty knew of this one and one at the Pink House Gardens, another
bamboo patch I'd altered to suit myself in a huge back yard garden up
the block from us. When I was out too late and hadn't called, Marty
would check the hideouts he knew about, usually find me but leave me
alone, and report back to my mom I was okay and would be home soon.

It took me about twenty minutes to get there. It was an ugly single-
storied flat-roofed cinderblock building probably built in the early fifties. I left the little briefcase on the passenger side floor. If it wasn't safe
in the parking lot of a police station, what's the use, I thought?

Inside it was uglier than outside. The floor was bare concrete. The
reception desk had a formica top with a chrome strip around the edge.
The female officer was pleasant though.

"Hi. Can I help you?"

"I'd like to see Detective Phillips, please."

"Is he expecting you?"

"No."

"Your name?"

"Kurt Goldman."

Behind her the huge room was a collection of grey metal desks grouped under little flat wooden signs about the size of a carton of cigarettes, identifying Traffic, Burglary, and Detectives in black letters on white backgrounds, hanging from small-linked chains attached to hooks screwed into the once white, now yellowish acoustical tile on the ceiling. Phones rang in every direction. If the acoustical tiles were supposed to dampen the noise level, it wasn't working. Florescent light fixtures ran in long over-bright rows, giving off a harsh abrasive light and buzzing loudly. Along the right hand side was a door to a unisex bathroom with both male and female figures on it, and one to a glassed-in office. The second door said Division Captain. The lights were off and it was empty now, and had the look of being empty most of the time. Maybe the Captain had somewhere better to be, I thought. Almost anywhere would qualify. It was an informal place. The receptionist didn't use the phone in front of her to ring or buzz Phillips, she just walked back to the group of desks under the Detectives sign, tapped him on the shoulder and pointed to me. He had a phone to his ear and swivelled in his chair to see me. He said something into it and hung up. He motioned for me to come to his desk. The receptionist came back and lifted a section of the counter to let me through. He motioned me to a chair huddled close to the side of his desk. He was about forty-five, dark, good looking, roughly my size and dressed pretty well considering his salary probably wasn't much to brag about. He looked like he liked his job.

"Nice place," I said.

His eyes followed mine and he smiled. He told me for thirty years it'd had been a temporary situation.

"And you," he smiled, " I feel as though I already know you."

He dug through a pile of papers on his desk and carefully slid what he was looking for out from under the rest of the mess.

"Here we go," he said pleasantly, "a Kurt Goldman signs the ID papers for the Coroner's Office at about 2a.m. and punches the security guy on his way out." He looked up at me for confirmation but went on when I said nothing. "Santa Monica PD takes the call and writes it up at 2:35a.m. Story's not too tight. Coroner's guy didn't see it, tells the cops the security guy's an asshole, probably had it coming so they shelve it - tell the security guy to put ice on his nose and forget it." He smiled at me, dug through the mess and came up with another paper, "Here we go; earlier the same night there's a hit 'n run behind Sandy's in Venice and our report's got your name in it - says you were there. Any comments?"

I shrugged. There wasn't much I could say.

"Next thing I know one of our outstanding citizens from Brentwood, a Mr. Robert C. Thorne, attorney at law, is calling from Saint John's Hospital in Santa Monica where they're reconstructing a coupl'a fingers for him, and what d'ya know? He wants a Kurt Goldman arrested for assault and battery. Any comments now?"

I watched my hands. I had my fingers laced together, my wrists resting on my thighs. My thumbs were playing chase with each other, first one direction, then the other.

I looked up at him. There was no hostility in his manner, but signs of growing impatience. I shrugged again.

"Look," he said, "I know about your brother. I'm sorry. I made the call on your sister-in-law after the black 'n white called it in." He watched me fooling with my hands. "You listening to me?"

I looked up at him. "Yes."

"Good. Like I said, I'm sorry about your brother, but I can't let you run wild around my town. Understand?"

"Yes."

"Your sister told me what she saw with Mr. Thorne. I called him back and he hedged, but finally admitted he may have put his hands on you and you may have warned him to take them away - like your sister says."

He was waiting for confirmation from me again. I didn't say anything. I was thinking about what Nick had said. Trying to decide if this guy could be any help. Could even be trusted.

"Is that about the way it happened?"

"Yes."

"Just a bundle of information, aren't you?"

I shrugged. He sat back and tossed a pencil on his desk and regarded me.

"Are we going to have a problem?" His tone was a lot more official sounding.

"I hope not."

"You hope not." He raised his brows like that wasn't good enough. He wanted an iron-clad promise. "I don't think you're getting the picture. Your brother kills himself. You show up to take care of family stuff. Fine. Suddenly your name is popping up in police jurisdictions all over the place. Before I get unfriendly, let me try this another way. Is there something I'm missing here?"

I thought some more about what Nick had said.

"Did you see the LA Times today?" I asked him.

"You mean about your brother?"

"Not the weather."

"Yeah, I saw it. It's a load of shit. I haven't heard anything from Downtown or the DA's office, and believe me, if something were going on, I would. And as for burglaries, there've been exactly three in the general area in a four month period-not exactly what I'd call a rash. There was absolutely nothing at the scene to indicate anything other than suicide."

"Would you tell me about it?"

He looked unsure, like maybe I was some morbid nut case. "Like what?" he said cautiously.

"First, what time was he found and what time were police first there- and you?"

He opened a desk drawer and fingered his way through files until he got to the report on Marty. He looked it over and spun it around for me to read. It was short. The end of a forty-six-year-old man's life and it fit on a two page form. He pointed to several entries. They were called by Roberta at 11:25 a.m. Officers got there at 11:45. He arrived at 12:10.

"Roberta Goldman stated that she had gone shopping in the morning, left the house at around 9:15. Her husband, Marty Goldman, was work- ing in his office at home. She returned around 11a.m. and knocked at the door of her husband's office and got no reply. She entered and found him on the floor near his desk. She called the police." They believed he was sitting at the desk and shot himself in the right temple with a Smith & Wesson short barrelled .38 Special. Not registered and no record of purchase. Roberta claimed she didn't know the gun was in the house. He'd probably fallen to his right from the chair in reaction to the recoil of the gun and the reactive force of the bullet to his head.

He'd had a meeting scheduled for 10:00 a.m. with Victor in Century City. If he'd planned on going, he would've had to have his briefcase packed up and ready to go not much later than 9:30. If Roberta left around 9:15 it should've been obvious to her if it looked as though he were planning to go out or stay and work at home. Or kill himself, if that's what his plan had been. How was he dressed? Ready to go out or not? Had he said anything to her before she left? I flipped the second page over. Roberta had told Phillips Marty had complained to her be- fore she left that he "didn't want to live this way any more". Phillips notes indicated Roberta took that to mean "under the pressure of busi- ness problems he was encountering".

"How was he dressed?" I asked.

"What d'ya mean?"

"Robe and slippers? Shirt and tie? Jeans and T-shirt? Was he dressed to go to his office or was he dressed to stay at home?"

Phillips was wary now. "What're you gettin' at?"

"I'd like to know how he was dressed."

"Why?"

I hoped Nick was right.

"Because he had an appointment at 10:00 that was important to him. If he'd planned to keep it, he would have already been dressed and ready to go by about the time Roberta left the house. He would have needed to leave by 9:30 to get there. So I'd like to know how he was dressed."

"Suit and tie. Jacket neatly over the arm of the couch. Ready to go," he said a little reluctantly.

I told him about the Key Man insurance policy, about Goldman Marshall & Wolf's financial plight without it, about the autopsy, about something fishy Marty suspected in the accounting of Warner Warner and Carpenter. I told him, without naming him, about Ron Lawton's suspicions that someone had been shadowing Marty. I told him about the guys in front of Sandy's and the hit and run and some guys, maybe the same guys, maybe not, chasing me last night near Sandy's. I didn't tell him about Tate or about anyone else from Ron. I hadn't seen them, and didn't think they'd been covering me anyway. I didn't tell him about the coded files or about getting into Wolf's GOD file. I didn't tell him everything, but I'd either told him enough or too much. He looked concerned, shaken out of his complacency, but not convinced of anything. Then again, neither was I.

"And you think you're going to play detective now?" he said sarcastically.

"No. I'm going to try to bury my brother. If Thorne or Wolf or anyone else gets in my face or puts their hands on me, I'll do my best to discourage them. Is that okay?"

He looked at me like there was a lot he wanted to say. He pursed his lips and let it slide.

"Don't let your grief become an obsession -make you nuts- and try to stay out of trouble," he advised.

"No problem," I said, but I didn't get up to go.

He gave me his best the-interview-is-over look. When I still didn't move, he said, "What?" with irritation in his voice.

"I'd like to see the gun."

His mouth dropped open before he recovered and gave me a meaningful stare. If there'd been a question before about my being a morbid nut, he seemed to think I'd just answered it.

"You'd like to see the gun?" he repeated, his tone like I'd asked to use the phone, but the underlying sarcasm making it sound like I'd asked to borrow his wife.

I had the feeling he'd have liked to tell me it was sick. That I was sick. Maybe he'd have been right. But I still had the urge, maybe the compulsion, to hold it. To see and feel the thing that had ended Marty's life. How could he have been alive one minute and dead the next? It wasn't possible. What evil magic could make that happen? I thought that if I held the gun in my own hands, the answer would come. I'd understand. He shrugged and unlocked the bottom drawer of his desk, reached in and sifted through some junk and came up with it. It was in a clear plastic Zip-lock bag. He put it on the desk between us. He'd let me pick it up if I wanted to, but he wasn't going to participate by actually handing it to me. I picked it up. I opened the bag. I looked at him, asking with a gesture if it were alright to touch it.

"Go ahead, it's been printed," he said with a look of distaste.

I took it out and sniffed it. It still had the slightly sulphurous smell of recently fired gun powder. There were five live shells and one spent one in the bag with the gun. It had been completely loaded. It occurred to me that one would have been enough. Why would Marty load six shells? Even a bad shot could do it with one. Nick and I could have a field day with that, but I suspected Detective Phillips wouldn't see any humor in it. It was heavier than it looked. Holding it didn't answer any of my questions. The evil magic lay elsewhere.

"I'd like to take it with me," I said.

"No way. Absolutely not," he said shaking his head.

"Why not? It was my brother's property and I'm the executor of his estate, so that makes it mine now. I want it."

"It's part of an official investigation," he lied.

"You just got done telling me there's no investigation," I reminded him.

He sighed. A weary pained look came over him.

"Don't do this. You're not in a very good state of mind. Look what happened with this Thorne guy and the security guard. What would've happened if you'd had a gun? You don't need that kind of trouble. Neither do I. You can't legally carry it, so what purpose does it serve? Carry it, and you're breaking the law before you even think about using it. I don't know what the hit and run is about, but if you're worried, I'll look into it. Just forget about the gun."

"I'd like to take it with me," I repeated, "do I have to sign something?"

"God dammit!" he slammed his open hand on the mess of papers on his desk. I was prepared to wait him out, and he knew it. He sighed again and shrugged. Apparently, he had no legal reason to keep it from me. "Have it your way," he said. He dug through the file drawer of his desk and put a form in front of me. "Fill it out. Completely. I want a local address and phone number. Got it?" He tossed a pen at me and got up in disgust. He walked to another of the detectives' desks and talked with the guy there getting ready to leave. It looked as though it were quitting time. All around the room they were straightening up their desks and putting on suit jackets, putting things in drawers. He came back to me and read the form over my shoulder. "Sign it there," he said, pointing. I did. "Whose address and phone is this?"

"My dad's."

He put the gun back into the Zip-lock, sealed it and dropped it in my lap. He walked off without another word.

I figured I'd made a friend for life.

Outside, in the parking lot of the West LA Police Division, I got in the little Mercedes, reached down and got the briefcase from the floor and put it on the passenger seat and slid the Zip-lock bag into it. I started the car. Before I could shift into reverse someone was at my window.

"Excuse me, sir, would you shut off the engine and step out of the car please?"

It was the detective Phillips had been talking to.

"Why?"

"Step out of the car please."

His voice was firm, no nonsense. I shut it off and got out of the car. I thought about having to make a call to Nick only an hour after we'd joked about it. Somehow, I had the feeling even Nick wasn't gonna find it funny.

"Place your hands on the roof please."

He was polite at least. I obeyed.

"We've had a report of a concealed weapon. I'm going to search your car."

"What!? What are you talking about? What report?"

He ignored me. He looked under the seat and in the glove box, then had a brainstorm and checked the briefcase. He took out the Zip-lock bag.

"Do you have a permit to carry this?"

"I'm not carrying it," I pointed out.

"If you don't have a permit, it's illegal to carry a weapon in the car where it can be reached. The trunk would be acceptable. Also, the bullets must be kept in a separate location. The glove box would do."

I was beginning to hope he was just giving me a cram-course in fire-arm safety regulations and was going to send me on my way, chastened, but a better person for it just the same.

"I'm gong to have to confiscate the weapon for seventy-two hours," he said.

"That's bullshit! That's fucking bullshit!!" I yelled in frustration.

He held up a hand like a traffic cop to silence me. "You may return here to pick it up Wednesday morning. If you like, you may apply for a permit to carry with the LA County Sheriff's Office. That might take as long as six weeks before you hear back from them. Thank you for your cooperation," he smiled.

I watched him walk back to the station house where Phillips held the door open for him and clapped him on the back as he entered. Phillips gave me a little smile and wave and mouthed the words "Bye bye" to me as the door closed.

At first I was mad as hell and cursing Phillips every inch of the way. As I drove back along Santa Monica Boulevard, I felt defeated. But sur-prisingly, I also had a not altogether unpleasant feeling. Like an addi-tional load had been lifted from me. The more I thought about it, the more I knew Phillips was right. I had no business with a gun. It was a relief not to have it. I had to laugh at how cleanly he'd had his way.

The only thing I knew for sure was that I was hungry. I hadn't had anything to eat since the toast and coffee this morning, and the farewell smile on Vann's face had been the only bright spot in an otherwise dis-mal day. Connie's little smile was worth considering, but working for Thorne put her out of the picture. And her ex-boyfriend's Porsche should

have been all the warning I really needed anyway. I took Santa Monica
to Wilshire then left on Beverly Drive back to Il Fornaio.

It was 5:40 and the streets throughout Beverly Hills were still sunny
and hot and busy with fancy cars and fancy people going about their
business with what I thought was one eye on where they were going, the
other on how they were being seen. Me too. Only I was worried about
who might be seeing me. I hadn't seen anything that looked like the car
that'd missed getting off at Mesmer and the cemetery with me, and I still
hadn't seen anything that looked like Ron's guy. If nothing else, maybe
the trip to the police station had served to scare them off.

The public parking lot just up Beverly Drive from Il Fornaio had a
Full sign in the driveway, but a spot opened up not two spaces from
where I'd parked on the empty street in the morning. I waited a car
length back, my blinker indicating I was waiting for the space, while an
old man, with an equally old wife as passenger, carefully tried to make
the transition from his parking space back into traffic. Since I was blocking the lane for him, he didn't have much to worry about, but he was old,
very old, and things probably seemed to be moving too fast and too dan-
gerously for him and he needed to take a little extra time to be sure. He
had six feet to the car ahead of him, but to be safe, he backed a second
time to get a little more clearance. Suddenly the air behind me was filled
with the sounds of a blaring horn and the angry shrieks of a young woman
in a Silver-blue Porsche convertible. Not just an impatient tap on the
horn, but a full-blown lean on it, as though the harder she pushed the
more successful she'd be at removing this outrageous obstacle to her life,
liberty, and pursuit of happiness. When traffic allowed, she peeled rubber getting around me into the next lane.

"FUCKING OLD PEOPLE!!" she snarled as she roared past.

She was very good looking in an over-made up way, and from what I
could see, had a wonderful body. She looked like a younger version of
Roberta, I thought. Someone's idea of a dream date. Someone was in
for a rude awakening down the line.

I debated about taking the little briefcase with me. I didn't like haul-
ing it around, but I surrendered to paranoia or sound judgement or whatever, and took it.

I was surprised to see Vann still there. I figured she must be working
a twelve hour shift. She greeted me like a long lost pal. After the way the
day had gone so far, I would have been overjoyed with a smile.

"You're back! It's good to see you again and so soon!"

Her hand patted my back, giving it a tentative but familiar little rubbing stroke as she came around and led me to a table once again along
the Dayton Way side. Obviously, not a morning person, I thought. At

this rate, we'd be old friends by quitting time, which I reckoned ought to be soon, probably at 6. I couldn't imagine that she'd work longer than that. When I sat she placed the menu before me and folded her hands across the little white apron hanging mid-thigh in front of her black pants. Her smile was radiant, her eyes sparkling, expectant.

"Are you free for dinner?" I blurted, caught up in her change of mood. It also made sense from a practical point of view, I told myself. If she said yes, I wouldn't eat much now. If no, I intended have an early dinner here and now.

Her brow wrinkled. "We're not allowed to date customers." She seemed genuinely disappointed. So was I. But I was hungry enough for it to have been a toss-up. As terrific as she looked, food sounded equally good to me.

"What if you came to my place for dinner?" she suggested. "Nothing fancy. Just food. That wouldn't be a date now really, would it?" She smiled mischievously.

"Not even close." I agreed.

She took out her order pad and asked what I wanted.

"Just the house salad, vinaigrette dressing, some bread, and ice-water."

"Good," she said, maybe approving of saving my appetite for dinner with her.

When she came back with my order she also placed the little tray with the check on the table and left. Underneath the check was a slip of paper with her name and address and phone number: Vann Quintana, 701 Valparaiso Drive, Palms (213) 318-2213. Under that she'd written, "can we make it a little late? I've worked since 6 and I'd like a nap. We could eat by 8:45. Is that too late? Could you be there by 8:30?" With bells on, I thought. I watched her work while I ate. She moved quickly and surely and had a smile and a friendly word for customers and co-workers. She didn't linger or chat, just worked steadily with purposeful ease. What a change from this morning. How could she be so different? I thought. Then I had the fleeting and stupid and troubling and unkind thought that she might be a plant. That between this morning and now someone working for Wolf or Thorne had gotten to her and paid her to keep tabs on me. Make friends with me and find out what she could. I tried to be rational. Wolf and Thorne wouldn't know I'd come here. Even if someone had followed me this morning, they wouldn't have known I'd come back. On the other hand, they might've bought her co-operation just in case I did show up again. No, it was too far-fetched. Too preposterous. She turned from setting food before a customer and saw me looking at her. She smiled a warm, friendly and open smile. Nah, no way - couldn't be. Although, no! no! no! I hated how easily I could let myself get caught up in the dime-store intrigue of these guys and even if it were only mental, question the decency of someone showing a little interest in me. I nodded agreement about her note. She smiled and gave me a little nod in return to acknowledge we were on for 8:45.

I needed to focus on something else. I thought I should be looking for Ron's guy. Or Wolf's. Or trying to sort out who would have been following me the first night if they weren't the same guys Tate had intercepted, the guys Ron seemed sure were the ones we'd seen with Wolf. I looked around Il Fornaio and out the windows to both Dayton Way and Beverly Drive. There were hordes of people everywhere. If Wolf's guys or Ron's guy were around, I'd never know it unless they came up and introduced themselves. I tried to focus on the idea of two distinct groups of thugs following me around, but I couldn't make much sense of it and put it aside. I wanted to watch Vann for a while. That made sense, I thought, but I didn't see her. I finished eating, left a tip, and paid the cashier up front near the bakery section of the place. I wanted to catch Vann's eye before I left, but still didn't see her and thought she must be in the back somewhere. Then I realized it was after 6:00, nearly 6:30, and she'd probably gotten off and gone home for her nap. How nice, I thought, picturing it as I left.

I drove out to the beach. I had two hours to kill and decided if I could get into Marty's office unseen, I'd print Wolf's GOD file before my welcome there was completely used up. I took a round-about route, checking the rearview mirror often, but saw no one suspicious. I went down the ramp and had to stop to put the magnetic card in position to open the gate. While I was stopped there, Gary Weiselman came up the ramp on the exit side where the gate went up automatically as he approached. He didn't have to, but he stopped across from me. So much for being unseen.

"Don't fuck with Millennium!!" he growled at me. He punched the accelerator and the squealing sound of his tires continued to echo inside the garage as I went in, past the uplifted gate.

Nice to see you too.

It occurred to me to take the elevator up from inside for a change, break the pattern of my habit since it was so obviously a habit, just in case someone had followed me, but then thought, fuck 'em. If they're following me, they're following me. It wouldn't make any difference. It occurred to me it might make a difference when I leave though. I walked part way up the ramp, thinking that if no one had followed me here, maybe even lost track of me because of my trip to the police station, maybe no one, except Weiselman, knew I was here, or where I was. I had a nagging feeling as I got close to the street. What if they were out front waiting to see if I'd show up here? Waiting to pick me up again? Why tip them off? I changed direction and went back down the ramp and took the elevator to the lobby.

I was disappointed that Ron wasn't there. There was a buffed up white guy in his late thirties, dirty blond hair, dead eyes, shaved, but unshaved-looking. He seemed like one of those guys who'd never be happy in their work. Whatever it was. He didn't seem to have been told anything about me. Worse yet, it seemed he couldn't have cared less. But when I asked him for the clipboard, he shook his head no.

"You're Kurt, right?" he asked.

"Yes, I am."

"Ron said you shouldn't sign in."

His eyes had taken on a focused and defiant look. We were fighting the system, and he was glad to be in on it. I quickly looked over the clipboard. Ronnie Hook was signed in at GMW, but no one else. I glanced across the street to the park. There was a big dark windowed sedan parked there. Seeing it sent a shudder through me. Funny, I thought, how intuition can rise up and guide you. I hoped they hadn't noticed me here in the lobby. I wondered if this guy had noticed them, or even been on the look-out for them.

When I got off the elevator I went straight down the hall to Marty's office. Ronnie was at her desk clearing out. She looked up when she heard me approach. She seemed embarrassed, but determined.

"What's going on?" I asked.

"I've decided to quit. There really isn't much I can help you with and I don't want to be here. I'll tell Mr. Wolf at the service tomorrow. I don't want to be here another day."

I wanted to protest because I knew she'd be of help.

"Would you consider staying until the end of next week? Please?"

She was shaking her head no. I thought about tagging on for Marty's sake? but it would have been too low.

"For Marty?" I pleaded. What the hell.

She looked helpless. Not wanting to say yes but now not feeling she could say no.

Low is as low does, my conscience chided.

"Alright," she said finally, "but not a day past next Friday."

"Thank you," I said.

She looked at the little briefcase, then at me.

"Do you need any help with anything?"

"I don't think so. How long will you be here?" I asked.

"Why?"

"Before you go, would you show me how to print something from Marty's computer?"

"Sure," she said.

The printers were in the room with the copy machines and were on line all the time. There were six of them and each was set up to take the overflow of the one engaged before it, so even large projects rarely took long to run. All I had to do was print whatever I was working on and go retrieve it. When she was sure I was clear on how to operate it she took her purse from the top of her desk and said good night.

"I'll see you tomorrow," she said.

I drew a blank.

"At the service," she reminded me.

"Right. Thanks."

She turned to go.

"Ronnie..."

She turned back to me.

"Marty's percentage of the partnership at DBS was 16%, right?"

"I believe so. It went up over the years."

"Were the changes in writing?" I asked.

"Of course. They revised the partnership agreement every two years, incorporating changes, amendments, new partners, deleting departing ones-it's a constant process. Why?"

"I'm trying to find stuff like that. It wasn't here. Where would it be?"

"Did you look through his files at home?"

"Yes, but I didn't-"

I was going to say see it, but of course I had. The rubber-banded old DBS stuff. On the closet shelf at my dad's.

"It should be there, or maybe since it's such old stuff, he put it in his garage?" she suggested.

I smiled, relieved that I knew where it was. "Thanks, I'll find it. One other thing."

"Yes?"

"You knew about the car at The Beach Club?"

Her lips played with that little smile of hers.

"Yes. I told you the bills for The Beach Club came here? So did the insurance and registration for the car. It's beautiful, isn't it?"

"You've seen it?"

"He showed me a picture after the first bill for insurance came here to the office and I asked him about it. He swore me to secrecy. He joked about it, but we both knew he was serious. Why would he keep it such a secret? I'm sure Roberta doesn't even know about it."

"I don't know," I lied.

I told her about the floppy disk with '37 Pack on its label. That I'd tried it as Marty's password but it hadn't worked. I explained what I thought was the incongruity of having just one directory on the disk and having it be coded if it were about the car. What would be the point? On the other hand, if it were his back up, what was '37Pack if not the code? She agreed it seemed strange, but couldn't explain it. She clutched her purse to her chest.

"If you're looking for the code, keep in mind the maximum number of characters is six."

"What d'ya mean?"

"With the program we use a code can be from one to six characters, but not more. Good night," she said.

"Good night, Ronnie, and thanks for staying 'til Friday."

I locked myself in Marty's office and sat down at his computer. I was excited but trying not to let it run away with me. I didn't know what to do first, copy Wolf's files or see if I could get into Marty's. I decided on Wolf's. I booted up and was about to change to the A> prompt, but decided to print from the C Directory and leave A free for Marty's stuff. I hit F5 to list the files. I highlighted the CODED Directory and answered the prompt for the password with GOD. In like Flynn. I didn't think I'd have time to pick and choose so I printed everything. A message indicated the files were in the printer's memory and presumably printing. I went to check. Page after page was emerging from the magic kingdom of micro-processing. It was going to take a while.

I went back to Marty's office, changed to the A> prompt and put the '37Pack disk into the A drive. I hit the F5 again and got the Coded Directory listing and highlighted it. When I hit Retrieve I got the dreaded Enter Password instruction. I jotted down '37Pack. If you counted the apostrophe there were seven characters. I typed 37Pack, crossed my fingers and hit Enter.

I was in.

The '37Pack Directory consisted of 18 files; it was all here! I scrolled down through each of them, stopping only long enough to get a sense of the huge discrepancy between what Marty knew he had coming and the garbage offer from Malovitch. Everything I needed to know about the separtation agreement, about Wolf and GMW, and something called Packard Productions was here.

What a bonanza! I wanted to yell out the windows, to tell someone, anyone! I wanted to run up and down the quiet halls of Goldman Marshall & Wolf and bang on doors! Instead, I checked the time. It was 7:45. I did the same with Marty's files as Wolf's, and printed the whole mess. GMW didn't seem like the place, and now wasn't the time to dig into it. I'd find somewhere quiet and private and safe and read it all. It would take another fifteen or twenty minutes for the printers to crank it out, so I thought I'd close up shop here, go to the printer, and organize Wolf's GOD files, before Marty's files began to emerge. I exited Marty's computer and locked up the office.

In the printer room there was a binding machine that put plastic covers on the front and back of whatever you wanted and bound everything together with plastic rivets. It worked on anything from one sheet to five-hundred. Wolf's files went to just over 400 pages. I collected batches from each of the six printers and bound them. Marty's stuff was beginning to come off the first printer, now free of Wolf's files. As I gathered it up I heard the elevator bong. My heart started to pound. I wanted to get this done and get out. The last thing I wanted was to be seen. I opened the door a little more and could see Wolf and his two cretins get off and head towards his office. He was angry and I could hear him clearly.

"How could you be so stupid?!! I don't want you both here. One of you can watch for him-the other one, I don't care who does what-the other one should try to pick him up. Try the places you know he's been: Cox's, Il Fornaio, his father's place-maybe the house in Brentwood-just get on it! If you can't find him tonight, make sure you pick him up tomorrow at the service. If it's not practical there, he'll be at a gathering at the Seascape house in Brentwood after the service. Just don't lose him again!"

The last of Marty's files were coming out of the second and third printers. I eased the door closed and gathered it up. I wanted to bind it too, but was afraid of the noise it made when the rivets were fixed through the stack of papers. I put everything into the now bulging little briefcase and prepared to sneak out. Then I saw it.

Next to the door was an electronic monitoring device that was flashing as letters and numbers began to appear at the bottom of a long list of jobs previously printed. The two new entries read:

Wolf/Coded/*.* all files/426 pages
M.H. Goldman/Coded/*.* all files/197 pages

So much for anonymity.

I thought seriously about smashing the thing, but the noise would bring them sooner than the discovery of what I had. There was no reason to think they'd check the list of items printed, especially on a Saturday. I was better off taking my chances with them finding out what I'd done sometime in the next few days than bringing them down on me by breaking the thing. It might even be wired to an alarm to signal malfunctions. Why risk it, I thought. If I could sneak out without them knowing I was here, I'd be ahead of the game. At least for awhile. There was a door across from the elevator that I'd always assumed was a stairwell. I was hoping it was. If I rang for the elevator they might hear the bong when it arrived. I snuck along the back hallway towards the reception area. The briefcase was heavy and awkward now. When I got there I heard Wolf's voice as he came out of his office. The door I'd seen was locked. Wolf's voice was getting closer. I fumbled for Marty's keys and found the one marked Mstr and slipped it into the lock. It opened and I slipped into the stairwell and eased the door closed as Wolf and his pals approached the elevator and punched the button for down. When my breathing slowed, I started down the stairs. I took my time. No point bumping into them in the lobby. I had to shift the heavy briefcase often from hand to hand.

When I got there and peeked out, only the security guy was there.

"Had me worried for a bit," he said. "I thought those goons might bring you down in a body bag."

He smiled. I tried to smile back, but it was forced. Hearing Wolf ordering those guys to find me made it sink in. This was for real. Where the hell was Tate or whoever else was supposed to be watching me? Funny how quickly I'd come to rely on even the suggestion that Ron's guys were looking out for me. I thought about asking this guy where the calvary was, but let it pass.

"How long they been gone?" I asked him.

"Long enough," he said, "I seen the boys go acrost the street, and Mr. Wolf's car drove past here a minute ago."

I wondered if the boys had both left in the big sedan to go get another car, or if one had stayed behind. The light in the lobby made it impossible to see across the street into the darkness.

"A cab came an' got one of 'em," the security guy told me. "The Buick's still there."

"Thanks," I told him.

I took the elevator to the garage. When the doors opened I expected to be gunned down. Too many movies. I came out cautiously just the same. The garage was quiet. Not a sound. I went to the little Mercedes, got in and started it in one fluid and highly motivated motion. The sound of the engine filled the garage eerily. I was glad to get out of there. When I got to the street, I turned left on Arizona, away from Ocean Avenue and the waiting sedan. The clock in the car said 8:12.

At Bundy, I turned right, then left on National. When I got to Barrington I pulled to the curb and stopped to check the map. I knew I was close, but I didn't know exactly where Valparaiso was. I turned on the dome light and got the map and found it. I was about a mile away. I put the map back, turned off the light and shifted back into Drive just as high-beams flooded into the little Mercedes from behind, a big sedan bearing down on me at high speed, then screeching to a stop. I thought they'd hit me for sure, but they stopped next to me and a little ahead, angled to pin me in, so close I couldn't have opened my door if I'd wanted to. My heart was pounding wildly. They were so close the guy on the passenger side couldn't get out either. The driver's door opened and a tall slender guy in a black sweatsuit got out, walked around the front of his car to the front of mine, extended his arm and pointed a gun at me through the windshield of the little Mercedes. Wolf must have these guys growing on trees, I thought, because this wasn't one I'd seen before. Neither was his passenger. Nor the car. Classy, I thought, a huge four door Mercedes sedan, this time. I thought about Marty's gun, wishing now I had it, and my clever pal, Detective Phillips, who'd made sure

I didn't. I pictured this guy firing his gun, the windshield shattering into a thousand little nuggets of glass. I had the thought flash through my head that Marty's insurance might not cover it. I was immobilized with fear, but snapped out of it to instinctively shift to Reverse keeping my foot on the brake. There was a small telltale thud as the transmission changed directions but he didn't seem to notice. He raised his other arm and summoned me with the universal come-here motion of his index finger. I couldn't think of a polite way to decline. Just as I floored the accelerator there was an explosion of noise and glass and metal. I must have momentarily closed my eyes in anticipation of what was to come and stood on the brake, expecting to feel a bullet smash into me, because when it didn't and I opened them, I saw Tate emerge from a battered old Pontiac Coupe that he'd just crashed into the back of the big sedan. The sedan had lurched forward crookedly from the impact and knocked the gunman off his feet. The passenger tried to get out, but was too slow and Tate pulled him through the partially opened door and forced him face first to the pavement, a gun held to his back. I'd already backed enough to get behind both the sedan and Tate's car to go around them. The passenger struggled until Tate stepped on the back of his head. A motorcycle roared up next to the curb and slid to a stop. As it did, the driver put a well-aimed boot in the face of the gunman as he struggled to get up. He fell back to the ground. Tate waved me away, like a traffic cop annoyed with rubber-neckers at the scene of an accident. I floored the little Mercedes. I was surprised to be alive, surprised more of Wolf's guys had found me so quickly, surprised Tate and the motorcyclist had been covering me, surprised at the power the little car had when coaxed.

When I got to Westwood Boulevard I went right on a little chunk of road called National Place, right on Malcolm to the end where on the left it became Valparaiso. I didn't like the idea of being trapped in a dead-end street, but since Tate seemed to have things under control, I figured I was as safe at Vann's as anywhere. I turned the car around so I'd at least be pointed out.

701 Valparaiso was dark. The whole street was dark. The nearest street light was back at the corner where Valparaiso met Malcolm a hundred or a hundred and fifty feet or so, and what light it threw had a melancholy dispirited feel. There was enough moonlight to see it was a run down cottage, beige or dirty white, fascia boards rotting, gutters broken, ivy well on its way to reclaiming the site by burying the house with thick strong vines. It sat at the end of the dead-end key-hole street, overgrown lots on either side. It would have made a hell of a haunted house on Halloween. I sat in the little car trying to think. My breathing had slowed almost to normal and I was trying to recall if there could have been any way for Wolf's guys, parked where they'd been on Ocean Avenue, to see me leave the garage on the Arizona side. It wasn't pos-

sible. No way. The guy that'd taken off in the cab couldn't have come back that fast. And besides, he was supposed to be out looking for me in all the other familiar places. So who were these two tonight? I was sure I hadn't seen either of them with Wolf at GMW. And they weren't the guys from in front of Sandy's. I couldn't say if they were the guys Tate had intercepted after I'd left Tina Cox's since I hadn't gotten a good look at them. At this rate there was going to be a massive traffic jam when all these clowns converged. Unhappily, I seemed to be the point of convergence.

I looked at the clock in the car. It was 8:45. Vann's nap was running a little late, I thought. If no lights went on in the place by 9:00 I was going to leave. I was tired and hungry. I thought about going to the house and ringing the bell or knocking, but I felt safer locked in the car. If something looked like trouble, I'd start it and blast the hell outta there. If I got out and approached the dark house, and if she weren't even there and I couldn't get in, I'd be exposed and helpless. I'd give her 'til 9:00. I put my head back and closed my eyes. I began to doze off. Headlights suddenly flashed and I heard the sound of a car and motorcycle coming fast. I opened my eyes and saw the big sedan and the motorcycle approaching from Malcolm. In a panic-I'd like to think of it as a controlled panic-I reached down to start the car, fumbling with the keys. The big sedan went past me and pulled into Vann's driveway. The motorcycle stopped right in front of me, blocking my escape. The biker pulled off his helmet. It was Vann.

Inside, the little house was clean and neat. Tate had the two guys from the sedan tied to 50's chrome-and-vinyl kitchen chairs. The passenger's face still had bits of pebble and asphalt imbedded in it. The tall slender guy was subdued, but defiant. His black sweatsuit was dusty and he had a nasty bruise and cut along his left jaw and neck where Vann had planted her boot, but inside he seemed unruffled. His dark hair was pulled back against his head in an eight inch pony tail. Tate hadn't said a word. He'd marched them in at gun-point and he and Vann tied them up. I watched. Ruffled.

Vann smiled, "Dinner's gonna be late."

She excused herself and went into the kitchen and took boxes with the Il Fornaio logo from large paper bags on the kitchen table. She took cannelloni and tomato and cucumber salad from them and looked at Tate.

"You hungry?"

He shook his head no. So far, he'd proved to be a man of few words. If he hadn't said something to Ron in Sandy's, I wouldn't know for sure if he could talk.

Vann put the covered baking dish with the cannelloni in the oven to heat and set the table for just the two of us. She poured three glasses of red wine from a bottle with a nice looking label. I judged wines by their label. Dinner was going to be very romantic. I could tell.

"You work for Ron, I assume." The idea had been taking shape over my interior objections, my preference being that she'd taken a shine to me at Il Fornaio. I was greatly disappointed. Never mind that she and Tate had probably saved my life.

"Yes, I do," she said. She ran her hand through her hair and looked things over. "Excuse me, I want to change."

She went down a short hallway. I could see the light go on and spill out the partially open bedroom door to the hallway floor. She called to me.

"Are you okay? Why don't you start on the wine - it'll relax you. I'll be right there. I'm gonna jump in the shower." I could hear the water run. A moment later I could also hear her talking on the phone.

Tate was sitting on a worn brocade couch watching his two charges. They didn't seem to be too uncomfortable. Tate's eyes had a relaxed look. Like a lion or tiger after a large meal. A hundred pounds of raw meat, and he was easy. He sat with his legs outstretched and crossed at the ankles. He looked at me, his eyes steady, his lips closed, breathing slowly and evenly through his nose, his long black hair tossed back behind his shoulders.

"You're startin' to draw a crowd," he said. No smile. No follow up. He didn't invite or seem to want a conversation.

I shrugged. Some people got it, some don't, I wanted to tell him, toss it off casually, but the shaking inside was only now beginning to subside, and I'd never have gotten the words out. The shrug was pretty good.

Vann came back into the kitchen, her short dark hair wet from the shower, wearing jeans and a white T-shirt, her bottom rounder and sexier in the jeans than the black pants at Il Fornaio, but the strength and power of her legs, even her arms, evident now. She had on little gold earrings, the size of small pearls against the pierced lobes of her ears. She wore Mexican sandals. I noticed her feet were tan. She checked on the cannelloni and sipped at the wine she'd poured. She brought me a glass.

"Why don't you sit down? You look a little ragged."

I hadn't moved since she and Tate had steered me inside. I'd been standing in the same spot next to the kitchen table for at least fifteen minutes.

"Who me?"

She smiled, "Yes you. You've fallen into this right up to your neck. These guys are professional - not very good," she added with a smile at them and Tate, "- but professional. Ron's on his way over. He suggested we just eat and try to relax. He doesn't want us to talk to them. Okay?"

It was fine with me. I wasn't sure how much I'd enjoy the food, or how relaxed I'd get, but at the moment I was willing to forgo any chit-chat with these two. Vann smiled and approached and sort of led me to a chair at the table. I wasn't sure if she could tell, but my legs were strangely leaden and shaky when I tried to walk, the way they used to get after long hard sprint workouts in high school, running six 220's in about an hour, then finding my legs rubbery on the walk home. She took the cannelloni from the oven and served it. The tomato and cucumber salad was nicely vinaigretted. She sat across the little table from me. We sipped wine. She looked good. She smelled good. On the other hand, Tate was the ultimate chaperon.

We ate in silence. I had questions, but wasn't happy with what I thought were going to be the answers. For her part, she was doing her job, and didn't seem to have much need to talk about it. Which answered the questions I didn't want to ask. What the hell, I should be focused on Marty and DBS and GMW and staying alive. On the other hand, man does not live on bullshit alone.

We'd finished eating and Vann was cleaning up in the kitchen. I couldn't see myself going into the living room, joining Tate on the couch or sitting next to him in the easy chair, maybe saying to the two guys, with a smile, what's new, or maybe, you comfortable, can I get you anything. So I stayed in the kitchen and watched the magic lithe strength of Vann as she moved about. Stupid as it was with everything else that was going on, I had to admit to myself my greatest disappointment at the moment was Vann was being paid for her interest in me. Such was ego. Picked its own time, called the tunes.

There was a knock at the door, Tate answered it, and Ron came in. He looked the two over, looked at Tate, then across the room to me and Vann.

"Everybody okay?"

"Fine," Vann said.

Tate sat back down on the couch. I think he'd nodded to Ron, but if he did, that was it. Ron came into the kitchen and put his arm around Vann's shoulders and gave her an affectionate hug. He smiled at her.

"Long day?" he said.

"Very."

"But worthwhile - you done good, real good." He squeezed her to him.

My heart sank a little more. Stupid, I thought, but there it was.

Ron sat down in Vann's chair and took the third glass of wine. He sipped it. He closed his eyes like he were gathering strength. Opened them and smiled at me.

"How you hangin'?"

"Okay," I said. My fear had finally gone and what replaced it was the thought that Marty might've been pursued by these guys too. Only he didn't have Ron and Tate and Vann looking after him. Anger began to replace the fear. "Do you know who these guys are? They're not the guys that were with Wolf tonight. I saw Wolf and the same two guys you and I saw in the lobby yesterday there tonight."

"I know, Bud told me," he said, shaking his head no, but added, "We're about to find out."

Without getting up he asked Tate if these were the two from last night. Tate shook his head.

"This guy's drawin' a crowd," he repeated for Ron.

Ron took another sip of the wine and got to his feet. He was wearing Levis and a white T-shirt, the uniform of the night, I was thinking. His body was incredibly muscular.

"Vann, you and Kurt like to take a little walk? A little after dinner walk?"

He said it like a question but his look made it clear it wasn't.

"Let's go," Vann smiled pleasantly.

"I want to stay. I want to hear what they have to say. I want to know who sent them and if they had anything to do with Marty's...Marty's..." Death wouldn't come. I had to settle for Vann's hand on my back. Her comforting massaging of the top of my shoulder. My throat was tightening. Ron was shaking his head no.

"You don't wanna be here. You went to see that cop, what's his name?"

"Phillips," Vann said.

I gave her a look. I hadn't seen her. And she'd been at Il Fornaio before and after. How'd she manage that?

"Phillips," Ron continued, "so whatever happens to these two, you shouldn't be a part of."

He said it matter-of-factly, but it was clear whatever happens covered a lot of unpleasant ground.

"Let's go," Vann said, "you could take me for a drive in that cute little car."

"No," I said stubbornly.

Vann sat down in the easy chair, one leg over the arm, running her hand through her almost dry hair. Ron stood in front of the two sizing them up. I think he knew immediately the guy in the black sweatsuit was in charge, that the other guy was more likely to give up information. But he focused on the sweatsuit guy anyway.

"What's it gonna be? I'll keep it simple. I got three questions you gotta answer. Who sent you? How far you supposed to take it? And did you do his brother, Marty Goldman?"

The sweatsuit guy looked at Ron defiantly, eye to eye. No fear. No worries. The other guy was looking at the floor like escape instructions were written there. Ron looked at me.

"You really oughta go," he said kindly. "If Phillips ever ties this to me, security for your brother's building an' all, he's gonna pull you in - he's gonna be bad news for you. You don't need the hassle, man." He looked at Tate. "What about the car you used tonight?"

"Parked it. It's clean if it gets impounded."

"Good." Ron looked back at me. "How 'bout it?"

I shook my head. Stubborn is as stubborn does. Ron made a face showing his displeasure. He stepped behind the sweatsuit guy.

"Anything you want to tell me? It doesn't have to be rough," Ron told him.

The guy didn't move a muscle. Ron grabbed one of his fingers where his hands were tied behind the chair and twisted it until it broke. The guy grimaced, then shuddered, then finally screamed as Ron twisted it well past the first crunching. He panted huge groans as the tears ran down his face. He was gasping for air like he'd been under water too long.

"You got nine more - what's it gonna take?" Ron asked him.

"Let's go," Vann whispered to me.

"Okay," I said grateful for another chance.

Ron nodded approvingly. "Why don't you show Vann where you're staying? If it get's late here, you got room for her?" He smiled. "I mean, like a couch or something?"

"Sure," I said.

"You take care of her, hear? She's my girl." He waved a cautioning finger at me, like a father to his teenaged daughter's date. "Is there a phone in the room?"

"Yes. You remember?"

He cut me off with the wave of his hand, before I could mention the Pacific Hotel or the room number. "I remember," he said, "I'll call," he looked at his watch, "before midnight if possible. If it get's later than that, we'll talk tomorrow."

"I'm meeting my family at 10. The Service is at 2."

"I'd like to pay my respects," he said almost shyly.

"Of course."

"Maybe we could meet before you see your family? Where you met Vann?"

"Sure," I said, "how 'bout 7:00?"

"That'll be good. Maybe I won't call tonight. We'll just talk tomorrow. You should get some rest. I don't know what I was thinking," he said. "You two run along now." The indulgent parent. Vann picked up a little drawstring cloth purse from the entry table near the door.

"Later," she said.

He smiled affectionately at her and she smiled back. When he turned back to the sweatsuit guy he wasn't smiling.

Chapter 22

The clock in the Mercedes said 10:15. I drove back to National and headed for the beach. When in doubt, go to the beach. Vann put her head back to rest, but I could see her checking the side mirror often. Unless Wolf was running a one man full-employment agency - and with what I heard from him tonight about his two guys finding me again, that didn't seem likely - it seemed there were at least three independent sets of two thugs floating around with me on their one-track minds. Wolf accounted for one. But why? Their chance of getting the insurance money was slim at best. Even if I posed a threat, I was only a minor one. An irritant. I'd delayed them, and not even for very long. If they couldn't get the insurance money, and GMW was likely to fold, what was the point? And if Ron was right, and Wolf's thugs had been following Marty around, there had to be something in the Studio Sheets to pose a serious threat to Wolf. I'd never see it. I had to get the sheets to Victor. Maybe it would be obvious to him. If not obvious, at least he'd be more likely than me to spot it. I saw a pay phone and pulled to the curb at National and Sawtelle. Vann sat up.

"What's going on?"

"I gotta make some calls."

"Won't it keep 'til we get inside?" she said, worried about being exposed.

"No," I said as I shut off the car and got out.

She got out her side and took a flat black pistol from the waistband of her jeans at the small of her back and held it discreetly against her leg when she walked. Where I was exposed in the circle of light from the phone booth, she stood far enough outside it to be nearly invisible in the dark. A few cars passed, but none slowed or had any interest in me. I got Victor's card from my collection and dialed.

"Hello?" His voice was high and uncertain. It occurred to me he'd probably been asleep, went to bed early since he was routinely in his office at six or seven.

"Victor, it's Kurt."

"Oh, hello."

"I've got the Studio Sheets from Warner and Carpenter for GMW. I want you to go over them. There's gotta be something."

"Yeah. Marty said 'fishy'."

He said it like it were just a slightly annoying smell. Definitely not something you'd kill over. I didn't want to scare him with that idea, get him worked up, but I wanted some answers quick.

"I want to bring them to you."

"Fine. I'll get them from you at the service tomorrow," he said, sounding ready to go back to bed.

"I mean now."

"Now? It's after 10:00!" he protested.

"That's the good news, Victor."

"What d'ya' mean?" he said apprehensively.

"The bad news is it's important that you go over them tonight."

He started to protest, but I cut him off. "Victor, remember what you told me?"

"What?" he said suspiciously.

"That things were a mess? That you'd help get me up to speed? That you were pretty sure it had to be the studio sheets Marty was worried about?"

"Yeah?" he said plaintively.

"It's messier than you can imagine and I think it's much worse than fishy. I need to know, Victor, and I don't think I could spot whatever it is. I think you can. I think Marty knew you could. Please! Tonight."

"Okay, okay, bring it over."

He gave me the address. It wasn't at the beach. 5814 Oakwood Avenue near Martel was on the fringe of the Fairfax District.

"Thirty minutes," I said and hung up.

I called information and got Doctor Richard Rosen's number and called it. I expected an answering service, 10:30 Saturday night, but was surprised and momentarily flustered when he answered, thinking he must have it ring through to his house at night. Maybe he makes house calls too.

"Doctor Rosen speaking."

"Doctor Rosen?"

"Yes?"

"I'm sorry to bother you so late and at home."

"I'm at my office. Who is this please?"

"Kurt Goldman-Marty's brother."

"Oh. I'm so sorry. So terribly sorry. It's inconceivable," he said.

"To me too. That's part of the reason I called-I need some medical information about Marty."

"I'm afraid that's confidential."

"I know it is, but I'm Marty's executor."

The question was, would he take it on faith and over the phone. The line was silent a moment. I figured he was considering just that.

"What is it you want to know?" he said finally.

"First, did he have any condition or disease that you know of, and knew he was aware of, that was life threatening?"

"No, none. He was in very good health - a little overweight - as a matter of fact, he'd agreed to join me and some friends for golf once a week. This coming Monday morning would have been his first time."

"So you were friends? Not just his doctor?"

"Yes, we went to Beverly High together. He was a year ahead of me. We met again at Stanford." His voice was thick with one of those waves of grief that rise up from nowhere and choke you. "I can't believe it," he moaned. Like a chain reaction, I could feel it coming too, but pushed it back down.

"What about the pills? The 'Des-something?'"

"Desyrel?" he said.

"Yes. What's that for?"

"It's a mild anti-depressant. He'd..." He stopped.

"He'd what?" I asked.

"I'm not comfortable discussing this on the phone. I'll be at the service tomorrow-could we talk after?"

"Sure, that'll be fine, but let me ask you one more thing." He didn't respond one way or the other. "Could the pills have had any side-effects?"

"You mean have caused confusion? Worse depression? Led to...?"

"Anything like that?" I asked.

"Not from the literature I've seen, but you never know. If a patient over-medicates."

"Could Marty have?"

"Not very likely."

"Why not?"

"He came to see me Tuesday afternoon to tell me he'd taken only two of them so far and that he'd gotten light-headed and faint. He was upset - apparently it'd come at a bad time."

The meeting at Millennium. "And what did you tell him?"

"To stop taking them. That Blum and I would find something else."

"Blum?"

He hesitated. "Let's talk more tomorrow."

From the sound of his voice, that was it for now.

"Good. Thank you," I said, "I'll look for you tomorrow."

"I don't believe it," he muttered, "I just don't believe it."

"Neither do I," I said and we hung up.

Vann and I got back in the car. I got the pill bottle out of the glove box and handed it to her. I started the car and made a U-turn to head east on National, turned left on Sawtelle.

"What am I supposed to do with this?" she asked.

"Count them. Please."

She gave me a funny look then shifted around and took a handker-
chief from her purse and spread it on her lap. I turned right on Santa
Monica Boulevard. She emptied the pills into it and counted them back
into the bottle. I went right when we came to Wilshire. By the time we
reached Fairfax she'd done it three times. She'd also kept a close watch
on her sideview mirror.

"Ninety-seven the first time, niney-eight twice," she said. "I'm confident ninety-eight is right."

That confirmed what Rosen had said. At Oakwood, I turned right,
drove ten shortish blocks and found Victor's place. It was the kind of
nice stucco two storied box my grandmother had had somewhere in this
general area in the 'forties. Like hers, probably three bedrooms, two
baths, separate dining room. It was a well kept neighborhood that'd
been strictly middle middleclass until recently, when the scramble for
housing under $500,000 had pushed the prices from $80,000 to between
$250,000 and $325,000 overnight. The street was well lit with street
lights mid-block as well as at the corners. Victor's house had the porch
light on and the dull glow through curtains of maybe a single lamp in the
front room.

"I'll be right back," I told Vann.

I reached across her legs and took the little briefcase from the floor
at her feet.

"I'll come with you," she offered.

"I'll just be a minute."

She ignored that and got out anyway. She eased away from the car
thirty or forty feet along the sidewalk, then crossed the street. She stood
in the shadow of a large tree while I went to Victor's door. I rang the
bell. It made an elaborate series of sounds, like the preamble to some
concert piece. If anyone had been asleep in the house, they weren't anymore. I wished I'd knocked.

"Jeez," Victor said when he opened the door, "you'll wake the kids!"

"Sorry," I said.

"Come in." He closed the door behind me. "Let's go into my study."
The nasal twang more awake now.

It was a nice room. Small, but tidy and homey. He had pictures of
two boys around nine or ten and a girl, maybe five. The boys were
decked out in Little League uniforms. Some team pictures, some single
shots kneeling, a bat and ball on the ground, a glove dangling casually
from a wrist over the up knee. Happy smiles. I put the little briefcase on
his desk and pulled out the bound volume I'd put together at GMW.

"I haven't looked at it," I told him, "but with whatever else is here, the
Studio Sheets from Warner and Carpenter make up most of it."

"Jeez," he said again, flipping through the pages, staggered by the size
of it. "This could take days!"

"Just give it an hour or two - maybe a little more if you think you're on to something. Maybe you could sleep in a little tomorrow?"

"With them?" he smiled in the direction of the kids photos. "Not very likely. I'll take a look. I'll see you at the service tomorrow. If I find anything I let you know."

"Thanks Victor."

"You're welcome. Can you let yourself out? I'd better get started."

"Sure," I said and started for the door.

"How did you get this?"

"You don't want to know." I smiled at him, then added more seriously, "And you don't want anyone to know you have it."

I'd gotten into the car and started it before Vann came back across the street and got in.

"Everything okay?" she asked.

"No. Yes." I looked at her, then away. I shrugged.

I could feel her eyes on me. I looked back to her.

"Whadda I know?"

She put her hand on my shoulder and gave it a comforting pat.

It was 12:10 when we parked in the lot behind the Pacific Hotel. I locked up the car and we walked around to the entrance and into the lobby. The desk clerk greeted me in his usual polite and slightly formal manner.

"Good evening, sir. Madame. 211?"

"Yes."

He checked the boxes behind him. Vann was looking around the large and once grand lobby. "No messages," he said. There never were, but he checked every night anyway. Checking was included in the price of the room, so he checked.

"I'm going to be staying a little longer." I said.

"How nice." There was no sarcasm in his voice. He seemed to mean it. He looked in a little file box. "You're paid through tonight," he said, "how much longer did you have in mind?"

"Three, maybe four more nights." I got my wallet, took out three twenties. "Same deal for cash?"

"Of course." He took the money. "Four nights." He marked it down on the card.

"Have a good evening, Mr. Hammer." He smiled at that. A faint smile, but a smile. Vann gave me a look.

We walked up the wide, worn stairway. I ran my hand over the beautiful handrail as I'd done both nights before. Someone's fine work still giving pleasure sixty years later, I thought.

"Nice place," Vann said.

I turned expecting sarcasm on her face, a frown on mine, but she shook her head.

"No, really, I mean it, I think it's great!"

I smiled, "So do I."

"Mr. Hammer?" she asked. "That's not much of an alias. Kurt Hammer? "

"No. Mike," I said, trying not to smile.

"Oh please!" she laughed and grabbed my arm. "Not really!"

"Really," I said sheepishly.

We were inside my room. I put the little briefcase on the desk. The moon on the water wasn't as bright as the last two nights, but it was nice. I thought the dim light from the brass fixture had a shot at being romantic tonight. Vann went into the bathroom, looked around, opened the little window there and stood on the toilet seat to look out. She came back into the room, kneeled with one knee at the head of the bed to better look out the windows. She went to the door and locked it. Set a chain and then took one of those rubber wedges from her purse and forced it under the bottom of the door with a couple of kicks with the toe of her sandal.

"I think that oughta do it," she said.

She took the pistol from the small of her back and put it on the night table on the bathroom side of the bed. She pulled back the covers. The sheets had their familiar clean bleach smell.

"Hmm," she said mostly to herself.

I figured it was an endorsement for the sheets.

"Do you have a T-shirt I could borrow to sleep in?"

"Sure." I got one from my suitcase on the dresser.

She took it and went into the bathroom and closed the door behind her. When she came out she had her clothes neatly folded in one hand, my T-shirt coming mid-thigh. It hung loose at the neck and shoulders. It looked good on her. Very good. Loose as it was, I could see the points of her nipples. Her legs were strong looking, but smooth and tan. The dim light from the fixture seemed romantic as hell. She looked through the empty drawers of the dresser, put her clothes in the bottom drawer.

"Mind?" she asked.

"No, not at all."

She opened the closet door, looked around, took a blanket and pillow off the shelf, threw them into the easy chair and pushed the chair until it touched the foot of the bed on the desk side. The seat of the chair was about the same height as the bed. She got the gun from the night table, set it on the floor within easy reach and wiggled herself in, her legs stretched out across the bottom of the bed. She tucked the blanket around herself. It was still warm out and the one blanket would be enough. She fluffed the pillow and settled in. She'd stationed herself half way between the door and the windows and figured from there she'd have time to respond to trouble from either direction.

"Could you get the light? I'm bushed."

A fine romance this is, came to mind. With no kisses. "I'm gonna work a while," I said.

I turned on the desk lamp and turned off the overhead fixture.

"Good night," she said.

It was a warm good night, but good night just the same.

A few minutes passed while I pulled out Marty's stuff, put it on the desk and put the briefcase on the floor. I looked through it, arranging as I went.

"I'm sorry about your brother. Ron said he was the best," she said sleepily and was out.

I set aside the papers that related to GMW. I needed to focus on the Separation Agreement as Marty saw it. I took up the file marked:

> DBS/Marty Goldman Partnership Separation Issues: 1965 Partnership Agreement; 1968 Update; 1972 Update; 1976 Update; 1980 Update (Home office files).

I knew Malovitch was a silk-shirted lying thief! But this was unbelievable! He generously offers $580 thousand to Marty, to the Estate, and $16,500 a month to GMW when the reality, even allowing for the three times penalty for the Peters litigation, was more like $6 million to Marty and almost $60 thousand a month to GMW for the eighteen months since Marty left. And he was going to flat out stiff Cox, Woodman, Davidson, and Weiselman for $34,250. I was outraged for Marty and the others, but even more for myself. He wouldn't have dared pull this on Marty! What a rotten worm! I wanted to strangle his overly-perfumed neck!

I closed my eyes and tried to calm myself. I turned in my chair to look at Vann behind me. I could hear the regular breathing of peaceful sleep coming from her slightly open mouth. I stood to stretch and to see her face. She had the angelic look of a sleeping child, a clear, untroubled, innocent face. Very appealing.

I looked at the next group of papers.

> DBS/Marty Goldman International Distributors Agreement: On 9/17/73 M. Goldman, B. Malovitch, and Don Diamond agreed in the matter of International Distributors, the firm of DBS would undertake all costs; M.Goldman will bill hours against it; M.Goldman will DIRECTLY RECEIVE 26% of fees paid to DBS; the balance of 76% to DBS to be treated as income to the firm; partnership percentages applied against year received NET.(E.F.ccs to: MHG; DD; BM)

It wasn't as good as having Marty's copy of the signed note itself, but

having the date and what I assumed was the exact language would make
it hard for Malovitch to deny. I thought the next file was pretty straight-
forward, the dollar amounts both easy to confirm and indisputable, until
the part about a co-signature agreement with Jacobs sank in. I re-read it
a couple of times.

> DBS/International Distributors: Judgement; Appeal; Calcula-
> tions; Balance as of July 31, 1982; Fees: $7,002,080 in
> escrow; DBS/MHG co-signature to release per
> M.Goldman/J. Jacobs agreement of 1/1/81(TBC) No
> CP b.s.!

Marty had tied Malovitch's hands! He couldn't get into the escrow
account without a release from Marty! No wonder they'd used the phrase
"releases all interests in, or claims to, known and unknown etc." in the
agreement they wanted me to sign! I laughed out loud and clapped my
hands together in awe. Marty, you nailed him good! But how did you
know?!

Vann stirred, but didn't wake.

I could hardly contain my glee. Malovitch must've gone nuts when
he found out about it! The date, 1/1/81, was just before Marty left DBS.
He must've had reason to believe Malovitch, or DBS generally, couldn't
be trusted. Maybe he was just being careful after Diamond denying him
the name thing soured him on them, blowing the family feeling, or maybe
there was something more specific, but the important thing was he did
know, and must've gone to Jacobs, his friend, and worked out the co-
release agreement. It made sense. With the win over International Distributors, it was Jacobs' money, and it was his legal bill that created the
fees for DBS. Whatever provisions he might want to make to pay it
were his business. He and Marty had made sure that DBS couldn't get
their hands on more than their share. Oh, how sweet it is!

TBC had to be The Beach Club. He must've hidden the co-release
agreement there. The idea that he felt he had to hide it was disturbing.
My glee was being replaced by foreboding. What had happened that
made him think neither his office at the beach or at home was safe?
What was it Malovitch had said about Marty's call to him? "...calls and
dares to demand I release the funds to GMW or he won't..." what?
George Zeffaro had turned the tables and jumped in and shut him up.
Won't sign the separation agreement? Even if the one Malovitch'd given
me was garbage, he and Marty had been close to an agreement based on
the terms Marty had outlined in these files. I'd heard it from Tina Cox
and Ronnie. And in his own lying sack-of-shit way, Malovitch had confirmed it. They may have been close, but it was clear Malovitch was
using settling all issues at once as a device to put pressure on Marty to
settle differently from what was outlined here. It had probably become
increasingly clear to both Marty and Malovitch that GMW was struggling and needed the flow of money DBS was withholding. Malovitch
had surely been using that to get Marty to roll over on something more

important. Like Marty's vested interest in DBS? 12% versus 16%? Or
International Distributors? They both dwarfed everything else. What
if Malovitch had been trying to force Marty into accepting far less for his
partnership interest than the 16% of the $26 million appraisal of DBS
Marty referred to here and believed was due him? What if Malovitch
had been betting Marty would agree to almost anything in exchange for
the release of those funds to GMW, knowing Marty had placed his ego
above money when he left to form GMW. Wouldn't he do the same to
keep it alive? What if that was the hang-up to signing an agreement, and
then Marty had sprung his co-release agreement with Jacobs in that call?
The International Distributor funds were ready to be released from the
escrow account. And Marty wouldn't sign for their release if Malovitch
wouldn't release the funds GMW desperately needed. But that would
remove the leverage Malovitch thought he had over Marty on a reduction of his interest in DBS. On the other side, if Marty had simply agreed
to release the International Distributors escrow funds, he could have
easily underwritten the flagging operations at GMW. Only if he did,
he'd have been putting up his personal funds to subsidize not just the
product of his ego, but the excesses of John Wolf's.

I couldn't see Marty doing that. The International Distributors' money
and money coming from his interest in DBS were his. He may have
invested his ego and reputation in GMW, but I think he'd expect it should
stand or fall on its own merits, the money owed to it by DBS rightfully a
part of that, and he'd fight Malovitch for it. I couldn't see Marty going
out on that limb. Not his style. So, I figured he'd told Malovitch, you
release and I'll release. And it seems that possibility had never entered
Malovitch's deliberations. The co-release was a surprise. He'd thought
he was holding all the cards. His reaction recalling Marty's call testified
to that. What else did it reveal? How far would he have taken it? I'd
asked myself that about Wolf, I recalled. However far he might have
taken it, Marty must've assumed it would go as far as trying to get his
hands on the co-release agreement. But what good would that do? Jacobs
would have his copy, so whoever was in charge of the escrow account
would have to get instructions from him. I wondered who else knew of
it? Ronnie? Tina Cox? Weiselman? Not Weiselman, or Malovitch
would have known, I was betting. Probably not Ronnie or Tina either.
Just Marty and Jacobs? Intuitively, I thought that was right.

TBC. The Beach Club. What had I missed? Maybe in the trunk of
the Packard. Maybe in the closet somewhere. I hadn't looked carefully
there. I had to find time to go back. Try again. I wondered about the
"no CP b.s.". Maybe Ronnie would know. But this was getting good!
Forebodings or not, I tore into the next file.

DBS/Client Settlement Percentages re: Partnership Agreement
30% rule. Page 26, 1976 Update: "If any departing
partner has been responsible for 30% or more of the
firms gross billings in each of the three years prior to

departure, the departing partner's new firm shall be
entitled to his partnership percentage applied against
55% of his client billing stream, rather than the usual
60/40 split."

How could they expect to get away with this stuff? I took the partnership agreements for 1965 and 1976 from the briefcase. I was ready to
bet the farm that page 26 would have nothing about the 30% exception.
Nothing but the 60/40 rule in '65. I turned to page 26 in the '76. It had
the exception all right, but it was 60% not 30% that triggered it! From
what Tina had said, Marty had accounted for about 40% of the gross for
several years. It shouldn't be too hard to substantiate that. But to make
60% stick, Malovitch had to believe I didn't have Marty's copies of the
'76 partnership agreement. That the one he'd given me would stand.
What would make him think that? I looked again at the first file. Right.
(Home office files). Now at my dad's. I'd have to get over there and find
Marty's copy of the '76 Agreement. How could he be so reckless as to
give me a doctored copy if there were the slightest chance I had the
original? Weiselman wouldn't have been any help there. What would
he know about Marty's home files? And even if he knew, he wouldn't
have access to them. I was getting a bad feeling about it. I knew I wouldn't
rest until I could get to my dad's to check. I would have gone right then,
but sneaking out on Vann, or waking her to go with me, would have been
a problem. Maybe not a huge problem, but a problem. She'd obviously
been following me all day, working at Il Fornaio, when she knew I'd be
there, and leaving when I did. Coming back when I did. How did that
work? I'd have to ask her. But, worse, showing up at my dad's in the
middle of the night would have pushed him over the edge. Further. It'd
have to wait until tomorrow. Today.

I sat back, rubbed my eyes. I was excited and agitated by all this, but
at the same time tired. Really tired. I checked my little pocket watch. It
was 2:10.

Just a little more.

Vann had a slight snore going. There was something appealing about
that, too. I breezed through the next couple of files.

I did a few calculations and made a note to myself. Malovitch had
offered the Estate $580,000 and GMW $297,000. Zip for the little guys.

By Marty's estimation he was owed $6 million plus. GMW $1,080,000.
The little guys $34,250. The difference was a cool $6,237,250.

If Malovitch thought he could get away with it, was it enough to kill
for? The further he took it, the less he had to lose with the next step.
And if he'd thought he could get away with it with Marty and had acted
on it, now he had an even greater incentive to stop me. Any way he
could.

Nice.

It amazed me that I was actually beginning to believe it. The whole
thing was unbelievable. You read about this stuff. It doesn't happen.

But then, my reaction, and just about everyone else's to Marty's suicide was that that was unbelievable. It also occurred to me you read about it because it does happen. I put the papers back into the briefcase and with them my note.

I went into the bathroom, brushed my teeth and took out my contact lenses. How sweet that is. I rubbed my eyes longer than I'd brushed my teeth. I stripped down to my underwear, folded my pants and put them on top of the suitcase on the dresser and turned out the lamp. I looked out the window. My eyes adjusted and the glow from the moonlight on the water lit the room romantically.

What a waste.

I got into bed thinking I'd never fall asleep. All the numbers, all the deception, all the questions I had that needed answers were swirling around in my head. My eyes ached and I rubbed them some more. That was the last thing I remembered.

Until Vann woke me climbing into bed.

Chapter 23

SUNDAY

⎯⎯⎯◦◦◦◦⎯⎯⎯

I had nice dreams. Vann had cuddled close, throwing one leg across my thighs, her arm across my chest, her head resting on my shoulder.

"I'm cold," she'd shivered when she came in.

She was asleep again before I'd had a chance to consider the possibilities or my options, which pretty much restricted both.

When I woke the little travel clock showed 6:10. Vann was dressed in her Levis' and T-shirt, sitting in the easy chair with her feet drawn up onto the cushion. She'd moved the chair back to its place, put away the blanket and pillow and had neatly folded my loaner T-shirt and placed it on the dresser next to my suitcase. She'd already had a shower and was drying her hair with a Pacific Hotel towel.

"Hi," she said warmly with one of those morning after smiles.

I was uncertain as to how to proceed. Technically, nothing had happened, but there was the almost or might have been to be considered. It must've showed and she took care of it.

"I'm sorry if I crowded in last night, but it got cold," she shrugged. The morning after smile became a don't-think-about-it-too-much look. "You still gonna meet Ron at 7?" She nodded towards the clock.

It was sunny and the air had that refreshing morning crispness to it again. The sound and sight of the little waves breaking on the shore dashed across the sand to me, stopping me where I stood, about to get into Marty's little Mercedes. Beckoning, soothing, tempting me to play hooky from the day and what it would bring. Just stay at the beach, maybe get a raft, or body surf so long that resting on the sand after wouldn't stop the rolling sensation of the waves. A nice idea, but it wasn't going to happen.

When we pulled out of the Hotel parking lot it was 6:40. I'd liked to have had time to go back to The Beach Club, if not to surf, to see if I could find the co-release agreement, but there wasn't time. It was important, but it would have to wait.

"Do you need to go home?" I asked Vann.

"What for?"

"Clothes? For work at Il Fornaio?"

She smiled, shaking her head. "I don't work there. The owner's a client-friend of Ron's. When Ron said it would help if I could work there, come and go on short notice - or no notice - he okayed it."

I turned right on Ocean Park, drove past Bundy where it becomes Gateway and took that to the 10 East.

"So you came and went every time I did?"

"You had me jumpin', that's for sure," she laughed. "You'd told Ron you'd be there in the morning, so I was there ahead of you. Tate stayed at the beach the night before and followed you in the morning."

"I looked, but I didn't see him."

"That's the idea."

Her voice had a friendly, teasing tone.

"And you followed me around all day?"

"All day."

"On the motorcycle?"

"On the motorcycle. When I was sure you were headed back to Il Fornaio, I raced ahead, to get back there before you."

"So you must have seen the car that tried to get off when I did at Mesmer? A big sedan?"

"Yes. It almost caused an accident trying to get off, but it was too late and had to keep going."

"And?"

"And what? I stayed with you."

"You didn't see them again? Didn't they try to get off at the next exit and come back?"

"Maybe, I don't know. I stayed with you," she said, annoyed.

Swell.

"You don't have any idea who they were?" I asked, a tone in my voice that annoyed her further.

"No. I wasn't checking ID's. I was there to cover you, not them."

She gave me a look, made sure I noticed it, then looked out the passenger window avoiding me. Asshole would have been a fair translation. She was quiet for a while, but she was stewing. It came to a boil.

"Ya know, Ron's goin' pretty far out on a limb for you - for your brother, anyway -" making the distinction clear, "we all are, and you don't think the service is good enough?! Get a clue! Tate got it right, you're drawing quite a crowd. I noticed you went to the cops. How much help you gettin' from them? I didn't see them savin' your ass last night. Did you?"

She was right, but the hell with her anyway. I didn't ask her to sign on. As a matter of fact, I didn't ask for any of it. The hell with them all.

I got off at National and made my way up Castle Heights to Beverwil and up Beverly Drive again. I should just keep my mouth shut, I thought.

That'll be the day.

"Are you getting paid?" I snarled.

It was a pleasant snarl, but still a snarl.

"By Ron, yes, of course."

"So quit!" I exploded. "Tell him you don't like the work. Tell him whatever you want! I got at least half a dozen guys I never met following me around wanting to do I don't know what and acting nasty and a dead brother I can't bury that maybe didn't kill himself after all and a shitload of assholes falling all over each other trying to screw each other out of more money than I can imagine and a touchy little body guard that climbs in and out of bed like parking cars! You're right - I should be grateful as hell! Thanks! You and Tate saved my ass. Thank you! How's that? Now get the fuck out of here. I don't need the extra aggravation!"

So, I'm not as good a sport as Tina Cox. Sue me. Everybody else is, I thought.

We were at Beverly and Wilshire anyway. It was only a block to Il Fornaio. I pulled to the curb and waited for her to get out.

"You're serious?" she said.

Her tone was a mixture of surprise, a little hurt and a load of contempt. When I didn't say anything, she bolted out the door and slammed it shut. I punched the little Mercedes and peeled the tiniest bit of rubber. I found parking on the all but empty street.

Ron was waiting. He was at a large table and already had coffee, hot cereal, eggs and toast and a sweet roll in front of him.

"Where's Vann?" he asked, a mouth full of everything.

"She decided to walk part of the way," I said as I sat.

He looked at me, waited for more, then shrugged his face and went back to his breakfast. The waiter came to the table for my order.

"De-caf Latte and the seven grain toast."

Ron finished what he had in his mouth. He looked past me towards the door. Vann had come in and taken a small table for herself near the front. The waiter had come and gone with her order. Ron shot me another look.

"What's goin' on?" Puzzled. Then a little stern. "I told you, she's my girl. You two got a problem?"

"A failure to communicate, as they say."

"Well, we ain't got the luxury just now."

He waved her over. She pouted but came. She steered clear of me and sat on Ron's side of the table.

"This asshole kicks me outta the car and makes me walk the last block! I quit!" she fumed.

Ron gave me an injured saddened look. I was in this ass-over-eyebrows, lost in a tangled thicket and I was antagonizing the only help I had. And not just any help, but his girl, whatever that meant.

"Let's sort that out later. Either of you interested in what your friends from last night had to say?"

I let my thoughts of Ron's girl Vann and our failure to communicate fade away and gave Ron my undivided attention.

"The guy in the sweat suit?" I asked.

"No," Ron smiled, "his pal. The sweat suit was pretty tough," he said admiringly. "I thought he'd be, but I was pretty sure the other guy would spill whatever he had when we got through a coupla fingers on his pal."

The waiter brought my toast and Latte and Vann's croissant, grape-fruit juice and fruit bowl.

When the waiter had gone, Vann smiled a grim slightly nasty smile. "How many?"

I had visions of her wishing it had been me.

"Three." Ron made a face, winced a little, at the recollection. A regrettable part of his business. "They work for a guy that works for a guy. You know the game," he said to Vann, "to put some distance between the hands-on guys and the guys pulling the strings."

"So did you find out who's pulling the strings on these two or not?"

Vann gave me the look again, the one from the car, the one that said what an ingrate I was, then passed it to Ron, a see-what-I-mean kinda look.

"Yes and no," Ron said.

Swell.

"How 'bout telling me the yes part," I suggested.

They exchanged a look. Ron was silent a moment giving me a chance to reconsider my position. My attitude. "Why you so testy?" he said, "I know you got too much on your mind and today's gonna be rough, but ease up a bit. Okay? We're on your side."

Vann's eyes were saying, like hell, you've got my resignation.

I settled myself down. "Okay," I said.

His impressive size and muscularity played only a small part in my change of attitude. He was right. I had other things on my mind and was avoiding them by pissing on him and Vann. A smirk played across Vann's lips.

"Do you know someone named Salio?" he asked me.

"No. What's the connection?"

"After the first finger, you know, the one you were there for? Just after you left, the junior partner's getting worried, tells the sweat suit guy to tell us what we want to know. He figures if we get to ten he's next in line for the finger bending. He got really panicked after the second finger - was yelling at the other guy to talk, hopin' not to do it himself- maybe he won't look so bad with this Salio guy that's in charge. But after the third finger he's had enough!"

Ron looked at Vann, one professional to another, for an appreciation of the irony.

"I told you they weren't very good!" she said to me.

I was wondering how many of her fingers it would take. Me, just the threat would do.

"And the connection? Salio?" I repeated, thinking the name sounded familiar.

"Salio's sort of a sub-contractor, but the guy who talked said he thought the guy Salio was working for was in the movie business somehow."

"Christ, who isn't!?" I groaned. "That's like being in the ocean and talking about who's wet."

Vann had half a look heading my way. I shrugged. "I retract that," I smiled at her. She stuck her tongue out at me, playfully. Maybe.

"Yeah," Ron said, "but in the makin' end of it, at a studio or somethin'. This Salio tells them they're supposed to scare you off 'bout some lawsuit your brother had goin' - now you're involved in - hurt you just enough this time to make it real clear you're doin' the wrong thing. Let you know it'd get worse if you didn't leave it alone."

Millennium! Salio was the silent guy at the meeting with Marty and the others at Millennium that Ronnie Hook mentioned. I told Ron I did know the name and from where. But how did they get wind of it so soon? Who'd have rushed to tell them? And why?

Weiselman!

That snivelling worm, it had to be him. Dealing information to Malovitch to cut a better deal for himself there; and with Millennium out of fear of Faustini and Perry? Seemed likely.

He said, "There's more."

I waited. He was giving me time to prepare for something.

"What?" I asked.

He took a deep breath. "They were on your brother too." He looked unblinkingly at me trying to decide if it were a good idea to tell me.

"What?" The rising sense of alarm, the familiar mix of apprehension and anger and grief again tightened my throat, made me feel I was strangling. I wanted to let it out, roar so loud and powerfully the jungle would fall silent, the other animals would stop in their tracks, afraid to move in any direction, and the animals tearing at Marty's flesh would stop, would leave off and run while they could. "Did they kill him?"

"No," Ron said, "and I believe them."

"Why?"

"The guy says they were supposed to - that they'd followed him, kept track of him for a couple of weeks when all of a sudden Salio tells them to take care of it, force him off a cliff along the Pacific Coast Highway. Says he goes out there in some old car now and then. If that don't happen, get him at home and make it look like a break-in. It's a rich neighborhood - shouldn't be too hard."

Christ, Marty! Good God! The pressure in my chest was unbearable. Tears came, but the roar was stuck in my throat, choking me. I could hardly breathe. Poor Marty, poor poor Marty. I couldn't look at Vann, and as much as I wanted to I couldn't look away from Ron. I think he wanted to reach out, pat my hand or something, but he didn't. He just waited for me.

"They swear he was dead when they got there," Ron said.

"And you believe him?"

I thought Ron would cry. His face clouded up and he bit his lip to stop it from trembling. "I didn't want to. I wanted to believe those punks - they did it. I had em' right there and I wanted them to be the ones. I broke one of his fingers to make sure." His eyes were wet too. "Those punks were gonna do it," he said, "they were just too late, that's all." Tears ran down his face now. He wiped them away, he shook his head. "They weren't the ones."

The waiter came back to re-fill coffees and Vann waved him off.

"So where does that leave us?" Vann said.

"What us? You quit, remember? Nobody's re-hired you yet."

She smiled and reached across the table and squeezed my hand. She took one of Ron's too.

"I've retracted my resignation," she said picking up her croissant and taking a bite.

Ron shrugged. "It means the guys at Millennium decided your brother had to go. It means they want you to understand you shouldn't fuck with them."

"It also means there's someone else out there who feels the same way and got there first," Vann said.

I didn't give them much detail, but I let them know that the gist of what I'd learned last night going through Marty's DBS files was that DBS had a huge stake in getting rid of Marty. And maybe me.

"The clowns that were on you Friday night were Wolf's - Tate is sure of it. So if the guys we got now..."

"You still have them?"

"I'll get to that," Ron said, "but we know they're with Salio and you think that means Millennium and this Perry guy."

"If they're with Salio, they're with Faustini and Perry, and from what I've heard, no one would dare do anything without Perry's approval."

"So that leaves the guys from in front of Sandy's on what? Thursday night?"

"Right, Thursday ."

"Busy week," Vann said.

"You think Mr. Malovitch had anything to be worried about concernin' you? So quick after you got to town?"

"He's got a way with people," Vann suggested.

Ron frowned at her. She smiled at me. Pals.

I thought about it. I wanted to think about it alone for a while.

"It's a good question." I said, "I've got to make a call. I'll be back in a minute. Why don't you guys finish eating."

I went past a dozen empty tables back to an alcove on the right with bathrooms and a pay phone. It was 7:45 and I figured Sara would already be at my dad's. Helping him get it together for today. But on impulse, I called Jason instead. His mother answered. She got it on the first ring.

"Hi, it's me," I said.

"How are you?"

"Okay. Is Jason up?"

"He's right here. Kurt, I'm so sorry. Are you okay?"

"Yes," I said, thinking, no or barely. A good woman. Sara was probably right. She put him on.

"Dad? Are you okay?"

"Hi." It was good to hear his voice. I could picture him. His sweet sweet face troubled by what he couldn't understand. Not that I could.

"I miss you," I told him.

"Can I come to the funeral?"

"I don't think so."

"Please? I want to be with you."

"I'd like to have you here - it helps to know you want to come. But there's just so much going on."

"I love you," he said. He started to cry.

"I love you too," I said and we hung up.

Sara got it on the second ring.

"It's me," I said. "How's dad?"

"Not good - still listless, like he's drugged."

"Has he taken anything?"

"Not that I know of."

"Keep an eye on him. You know how he likes to prescribe for himself from his stash of old prescriptions."

My dad the hypochondriac apothecary.

"I will, only I think he really could use something."

"Let's wait a few days, see how he's acting."

"He's so depressed."

"What do you expect?" I regretted the tone. "Look," I said evenly, "depression is appropriate now. If he doesn't improve at all in the next week or so, we can take him to a doctor."

"Okay."

"Is Nick there?"

"Not yet."

"You know that stuff I brought there yesterday? The stuff Nick helped me carry upstairs?"

"What about it?"

"In one box there's a bunch of papers rubber banded together - Diamond, Bernstein and Silver partnership stuff. When he gets there would you ask him to get it and bring it with you when you guys come into Beverly Hills this morning."

"They already got it."

"What are you talking about?"

"The men you sent got it last night. Dad gave it to them."

"WHAT ARE YOU TALKING ABOUT!! I DIDN'T SEND ANY-ONE!!" No no no! Please no.

"Do you want to talk to dad?"

"No, no, just tell me what happened. What men-what did they say?"

"Two men woke him up about nine-thirty and said you'd sent them for the boxes."

"How could he be so stupid!?"

"Kurt! He's confused. He thought...they told him it was important for you!"

"And he let them take them?!"

"He thought it was for you. How else would they know the boxes were here? What's going on? You didn't send them?"

"No, I didn't send them." Malovitch did. I had a sick feeling in my stomach. "Don't worry about it. I'll take care of it." Right.

"Where are you?"

"Across the street from the Bronx Deli, at Il Fornaio."

"How come?"

"I'm meeting with some people."

"What people?"

Jeez. "Just some people. I'll see you guys at 10:00." A small glimmer of hope flashed. "Did they take all of the boxes or just the one with the rubber-banded stuff?"

"All of them."

Shit. What a nightmare.

"I'll see you at 10:00."

We hung up.

I had to focus. What did Malovitch know or need to know about me or what I was doing as early as Thursday night? I'd just met him that afternoon and he wants to get together to finalize his and Marty's agreement. I'd start backwards. By the end of our meeting yesterday morning he could be sure Weiselman's information that I didn't have a thing was accurate, assuming Weiselman was the pipeline to Malovitch, and I thought that was a virtual certainty; no proof, no documents, no notes from Marty, no signed notes from their meeting. But I'd let him know I at least knew about the International Distributors' money, the 16% partnership stake and had an inkling DBS owed GMW more than the $297,000 they were withholding. He'd know that information could only come from a few people. The most likely being Ronnie Hook or Tina Cox. So if Weiselman reports I was standing in the street talking to

Tina, maybe Malovitch wastes no time and has someone following me from the time I leave Seascape. Trying to keep tabs on me to make sure I don't get any information that might make me reluctant or unwilling to sign the agreement he says was all but signed by Marty. Or if it looks like I might have come across information like that, make sure he's aware of it before we meet. Where'd I go? To Groman's; to see John Goodman at the Bradbury Building; to the beach. To Marty's office at 81436 Ocean. If they'd followed me there, Malovitch might've had to assume I'd gotten something. And after that, Sandy's and Tina. Our walk on the beach. If Malovitch was worried I might've found something in Marty's office at home or at GMW, and met with Tina Cox for the second time that day maybe to confirm it or get filled in on some details, he might've had the two clowns try and run me down in the parking lot. A crude preemptive strike. He wouldn't have known until Friday after the meeting at GMW and my confrontation with Weiselman that I didn't have the second DBS file on separation matters. Assuming Weiselman had Marty's copy of Elaine's initialled memo on International Distributors, Malovitch knows I don't. And even if Weiselman doesn't, my asking him for it made it clear I didn't, so Malovitch would know that. So by Friday, Malovitch would know I didn't have anything that could hurt him. He can call off his dogs. But by Friday night Wolf's not so fond of me and his guys are following me around. Until Tate does whatever Tate did to make them go away. Since it was Malovitch's guys the night before, Ron was right thinking the guys Tate scattered weren't the same ones and didn't know I was probably heading for Sandy's. By Saturday morning, Malovitch was sure enough of his position to try to shove his bullshit agreement down my throat. Until I play the wise guy with my workman's lien plan, and set him off again. So maybe he cranks up his two guys and has them follow me around Saturday after I leave his office. I went to Seascape, cleaned out Marty's office, gave Thorne a crude manicure, then went to my dad's. No. I went to see Krasznik! And the car that missed the off ramp was Malovitch's guys! They must have taken the next off-ramp and come back and followed me to my dad's, seen me and Nick take the boxes up. Maybe they followed me to the West LAPD. If they reported that to Malovitch, maybe he thought I had some idea he'd had me followed. That I'd gone to the cops. No! That I'd found something in Marty's home office that I wanted to hide at my dad's before going to the cops about it. So I go to the cops, then back to Il Fornaio then back to the beach. Whatever I'm up to, Malovitch doesn't like the look of it. And if I go to the trouble to stash it at my dad's, he wants it. Never mind that I didn't get into Marty's coded file until last night at GMW. Didn't read the stuff 'til 2 this morning. Didn't find out what a sleazy bucket of scum he is, at least not for sure, until then. He doesn't know that. He knows I'm threatening him about a workman's lien, for whatever that's worth, and he knows I've taken papers to my dad's then go to the cops. That's enough for him. His guys tell my poor grief-stricken and confused dad he can help his son by giving them the papers I'd stored there. So he does. Malovitch may not have gotten much for his trouble, but he got everything I had. As far as he knows.

All he really had that I needed was proof of the exception to the 60/40 rule, and the documentation of Marty's 16% partnership stake.

What I had that he didn't know I had was all of Marty's files, calculations, and estimates based on the 16% and the exception to 60/40 rule! If not proof, it would surely be enough for Winters to get a court order for DBS to produce undoctored partnership information.

I thought about that stupid monitor in the copy room at GMW. As soon as Wolf realized I'd copied those papers, I'd have his guys on my ass again. And worse yet, if Weiselman found out I'd copied Marty's coded files, Malovitch would know, and he'd know what he had from my dad's wouldn't begin to protect him from what I now had. Actually, as soon as he went through it, he'd know it wasn't anything for me to have gone to the cops about, which might already be bothering him.

Another unhappy thought hit me. If he was willing to have his guys run me down on Thursday night before he knew for sure from Weiselman I didn't know anything, knowing I'd gone to the cops about something, and obviously not something in the papers I'd stashed at my dad's, he'd have to believe I knew something else, something more important, more incriminating or dangerous to him. Worth going to the cops about. Like him having Marty killed. Making it look like a suicide. Not taking a thing. No break-in, no burglary, like the Millennium guys had planned. Just a man with business problems ending his life. What would he think I had or knew about that would tie him to Marty's death and send me to the cops?

My head was spinning. Ron had asked the right question: "You think Mr. Malovitch had anything to be worried about concernin' you that quick after you got to town?" If he had Marty killed, sure he did. That I might find out. And as soon as I went to the cops he had to figure he now had more to worry about than the $6 million he had killed Marty for. But what did I know? What did he think I knew that would make me think he killed Marty? He'd been in control until I raised the possibility of a workman's lien. Then he'd lost it. No, that was only part of it. He'd lost it when I'd gotten cute and told him he'd be frozen out of the International Distributors' escrow account! That's what set him off. What if he thought I'd come across the co-release agreement? I winked at him. Like I knew I had him cold. I didn't know it then, but it had to be on his mind, and I get cute and wink at him, telling him not to start spending that money just yet. It's a wonder he didn't shoot me on the spot. Since I went to the cops, he probably wished he had. Which made my immediate future cloudy. Another thing bothered me. Why would Weiselman be tipping off Malovitch that I was talking to Tina Cox at Seascape on Thursday? Why was I assuming Weiselman? Malovitch might have seen me himself. He was there and at that point I didn't know who he was, so if he had, I wouldn't have been aware of it. That could have been what set him in motion. But somehow it didn't feel right. The way Malovitch acted when I met him, untroubled, in control, Marty's good friend devastated by the news, reluctant to bring it up but nevertheless anxious to get the separation agreement signed, all indicated someone unconcerned and unaware of any problem I might pose. I was sure I'd met him after I'd talked to Tina in the street. After his performance yesterday morning I knew, when riled, his control ebbs fast. I didn't believe he was a good enough actor to stand there with his wife offering condolences and trying to set up a meeting, if he were agitated about me and Tina talking, and simultaneously making plans to have guys follow me around, maybe run me down. That brought me back to Weiselman. He had to have been involved with Malovitch before I showed up. Before Marty died. Maybe he'd been busy working against Marty for a long time. I wondered if Marty had known or suspected. Something was gnawing away at the back of my consciousness, something from the files last night. I couldn't place it, but I knew it was relevant, knew it was in the files. I'd try to take another look sometime before the service.

Oh no! I'd left the little briefcase in the car! What an idiot! That's all I needed! I ran back through the restaurant.

"Be right back!" I said to Vann and Ron as I went past them.

I was out of breath when I rejoined them. I had the little briefcase and put it on the floor at my feet. It was safe. I wasn't going to let it out of my sight again. I wondered what I could do with it during the service?

They were nearly finished eating. My coffee was cold and I motioned the waiter for a warm up. Vann had been eyeing me, and when he'd gone she asked,

"What's with you? You look a little off."

"You mean, more than usual?"

I filled them in on the possibilities I'd been entertaining. Maybe entertaining was a poor choice of words. In any case, Ron took it seriously.

"I want Vann to stay close to you," he decided.

I was going to give her a little lascivious look, but things were too ugly, too threatening, and like she said, I was a little off. Then again, if life goes on, life goes on. I leered at her. She smiled. If I lived through Marty's funeral, my future might be looking up.

"I want her with you at the service. Like she's a friend of yours - you're the brother ain't married now, are you?"

The way he'd asked it, yes and no seemed appropriate, but I knew what he meant so I didn't play with it.

"No, I'm not."

"Got a girlfriend joinin' you at the service?"

It seemed like another lifetime. Vann surveyed my hesitation. Seemed relieved when I answered.

"Not really."

"Then let's have Vann join you - as a friend."

He looked at Vann first, and she nodded agreement. Then me.

"Fine," I said.

"I'm gonna cover you long - me or Tate - Vann up close. If Mr. Malovitch," I loved his use of Mister for Malovitch, whom I now thought likely may have killed Marty, and may be trying for me, but to Ron, who'd been doing janitorial work at the Wells Fargo Building and seen the guys in the Armani suits from DBS coming and going, it was going to be Mister Malovitch for all time, "or anyone poses a threat, Vann'll be there to stick 'im. From now on if we see someone's on you, we'll do more than keep tabs or scare 'em off."

That reminded me of the two guys from last night. I asked Ron what he'd done with them. Where were they now?

"Bud's at Vann's with 'em - a kinda detention," he smiled. "Question is, what to do with them?"

"What about the cop he saw?" Vann asked. "Phillips?"

Ron said, "He's a good cop. Takes his job serious. Whatdja'all talk about?"

I told them about Thorne. The gun. Vann got a kick out of that. She'd seen it but didn't know what was going on. About my suggesting to Phillips maybe it wasn't suicide.

"He take any interest in it?"

"Not much. You wanna turn those guys over to him?"

"We gotta do something with 'em, and we don't want 'em back on the street."

"What about their fingers? After Thorne, he's gonna assume I had - you should pardon the expressionn - a hand in it. Even if he doesn't, you don't need the hassle either."

"Tell him somethin's goin' around, like the flu," Vann said through a sip of coffee.

I thought about it for a minute, then said, "Can you keep them a little longer while I look into something?"

"How much longer?"

"A day or two? Three tops?"

He and Vann looked at each other. Maybe kidnapping charges on their minds. Ron apparently decided that the difference between one day and four was academic.

"Yeah," he said, "but three days tops, right?"

"Right," I said.

Vann was shaking her head, like, who needs this?

It was 8:20 when we left Il Fornaio. On the way out I reminded Ron that Wolf was aware of Il Fornaio as a hang-out for me and had told his guys to watch here or look for me at the service. I assumed Malovitch's guys were back on the job now too, particularly if he'd decided nothing in the papers from my dad's were interesting enough to send me to the cops yesterday. Tate was right. I was drawing a crowd, and today looked like the day they'd all converge. At least the guys from Millennium were accounted for. I was assuming no one had missed them yet and sent out replacements.

"Where you headed now?" he asked.

"To the beach. It's important that no one know I've gone there. If someone's following..."

"Don't worry," he said, "I'll take care of it."

I checked my pocket watch. "I think there's time to get out there and back before I meet with my family at ten."

"Where?"

"Across the street - the Bronx Deli."

"That's sorta funny," Ron said.

"What?"

"I read where Garvin Perry owns it."

" Swell. Maybe I better have Vann taste the food for me."

Chapter 24

The traffic was practically non-existent and we got to The Beach Club at 8:45. On the way, Vann told me her father had been killed in Viet Nam when she was ten. He was being evacuated for treatment of wounds when the helicopter was shot down. Ron had been in the same company, the same platoon. They were close, looked out for each other. Ron'd been looking out for her ever since. He'd taught her all kinds of martial arts stuff as a teenager, and when Marty helped set him up in his security business, she was just getting out of Santa Monica City College. Ron wanted her to work with him, had it in mind to have her run the office, but she decided to take it a couple of steps further and got a PI License. It gave her a lot more latitude, and she liked that. She could do body-guard work for some of Ron's clients when they needed it. Things like that. Ron didn't like it at first, but he knew she was good and could take care of herself.

I pulled through the gate into the court yard, stopping at the booth to show the attendant my card. I pulled into the parking area at the south end of courtyard. We locked up the little Mercedes and walked around the end of the front row of garages to the row behind. I had the briefcase with me.

"I want to show you something," I told Vann.

I didn't think I had to tell her any of the history of why Marty had the car, why it was important to him, just show her how lovingly he'd re-stored and kept it. It seemed important that she have a sense of him. I told her we'd grown up broke in Beverly Hills. That I used to sneak in here. That he didn't. Wouldn't. I opened #26. It took her breath away. She saw it, turned to smile at me, then ran her hand over the smooth sensuous fender to the top edge of the door, gave me a look to see if it were okay to get in. I nodded. Behind the wheel she seemed trans-ported. She ran her hand across the burl-wood dash.

I was pleased. "Take a look in the glove box. Under the envelope."

She found the photo. Stared at it quite a while.

"We better get going. I gotta look for something."

She put it back.

As we crossed the lobby Eric saw me from his office. A warm smile spread over his face, and he came out to greet me.

"How nice to see you so soon," he said, "can I help you in any way?"

"I need to check my brother's closet."

"Well, you know where it is. If there's anything I can do, I'll be here."

"Thank you."

I told Vann what we were looking for and she helped me, drawer by drawer, suit pocket by pocket, shoe by shoe.

She found a manila envelope taped to the underside of one of the drawers.

"Is this it?" she smiled proudly.

I had this funny feeling about the fact that, one, I would never have thought to look there, and two, that she had, and three, Marty had thought to put it there. He must have had a pretty clear picture of his predicament. I took the envelope from her and opened it.

Jackpot!

Not only was the co-release agreement there, so too was Marty's copy of the DBS memo about International Distributors.

I found Eric and asked to use his copy machine. I copied the memo, the co-release agreement, and half a dozen pages of Marty's DBS Settlement files from the little briefcase. Enough to put Malovitch in one kind of box or another. When I'd finished I asked if they had a safe. They did, and I had Eric put the envelope and the little briefcase in it. No one was to have access to it, with one exception. I wrote down the name of Bob Winters. Just in case.

"You seen Ron?" I asked Vann as we parked once again on Beverly Drive.

It was 10:05.

"Not since we left here," she smiled, "but I wouldn't have expected to."

"Maybe he just pretends to follow. Maybe he's having a beer."

"Not likely," she scoffed.

We went into the Bronx. It looked liked what I imagined a New York Deli, a big one, would look like. The floor was tiled with small off-white tiles, bordered by small black ones with occasional decorative accent patterns in the middle. Booths were separated for privacy by shoulder high wooden walls with beveled and frosted glass panels at the tops. The place had the look and feel of 1910 New York City. Rich. Maybe I'd stiff Garvin Perry for the tab.

Nick and Sara and my dad were in a booth in the back. I introduced
Vann. My dad's skin was grey. His eyes were without luster. He'd always taken pride and pleasure in a shower, a close shave, some after-
shave, and being well decked-out. Today, he'd gone through the motions, but there was nothing behind it. He was an empty shell. Nick and
Sara were subdued. They ordered breakfast for themselves and my dad.
Vann and I had coffee. We talked about the service this afternoon, about
going to the Seascape house afterwards, about anything and nothing.

Nick didn't miss Vann's watchfulness.

"I need a cigarette," he said after a while, "let's go outside."

Vann gave me a sort of helpless look. It would be awkward if she
came, dereliction if she didn't. I smiled at her. I understood. Don't
worry. It'll be okay, I tried to tell her with my eyes.

"Finish your coffee," I told her, "we won't be long."

"Who is she?" Nick asked without preamble when we were out on
the sidewalk. He lit up, blew the smoke up and away.

"Just a friend," I said.

"I told you, you're not in this alone. She's a cop or something. Right?
I know the look, the posture. The watchfulness. What's going on?"

What purpose would it serve to tell him? There wasn't anything he
could do. Why worry or involve him? Why confuse the issue of Marty's
death with suppositions of murder?

"Just a friend," I repeated.

His lips tightened on the cigarette. His whole body tightened. His
feelings were hurt. He'd turned away from me slightly, and when he
turned back, his face was drawn and his eyes were red and wet.

"I became a lawyer because he was a lawyer. He was too much older
to really be a brother to me, you're my big brother, but he was like a
father. Dad was down the tubes by then, never home, always trying to
get something going. It's Marty I remember. He was always there. He
advised me about scholarships and offered to help if I didn't get one. He
offered to help get me into Stanford Law if I didn't get into Boalt. He
used to call from time to time when I was in law school. Make sure it was
going okay. He made it clear I wasn't alone just because dad couldn't
help - maybe I can help now." He wasn't offering; he was pleading. I
knew the feeling.

Maybe I shouldn't have, but I gave in. I told him everything that'd
happened and what I'd discovered so far. As I heard myself talking, it
sounded preposterous. As unbelievable as his suicide had, which in itself, should have made it all the more plausible. I had to admit it was a
relief telling him. He kept shaking his head, like he was thinking it was
impossible, Marty's world, the people he knew and worked with, couldn't

be like that; or maybe with the thought that I was crazy to get caught up in it, pulling another of what he thought of as my patented hairbrained moves again, like Thorne's fingers; or God-knows-what else he might have been thinking. I wasn't sure exactly how he meant it until I heard him muttering "Miserable bastards, miserable fucking bastards", almost spitting the words, the way we'd both learned to utter that particular turn-of-phrase at our father's knee. More accurately, over it. In any case, I told him how Vann was connected to Ron and Ron to Marty. About DBS, GMW, Millennium, the papers taken from dad's, The Beach Club, the '37 Packard, everything. The '37 Packard brought a bitter-sweet smile from him. He was too young at the time, but he'd heard the stories later.

"Twice, Marty asked me to represent people on criminal charges. Drug charges. Once a client, once an associate. I can't violate client privilege, but you've mentioned both their names. It may figure into this."

"Weiselman," I said, "that's no big mystery. The guy's a mess. He's got a nose habit and it's running his life. He makes what I'd call a ton of money and he's on the ropes."

He smiled.

"Have you met this Sutton guy?" he asked.

"No, not yet."

He smiled.

"Thanks," I said. "I'll see where it goes."

He finished his cigarette and we went back inside.

Sara and Nick were going to take my dad to the Cemetery early. He insisted. He was inconsolable, and restless, and permeating everything else, he had the same sense of religious violation as Krasznik about not burying Marty's body today. I think he wanted a dose of Jewish absolution, in whatever form that might take, in whatever way Krasznik might be able to provide it, against this trespass.

Vann and I both needed a change of clothes for the service. It was 11:30. We had plenty of time, but I had the feeling I'd forgotten to do something urgent.

Chapter 25

All the intrigue and the threats posed by Wolf's guys and Malovitch's and Salio's guys couldn't overshadow or lessen the dread I felt as I drove the little Mercedes into the Hillside Memorial Park Cemetery. Nothing was going to make Marty be alive again, and everything else was just swallowed by that. The Park lawns had the emerald green look generous helpings of nitrogen imparted, and the scores of trees scattered over the rolling hills looked strong and healthy even as they breathed the thick brown air from the nearby 405. It was only 1:35 but from the traffic inside the Cemetery, I had the feeling we were late. There must've been two hundred cars there. Five or six hundred people in the process of leaving cars, and entering the Service Chapel.

"It's a good thing we've got reserved seats," I said out loud without thinking.

Vann gave me one of those searching, disbelieving looks I'd been getting used to from Tina Cox that kept making me wish Nick were with me, but then after a moment laughed in spite of herself.

"That's terrible!" she said still smiling.

But at the same time put her hand on the back of my neck and pulled me to her a little and kissed my cheek.

"You okay?" she asked.

"So far," I told her.

Parking wasn't a problem. There wasn't any. She looked at me like we had a problem. I was thinking maybe we could just leave. Skip the whole fucking thing. I almost said it, but thought why press my luck? Where's Nick when I need him?

"What?" she said.

I told her, but it wasn't as funny as it would have been with Nick. In fact it brought tears to my eyes. Something did. She took my hand and held it in both of hers. Nick could hold off a while.

I snaked though the everywhere double and triple-parked cars and made my way to the back of the chapel just as a flower van was pulling out. The space was reserved for the Rabbi, but I figured if he weren't here already, parking was the least of his problems. I pulled in. We were

ten feet from the back door to the hallway that lead to Krasznik's office
and the Family Anteroom.

Vann and I went in through the back door. The scene was chaotic.
And noisy. Much too noisy. My dad and his brothers Edward and Bernie
stood clustered together just inside the door to the Family Room, black
paper yarmulkes bobby-pinned to the back of their heads. Nick and
Sara and Marty's daughters, Maia and Eli, and their mother Ellen, were
in the hallway where Roberta stood between them and the door to the
Family Room like Cerberus at the Gate. Roberta had her hands on her
hips and was hissing something at Ellen. I didn't have to get any closer
to hear her, but I approached anyway. I was in the neighborhood.
"You're not immediate family. This is for immediate family." Roberta's
voice could have scratched glass.
"She's the girls' mother," Sara argued, trying to keep her voice under
control. "They want her with them."
"There's no room!" Roberta persisted.
Nick stood back from the scene a couple of feet. From his expression,
he wished it were a couple of miles. Roberta's daughter, Lucy, thirteen,
huddled close to him and his daughter Martha, eleven, son Grayson,
eight, and his wife, Kayla. Sara's eight year old daughter, Grace, leaned
against the wall, arms folded across her chest, eyes blazing. Her father,
Jim, next to her. Eli and Maia were both crying, Ellen's arms over their
shoulders trying to comfort them. My dad and his brothers and their
two wives wanted no part of it, staying within the protecting confines of
the disputed territory, maybe fearing their seats weren't safe either.
Vann gave me an uncertain look. I told her to find a seat out front.
She didn't want to leave me, but could see it wasn't practical to insist on
staying at my side. Although I was beginning to like her there.
"What's the problem?" I asked Sara.
"There's usually twelve chairs in there. They've stretched it to eighteen for us, but we've got nineteen all of a sudden." She made a face as
she said it, telling me the nineteenth was someone far more questionable
as immediate family than the girls' mother.
In a test of her new widowhood status, Roberta's voice dropped to a
piteous plaintive wail, "My husband is dead! I need him with me! I need
him!" It was unclear to me if she were talking about Marty's absence or
filling the non-existent nineteenth chair with the mystery guest. She
resolved that when she sneered, "The problem is her!" She pointed a
long well manicured and finely painted fingernail at Ellen.
It was 1:55 and I for one didn't want to be involved in this tawdry
display when Krasznik emerged from his office. I was in enough trouble
with him already. Ellen hugged the girls.
"You'll be alright. I'll sit down front, close. You'll be able to see me
through the curtain."

"Noooo!" Eli wailed, no longer a teenager, but now like a kid being dropped off at child care for the first time, "Noooo!"

Maia looked too stunned and numbed to make a sound. And pale. I thought she was on the verge of fainting.

"Who?" I asked.

On cue, from the large doors further down the hall that led to the main Chapel room, Bob Thorne approached.

Nick, lips compressed into a thin line, corners down-turned, raised his brows about four notches, making his eyes go wide and tipped his head in Thorne's direction. I was dumbfounded.

"Thorne?" I said to no one in particular. "You're kidding!"

I looked at Sara and she made it clear they weren't. I took a couple of steps in his direction to intercept him before he got to our little gathering. I had to make this quick. Krasznik would be out here any minute. Unless he was looking for parking. Thorne stopped in his tracks when he saw me. He had on these huge gloves like you see on defensive linemen, small pillows really, and his eyes went wide. I liked to think his fingers began to throb and ache a little more at the sight of me. When I'd gotten close enough to him to where I thought I could whisper, he sort of backed away, retreating, so that I had to go forward again and felt like I were chasing him in slow motion back down the hall to the main Chapel room. Whatever works, as they say. Finally, at the two large doors, he stopped. Here he'd make his stand.

"Keep away from me," he growled.

"We've got a little problem," I began.

I had my arms out, hands palms up, in a gesture of openness and conciliation. Supplication, really. He took it all wrong.

"Keep back!" he shouted. "You're the only problem around here."

"Take it easy," I said, approaching him the way a dog catcher might a skittish stray.

He started to raise his hands in a defensive, reflexive gesture, but they'd been there, done that, and once was enough. I finally got close enough to whisper.

"Bob, there're only eighteen chairs and it's either you or the girl's mother. I'd appreciate it if you'd help calm Roberta down - tell her you'll be glad to sit out front; that it'd be a good thing for the girls to have their mother with them."

"Roberta's all alone," he said.

I looked over my shoulder. "Lucy's with her."

"Not the same thing."

Ever the lawyer.

Krasznik's secretary came out of his office door. He wouldn't be far behind. It might only be a matter of seconds. My pulse rate surged. If I were going to have legal problems, I'd choose Thorne over Krasznik any day.

"You got ten toes, you slimy fuck, how'd you like to be wearing fluffy pink slippers the next few weeks?" I hissed at him. I eased up and added, "Please." This time, it seemed to make all the difference.

"Okay, okay," his eyes and voice still defiant, but his toes signing the unconditional surrender.

Just then Krasznik came through his office door into the hallway, filling what space was left.

"What's this!" His voice came like distant rolling thunder, but I could tell it wouldn't be long before lightening bolts were flying my way. "You should all be seated! We're ready to begin!"

He swept into the Family Room and embraced my dad. He seemed to transfer energy and strength to him. He said a few words. My dad nodded, looking directly into Krasznik's huge presence and finding comfort there. Krasznik shot the rest of us a look like late-comers to a play, about to squeeze past to their seats. We filed in. Roberta stayed behind to confer with Thorne. Krasznik passed through the curtain to the podium, looking back, aware Roberta wasn't seated yet. I could hear her angry tone, but not the exact stream of words washing over Thorne. Krasznik gave me that look of his. I was the oldest brother. This was my responsibility. Take care of it! I went back into the hallway.

"Roberta, the Rabbi's waiting!" I said.

So too was Lucy, standing there wanting to go in and sit down, wanting her mother to stop making a scene, wanting to be someplace and maybe someone else. It was not a good day for her. Marty married Roberta when Lucy was six. They were close from what Sara told me. Sara said she was a good kid; loyal, tough, but kept it all in. It was taking a toll today.

Thorne tried to gentle Roberta, soothe her. It didn't work. She pulled back from him abruptly, her expression like he'd told a dirty joke. He went back down the hallway. Roberta and Lucy went into the Family Room and sat down.

Krasznik invited first Maia, then Eli to speak. With composure and grace and intelligence they did. I was proud of them and amazed. I couldn't have done it. I couldn't have uttered a word. Krasznik had escorted each of them back to their seats in the Family Room, and each time he gave me one of his terror-inducing looks, telling me with his eyes, I must speak. I stood toe to toe with God, and shook my head no. My failures in his eyes knew no bounds. If he didn't understand and forgive me, I hoped that at least Marty did.

Krasznik began slowly, in his folksy way. Then building, saving the thunder and lightening bolts for later.

"This was a good man," he said, "not a saint, not even a very good Jew." He looked out past the podium to the overflowing crowd of high-livers and sharp dressers and said, "Like most of you, I fear. But I've talked to you, his family, his brothers and sister, his father, his wife - both

of them." He paused, looking over his little half-glasses, to let his disap-
proval sink in. I could feel the collective squirm of the multi-married in
the audience, which covered most of them, I thought. "And you've heard
from his daughters," he looked through the curtain at us in the Family
Room, then back to the gathering, "two children that alone would make
a life worthwhile. I know this man." He looked at the closed empty
casket, helping perpetrate the small fraud, Marty missing his own funeral, due, of course, to circumstances beyond his control. But not mine,
Krasznik's slow deliberate look in my direction reminded me. "I married him. I presided at the marriage of his sister and the burial of his
mother, ceremonies that lifted and dashed his spirit in equal measure." I
was mentally putting his marriage to Roberta into the second column.
"I know how much this man cared about his family and how much he
meant to them. But what has surprised me - no - what has AMAZED
ME, were the calls I've had in the last two days from a HUNDRED
maybe TWO HUNDRED of you that knew him as a friend. A ROCK!
His brother told me he was a rock. I listened. He said a rock. I thought
'A good man'. Then a caller, then another, and so many said, he was a
rock! You could count on him. He was always there. You didn't have to
ask. He knew. HE cared enough to ask, to find out. And he helped.
Because he could, he took it as his duty, and he took pride and pleasure
in that duty. His hand was touched by God's hand, and he reached out
with it and found a way to touch all of you. That's why you are here. You
have lost from your lives the hand that God touched and the loss is OVER-
WHELMING." Krasznik's voice was thundering now, his eyes flashing, his big hands gripping the sides of the podium like he would lift it
and hurl it into the audience, Moses with the Tablets, "It is supposed to
be! You are supposed to know what you have lost! It is supposed to hurt!
You have cried over the phone, mourning your loss, telling me it is too
much to bear, but I've told you and tell now again, THIS IS GOD'S
LOSS, this man is God's loss more than yours. God touched him and
gave him this deep warmth and caring nature and now, unaccountably,
he is gone from our midst, and we have no answer. Only God can give
and give and give without end. No man can be a ROCK! The brother
likened him to a rock in a stream, a resting place for those too tired to
swim on, a resting place to regain strength, before finishing the journey,
a rock that itself resisted the rushing waters, until it could resist no more
and gave way. He was no rock! He was a man! He was a good man, but
he learned what we must all learn. God is the rock! God is the resting
place! Without God, the rushing waters claim us all! Where was Marty's
rock? Who could he turn to? Who amongst you could he turn to? Was
it a surprise he could find no rock amongst you? There are none! There
are six hundred of you gathered here who know you have lost a fine man,
a man who was a rock for you." His voice still filled with thunder.

The room held three hundred, but was overflowing out large double
doors on both sides and in the back, easily making six hundred possible.

I was thinking we could get it down into the mid-five hundreds if we got rid of anyone possibly linked to his murder.

His voice grew soft. "But you were not his rock. You couldn't be. There is no shame. God is the only rock. Did Marty seek him at the end? That is between Marty and God now." He was quiet. He stood motionless long enough for the crowd to approach restlessness. His searing eyes scanning the room put an end to any would-be rebellion. Then he bellowed at them, us, "YOU DON'T HAVE FOREVER! DO YOU THINK YOU HAVE FOREVER!?? YOU MUST FIND THE ONE TRUE ROCK! THAT IS MARTY GOLDMAN'S FINAL MESSAGE TO YOU! FIND THE ONE TRUE ROCK!" Then quietly again, but panting from his efforts, "You must find the one true rock! That is Marty's legacy to you. You must find God and trust in Him. He can bear your weight. He is the rock."

Krasznik came back through the curtains into the Family Room. My dad stood on shaky legs and thanked him. Krasznik shook his hand and then bent his huge frame down to my dad and kissed the top of his head.

"He is in God's hands now. Try to take comfort that he is in God's hands."

Krasznik went past the rest of us like we were road kill.

Wild Bill. Ya gotta love him.

The crowd in the Chapel dispersed through the three double doors into the hot August afternoon, joining the hundreds who couldn't fit inside, milling around on the lawn and front steps. Since there was not going to be a burial, there would be no grave-side service.

Krasznik had gone somewhere, then returned to the Family Room to escort Roberta from the Chapel to formally review the troops on the front steps, to accept condolences. He stood with her and Lucy and Eli and Maia and Bob Thorne and my father, forming a receiving line. I stood off to the side by myself listening. Nick and his kids and wife joined me, then Sara, Grace and Jim. We didn't talk. Just watched.

Tina Cox came out of the Chapel with red wet eyes. She was wearing a dark blue suit like a man's, but definitely tailored for a woman. Her honey blond hair was wound into a French braid that was itself wound like a tail-piece above her collar. She was with Mel Davidson and a woman I assumed was his wife. They made their way to Roberta and the girls and my dad and I presume said the things people say. She shook hands with my dad. He seemed to be in a trance again, but I thought that was good because it seemed to be a protective trance, and he needed all the help and protection he could get. Tina looked up from her handshake with my dad and our eyes met. I tried to will her off without being too obvious. I had a lingering feeling of unease since meeting with Malovitch yesterday. It still seemed inescapable that she'd let Weiselman know I couldn't get into Marty's files. That Malovitch had the information through her if not actually from her. There's a thought. What if she were having dealings with the big M? I looked at her face. Tried to decide if it were capable of that kind of duplicity. Nah! I smiled to myself at my inability to impugn such a face with such a thought. What a sucker I was! Thought of Nick and my dad and the Goldman way with women. What a bunch of suckers! I must have done more than smile to myself, because Tina smiled in return and came over.

"Hi," she said. "How are you?"

"I've been better," I said.

She hesitated a moment, trying to read my eyes. With her this close, with the look and warmth and the smell of her, I'm sure they were sending mixed messages. None saying stay away. She threw her arms around my neck and clung to me. Over her shoulder I saw Nick sort of purse his lip and raise his brows, like, what's this? Past Nick I could see Vann. She'd hung back either out of courtesy to this being a family affair, or to gain a useful perspective, or both. I'd been aware of her taking stock of Tina, not missing a look, a gesture, or a nuance of a gesture. But all that turned in an instant to naked surprise when Tina's arms went around me.

Tina whispered in my ear, "If I don't get a chance to talk to you at the house later, I wanted you to know, I'd like to see you tonight. Call if you can - or just come by - please!" She hugged me a little tighter, then stepped back. She shook hands with Nick and Sara, said how sorry she was, then left.

Then Mel and his wife. Then others. Far too many others. Maybe there's something to the notion of sharing grief to loosen its grip on you, to accept it, then dispel it, and finally begin to get past it. But the tears and condolences, real and fake, the display of it was bread and butter to these movie people, and being around their performance was becoming demeaning. I was aware of grass and trees in the distance. I nodded to Nick and started walking.

Much of what Krasznik had said had struck home, and not just with me. Even if they didn't know much specifically about what was going on, these wealthy, hard charging and hard working lawyers and doctors and accountants, not to mention the actors and directors and producers gathered here like an opening night at the old Grauman's Chinese Theatre, couldn't escape the sense that, there but for the grace of God go I. I could see it in their faces. I could feel it weighing on them, not only in the fragile sense of our existence that Krasznik brought home so unequivocally, but I could see in their faces the realization that if Marty Goldman, the best and brightest, the most sure-footed of them all could come to such an end, how much more precarious were their own little paper-mache worlds? For me, Krasznik's words, and his penetrating looks, twisted the knife that had already cut so deep. I had not been my brothers keeper, not even close, and it hurt. It should. When he needed help, I was there all right, but asking for his, the day after Jerry's drill rig collapsed the embankment. Hurt by being what I thought was brushed off. So intent on my little world, my little problem, I couldn't or wouldn't hear his. I wanted to crawl off and feel sorry for myself. Let my grief overwhelm me and provide escape from the relentless reflections on my failures. And at the same time, from the arrogance of thinking I might have made a difference. Not incompatible, or mutually exclusive, really. It's the trying to make a difference that would have counted, and I hadn't.

I'd gotten about fifty or sixty yards away from the Chapel. I was headed for a group of cypress trees on a grassy knoll. I sat in the shade at the base of one of them and put my head back and closed my eyes. If you let it, the traffic noise from the 405 filled the air. Loud enough to wake the dead. What would Krasznik think if he knew Marty had not taken his own life? If he knew some of these scum sucking pigs had killed him? It wouldn't change a thing, I decided. Krasznik would see it as living in a sewer. Did it really matter how you drowned? If you were pushed under or just let yourself sink? If you didn't try to get out, what was the difference? I was wondering where the sewer notion had come from. How it had entered my mind now? Marty. He'd said, "...it's a sewer - a fancy expensive one, but a sewer just the same - time for a change." I'd told Tina Cox about that. Everywhere I looked, Marty had been doing what he could: pressing to get the goods on Wolf from Warner Warner and Carpenter; planning to file against Millennium; assembling all the information for a fair separation from DBS, and going so far as to get the co-release agreement from Jack Jacobs. What was he doing about making a change? Getting out of the sewer? Everywhere he'd defined the problems, and taken steps to overcome them. Where were the steps to make a change?

"I'm gonna leave now."

I opened my eyes. Ron stood there, his eyes wet and red-rimmed. I started to get up.

"Sit still. Vann's over there." I followed his look to Vann near the Chapel steps talking with Nick, but watching me and Ron. "She'll stay with you. I'll be around." He smiled. "I think it's gonna heat up some now, I can feel it. We'll get together later. Where you gonna be?"

"There's a gathering at Marty's house at 4:00. I'll head back there in a bit - you're welcome to come."

"We'll see. Thanks."

He reached down and shook hands with me, then started down the knoll, turned and said, "He was a fine man," then continued down. He passed Victor March who was headed my way.

"I've been looking all over for you!" Victor said breathlessly. He looked around as though he expected a chair to materialize. Sitting on the grass wasn't on his list.

"You found me. Sit down. It's dry."

He made an involuntary face, wrinkling his nose, looking around. Still no chair. He took off his suit jacket and sat. He seemed to be willing his bottom to make as little contact with the ground as possible. He knees were up and he held one in each hand, his jacket across his lap.

"Find anything?" I asked him.

His voice was high and agitated and he didn't seem to want to come right out and say it.

"Not for sure," he hedged.

"Try possibly and let's see where that goes."

"There's something fishy - that much is certain. It's very complicated. The amount of material is huge."

"Come on Victor, what looks fishy? In what way?"

"I'm not sure, but possibly the operators shift. They start out as one thing, and I track them through several applications and they seem to shift."

"What's an operator?"

"Specifically, I don't know. But it doesn't matter. They could be percentages of percentages about revenues or residual clauses, anything in a contract between the studios and the firm's clients; all the things Marty would have negotiated on behalf of his clients. The operators are just numerical considerations that were agreed on to be applied against money the studio says they've received for a given project."

"So why doesn't it matter?"

"Say there are ten operators in a contract - maybe there's a hundred, but let's just say ten - so every time they show up the dollar figure that preceded it is affected, and the number on the other side is reduced by that particular operator."

"So?"

"So, what I think I'm seeing is the same operator is not always producing the same result."

"I don't understand what you're getting at."

"If in a complicated contract the studio sheets come to WW and C, they're supposed to be programmed to take the numbers and run the operators against the studio's figures to verify them. With the sheets, the studios send checks for huge sums of money that cover dozens of projects. What WW and C does is verify, divide the money between the firm and the clients, and send out checks. How can an operator in a certain contract function one way one time, and another way another time?"

I let it sink in for a while. A little light came on.

"Let me guess. When it operates differently from what you think is normal for that particular operator it always produces a lower number?"

"Yes!" he said. "A glitch might produce a random difference, but it would probably vary high one time and low the next. Always in one direction makes it suspect. But it would take an enormously complicated program to do that on a sufficiently random basis to hide a pattern. If you did it too often, not randomly enough, it would show up in any audit. If it were done truly randomly, allowing the normal operator to function most of the time, and substituting a lower figure for a variety of operators in the same contract, it would be almost impossible to uncover."

"So, basically, they're skimming," I said.

"I think so," he stressed. "I'd have to do a lot more work to nail it down."

"How long?" I said.

"If I did nothing else, and got our computer guy Derrik Vass to help, maybe by tomorrow night."

"Do it, please."

"You know if they're doing it, it would have to be a very sophisticated program. And the amount of money involved, even if they weren't being too greedy would be phenomenal, and..." he paused. I could feel a building sense of vindication in his voice.

"And," I said, "it would account for Wolf's insistence that WW and C handle the GMW accounts - his old clients, and Marty's to boot."

"Yes," he crowed, "They've been with Wolf for such a long time!"

"If you were to take a guess, what kind of dollar figure would you put on it?"

"At this point, I couldn't begin to...." he shook his head.

"You must have some idea? Order of magnitude? Ballpark? Something," I prodded him.

He was still shaking his head. "A wild guess?" I tried.

"Order of magnitude," he said, "given the dollar volume I've seen so far?"

"Yes, Victor, whatever. I know you'd like to be more precise, but I'd like to have even a rough idea."

"Seventy, seventy-five thousand a month."

"WHAT!!"

"Well, that's just a guess. You can't quote me on that! It might be more."

"MORE? Good God! That's enough..."

I left it there before finishing the thought. Victor and I were both quiet. I think we must have seen Thorne and Wolf and Marshall talking to Roberta on the Chapel steps at the same time. But, seventy thousand a month was more than enough reason for Wolf to make sure Marty never saw the studio sheets, enough reason to get as nasty as he had to. If he'd been ripping off his clients for years before the formation of GMW with the artful and sophisticated help of Warner Warner and Carpenter, I'd have thought he'd have a sizable nest egg put away. The fact that he didn't would make him less willing and able to just cut his losses and walk away from his current difficulties at GMW. It figured he'd fight like a cornered rat.

This put Wolf right back up there in the running with Malovitch for possible assassin of the month honors. And on a more personal note, the month was far from over. I was beginning to think it might be worthwhile to go back to GMW and break that page counting monitor in the printing room before anyone got there tomorrow morning. Once he found out I had the sheets, things would start to boil, all right.

Ronnie Hook was coming up the little knoll with two men, both in their seventies, both with faces that looked familiar. She measured her steps against their struggling ones.

"If it's so hard to detect, how did you find it in a few hours?" I asked Victor before Ronnie got close.

"I think you're about to find out."

Victor and I both stood to greet Ronnie and the two old guys.

"Kurt, this is Lew Sykes and Andy Hall. They're both long time clients and friends of your brother."

We shook hands. Ronnie introduced Victor.

Lew Sykes was an actor. A gentle old guy with a great face. Troubled now, but almost as familiar to me as Jimmy Stewart's or Gary Cooper's.

"I'm terribly sorry about Marty. He's been a good friend to me. And I hate to bother you at a time like this, but I talked to him just last Monday and he was going to look into a little problem for me. Would you know anything about that? Andy here had the same problem."

I remembered their names from Marty's desk calendar. I started to say no, when Victor spoke.

"I'm Marty's accountant, Mr. Aryes. He called me after he called you. You're checks have been a little smaller?"

"Yes. They go along year after year like clock work while we were at Diamond, then all of a sudden they shrink a little - oh, not a lot, but I couldn't understand why. I didn't say anything for a while. I knew how busy Marty was with the new firm and all, but it kind of bothered me, you know? I knew Marty would get to the bottom of it for me. Isn't that your situation, Andy?"

"Exactly," he said.

"I'm looking into it personally, Kurt and I are, and we should have it resolved for you soon," Victor promised them.

"Thank you, thank you both. It's such a tragedy, isn't it?" he looked around, confused by it all, but sure of one thing. Marty would get to the bottom of it. Dead or alive.

They started back down the hill. I thought I remembered what I'd forgotten, what had been nagging at me.

"Ronnie," I said, "before you go, could you tell me something?"

"I'll catch up to you," she told Lew Sykes and Andy Hall as they continued down the hill. Gravity being the deciding factor.

"I got into Marty's coded files."

"That's wonderful."

"I found a notation Marty made in a file about the International Distributors money over differences he and Malovitch were having. He and his friend Jacobs signed a co-release agreement, so funds can't come out of escrow for legal fees until both Marty and Jacobs sign. Did you know about that?"

"No, I didn't," but a rueful smile said she liked it. "When did they do that?"

"In January, 1981," I said, "just before he left DBS."

"Just before Mr. Jacobs died," she said.

"Oh no!! How!? He had to be about Marty's age."

"Heart," she said simply.

The implications sent my mind spinning again. If I were right about having set Malovitch off by inadvertently making him think I knew about the co-release agreement, even though it wasn't true at the time, now that it was, his knowing Jacobs was dead would also lead him to assume getting rid of me would solve his immediate problem. If someone didn't know about it, my successor for instance, they wouldn't balk at signing a separation agreement with the release-of-all-claims-known-and-unknown provision. Malovitch would go to great lengths to keep it from surfacing. But from his point of view, he'd have to act quickly, before I could make it known. I'd mentioned talking to Winters tomorrow morning. How shrewd of me. It was beginning to look as though it would be neck and neck between him and Wolf. The prize, of course, being my neck.

Victor was standing with his mouth open, appreciating Marty's stymieing of Malovitch. Maybe he'd wanted the DBS account at one time too. I forced my mind to un-spin and came back to Ronnie.

"Well, what I wanted to ask you was, just after the entry indicating the date of that agreement, it said 'No CP b.s.' with an exclamation mark. Any ideas?"

She thought about it for a minute, then said, "I don't want to pry, but has Mr. Malovitch been difficult?" She hastened to add, "I really shouldn't say much, but I know that Marty and Mr. Malovitch had been having some strong differences about the International Distributors money, before coming to what I believe was substantial agreement; and there were other contentious issues relating to the separation agreement. Have you seen evidence of that?"

I smiled. "Some."

"Well, the reason I ask, Marty refused to go along with Mr. Malovitch and others at DBS in a suit involving another departing partner, Colin Peters. Marty thought Mr. Peters had been treated badly in his separation negotiations, and when he sued DBS, Marty wouldn't contribute to the litigation fund. It caused quite a fuss. My guess would be that Marty was not about to put up with the," she cupped her hand to her mouth and quietly said, "b.s. Mr. Malovitch had subjected Colin Peters to. That's my guess. He's here," she said, "I'm sure he'd be glad to talk to you. He was very appreciative of your brother's support. He won, you know. DBS has appealed the verdict, but they'll lose," she said confidently.

"Thank you, Ronnie, I'm sure that's it."

"Don't turn your back on Mr. Wolf," she warned in an unusually direct way, "he's worked up even worse than the other day. I overheard him and Mr. Thorne, about Mr. Thorne's accident." She smiled and held up her hands, "Your name came up."

I'll bet. Before she started back down I asked her, "Did Gary Weiselman ever go out to Millennium?"

"Yes, of course. He and the tax experts from Millennium met several times to clarify issues on the Sutton contracts, paving the way for Marty and Mr. Faustini."

"Thanks again, Ronnie."

When she got far enough down the hill, with renewed panic, Victor asked me, "Does he know!?"

"Does who know what?"

"Wolf! That you've got those sheets? That I've got them?!!"

"I don't think so. Not yet, anyway."

"Jeeez, jeeeeez," he said, his eyes wide, his hands going to the sides of his head, reminding me of Eddie Cantor, "I don't want to be seen with you!!"

"Thanks."

"No, really! I mean it! Let's communicate by phone."

"Fine, but tell me how you saw the connection ."

"What connection?"

"To the skimming."

"When Marty called me about Lew Sykes and Andy Hall my first thought was glitch, but coupled with the operators looking funny, it just popped into my head about Marty saying something seemed fishy, so I was inclined to narrow my focus on the operators last night."

He went back down the hill. I could sense from his body posture he was attempting to get to his car without Wolf seeing him coming from my direction.

Chapter 26

———◦◦◦◦———

Nick was pointing me out to two men in their forties. They started up the hill to me. At this rate, they'd have to re-sod the area.

"I'm Rick Rosen," the taller one said as they arrived. He was nice looking, a trim dark beard with touches of grey in it, longish hair in a short pony tail, thin-rimmed Tortoise shell glasses. The other guy introduced himself as Arnold Blum, short, squat, slightly rumpled, slightly bald. "Can we sit?" Rosen said.

"Of course. I'm glad you looked for me. I thought I'd run into you at the house, later."

"Better here," Rosen said.

They both took off their suit jackets and made themselves comfortable on the grass. Blum stretched out his short legs and crossed them at the ankles. Rosen sat next to me against the same tree. It wasn't my tree.

"We're going out on a limb here," Blum said, giving me a funny look when I smiled, but continued anyway. "I understand from Rick that you're Marty's executor?"

"That's right," I said.

"Have letters testamentary been issued by the Probate Court yet?"

The guy knew his stuff.

"Not yet. I expect them tomorrow." Maybe. That was the thing I'd forgotten. I had to get the will to John Goodman!

"Like I said," Blum continued, "we're sort of out on a limb - talking to you if you're not court appointed yet."

What could I say? Sometimes it's best to say nothing. Rosen jumped in.

"I'm sure it'll be okay, Arnie."

"The first thing I'd like to say is there's been no evidence of psychophobic reaction to Desyrel in the literature, no contra-indications, none at all."

The guy should have been a lawyer. Or a fan-dancer, the way he was covering his ass.

"Only in cases of over-medication," Rosen was saying when Blum interrupted him.

"You said he only took two!" Blum protested unnecessarily. "And that in two days!"

"Relax Arnie, Marty told me he'd only taken two."

"I counted them. It was a bottle of 100 and there were 98 left, so I think we can rule out over-medication. What I first would like to know is what brought him to you Dr. Blum? And why the pills?"

Blum looked to Rosen for guidance. Rosen took the lead.

"Marty had been having trouble sleeping. He was depressed. It had persisted for a couple of months. I thought the golf would help with that as well as with his general need for exercise. He put me off several times about the golf, then finally bought clubs and agreed to Monday, but a month ago I suggested he see Blum. He'd asked for sleeping pills but I didn't want to prescribe them if an underlying depression was the cause. Anyway, he agreed." Rosen looked for Blum to pick it up from there. You'd have thought his malpractice insurer was sitting in with us.

"I only saw him twice - three times if you include the initial visit." He shrugged, as if to say, "What more can I tell you?"

"And?" I coaxed him.

"He wasn't very cooperative. He mentioned a host of business problems, sort of rattled them off like a list of things to do, but while I could tell they were a source of frustration, I didn't feel they were overwhelming him; they were only a part, maybe even only a small part of his depression - and he was depressed. It came out in subtle ways, even though I think he was going to some length to avoid talking about it, which is why I say he was not cooperative."

"What ways?" I asked.

He looked at Rosen again. He knew he was definitely crossing the line into doctor/patient privilege and was still worried I may or may not have been entitled to the information. He shrugged. He'd gone this far and I suspected any line he drew now he knew would be not only arbitrary, but late.

"He was easily distracted from whatever he happened to be talking about at the time, to whatever was really bothering him. He would mentally drift off into silence, listening to interior conversations that troubled him. He couldn't seem to stay away from whatever it was."

"But he didn't talk about it? Or give you any hint?"

"The closest he came to talking about any substantive issue was your father." This time he looked both at Rosen and me for reassurance. Did I really want to hear this?

Sure, I thought, why not? I wasn't planning on sitting down with my dad and saying, "Guess what?"

"He was terribly afraid of collapsing, like your father - like he perceived your father, I should say, collapsing emotionally, financially, just having it all come down. He said your father was about his age, forty-six when things fell apart for him - business things?"

I'd say that was about right. Both the age and the perception. Poor
Marty, I thought, the spectre of dad's decline eating away at him until he
feared it was a genetic curse that had begun to rule him, would under-
mine his success now from the inside as it had his strivings as a teenager
from the outside.

"Other than that," Blum finished," he really wasn't willing to open
up." He shrugged again, a visual period.

"Dr. Blum and I agreed the Desyrel was indicated. We wanted to
break the cycle of his depression."

"Would you be comfortable telling my lawyer, the estate lawyer," I
began but I sensed Blum's nuts seeking shelter when he heard the word;
he shifted uncomfortably on the grass. I pressed on, "that Marty was in
good health, no life threatening medical problems, no medications that
might have provoked…"

"Just what are you looking for?" Blum jumped in, his blood pressure
going wild if I could judge by his change of color.

"His partners want to have an autopsy performed to try to get around
a suicide clause in an insurance policy. I'm told they'll get their way, but
I want to go on record objecting on the grounds there isn't a shred of
evidence to suggest any condition he had, mental or physical, that would
have made him unable to understand the nature of his actions."

Both Rosen and Blum seemed unsure. On the one hand, they had
been treating him for depression. Was he depressed enough to kill himself? Obviously. He did it, didn't he? They thought so. Almost everybody did. So the next question was, did he understand the nature of
what he was doing? Was he so depressed he thought he'd relieve his
headache and sleeplessness with a .38 special? Take two and go to bed?
Or one? Not likely. But on the other hand, once the partners found out
he'd taken medication, they were sure to push the notion that he'd re-
acted adversely to the drug, killed himself without meaning to. Maybe
the partners would look to sue the good doctors, here. If that came to
pass they'd be saying the same thing then that they were telling me now:
he only took two pills in a 48 hour period, when the literature showed no
problems with the recommended dose of 12 pills in that amount of time.
After a few moments thought, Rosen had come to the same conclusion.

"No, I don't have a problem with that," he said.

Blum nodded agreement.

"Could you call Bob Winters at Goodman Winters Callan and Street
before 9:00 tomorrow morning? I'd appreciate it."

"Yes, I'd be glad to," he said.

I took Winters' card from the collection in my wallet. He copied
down the number. He and Blum stood. Blum had something else on his
mind. He looked at me but was undecided about saying it. Rosen waited
too.

"The way Rick described your brother's reaction to the Desyrel suggests the possibility," he looked to Rosen for support but Rosen didn't

seem to know where he was going with it either, "that he might have been having a panic attack. It's not well understood, but along with depression and suicide and drug sensitivity it can run in families. I never had much of a chance to get into family history with him. If he was so sensitive to the Desyrel that two pills provoked a drug-related fainting spell, it could as easily revealed or triggered a panic syndrome waiting to happen. Which itself might have been brought to the surface by the depression." He looked at me now with fixed eyes. "Sound like anyone else in your family?"

My mother's brothers. Of five, two were suicides for sure, a third likely, and two heart-attacks. Somehow I felt like a co-conspirator with Thorne and Wolf linking even in my mind Marty's spell at Millennium, whatever had caused it, and his death. I think it was his saying "waiting to happen" that bothered me. It never happened before. Get off his fucking back, I was thinking. Not only didn't I think they were linked because of what I suspected or knew of Malovitch and Wolf and Millennium, all that aside, it just didn't feel right. Didn't feel like Marty. Before I could lie about my uncles, which I'd planned to do, he wound it up.

"I just thought I'd mention it. I know this must all be very difficult for you. Just don't get pulled in over your head. If it does run in your family, you never know when or in whom it's going to pop up - what might set it off." He reached down and patted my shoulder awkwardly, but with genuine concern.

"I'll keep it in mind," I smiled at him as we shook hands.

Rosen shook hands with me and said, "I'll see you at the house. My wife and I are going to pay our respects to Roberta."

As I watched them go I noticed Nick waving at me to come down the hill. He was ready to go. I waved for him to come up. He made gestures intended to make it obvious he had Kayla and Martha and Grayson with him and I was alone. What made more sense? I motioned for him to gather them all and come up. He flipped me off, but humored me and came. Sara and Grace and Jim and my dad did, too. We sat together on the grass under the tree without talking for ten or fifteen minutes. It was nice. There was more than just the sense that we were connected by the present tragedy, there was an overriding feeling that we were part of a single fabric, not just connected, but woven inextricably together. Sitting there, joined right down to scraps of our DNA, I had the feeling that we could make the tear in our fabric mend. Just will it to reweave and bring him back. In a way, it worked.

I saw Vann down by the Chapel talking to Ronnie Hook and someone I didn't know, so I presumed she didn't either. I waved to her to come up, but she shook her head. Even at that distance, our eyes met and held and I could see the warmth in hers. Respecting our privacy, I thought.

"We'd better get out to the house." Sara sounded reluctant. "You're coming, aren't you?"

"Pretty soon," I told her.

We all stood and hugged. My dad used to be six feet half an inch, 205 pounds of muscle. At five-ten I was taller now, and he felt like smoke, a little thicker than air, but not enough to hold up a suit.

Nick and Sara stopped to say something to Vann and Ronnie Hook, and when they left, Ronnie did too. Vann came up my little knoll with the guy she'd been talking with. When they got to my tree she introduced him.

"Kurt, this is Colin Peters. Colin, Kurt."

We shook hands. Vann was about to leave, but I patted the ground next to me. She had a funny expression on her face and wrinkled her brow. I thought maybe she thought this was too private for her to hear. She sat on the grass, but purposefully not very near.

Colin Peters took off his suit jacket, his tie and opened his collar and rolled up his sleeves a couple of turns. He was in his late fifties, I guessed, a little over-weight, but more pronounced was his general look of ill-health. His skin color was more grey than pink, and his eyes were cloudy, like those of a much older man. But he had a fine smile, and it brought a little life to his face when it came.

"Today may not be the best time for it, I suppose, but I don't know when we might find another." He smiled.

"For what?" I asked.

"Personal reminiscences, maybe a little business. Ronnie told me," he laughed pleasantly, "my initials came up in some notes of Marty's."

"If you don't mind telling me about it, I'd like to hear."

"I think it might help you," Peters said. "Ronnie says you've already been in touch with Barry Malovitch about Marty's separation from DBS."

"That's right."

"The notion that DBS is family has been an illusion for some time," he said. "It was brought home to Marty when he asked to be included in the firm name - an entirely appropriate change, I might add - but it had become clear even before that, when I decided to retire from DBS. Moe and Al and Don had become increasingly dependent on the revenue generated by Marty and myself and Larry Klein. To a lesser extent by Barry Malovitch and George Zeffaro and the younger associates. At the time I first mentioned retiring, overall revenues had been down. Our billings had been good, but studios and individual clients were becoming slow pays. The recession was being felt, even in the more glamorous circles we travel in. So the 6% partnership stake I had suddenly became a problem. The firm was worth at least $20 million. I planned to take my $1,200,000 and start a little firm of my own. Slow down - get out of the fast lane. I had a heart attack, not too big, but a serious warning. I was under too much pressure, too many deals; just too much for me and it was time to make a change. I was ready for one, really, even before the heart problem. But Barry Malovitch and George Zeffaro and Moe disputed the $20 million dollar figure. I thought it was quite low, actually, more than fair to them. It got nasty. The real problem, of course, was the lack of available cash to buy me out, and I did want the bulk of it in cash which I'd need to start my own firm. In any case, I paid for an appraisal of the firm's worth. It came back at $26 million. There were all kinds of peripheral issues, but for the most part, I wanted my 6% of the $26 million and consideration if and when the International Distributors suit was settled. Malovitch and George Zeffaro combed our 1965 Partnership Agreement, found a million marginal considerations, and proceeded to interpret them in a most dishonest way. They offered me $480,000. Take it or leave it. Barry figured to bully me into accepting rather than get involved in a protracted lawsuit. Marty and Larry Klein took my side. Marty suggested DBS take out a loan to buy me out, but they were out-voted by the others. Marty refused to contribute to the litigation fund when I sued DBS over the separation agreement they offered me. I think it figured heavily in their denying him his name on the door."

"And you won?" I asked him.

"Yes," the greyness returned to his face. "But Malovitch is a very petty man. Vindictive. He knows my health isn't good. They used every delaying tactic possible during the original trial, appealed on a variety of technical issues when they lost, and have been dragging out the final appeal process. It's been four years."

"But you expect to prevail?"

"Yes."

"Soon?"

"Yes."

"So DBS will owe you $1,200,000?"

"With interest and legal fees and a return of the appraisal fees I paid, it's more like $2.25 million," he smiled grimly, "if I live long enough to collect."

"Did you start your own firm?"

"No, I didn't have the money. I had savings enough to make it through, that and your brother was good enough to engage my services in the formation of Packard Productions. Do you know about that?"

Marty's files. But I'd skipped it to focus on DBS.

"No," I told him.

He looked at his watch. "It's almost 4:00. Are you going to the house?"

"Eventually. Are you?"

"No. It's not a setting I'd be comfortable in. Barry Malovitch and certainly Don Diamond will be there - this was a neutral enough setting, if you know what I mean."

I nodded that I did. "I saw a file marked Packard Productions but didn't have time to go through it. What can you tell me?"

"When Marty left DBS, part of the reason was to get the recognition he thought he deserved-and he did-but he was looking for a change too. There's only so long you can do these deals. In the beginning the people seem interesting and the money is amazing, but sometimes something special happens, art happens, and I can't tell you what a thrill it can be to be a part of it. A guy like Marty made that happen more than most because he looked to make it happen, bringing together the people who were likely to make it happen. That's why he brought so many new talents into the mainstream. He could spot them and was willing to take them under his wing and help them get into a position to utilize their talents. Look who's here today - almost every important person in the business: all of the producers, directors, and actors that have made a name for themselves in the last ten years - or will in the next ten - most of them Marty's clients. Most of them got in the door because Marty held it open. He thought starting GMW would be enough of a change, but besides the problems that cropped up there between himself and John Wolf, he knew in his heart it was just more of the same old thing. He'd turned down offers to run studios more than once, but the idea intrigued him. He kept coming back to the creative side of things as the change he was looking for. Packard Productions was the result."

"A production company?" I asked.

He laughed, shaking his head. "No, not with Marty. He had much more in mind. It was a mini-studio without a roof. It was an unbeliev-able synthesis of talent and experience and seed money. He'd organized clients that wrote, directed, produced, and a list of actors that reads like a who's who in the Screen Actors Guild; he had investors for project money, and he'd already orchestrated the first stages of development on half a dozen projects." The stuff from the trestle table, now in the hands of Malovitch. "He'd do the legal work on them, with me assisting. He planned to bring one of his kids from GMW when he was ready. The most fantastic thing about the whole venture was it was based on a co-op model. A quality end product was the goal. Everyone had to be com-mitted to that. To assure it, everyone who came into a particular project was paid the same. A flat fee. And everyone would receive points in equal measure against potential profits. It was ingenious. For the estab-lished people, it was a chance to do fine work, maybe their best work, in an atmosphere that encouraged it again, without the constant battles over money as a pecking order consideration, without studio people, quasi-bankers really, pulling the strings. Once a project was undertaken, making it happen and making it right was the foremost consideration. For the newcomers, it was a chance to work with some of the best people in their respective fields. Find their way in a protected and supportive environment, and leverage their way into higher earnings at the same time. It would be a development company for talent as well as product. It is - was - to be the culmination of all the best Marty knew this art form could be and the attempt to eliminate the evils it so easily engenders."

"And now - without Marty?"

"It's dead too."

It raised new considerations.

"Who else knew about it?" I asked him.

"Early on, it was a well kept secret. But as Marty pulled more and more of the top talent into the circle, excitement began to build, and even though it was only a rumor, Marty was getting inquiries. His plan was that the co-op model would extend to personnel. Marty would get it up and running with people he'd invited in. After five years, inclusion of new talent would be by invitation of the existing membership, with a cap on the total number of people involved to preserve the intimacy and integrity and commitment he'd intended in the first place. Wild rumors were circulating. It was becoming one of those Hollywood status things to be a part of it, even if it weren't clear it was for real. A problem if you weren't. Also, some of the other firms in town and the studios were beginning to get wind of it and fear it amounted to a raid on their talent pool. Thom Reynolds at United, Faustini at Millennium, Dinwiddie at Paramount had all put out feelers. They wanted to know what was going on. How they fit in. Basically, how much of a threat to them was it. I know DBS was alarmed about it. Since Marty left, their financial position has deteriorated. The clients that went with Marty did damage enough. But with Packard Productions in the offing, others who'd stayed behind and were looking to leave, used the suggestion of it. Marty hadn't invited them, and consequently Malovitch had nothing to worry about on that score, but it was a convenient excuse for some of DBS's core clients to jump ship. Even if Packard Productions wasn't really going to be their landing place. With Marty's death, there's going to be significant realignments all over town."

"What do you mean?"

"His clients are the top people. It will be a feeding frenzy among the other firms in town trying to sign them."

"Like DBS?"

"Sure. They'll try to get some of them back and GMW will try to hold them, but there are half a dozen other firms in town that will jump at the chance to sign the big names that will suddenly be available."

"Were participants in Packard Productions free to work on other outside projects?" I asked.

"Of course. Participation was on a project by project basis. It allowed great freedom to do the usual elsewhere, and preserve the unusual and intimate and committed nature of these special projects. It was a marvelous idea."

"Had Marty made that clear to Malovitch or the studio people you mentioned?"

"I don't know."

"Was Sutton in?"

"No. He's an ass. He's what's wrong with Hollywood. A noisy, fearful man with a little talent and a lot of ego. Marty wanted to settle the contract differences with Millennium. He wanted GMW to be free of any complications when he left."

"LEFT? You mean he had a time-table?"

"Of course. He could see nothing but trouble with Wolf. He was going to get GMW on sound footing, leave those clients not invited into Packard with the best of the associates there he'd been grooming, if that's what they wanted, or let them find new representation if they wanted, and then step away."

No wonder he wouldn't consider using any of his separation money from DBS to bail out GMW from Wolf's excesses. He had plans for it. It put a whole new slant on most everything. Especially suicide.

"Have you met Larry Klein?" Colin Peters was asking me.

I snapped out of my thoughts.

"No. Glad to meet you," I said.

"I should be going," Peters said.

He and Klein seemed to have a silent agreement not to dislike each other even if they were on opposite sides of a legal dispute. But it apparently didn't extend to overt friendship either.

He stood and we shook hands.

"Thank you," I said.

"Thank you for your brother," he said. "He was a fine man."

He started down the hill. Klein gestured for permission to take his place. Vann had stretched out, hands behind her head, legs crossed at the ankles. If I hadn't known better, I'd have guessed she was sleeping. I hadn't noticed when we'd gone back to her place for clothes if she'd kept her gun on her. I tried to picture where it was, how she could hide it in the smooth well-fitting pale blue silk pantsuit she was wearing, but failed. Klein looked at Vann. His look said can we talk? With her here? No problem, I let him know with a nod of my head.

"I'm sorry about Marty. He was a wonderful guy. We came into DBS at about the same time. Me in '64, Marty in '65. I'm just devastated."

He seemed sincere, but his devastation wasn't going to deter him long from whatever he had on his mind. "Let me get to the point. You have a serious problem with Barry."

"Malovitch?"

"Of course," he said irritably.

Maybe he didn't know any other Barry's. Maybe I did. Although, off hand, I couldn't think of any.

"I don't want any part of his plans, so I'm telling you to be careful. He's hired some people who make problems disappear."

"You mean, sort of, hokus-pokus?" I waved my hands in the air like a magician and smiled at him nonchalantly, not a care in the world.

"I mean I think he's going to have you hurt - seriously hurt!" He was both yelling it and trying to keep his voice down, the effect of it squeezing the words into an odd sound. "He's gone totally nuts! Just totally out of control!"

Vann sat up, gave him a look.

"It's okay," I told him, meaning her. Not the part about having me hurt.

He was doubtful, but wanted to say his say and be done with it. He spoke to Vann now as much as to me, to make sure everyone understood his hands were clean.

"You can go to the police, but I don't know if they can help. Barry didn't come right out and say it, so there's nothing I could really tell them - no proof. But I wanted to warn you, and I have."

He stood.

"Any names?" I asked him.

"No, but he made it sound like it would be taken care of by tomorrow. I'm sorry, but that's all I know. Good luck."

"Good luck?" I half laughed.

Like I'd bought a Lottery Ticket in a 7-11 store, and the clerk wishes me good luck. He was half way down the hill when I saw the appreciative smile on Vann's face.

"He might have said 'it was nice knowing you'."

With the $2.25 million DBS was going to have to pony up for Colin Peters, and the $6.25 million difference between what Malovitch had offered me and what Marty's files indicated the separation was worth, and the declining fortunes of DBS, it was no wonder Malovitch was having trouble maintaining that family feeling.

I was hoping Vann had her gun hidden somewhere.

"I'm sorry I'm meeting your family this way. I really like them," Vann said as we walked down the knoll. "I wish I could have known your brother." She started to take my hand but thought better of it and stopped herself.

The cemetery had pretty much cleared out. It was 4:15. By the time we'd gotten back to the little Mercedes there were only a few other cars parked behind the Chapel. I unlocked the door for Vann and she got in. As I opened the door, I could see the Rabbi about to get into a Lincoln Town Car pulled up over a curb, all but the rear wheel parked on the grass. When he saw me he stopped. I'd forgotten to give him the envelope with his fee. I told Vann I'd be right back. The Rabbi's eyes were fixed on me as I walked to his car. Every step of the way. He tugged at his beard. When I got to him, I handed him the envelope and thanked him for the service. He looked at the envelope in his hand. For a minute I thought he was going to open and count it, but he looked back at me and tapped it against my chest.

"This doesn't include parking in my space."

He gave me a big wink and a nod to punctuate it and got into his car, backed off the grass and drove for the exit, one of those big hands waving good-bye to me out his window.

Chapter 27

Since Wolf had told his guys they could pick me up here if they didn't find me before, I assumed they'd be following. And since Malovitch now seemed to have a deadline, so to speak, of tomorrow, I expected his guys to be tagging along too. If Salio had sent out replacements for his missing boys, Heckle and Jeckle, the best I could hope for from the long awaited convergence was a traffic accident. I mentioned it to Vann. We were just pulling out of the cemetery.

"If they'd at least timed it right, we could've got a two-fer discount at the cemetery. Now it's too late."

"Very funny," she said, giving my hand a comforting pat. I noticed she'd pulled down the vanity mirror on her side and was using it as a rear-view, and constantly checking the passenger side-mirror as well.

I got on the 405, planning to take it to Sunset and Marty's house. We'd gotten as far as National when I saw the sign for the 10 West, and delaying as long as possible, I abruptly cut across a couple of lanes to take the off ramp.

"Hey!" Vann complained as the little car lurched in response, "what'ya doing?"

"A change of plans."

I watched the rearview, thought I saw a big sedan, fast becoming my least favorite body style, follow across traffic for the offramp, but couldn't tell if it were pursuing. Too many cars on the off-ramp behind me.

"Not yet," Vann said, responding to what I was thinking.

"But soon?"

"I'd expect them to pick you up when you leave your brother's house. Right now you're expected. Later, you're just off here or there. It would give them more leeway. Where're we going? You told Ron you'd be going to the house. He might have expected to pick you up there."

"You don't think he's following us?"

That was my leeway.

"Maybe Tate," she shrugged.

I got off at Centinela, turned right to Pico, then right again. It's a working class neighborhood, a mix of slightly run down houses and even more run down businesses. A mix of old whites, middle age Chinese and young Mexican families. There's a hardware store on Pico between 29th Street and 30th, a little parking lot behind it, south of Pico, you get to from an alley. I was going to park back there until I saw how narrow the alley was, how easy it would be to get bottled up. Paranoid maybe, but like they say, even paranoids have enemies. I parked on 30th street pointed towards Pearl, away from Pico, a few cars past the alley.

"I'll be right back," thinking she could just wait in the car.

"Sure," she said as she got out. "Like I'm gonna sit here while you wander around. Ever seen Ron really mad?"

"No."

"Try to imagine it."

I shrugged. "I'll be right back, " I repeated.

I'd almost forgotten it was her job, but was glad she hadn't. She followed about thirty feet behind me, walking with an aimlessness belied in this neighborhood by her silk pantsuit.

It was an old hardware store, dark, small, musty smelling and crammed full of tall shelves in too narrow aisles, not giving up usable floor space unnecessarily. Creaky wooden floors and pegboards with hooks full of ninety-nine cent to $3.98 bargains. For $3.98 I bought one of those combination screwdrivers that had one slotted bit magnetically held in place in an octagonal sleeve, and five additional bits hidden underneath a screw-on cap in the plastic handle, a big and small Phillips head, big and small Torque and a small slotted. I paid the Chinese guy that owned the store and took my little treasure out into the still bright sun. I didn't see Vann. I thought she might be back at the car. I was busying myself changing the large slotted bit for the small Phillips as I walked. It was just a guess, but I was thinking it would probably be the small Phillips. I turned the corner at 30th still fiddling with the bits.

Then I was at the alley. I didn't see Vann when I looked up from screwing the cap back onto the handle. There was the roar of a big engine and the squeal of tires. I looked to my left, back towards Pico and the traffic, but didn't see anything, then turned to the alley in time to see the big sedan bearing down on me. I was momentarily frozen, then tried to step back, out of its path, but could see there wasn't going to be time. I was aware of the screwdriver in my hand, but had the feeling it wasn't going to be much help. I threw it at the car's windshield anyway. There was an explosion. The windshield was suddenly transformed into an opaque web of small nuggets held together by an invisible film. "What a throw!" I was thinking as I jumped and rolled in the air, turning my face away from the on-coming car. I cleared the hood but was hit by the driver's side of what was left of the windshield. There was a second explosion as I came to rest on the edge of the sidewalk near the gutter ten or twelve feet closer to Pico than I'd started. I noticed the acrid smell of burning rubber, had a sense of whitish-blue smoke floating all around me. I was aware that I had a problem, but couldn't seem to focus on it. I thought I heard my name shouted, but wasn't sure. I had this strange sense that I was alive, and that it was improbable and that I needed to take stock. I thought a body-part inventory was in order. See what was still there and what worked. That was the general direction of my thinking, but it was happening in some kind of slowed time. I got to my hands and knees. I heard the sound of the tires squealing again but couldn't imagine it had anything to do with me. I thought I heard my name again, someone yelling at me, but it was coming from so far away, I thought I must be mistaken. I got myself sitting on the curb, my feet in the street. I thought I saw the big sedan coming backwards through the cloud of smoke. The tires were spinning furiously. I tried to make sense of it. The idea formed that after the car had hit me it had crossed the sidewalk into 30th Street, and now was backing up. Why would it do that, I wondered? I thought about it as the trunk began to emerge through the smoke, then the back windshield, as the spinning tires were beginning to produce some movement in my direction. The car was backing up to run me down! That was it! I was enormously pleased with myself. What a breakthrough that seemed! My head was clearing! Here they come! Then it dawned on me, I gotta get outta here! I told my legs to get me moving but they weren't listening. The best I could do was roll to my left. It would have to do. I heard two more explosions as the car, backing now at a pretty good clip, hit the curb, bounced over it and slammed into the brick wall of the building behind me. I had a renewed sense of urgency and managed to get to my feet. I stumbled a few steps and found myself leaning against the brick wall, unable to stand on my own. The smoke still hung in the air and now there was steam and hissing. I could see the car clearly now, but suddenly I was being pulled backwards, then tripped. Someone tripped me! I hadn't been steady on my feet to begin with, so it seemed pretty unsportsman-like for someone to trip me! I looked up from the sidewalk, saw the driver's door open and someone got out pointing at me. There were two more deafening explosions just over my head and he stopped pointing. He seemed to jump backwards into the car. I tried to get up. I was doing pretty well, using the wall for support.

"STAY DOWN!!" Vann yelled at me as she hooked my feet out from under me with one of hers.

Where'd she come from I wondered? When I was down again she put a foot on my chest to keep me there. She had that huge black gun in her hands and it was pointed at the car. I wondered again where in that sleek silk pantsuit it could have been. The passenger door opened and someone got out. I could see their feet under the car.

Vann yelled, "DON'T MOVE!"

Whoever it was wasn't as cooperative as I was. He used the car for cover, made his way to the alley, and ran. Vann was poised to shoot but didn't. Another car turned the corner from Pico and came to a screeching halt.

"WHERE THE FUCK WERE YOU?!" Vann yelled at Bud.

"I lost you! He okay?"

"I don't know. Down the alley - go after him." She waved him off with the gun.

Bud's car dug in and hurtled through a turn into the alley. I could hear the throaty sound of his engine bellowing as it gained momentum, then fade as he got further away towards 29th Street. I'd had my head lifted high enough to see, but was getting dizzy and I let it come to rest on the concrete. When I felt better, I touched her foot on my chest.

"Can I get up now?"

Detective Phillips was in a sour mood. It was Sunday and he was off. He was on call as backup, but he was supposed to be off and had hoped to stay that way. Seeing me made it worse.

"I thought we had an understanding," he growled at me, his face close to mine.

Vann was in the driver's seat. I was sitting next to her in the little Mercedes on the passenger side, the door open, my head against the back rest, with one of those gelatinous ice packs the ambulance driver had given me against the back of my neck, my eyes closed. Keeping them open for very long was impossible. I had this narcoleptic urge to let them fall shut that came in dizzying waves. Phillips was squatted down next to me, a notebook and pen in hand. If he saw it, he didn't say anything about the screwdriver at my feet. When Vann had let me up, over her protests, before the first squad car showed up, I went looking for it. I was pleased when I found it. I should have it bronzed. After all, I thought, how many times you gonna break the windshield of a car trying to run you down armed only with a screwdriver? It took several tries for Vann to convince me otherwise. That she'd shot it out at the same time I threw. In any case, I'd paid $3.98 for it and it was mine.

A Santa Monica squad car had responded to the first shots fired call. Before the smoke had cleared there were two more and an ambulance. I thought the ambulance should have been for me. Originally it was. Some-place comfortable to lie down and collect myself. Finish the inventory I'd begun. I was feeling better now, mostly bruised and beginning to get stiff and sore, a few cuts, but remarkably, nothing serious. Instead, they treated what they could see and decided, a little too quickly I thought, I was okay and they were going the use the ambulance as a meat wagon for the guy Vann had brought down. I would've liked to have told him it's not polite to point, but Vann had done it for me. In her own decisive way. He'd been pointing a long barreled something at me that they'd found clutched in his dead hand. It must've been a favorite, because even now he seemed to be planning to take it with him.

We were five blocks from West LA so, technically, Phillips could have begged off. His pal, the guy that'd taken Marty's gun from me, had been on duty at the West LA Division and monitored the call from the SMPD squad car asking for the ambulance, heard my name, and called Phillips.

"I told you I didn't want to have a problem with you. You were gonna stay outta trouble. Just bury your brother. Remember? Now you've made this mess here and say you don't have a clue who this guy is? You expect me to believe that? Yesterday you were full of theories. This guy must fit in somewhere - start talking."

"Lay off!" Vann challenged him. "The guy tried to kill him. Now it's yours. Do your job. Maybe if you'd 've taken more of an interest yesterday?"

"I am doing my job! We still haven't gotten to you," Phillips shot back, "how you figure in. What you're doing here with him."

The squad car guys had taken Vann's gun, checked her permit and begun to take a statement until Phillips showed up and took over. He made her go through the whole thing again. He was satisfied about the shooting when an older Chinese couple who'd been on the corner of Pico and 30th, about to cross to the block with the hardware store, verified her version. He eased off on her and had come back to me. Now, starting in on her again.

"We're friends," she said. "I accompanied him to his brother's funeral."

"A friend. At the funeral. Who just happens to be carrying?"

"You saw I have a license to carry."

"So, my pal Kurt here is in town, what - four days now? - and he just happens to make friends with a chick with a Private Investigator's license and a permit to conceal?" He turned back to me. "I thought I told you not to play detective. That I'd look into it."

"Did you?" I asked.

"Chick?" Vann scoffed.

Phillips was a little embarrassed. On both counts. "Not yet," he said to me. To Vann, "You know what I mean. How is it this comes about is what I want to know? He hired you, what? - yesterday after we talked?" He looked back and forth between us. "Before that? On his suspicions?"

"Not yet. Does that mean you had it on your calendar of things to do if you couldn't think of anything else? No parking tickets to write? No broken taillights? What was it gonna take?" Vann needled him.

Phillips colored but didn't say anything. We were ganging up on him and he didn't like it. I felt a little sorry for him. It had been only yesterday, and it sounded far fetched no matter how you sliced it. At least then. At least to someone outside of it.

"I met her," I said, "just lucky. Besides, it's been at least twenty-four hours since we had our understanding. I think I'm doing pretty well - considering."

"Considering what, wise guy?"

There, in a nutshell, was the problem. What could I tell him? That

I'd heard Wolf tell his guys to find me? While I was busy printing his files I'd broken into? That Wolf had more than one motive for getting rid of Marty? To remove Marty as an obstacle to a hurried DBS settlement and get the money GMW had coming. And the skimming. How'd I know? Victor. Would he confirm it? Not yet. How'd he think he knew? Back to the files I'd stolen. Or Malovitch and the co-release agreement and the $6.25 million difference of opinion we had going? That someone, almost certainly these two today, on Malovitch's behalf, had conned my dad into giving them private papers relevant to our differences? Did I even want to tell him there'd been a second guy that Bud went after? I'd noticed Vann had said this guy, not these guys. She wasn't ready to trust him. Why should I? Or tell him what Colin Peters had told me? And Larry Klein, warning me? That was pretty strong. Except Peters had an axe to grind with Malovitch and Klein only inferred it. There was nothing to connect this dead guy and the one that got away with DBS. At least not yet. And Millennium, for whatever reasons Faustini and Perry might have thought they had for getting rid of Marty, and now me, did I want to let Phillips know we'd busted fingers to make their guys talk? That it was over a lawsuit? Or maybe an incipient mini-studio they felt threatened them? The whole fucking thing seemed nuts! It was nuts! Then again, here was this guy, dead.

My eyes were open more than they were closed now. Vann seemed to have followed my thinking. Before I could respond to Phillips, she touched my hand and had me follow her look. Bud had come up 30th Street from the direction of Pearl, seen the police cars and parked half way down the block from us on the opposite side. He was giving Vann the okay sign.

"Just tell him," she suggested, "so we can get outta here. You're supposed to be at your brother's house."

I had no idea where she wanted me to go with it. Before I could say the wrong thing, or anything, she said, "I work for a friend of his brother's. We thought the problems he'd been encountering warranted concern."

"And the name of this friend?" Phillips asked.

"Is confidential," Vann answered him.

"And neither of you has the slightest idea who might be behind this guy?"

Phillips caught me looking to Vann for direction. Didn't like it.

"Not a clue," she said. "Maybe it was random - like a drive-by?" She shrugged.

"And you, you think it was random?" he said, exasperated with us, squeezing my knee for emphasis and to assure my complete attention, "I suppose your theories from yesterday don't figure in now?"

I shrugged. I just wasn't ready to trust him. Let him do a little investigating of his own.

"I want an answer!" he yelled.

I turned my head to look at him. My neck was getting stiff and it hurt.

"Who can say?" I said.

He stood, closed his notebook, put it in his inside suit-jacket pocket, then repeated, "Who can say," shaking his head.

"What about my gun?" Vann asked.

"You'll get your goddamm gun back when I'm good and ready!"

"When might that be?" she persisted.

"Tuesday or Wednesday. Whenever the investigation of this shooting is complete."

"Make it Wednesday," I said, "we can save a trip and get them both."

Vann gave me a funny look, not understanding. Phillips did.

"Yours and Marty's," I said to Vann.

"Can we go now?" Vann asked him politely.

Phillips just walked away from us.

Vann did the driving. She headed south on 30th, mouthing the word "home" as we passed Bud. I watched him in the side mirror as he started his car and drove oh-so-carefully past the police cars and the ambulance and turned right on Pico. Vann went all the way down to Ocean Park then left, continued past Bundy where it became Gateway and intersected Pico about three quarters of a mile down. She turned right on Overland and came into Valparaiso off Queensland to Malcom. Bud was already there, his car parked in the driveway, standing next to it lighting a cigarette. Vann parked the Mercedes behind Bud's car blocking the driveway. She got out. I didn't.

"Where is he?" Vann asked.

Through a cloud of smoke, Bud tipped his head towards the back of his car, "In the trunk."

"Alive?" Vann asked.

"Of course. Whatdya think?" he sounded injured. "Whatdya want me to do with him?"

"Leave him there until I can talk to Ron. I'm gonna page him." She turned to me, "you wait there."

I hadn't planned to move. I didn't think I could. I was getting stiff from head to foot. I supposed she thought it best I didn't come in and see the two guys on sabbatical from Millennium. I was curious, but all in all, would prefer to have been somewhere else. Even Seascape. I was looking forward to seeing Malovitch there. To his seeing me there. Alive. In a few minutes Vann came out of the house.

"Ron's on his way. He's really pissed." She shot a look at Bud, then me. "He thought you were going straight to your brother's house." The implication being not only Bud, but I'd really fucked up too. "He says to head on out there. He and Bud will take care of things here. Find out for sure if these guys were sent by your friend Mr. Malovitch."

"I'm not done with my side trip yet," I told her, "I need to go somewhere."

"Great!" she rolled her eyes. "And just where is that gonna take us? You don't seem to be getting the picture!"

"Why don't you just stay here then?" I suggested. "Sounds like I'm putting you out."

We were almost back to the fuck you stage.

"Where is it you need to go?" she said with mock sincerity.

I struggled to get out of the car. I got lightheaded when I stood and had to lean against it for a minute.

"I'll drive," I said.

"Oh, that makes sense!"

My head cleared and I smiled at her. "You're not insured. It's already been a problem."

"You weren't complaining a few minutes ago."

"I forgot about it then. Besides, that was before I'd seen your driving. You coming?" I said as I got in the driver's side.

She rolled her eyes. "Where are we going? I should leave word for Ron."

"A quick trip to GMW," I said.

"You got that?" she said to Bud.

"Yeah, I'll tell Ron. Eric's there today," he said as I pulled away.

Eric waved us past without having me sign-in. Ron had covered that pretty well. Vann was opened mouthed at the GMW offices. The packaged opulence. We went down the hall to Marty's office. I wanted to check, make sure no one had been in there, that no one - Wolf - had moved in there. Vann looked around the room. Gave me a funny look when our eyes met. I think she was having the same feeling I'd had the first time. That it was rich without character, expensive, but cold and distant and antiseptic. I wanted to defend Marty in her eyes.

"Roberta did it," I said.

Vann shrugged. It was nothing to her.

"Marty was here for the ocean."

She went to the big windows.

"He got that right," she said.

I locked up Marty's office and we went back through the reception area to the Copy Room.

"You never been here?"

"I don't do lobbies," she said coolly. Now that the bullets had stopped flying, everything about her seemed cool.

When we got there I checked the little monitor. There was nothing on it after the two jobs I'd run, so it was likely no one had seen it yet. I took the screwdriver from my pocket. Sure enough, the small Phillips did it. There was a little screw on the bottom edge that allowed the cover to come off. Vann looked over my shoulder and saw what I was doing. Saw the monitor and figured out why. Underneath the cover there was a re-set button. I pushed it and the LCD screen cleared. No more Wolf files, no more Marty's files.

"Covering your tracks?"

"Trying to," I said.

I smiled at her, pleased with myself.

Chapter 28

When we got to Seascape, the parking situation looked like LA International on the day before Thanksgiving. The street was filled with cars for a long block on either side of the house and the driveway and front lawn were both filled. The idea of parking a block away wasn't so bad, but the idea of having to walk back to the house was. When we got to within fifty yards I could feel the hum of bad vibrations emanating from the house. I was going to see how my dad was, put in an appearance and get out of there as quickly as I could.

There were thirty or forty people on the front porch and walkway and what was left of the front grass after the parked cars. Nick and my dad's brother Edward were there, Edward with a pipe, Nick a cigarette. Nick watched me over Edward's shoulder doing a stiff-legged shuffle as I approached. I hadn't given it any thought until now, but I wished I'd used a bathroom at GMW to clean up. I ran my hands through my hair and dusted off the more obvious signs of having been run down.

"Don't bother," Vann said, "it's not helping."

As I got closer, the alarm in Nick's eyes increased. When I was close enough for him to examine me, he moved past Edward and came the last few steps to me like he thought I might not make them on my own. Actually, I felt better. Just moving around helped. It hurt, but helped.

"What happened to you!?" he said.

I tried to smile. "I wasn't watching what I was doing crossing a street. I got hit. Sort of."

"Sort of?" Nick looked at Vann. She closed her eyes and raised her brows. If you believe that, I got a bridge to sell you. Nick looked from her to me, pressed his lips together so tight I thought he'd launch the cigarette like a tiddly-wink, but let it pass.

"Did you get examined? Did you see someone?"

"Yeah, some paramedics. I'm fine - just a little banged up. Don't mention it to Dad. He doesn't need more right now."

Edward took it all in, puffed on his pipe. Edward's an academic. For him, everything's academic.

The crowd was immense. I decided I had to make at least a cursory pass through the house and say hello to those I knew and then get outta there before my being there set Roberta off.

"Is Sara with Dad?" I asked Nick.

"And Roberta," he warned me. He smiled, "Bob Thorne's with them too, wearing his mittens. I offered to shake hands, but he demurrrred." Nick smiled.

"I'll see you in a bit," I said to both Nick and Vann.

I squeezed past the throng pushing to get in or out the door. It was impossible to tell which. Inside, the house was packed. There were half a dozen catering company people attempting to circulate with trays of hors d'ouerves and drinks. There was a little bathroom off the entry, near the dining room. I had to wait for the woman who'd been in there, and the two ahead of me, but when my turn came, I washed my face, combed my hair and with a moistened towel, cleaned my clothes. I thought I looked pretty good, considering.

My dad and Sara and Roberta were on the couch where I'd found them Thursday, my dad in the middle, Thorne hovering nearby. My dad looked better. Krasznik had helped. Had brought some finality to Marty's death that eased the burden of whatever my dad wished he might have done differently in the past. He looked tired and drained, but no longer haunted. I couldn't say the same for Roberta, or for that matter, Thorne. I could feel Thorne's unease when I pushed past the last few people between myself and the couch. Good, I thought, fuck him. Roberta had a drawn, haggard look. But quiet and subdued. It must have been the quiet and subdued part that threw me. She saw me coming, but it hardly registered. I knelt down in front of my dad. I held his hand.

"How ya doin'?" I said.

Sara had her arm around his shoulders. A family in mourning.

"Better," my dad said, managing a little smile. "Rabbi Krasznik is here somewhere."

Roberta looked at me, then away. I wanted to give her the benefit of my doubts and assume some of the reality was sinking in. That she was mourning him. It could happen.

But not in this life.

"How dare you make things worse with Barry Malovitch!" she said in a low grinding voice. A Model A taking on Pike's Peak. "He and Marty were in agreement!"

"Not now, Roberta, not now," Thorne implored her, suddenly a pillar of propriety. "We'll get things resolved tomorrow. "

I wondered if he and Malovitch had discussed a timetable. Probably not. I wondered if Thorne were close enough to Wolf to be privy to the skimming. Probably not. No, certainly not. Wolf would use him and Roberta as long as it suited him for the insurance money, but wouldn't run the additional risk of confiding anything else in him. Thorne was a tiger without claws, I decided, enjoying his mittens all the more.

Sara noticed my cuts and bruises. "What...?"

I flashed her a look, then a quick one to my dad. She got the message.

"I'm gonna eat something. You want anything?" I asked Sara and my dad.

"Some 7-Up," my dad said.

Sara shook her head no, then said, "I'll come with you. I'll get Dad's 7-Up."

We made our way through the crowd. I saw Wolf and Marshall in the far north corner of the room with Davidson, his wife and Woodman. I hoped they were hatching contingency plans for when they didn't get the insurance money. Tina Cox was at the fireplace deep in conversation with four very famous, very visible clients of Marty's: Gene Steadman, Al Padino, and Myrel Stamp. Malovitch had his back to me. He was hovering just outside the circle around Tina. I had the feeling that the realignments were already underway, and Tina wasn't going to be outflanked if she could help it. I thought Malovitch was waiting for an opportunity to make his own pitch to these guys. Bring them back into the family at DBS where they belonged. Tina saw me, smiled warmly. I could feel Sara stiffen ever so slightly.

Every inch of the house was filled with bodies. The sense that I'd had at the cemetery - there but for the grace of God - was already fading. It was being replaced by a smugness on their faces now that reflected history being rewritten in their minds, something to the effect of, he wasn't so hot after all. It happened to him, but could never happen to me! Hoooray for Hollywood.

The kitchen was crowded too. Another group of catering people preparing small sandwiches, some hot foods and drinks. Sara got the 7-Up while I made a couple of roast beef sandwiches with lettuce, tomato and pickle. And lots of mustard. I wrapped one up in a napkin. The mustard was oozing out so I wrapped it in another.

"Lunch and Dinner?" Sara chided me.

"No, one's for Vann. She hasn't eaten since this morning either."

Sara looked me over as I bit into my sandwich. Mustard squeezed out the back.

"Who is she? Really? And what happened to you? You look like you got run over!"

"I did." I gave her the story I'd given Nick.

"Jeez, are you okay?"

"Fine - just banged up - and hungry." I attempted a everything's okay kind of smile.

"And Vann?"

Ever since Jason's mother and I divorced, a mistake as far as Sara was concerned, any woman I looked at, or who looked at me was automatically guilty of something. If we were Catholic, I could understand. When it suited them, all women were Catholics at heart.

"A friend."

The caterer's staff was falling behind on the dish washing. The sink was overflowing and the dishwasher was filled but needed to be started.

"Where's Maria?" I asked.

Sara rolled her eyes. "Roberta blew up at her yesterday just after you left. She fired her! Made her get out right then! The poor girl! It was really awful." From the look of things, she hadn't replaced her.

We squeezed our way back into the living room. My dad was alone now on the couch. Sara sat with him and gave him the 7-Up. I spotted Malovitch with his wife through the French doors to the back yard talking to another of Marty's client's and his wife and another couple near the gate to the pool.

"I'll be back in a minute," I told Sara and my dad.

When I turned, Vann was there. "Where're you off to?"

"Here, I made you a sandwich," I said and handed it to her.

"Aren't you the one."

"The one what?" I asked her.

"I haven't decided yet," she said as she unwrapped it.

"I hope you like mustard," Sara offered.

Vann got past the first napkin and saw the mustard leaking out of the sandwich, gluing the inner napkin to it. She carefully peeled the gooey napkin away and took a bite.

"Perfect! I love mustard. How did you know?" she said licking her fingers. A caterer came by and she took a coke from his tray. "Where're you off to?" she repeated.

"I'm going to say hello to Malovitch," I said quietly to her, "and give him the opportunity to see a ghost."

"You think that's smart?" she said between chews of her sandwich. "I don't." She had mustard in the corner of her mouth. I had the urge to lick it away. I must've smiled at the thought. "What?" she said.

I pointed to the corner of my mouth. She smiled and the tip of her tongue delicately flicked it away.

"I'll be back in a minute."

I was working my way across the densely packed room when a small hand took hold of my shoulder. I thought it was Vann.

"I said I'd be right back," as I turned, I saw it was Roberta attached to the hand.

"There's a call for you. A Detective Phillips," her grim nasty smile telling me I was in for it now. My overdue comeuppance for Thorne, she must have thought. "Take it in the office," she ordered.

I changed direction and pushed my way into the kitchen and then through to the office. Remarkably, it was empty. After the din and crowding throughout the rest of the house, the quiet there seemed eerie. Maybe it was common knowledge that Marty had died in here. I picked up the phone. I could hear the noise from the crowded house wherever the phone had been answered.

"I've got it," I said, and waited. It took a few moments before Roberta or someone else hung it up.

"I've got something belongs to you," Phillips said.

"Let's go," I said to Vann when I got back to the living room. She was washing down the last of the sandwich with the last of the coke.

"Where?"

"I'll tell you on the way."

I told my dad and Sara I'd call them at his place later that night. Then told Sara I'd look for Nick on the way out. She gave me a look to indicate I hadn't put in enough time here. The proprieties should be observed. I half turned to go. I was worried about Phillips. I didn't like his tone. Too much cat and mouse, him thinking he was the cat, so I was in a hurry. The problem was Sara had this kind of radar detector, like my mother before her, that alerts her so she can make it difficult to get away in direct proportion to your need to go. Like one of those dreams where you need to escape and the harder you try, the more tangled or paralyzed your legs become. It's a female talent, and not a rare one. After a few more minutes of dancing around the edges of where I was going and what I wanted to do that was more important than staying here with my dad, Sara reluctantly gave me leave to leave. I had Vann by the hand pulling her along behind me as I cut a path through the crowd to the front door. When we got a few steps out onto the porch, I heard my name.

"Kurt!"

It was Tina Cox. She was on the grass twenty feet or so from Nick. The guy with her I recognized immediately as one of Marty's clients, as famous as an actor could get. Brad Merlon. I supposed Tina was talking him up too. I had a funny rush, a combination of being star-struck and shy, wanting to gush, "LOOK WHO'S HERE!" and at the same time not notice him to preserve his privacy. He was fat now, but still intense looking with deep, strong eyes. Thin white-grey hair. That pouty lip. Up close, it was almost femininely sensuous. In fact, everything about him had a vaguely feminine air, except his eyes. They came up the stairs onto the porch together. There were fine beads of sweat on his face, at his hair line, and around the folds of flesh at his neck. Tina looked down to my hand holding Vann's. I instinctively let it go. Bad instinct.

"Brad, this is Kurt, Marty's brother." She gave my appearance a once over.

We shook hands. He stood still for a very long time with his hands clasped before him, his head tipped back slightly, his eyes almost closed, as though he were listening to the gentle breeze as it passed through the leaves, or maybe focusing his attention, Zen-like, on the intermittent buzzing of insects in the warm grass, but I suspected he was really allowing his presence to work its magic and set the stage. Just as suddenly as the rush had come, it was gone. I had the feeling I didn't like him very much. His eyes opened and the down-turned corners of his puffy mouth seemed to be forming words, but nothing came out. A subtle form of communication. Maybe I was supposed to guess. Maybe it was the Method. I waited, still impatient to be off. I remembered Marty once telling me most of his movie clients were spoiled insistent children you can't escape. I was having that feeling now. But I could see that Merlon was used to operating in his own time frame, not to mention his own zip code. Phillips would have to wait.

"And this is?" Tina looked to me to supply Vann's name for the introduction.

"Vann," I said. "This is Tina Cox."

Vann shook hands with them both. "Good to meet you Mr. Merlon, Ms. Cox." Merlon hung onto her hand like he might be planning to take it with him. She took it back before he could claim squatters rights. She turned to me, "I'll wait for you at the car." She walked away without so much as a glance back. She stopped where Nick and Edward were, said something, then kept going. Straight backed and square shouldered. I liked the way the light shone on her dark hair. There was a hint of auburn in it I hadn't noticed before. The light filtering through the huge poplar trees that lined the street played nicely off the pale silk suit as it rippled to her walk. I couldn't imagine where the gun had been. Tina watched me watch her go. She gave me a who's that look with raised eyebrows, but didn't say it. So I didn't answer it.

"Brad has a question for you." She looked for him to pick it up from there.

He mumbled a lot of preamble about how Marty had been like a son to him. How devastated he was about his death.

"Just devastated," he repeated. He shook his massive head sadly. Ran a hand through his hair. He examined the ground near his feet, looking for the words to express his feelings. I was hoping they were written there. He wasn't much of an improviser. Maybe I could just read them for myself, save him the mumbling. His speech magically got more intelligible when he finally came to the point. Money. "I loaned Marty $50,000 dollars," he informed me, "I'd like to get it back. It was a business loan. I was hoping it wouldn't have to go through his estate. Do you think you can be of any help?"

I didn't have a clue. The way he asked it, he had more than just a little doubt on that score himself. I assumed everything went through the estate. If I were going to put it on the list of things to do at all, it wasn't

going to be very high, and even then, I needed to know what it had been
for. I would have liked to see how the check had been made out. To
Marty? To GMW? To MHG, a Professional Corporation? I remembered what I'd thought was the out of character doodling Marty had
done. I was trying to recall what I'd seen about it in Marty's coded files.
I was doing a quick memory scan, when he interrupted my thoughts.

"It's an awful lot of money to be just floating around," the fleshy mouth
was saying. His oversized head rocked back slightly, then tipped side to
side while his right hand sort of stirred the air in front of him, the gestures suggesting a certain irresponsibility on Marty's part for dying and
leaving it thus. If you believed Marty killed himself, there was some
merit to the notion.

"I saw something about it," I told him, "but it seemed to fall into a
couple of either/or possibilities." It was starting to come back to me. I
wrinkled my brow for effect. Let him know he wasn't the only actor on
the porch. "One way it's a gift - right? The other way it's what? A five
year note? Or, if it's going to become a note, it can be increased and
invested in Packard Productions. Something like that? Am I close?"

Out of the corner of my eye, I felt more than saw Tina draw in her
breath. As far as she was concerned I didn't know about Packard Productions. From her reaction, she did. How could I? Unless I'd gotten
into Marty's coded files. I wondered if she had any idea what was in
them. I decided it really didn't matter. Most likely she didn't know
specifics. But she knew anything that complicated this situation slowed
it down, and from her point of view, that was an unhappy development
anyway you looked at it. For one thing, I wouldn't be as likely to be
pushed into a hasty agreement with DBS that would bring the money
needed to keep GMW afloat; and secondly, I might not agree to put the
estate out front against Millennium if I thought Marty was already making plans to withdraw from them. Where would that leave her and
GMW?

Merlon pursed his lips and wrinkled his brow, better than I'd done it,
I had to admit, really thinking about it. The oversize tub of lard knew
that was it exactly, but was trying to decide how much he had to or wanted
to acknowledge. "Hmmmmm," was all he came up with. He sort of
washed his face with that big right paw of his, allowed it to hold, then
pinched his chin in a massaging way. He put his left hand on his hip,
stared out into space, and let the right hand wander to the back of his
neck and made it clear he was really giving it some thought now. Not
Academy Award stuff. "I'd like to look at my notes. Can we talk in a day
or two?"

"Sure," I said.

"Let me give you my private line," he offered in hushed tones.

I didn't mention that I thought I already had it. It also occurred to me
the number was probably worth more than the $50K to the tabloids.
Maybe we could just make a deal: he keeps the number, I don't call the

tabloids, he forgets about the $50K to Marty and we call it quits. I didn't think he'd go for it. He handed me a card with no name, just an area code and number. Pretty cool. When I looked up from it, there was the merest hint of a smile on his lips. He thought it was cool too. Sort of gave himself away. I winked at him. Let him know I knew he knew I knew. Something like that.

This acting stuff wasn't so hard.

Before I got off the porch, Tina gave me one of those condolence hugs appropriate to the occasion, but whispered in my ear to remind me about seeing her later that night. She seemed more anxious now. Packard Productions probably had something to do with it, I thought. "Are you okay?" she asked.

"Fine. I had a little accident."

"Your brother said you got hit jaywalking or something?" her hand touched my forearm tenderly.

I was weighing the measured tone of sincerity. It was amazing how quickly my level of skepticism had risen.

Then she added in an offhand way. "Who's that girl?"

"A friend," I said, equally offhandedly.

Vann was waiting at the car. I'd been looking for a chance to thank her for saving my life. I unlocked the driver's door which automatically unlocked her side too. As we were both getting in I started to say it, but she spoke first.

"Sort of a touchy-feely type," she said scornfully when we were in the car.

"Merlon?"

"No, your Ms. Cox."

I tried to shrug it off.

"I think she was closer to Marty than she likes to admit. Even to herself. I think she had a crush on him," I suggested. "It's only been four days," I added.

"So she's transferring it to you?"

I gave her a disapproving look.

"You think they were having an affair?" she asked.

"No, I don't," I said. I didn't tell her that I thought Tina wanted to.

She made a face, skeptical, not accepting my explanation but not interested in debating it. Changed the subject. "Where're we going?"

"West LAPD. Phillips called and said he had something of mine."

"What?"

"He didn't say."

"Thanks for hurrying," Phillips said sarcastically, "this is supposed to be my day off."

My instinctive response would have been, fuck you, and I thought I might remind him what today was for me, but suddenly it seemed funny. I'm burying my brother, figuratively speaking anyway, somebody tries to run me down, shoot me, I got Roberta, Thorne, Wolf, Malovitch, Millennium, and now Merlon in my face, and Phillips is pissed off because it's his day off and I'm not here fast enough to suit him.

"Something funny?" he said.

"You got a funny town here, that's all. What is it you have of mine?"

Vann and I had pulled up chairs next to each other on one side of his desk.

"This," he said as he slid one of the boxes I'd packed at Marty's from around the far side of his desk. He had the rest of them stacked there too. "Recognize them?"

"Yes! They're my brother's," I said with obvious excitement and relief.

"So how do they end up in the trunk of a car just randomly trying to run you down?" he smirked, "if you don't mind my asking."

"I left them at my dad's apartment yesterday afternoon. Some guys came by and told him I'd sent...him to get the boxes. He gave them to him."

Vann had grabbed my thigh and dug in a fingernail at the plural. I hoped Phillips hadn't heard it, or noticed my wince.

"Guys? or guy?" Phillips said, his eyes narrowing.

"Ask my dad," I shrugged, "I wasn't there. But I'm really glad to get them back. Thanks."

"Thanks," Phillips repeated rolling his eyes. "Follow me on this," he said, " I want you to tell me, who might've known you had these papers? Who might have known you'd taken them to you father's? Who would want them? And if they already had the papers, why run you down?"

You want them chronologically or alphabetically? I wanted to say.

I was shaking my head, but before I could say it or put him off, he held up a hand, like, don't say you don't know. "Speculate. Take a wild guess here."

"Bob Thorne knew I had the papers. He was there yesterday morning, then had someone from his office catalogue what I took. That was part of our disagreement." I wiggled my fingers at Phillips as a reminder. He smiled unenthusiastically. "As far as who might have had an interest in them, there are several possibilities."

"Like?"

"Some of the papers deal with partnership matters at my brother's old law firm. Some of them deal with a future project he was working on. The old law firm, the new law firm, and several of the studios in town have taken an unappreciative interest in what he was doing. Any one of them might have wanted to get the papers."

"And run you down?"

"Any of them. All of them."

"I know how they feel," he smiled.

"Can I take them? You don't need them for your investigation?"

"Take them," he said.

"Did you find out who the guy was?" Vann asked him.

"Not yet; he wasn't carrying ID. I'll try prints when the lab opens in the morning."

Phillips reached down into his bottom desk drawer. Took out Vann's gun and put it on the desk close to her. "Maybe you better have this back," he said.

"Thank you," Vann said.

I looked at him. Raised my brows hopefully.

"Not a chance, cowboy. Wednesday at the earliest." When I looked at Vann she was smiling, stuck her tongue out at me. "Stay in touch. Keep me posted if you think of something," Phillips said ruefully.

"I'll do that."

"You're a one man circus," he said, "you come to town and suddenly I'm following you around with a shovel cleaning up the mess."

He helped me and Vann take the boxes to the car.

Chapter 29

It was 7:10 when we left the police station. I hadn't seen anything of Ron or Tate or Wolf's guys, who I figured must have picked us up at Marty's house if not before. But I had things I wanted to do. If they followed, they followed. I was a little less worried now that Malovitch's guys and the guys from Millennium were accounted for, and since they were the ones who'd been told to take care of me, Wolf's guys might have been day care providers for all I cared. It would be a different story if I hadn't altered the monitor, but so long as Wolf didn't know I was aware of the skimming, I felt reasonably safe. On the other hand, it occurred to me that whether or not Malovitch had seen me at Marty's, he'd almost certainly find out I'd been there. He'd know his guys hadn't taken care of me. I wondered how soon he'd be able to have new recruits on the job. Was there some Rent-a-Thug Agency in LA? If not, if I survived this, maybe I'd start one. It would be a great little money maker.

We got to The Beach Club by 7:35. I got the printouts of Marty's files and took them with me in the little briefcase. But I left the computer disks in the safe. Just in case. I took an envelope with the Club's logo in the return address place, addressed it to John Goodman and put the will in it. We were rolling again by 7:50.

Vann still had a standoffish expression and seemed sullen. I still wanted to thank her, but thought it would be better to wait until she seemed a little more receptive.

"You're goddamm welcome!" she snarled suddenly.

"What's the matter with you! I've been trying…"

"I know it's my job, but I can't remember anyone so completely ungrateful! Ever! I might have been killed too, ya know!"

"I was…"

"What?! Gonna send me a thank you note? In a week or two?! What an…" She threw up her hands in frustration at her failure to find a suitably vile description of my character. It didn't seem like a good time to tell her I'd been trying to thank her. She seemed to be still fuming, but quietly, so I thought I'd leave well enough alone.

"Before you set off on any more adventures, take me to my place," she said, "I want to change clothes."

Maybe take a Motrin or two.

"Maybe it's time to have Ron pull you off," I said.

She made a point of looking at me, glaring really, but didn't say a word. Like I didn't have a clue or something.

We got to her place at 8:20. No one was there. No cars in the street or driveway. She let us in. No Ron, no Eric or Bud, no Millennium guys or Malovitch's left over. I stood in the middle of the living room with the little briefcase in my hand.

"Where are they?" I asked her.

"How should I know?" she said still irritated, then, "Ron has a warehouse and garage in South Central. He probably moved them there," she said, putting her keys and the gun on the coffee table in front of the couch. She'd slid the gun under the seat in the car when we left the police station, so I never saw where she hid it on her.

"Why?"

She spun around with her hands on her hips and ended up so close to me I could feel the heat of her. She gave me another of those "You're clueless" looks, adding, "Because, for one thing, I live here! I like to come home once in a while and not trip over a bunch of hired assholes, if that's okay with you?"

Her face was inches from mine, her chest heaving with pent up anger or energy or something. There was dim light from the one lamp next to the couch that she'd turned on with a switch next to the front door. Up close, I noticed for the first time her face had only partially made the transition from the twelve-year-old tomboy she'd probably been. A sweet, strong face, but teetering between adolescence and adulthood. Her lips were very red and moist, but I didn't think it was from lipstick. I had this urge to kiss her. She looked up into my eyes, waiting. But for what? For a thank you? For a little more encouragement for her to withdraw from the case, if that's what it was for her? Or for a kiss? If I kissed her, or tried to, and she thought I thought that was supposed to be her reward for saving my life, I'd never hear the end of it. So I just stood there. Sometimes it's best to just do nothing. Leave things alone.

"I could just strangle you sometimes!" she said throwing up her hands and turning on lights as she went down the hall. "I'm gonna take a shower," she announced.

I wasn't sure what to do. I could wait for her. Sit around with my thumb in my ear, or I could look for a beer or some juice in her refrigerator, relax while she showered. Or I could just get the hell out. Her motorcycle must still be around. Maybe in the garage, so it wasn't like I'd be leaving her stranded. And it was obvious I was annoying her. The hell with her, I thought, I've got things to do. And having her along with me would be awkward if I decided to go see Tina Cox. What I really wanted to do was go through the Packard Productions stuff. All things considered, the hell with her, I thought, I'm outta here! I left her a note on the kitchen table:

> Take the night off. Take the week off. I've got work to do and I'm going home. I know you'll mind, and I'm sorry, but I borrowed your gun. I'll get it back to you tomorrow somehow.
> P.S. Thank you for my life. Kurt.

As I pulled away from Vann's place I was swamped with a hollow lonely feeling, and having the gun didn't help. It only served as a reminder of the trouble I was in. I had it in the little briefcase on the passenger seat next to me. I realized I missed the sense of protection she brought me. I missed her. Crabbiness and all. I wasn't more than a block from her house when I thought about going back. I was worried. Burying Marty, figuratively speaking, had brought a new clarity in two respects to my position as the prime target in all this. It underscored the fact that he was gone and out of it, and I wasn't. And that until the motives for Malovitch and Wolf and Millennium to have killed him were out in the open, they had every reason in the world to keep on trying with me. If Wolf's guys had been following us since the funeral or since we left Marty's house this evening, I hadn't seen them. And it didn't seem like Vann had either. I didn't want to lead them back to the Pacific Hotel and blow my relative safety there, but it seemed like the best place to work. On the other hand, having a secure place to sleep was worth preserving. I headed to Il Fornaio instead, relying on the vague hope maybe Ron or Tate were around somewhere.

It was a little after 9:00 p.m. when I sat down at a table on what I was beginning to think of as my side of Il Fornaio, but this time at the last table on the west end away from the remaining diners scattered throughout the room. I had the little briefcase with the printout of Marty's files and I'd sorted through the boxes of stuff in the trunk and retrieved Marty's copies of the DBS Partnership Agreements from 1965, 1976 and one from 1980.

It didn't take long to find the exception to the 60/40% rule. On page 26 of the 1976 and 1980 versions of the Agreement the exception read: "...in the case that a departing Partner has accounted for 30% or more of the firm's gross revenues in three or more years preceding his departure, that Partner shall be entitled to his Partnership percentage applied against a 55% diversion of his client's contract revenues to his new firm." I checked. In Marty's files he had figured 16% against 55% of $7,734,375. I knew the boxes contained years worth of old DBS year-end statements, clients' billings and so on, so it would be no great trick for Victor to prove Marty had exceeded the 30% threshold for the last three years. I could just drop this in Winter's lap and let him twist Malovitch into shape. Or maybe I could do better. Maybe there was another way.

I pulled out the file on Packard Productions. Colin Peters had it right. It wasn't just a business venture. Marty had invested his spirit in this. He'd been the best at what he did for twenty years, and this would have allowed him to use everything he'd learned to make successful both the art and commerce of movie making instead of allowing the usual haphazard opposition of one to the other to govern. Success would be the result of orchestrated planning, projects well chosen and talented people committed to them, well financed, with a stake in the outcome, not just hired hands. It jumped off of every page. I could feel his excitement from the outlined Statement of Intent and the list of potentials he'd made in every category he wanted represented, to the final list of invitees. It was as interesting and instructive in those he'd rejected as in those he wanted. His notes were frank and open. Not intended to be seen by anyone but himself. A lot of egos would be bruised and feelings would be hurt if they were. I read for awhile. Most of the names of actors and directors were familiar, but with a few exceptions, the writers and producers and money people were not. Once he'd decided who he thought was best suited to working in the fashion he'd outlined, he'd made phone calls to discuss their possible participation free of the inhibiting or restrictive confines of letter writing. There were dates next to names, often many. From the look of this, there must have been a lot of discussion without committing anything to writing. Strange for a lawyer, I thought. But next to the names of those he'd invited, he'd written IN and the date they'd agreed. I didn't see any instance of an invitee opting out.

He'd considered Tina Cox and rejected her. He'd taken on Colin Peters gladly, but knew it was temporary. Colin was a talented man, but wanted a quieter, less pressured life and would retire to a small office and a few clients as soon as he got the money DBS owed him. It was clear the help he'd provided in designating and securing some of the financial participants was instrumental. Marty had thought Tina was the most talented of his kids, and wanted to bring her in with him, but had decided working with her that closely would be a problem. He hadn't come right out and defined it, but it seemed clear to me her crush on him wasn't just a figment of my imagination. I had the feeling that he feared the more intimate nature of the work, the longer hours and greater sense of commitment and involvement that he envisioned for Packard Productions would only increase her attachment to him. What about him? It wasn't explicit, but somewhere here between the lines he seemed

to be protecting himself as well as looking out for her. And Packard
Productions. He hadn't hit on a solution to a replacements for Colin.
Of the projects laid out on the trestle table, I wondered how close any or
all of them were to being ready. It seemed they were. There must be a
Contract of Participation in each stack of papers. From what I was seeing here, that would be the governing document for each project, stating
who was going to do what and how much money would be made available and what the flat fee and percentage would be for the participants.
It depended on how many of the Packard Production people would be
involved. Money was considered another participant. Packard Productions would also be considered a flat fee participant. Assuming profits,
the money accumulated by Packard Productions would become a fund
to underwrite budgets that were going to run over. Jeez, it was all here!
Like a Ferrari with the keys in it begging to be driven.
    "I want it back!"

    I looked up from the mess of papers I had spread across the table.
Vann stood there with her hands on her hips, a dead serious look on her
face. It took me a moment to shift from Packard Productions to her.
    "Hmmm? Hi. What?"
    "You know goddamm well what!" Through clenched teeth she said,
"My pistol! Where do you get off taking it! You're completely out of
your mind! Putting aside stealing it, you don't have a permit to carry!
What were you thinking of?!"
    "Shooting back?"
    I smiled. Raised my brows. I wasn't in much of a position to argue.
She was right, but it'd seemed like a good idea at the time. She wasn't
buying it, so I didn't push. Besides, my mood had changed. Having
been immersed in the enormous potential of Packard Productions, and
Marty's excitement about it, had raised some new possibilities. I was
swept up in them, not the more tawdry problems the gun represented. It
was difficult to change gears. She was going to help me.
    She sat, continuing to glare at me, waiting for some answer or expla-
nation so she could berate me with its implausibility or stupidity.
    "How'dja know I was here?" I asked.
    "You're completely predictable! That's how!" Her eyes got wilder at
the thought. "You said you were going home. Was that to throw me off
the track or something? What's the matter with you?! We're trying to
protect you!"
    I told her about wanting to preserve the Pacific Hotel as a safe haven,
changing my mind and coming here. Asked her if Ron or Tate was around.
    "They're around," she said annoyed, like everyone was doing their
jobs but me. "Where is it?"
    "In the briefcase," I nodded to the floor at my feet.
    "I'm going to the bathroom," she announced.

Good for you, I almost said, then when she reached down and took the briefcase realized it was to take back and hide the gun. She was wearing light grey UCLA sweats and running shoes. It would hide well in there. Her look dared me to object. About anything. When she came back and put the briefcase back on the floor, she seemed more composed. She even smiled at me.

"Had anything to eat yet?"

"No. I was almost done here when you arrived."

"Going someplace?"

"Maybe. I've got a call to make first."

I was going to pack up the papers and take the briefcase with me but decided it would just offend her. God forbid I should do anything to offend her.

Tina answered on the second ring.

"Kurt?"

"Yeah. You still want me to come by?"

"Yes, of course. How soon can you make it?"

"Fifteen minutes or so. Maybe twenty."

We hung up. I wasn't sure what to do about Vann.

As I approached the table I could see Vann was craning her head, reading the Packard Production Statement of Intent, poking it with a finger to bring it around in her direction, make it easier to read, but not so much as to make it appear she were really prying, more like it was there and had caught her eye. Innocently. She was sipping at a glass of red wine and was dipping pieces of bread into a mix of olive oil and vinegar on a plate before her. It smelled good. My stomach growled.

"Have some," she said pushing the bread basket towards me.

Without sitting I helped myself to a piece and dipped it.

"'Scuse me," I said, taking the papers and putting them back in the briefcase.

She looked up at me with those big clear blue eyes and smiled. "Your brother was pretty cool. This would really have been something special, wouldn't it?" she said pointing to the papers. "I heard what that Colin Peters said, that it's dead? Really a shame. He thought the world of Marty, your brother," she corrected herself self-consciously.

"You talked to him?"

"On the steps of the Chapel, before I brought him up the hill to introduce him to you."

"Right," I said waiting for more.

She shrugged, dipped some more bread. "Mostly he just said how your brother was always there for people, stuff you'd expect to hear at a funeral, but I knew he meant it." That reminded her. "Jeez," she shuddered, "that Rabbi guy's somethin'!"

I had the briefcase packed up.

"So that's the end of it?" she asked, looking at the briefcase, "just like that?"

"Who knows?" I said.

She gave me a funny look in return, like she wanted to hear more, like we had this bread and wine and the two of us could just sit here and talk. But I changed the subject. "I'm going to see Tina Cox now."

Her expression hardened. It's a talent I have.

"It would probably be best if..." I was looking for a diplomatic way to say it. Not my strong suit in the best of circumstances.

"If I didn't follow you and wait around while...?"

She waited for me to confirm it. I made a face - so? - shrugged with my mouth.

"Whatever," she said with pointed indifference. "I'll leave the tomcat patrol to Ron or Tate. But maybe you should talk to Ron. He can't hold onto those guys indefinitely."

"My three days aren't up yet," I said. "Would you ask him to call me tomorrow morning at GMW? Please?"

"But not too early?" she sneered.

It was almost 11:00 when I got to Tina Cox's place. I took the brief-case with me and locked the car. There was a little soft light coming from the dormer. The rest of the house was dark except for the porch light. Good signs, I thought, under other circumstances. I crossed the porch and rang the bell. I heard the sound of bare feet coming down the wooden steps from the upstairs loft. A light came on in the living room and Tina opened the door.

"Hi, how are you? Come in," she said and stepped back to let me pass.

Her voice sounded a little strange, a little far off. But my attention quickly strayed from her voice. She was wearing only a long white T-shirt to mid-thigh. Maybe underpants, but no bra. He long blond hair hung loose to the middle of her back. The house was warm, embers still glowing in the fireplace.

"Let's sit there," she said pointing to the couch.

She poked at the embers to revive the fire and then put on another log. Even in the dim light of the one lamp and the low fire I could see her eyes were red-rimmed. There was a wine glass and a nearly empty bottle on the coffee table in front of us. Her evening appeared to have been a liquid Canticle for Marty. She saw me looking at the glass.

"Would you like some?"

"No," I said, but realized I did. "Yes, please."

"Red okay?"

"Fine."

She poured the remainder of the bottle into her glass then went to the kitchen, opened another and poured a glass for me and brought them both back. She sat with her legs tucked under her, the T-shirt pushed down between her legs for decorum. We were sitting at opposite ends of the couch. She was uncertain. So was I, but she had the advantage of almost a full bottle of wine's worth of reduced inhibitions going for her. What I had going was a couple of mental conversations with her that not only really didn't go anywhere, but definitely wouldn't bring us closer together. Like "What's on your mind?" since she was so anxious to meet. I assumed Packard Productions. Not much I was about to tell her on that. Or how about, "Loose lips sink ships" since she'd shot her mouth off to Weiselman. If I let myself think about it much, I could get mad in a hurry and wouldn't need the wine to loosen me up. The hell with her, I thought, she's just as much of a self-serving conniver as any of them! I wondered how her trawling for Marty's clients had gone. She'd worked the crowd pretty well. Maybe trying to line up a few big fish for what she might already be thinking of as her post GMW days. In fact I probably ought to get the hell out of here, I was thinking. This isn't going to do either of us any good. I'd decided to, but hadn't sent the message to my feet. Before I could, she slid towards me and put her head against my shoulder.

"I loved him," she said, crying. "I've never loved someone so much in my life and I never got to say it to him."

It hit home and hard. Get in line, I thought.

She was shuddering softly against me, not trying to hold back, but not out of control either. Gently, caressingly she put her hand on my knee. Or maybe Marty's. It made me think of what John Goodman had told me what now seemed like a lifetime ago, but had only been two days before, I now stood in for Marty in all things. Or sat. Not good. Bad timing. It could be worse. It could be Malovitch. Not funny. I patted her hand. I didn't say it, but I was thinking, "there there" a la Yossarian in Catch-22.

"I should go," I said.

Her arm came up from my knee and went across my chest hugging me to her.

"No, please, I don't want to be alone."

Along with Rent-a-Thug I ought to start Rent-a-Lug. I could clean up in this town. But at heart I'm a softy. As much as I hated giving my ego a back seat to anything, I was going to give her points for Marty. It was real. She was real. I'd cancel out Weiselman and chalk up her head hunting to necessary survival skills. We could start over. More than generous, I thought.

"You wanted to talk to me; before you got lonely, right? What about? I'm all ears."

She sat back and gave me an appraising look.

"Same something," she said.

"What?"

"You tell me. Same father?" she smiled wiping away tears.

I sort of got the drift and figured it was better not to let her explain. If Marty had his reasons for being standoffish with her, so did I. My ego would let me stand in for him only so far, for christsakes; besides, since he didn't and wouldn't, standing in in this case meant standing down. And it certainly had nothing to do with my dad. He'd have had his pants off as soon as he saw the T-shirt.

"Last chance," I said with a smile, "talk or I go."

She ran her hand through her hair and put the wine glass on the table. She delicately rubbed her eyes with the middle finger of each hand.

"I'm sorry, I know I'm not being fair to you. I like you, for you. I really do feel close to you, but you're right, it's because of Marty." She composed herself. "How do you know about Packard Productions? What do you know?"

I wanted to tell her everything. I wanted to trust someone. I wanted to tell her about Malovitch and Wolf and Millennium going after Marty - now me - but I couldn't.

"You shot your mouth off to Weiselman, right?" I smiled to soften it.

She sat back against the couch, sipped at the wine. "It was an accident," she said, her hand coming to cover her mouth. Nice gesture, but too late for that, I thought. "How did you know?"

I could tell her part of it. "Malovitch. He knew I couldn't get into Marty's files. I gave you the benefit of the doubt and assumed you weren't dealing with him behind my back. From other things I've seen and heard, it had to be Weiselman. Since you were the only one, other than Ronnie, that knew, it had to come through you, if not actually from you to Barry."

"You never thought Ronnie was a, what? Suspect?"

"Never. She loved him too," I shrugged, "in her own way. I think she's loved him a long, long time. Selflessly. She didn't worship him, but she was loyal to him and to her feelings for him. I think she knew him better than any of us. And became something of a First Wife in the old Chinese way." She gave me a funny look. "Ran the household, tried to make everything run smoothly for him, even if it meant being seen as part of the furniture by everyone else; as long as she knew he knew, that was enough for her."

"And did he?"

"I think so. But we digress. Weiselman was trying to cut a better deal for himself with Malovitch by giving him information that would allow Malovitch to force an agreement on me that wasn't even close to what DBS owes Marty. If Barry knew I couldn't get into Marty's files, I'd have little chance to dispute what he offered as the agreement he and Marty had all but concluded."

"I don't believe it! Why would Gary do it? Why would Barry? They're like..."

"What? Family?" I scoffed at her. "Your uncle Barry told me as far as you and Joe and Mel are concerned, you have nothing coming from DBS. Conspicuously absent from his list was Weiselman. He said if I thought you guys had something coming, I should take it out of what they were so generously offering me."

"What are you talking about!!??" she moaned. "Barry wouldn't do that!"

"Yeah, right. Without Marty's files, Malovitch was offering me about $580,000 for everything Marty had coming. For GMW they say they're putting about $16,000 a month in an escrow account. There's a little less than $300,000 being held now. As far as Malovitch is concerned that's it."

She was shaking her head in either disbelief or shock. "What does Winters say?"

"He doesn't know yet."

"What! He wasn't with you?"

"No, I met with…"

"You went alone! Are you out of your mind! No wonder!"

"No wonder what? Your uncle Barry all of a sudden decides he's got an opportunity to take advantage of the bumpkin?"

"I'm sorry, that's not what…"

"Fuck you! I went with Winters' knowledge and informed Malovitch I wasn't represented; that it was an informal meeting to get information. He felt free to press this shit on me because he knew I couldn't get into Marty's files because someone shot her mouth off!"

"Okay, okay," she held up a hand, "I'm sorry. I said I'm sorry. I'm just dazed by all this."

"Get in line, sweetie."

She started to give me a hurt or angry look, but laughed instead. "So where do we go from here?"

"That's yesterday's news, literally and figuratively."

I gave her a fetching little smile.

"What?" she said.

"I got into the files."

"How? That's wonderful!" she beamed. "And?"

"And they owe Marty more like $6 million." She covered her mouth with her hand. "Through Marty to GMW, they owe more like $56,000 a month, or just over a million for the eighteen months. From you and Gary and Joe and Mel another $2200 a month. Almost $40,000 total. Based on the deal Marty had struck with Malovitch, each of you has a separation bonus of around $7000."

The numbers were beginning to sink in. I could see her mind sorting through the possibilities. The hell with the insurance money, the stabilizing effect of nearly $1.1 million coming to GMW would immediately solve their problems. I could see she was buoyed, almost gleeful at the prospect.

"My God! Do you know what that means?"

Maybe it was the wine, or just the need for good news, but the reality of dealing with DBS seemed to be escaping her. Maybe she still believed in the DBS family. Maybe she was unaware of their treatment of Colin Peters, although I didn't see how she could be. In any case, I wanted her to be salivating at the prospect. I wanted them all to be.

"I think so," I said.

"And Packard Productions?" she said. "You found out about it in his files?"

Maybe she held her drink better than I thought.

"Yes, and from Colin Peters."

She winced ever so slightly at the mention of his name, then recovered. "And?" She smiled, just short of coy.

"And what?"

I waited while she thought about it. I thought I knew what she wanted. Why Peters and not her. If that was it, and she thought I'd found that out, what was the point in asking me now? If it was dead, it's dead. She made up her mind. She looked directly at me. No hesitation, no half-held breath. No shrinking violet.

"Why didn't he want me?"

It was a fair question. But I wasn't sure if it were a matter of professional or personal pride. I wasn't sure if I wanted to answer in either case. So I asked her one.

"Did you ever tell Marty you loved him?"

"No, I told you," she said, still waiting for an answer.

"Do you think he knew how you felt?"

Her composure slipped a little, but she hung in.

"Yes, I think so."

"So, if he'd acknowledged it, but had been unwilling to do anything, it would have either made the working environment difficult; or it could've led to an affair; or he'd choose to be with you and divorce Roberta."

She was biting her lip and her eyes weren't holding mine anymore. She was turning the wine glass in her hand round and round. I waited. When she looked up at me I told her, "If he'd taken you into Packard Productions those three options would have been on the agenda every day. He didn't want that for himself or you or Packard Productions. I think it came down to his having made a commitment to Roberta and honoring it." She looked up at me with tears in her eyes. "No matter how much he would have liked to do otherwise."

She started to sob, put the wine glass down and covered her face with her hands, then turned and buried it into the couch back. I put a hand on her shoulder, then brushed the mass of tangled blond hair away from the side of her face. I stroked her cheek with the back of my fingers.

"Whatever else he felt, he figured you to take his place at GMW. He thought you had the talent and feel for it. If he couldn't invite you into Packard, that was a pretty close second."

She continued to cry for a while and I continued to stroke. She seemed to calm herself. She reached up and took my hand and held it to her face.

I gently took my hand back. "I assume there'll be a partnership meeting tomorrow about the autopsy, the insurance money, the lease concessions?"

She was looking at my withdrawn hand. She smiled.

"Same father?"

I shook my head no. "Same mother. The meeting?" I reminded her.

"Eleven. After Thorne's hearing. Why?"

"As long as everyone's getting together anyway, I'd like to have a little meeting of my own. Actually, a couple of them."

"Oh really?" she said, "with whom?"

"The first one, with the GMW partners and Malovitch. If he won't come in person, then by conference call."

She smiled, liking it.

"Then you and Sandy Marshall and me and Winters and a mystery guest. A couple of other combinations after that. Think you can help me arrange it?"

"I'd love to!"

"Without explanations to anyone?"

She seemed less certain. Furrowed that smooth pretty brow.

"What do you mean?"

"I mean no shooting off your mouth, for one thing," I said.

She made a face to tell me, be serious, that's not a problem. Maybe not for her, but it was crossing my mind. She said, "I meant, why no explanations?"

"Because it's important, that's why. Can you handle it? Just get them there?"

"Fine. Yes," she said a little miffed. "Can I tell them you'll be there, or is that a secret?"

"Just tell them Bob Winters would like to meet with them. No point in getting anyone riled up about me."

"Anything else? Anyone else?" she said in a friendly challenging way.

"One more involving you," I told her. She raised her brows as a question. "If I can set it up, I'll let you know after the meeting with Marshall and the mystery guest. If I can arrange it, I'll want Gary and Joe and Mel and you there. Okay?"

"Great," she said with a note of irony. "Whatever."

She pouted a little, wanting me to tell her more, but sure I wouldn't, but not too unhappy, still riding high on the news Marty's files seemed to portend for GMW.

"What about Millennium?" she said. "Have you thought any more about taking the lead in a suit against them?"

"Let's see where we end up tomorrow. After these meetings. I think we'll be in a better position to decide."

"But you haven't ruled it out, right?"

Persistent broad. I made a face, held up my hands in a who knows gesture. "I've got to go. It's going to be a long day tomorrow." Today hadn't been so hot either, I thought. I got up from the couch and walked myself to the door. She stayed there on the couch. She could make a T-shirt amazingly sexy. She knew it, too. She gave me a coy smile. I thought she was going to ask me to stay.

"Who's Vann?" she said as I was going through the door.

Chapter 30

I left Tina's place at 12:30am. The traffic was light and I sailed across town. I got to the Bradbury Building and dropped The Beach Club envelope for John Goodman in the night slot.

When I crossed into Santa Monica, I drove in a circuitous route on my way to the Pacific Hotel and abruptly pulled to the curb and stopped several times to see if anyone was following me. See if they'd pull over too and give themselves away, or maybe drive past, then pull over afraid to get too far ahead. I did it the first time on California as I approached Lincoln. I slowed and let the light there go yellow, then cut across the street from the curb to the left-turn lane, turned and sped up as it went red. I checked the mirror. No one. I got as far as Rose and should have turned left to Main, but on an impulse went right instead. For a long block the Penmar Golf Course was to my left, then it widened and was on both sides of Rose for another long maybe quarter mile un-interrupted one block stretch. With no houses on either side and only one street light in sight, the darkened park would force anyone behind me to reveal themselves if they were trying not to. It got dark so fast after I passed the street light that only the lights from my car made the road visible, partially illuminating the low gentle roll of the golf course to my left and right, giving it a macabre effect. The tall eucalyptus trees stood like indifferent sentinels, unlikely to help if I needed it. Coming up on my right I could see the mouth of a narrow utility road, or maybe a cart path that went into the course and immediately disappeared behind a stand of the trees. Maybe they'd help after all. I slowed down and just before I got there I turned off the headlights. The complete darkness engulfed me, but I had one of those residual retinal images, like a camera flash that stays with you, and I followed it, driving as though I could see. Even going as slowly as I was, I bumped and pitched, but for the most part ended up where I thought I would, to the right of the road behind the trees alone in the darkness.

My lights disappearing might have at first suggested a tight curve to them, but as they came into the golf course they could see the road was straight. I could hear their engine go from loafing along to an uncertain acceleration to a panicked roar when they thought they'd lost me. They flew past the trees that hid me. When they got to the end of the stretch, near the end of the golf course, I could see their brake lights come on. Their car just stopped in the road like a tired runner, stooped, hands on thighs, getting his breath. For a moment their back-up lights came on and I could hear the higher pitched sound of the car coming towards me in reverse. They must have been discussing whether to come back or go forward to find me. After only a brief retracing they decided I'd raced ahead of them. The back-up lights went off and the engine dug in and they were gone. Wolf was gonna love them for this.

I waited for fifteen minutes. Minute by minute it felt like the green light from the dash clock was getting brighter and brighter, filling the little car to the point I thought it would give me away. When no one came I figured I was safe. Although it gave rise to thoughts of Ron and Tate. Where the hell were they? I fleetingly pictured Detective Phillips, hands on hips inside his open sports jacket, having arrested them for kidnapping and false imprisonment, looking at me and sneering, you're next, pal. Maybe I could make his day some other way.

I parked in my usual place behind the Pacific, got my usual friendly sardonic greeting from the desk clerk, and climbed the fine old staircase to my room.

"Hi," Vann smiled from the bed. "Nice work."

"You were there? I don't believe you! I looked all over for someone!" I said.

"So don't," she said evenly, "but pulling to the curb was good and going away from Main was even better. You fooled me, but then, I thought I knew where you were going and expected you to go there. What made you do it?"

"Just a feeling."

"And turning off your lights and ducking behind the trees? Had you planned that route? Scouted it?"

"No. I just saw the opportunity and took it. I didn't know anyone was behind me, not really, just a feeling. Where were you? I thought Ron or..."

"They couldn't make it. That left me," she shrugged.

"For the tomcat patrol?" I chided her.

She smiled pleasantly. Apparently I was forgiven and we were friends again.

"I didn't see or hear your bike. Where were you?"

"My bike's pretty quiet, special mufflers, and I had the light off."

"All night?"

"Yes."

"How could you see?"

"Look in my helmet," she pointed to it on the desk.

When I picked it up and looked in it I could see the face shield was especially thick, small buttons and instructions around its perimeter.

"What is it?" I asked her.

"A night screen, like night scopes for commandos. Same idea."

"And you can see in the dark with it?"

"About like on a foggy day."

She got up off the bed. She was wearing the sweats and a brown leather Bomber-style jacket but much heavier, like a flat-track racer's with the zipper hidden beneath a thick flap. She had on socks, her boots by the desk chair. She unzipped the jacket, took it and the UCLA sweat shirt off. Underneath, a long sleeve coarse knit thermal shirt. She threw the jacket and sweat shirt over the back of the chair and went to my suitcase, found the T-shirt from the night before and held it up, asking with her face if she could use it again. I nodded. A picture of Tina came to mind. Bad timing.

"Chair or bed?" she asked me with a sweet, curious little smile on her way into the bathroom.

"I've got some calls to make. You can take the bed."

"Now? It's," she checked her watch, "nearly two!"

"I know. Did you ask Ron to call me tomorrow morning?"

"Yes."

"Is there somewhere where I can reach him now?"

"Now?"

"Now."

She gave me a look. "You're sure?"

"I'm sure."

"He's gonna love this." She went to the desk and dialed for me. "Eric, is Ron awake?" She looked at me shaking her head, waiting for me to seal my own doom. I gave her a go on gesture. "Wake him," she told Eric. It took about two minutes. "It's me," she said, "I know what time it is! I'm awake too, aren't I? He wants to talk to you. Yes now!" She held out the phone like it'd just come out of the oven. "Good luck," she said as she went to the bathroom and closed the door.

"Ron?"

He cleared his throat. "This better be good."

A sense of my predicament settled in. A sense of Marty's. The frustration of knowing some, but not enough, began to overtake me. Maybe it was because it was late and I was tired. Maybe, but as much as I'd thought about what I needed to know from him, what I felt was creeping into it. I tried to push it down. One thing at a time. I tried to ask it with no more emotion than did he put the cat out?

"Did Malovitch's guy admit to killing Marty? Or say the one Vann got did?" The line was soundless. "Ron? I need to know." I waited but still he said nothing. "Ron? I need to know. Tonight." Still nothing. I could feel it rise. I could feel the anger and frustration come together and just shatter my resolve.

"DID HE FUCKING DO IT OR NOT?!!" I yelled, my voice sounding savage and unfamiliar.

I was on the verge of losing it completely, the carefully constructed pillars of my existence just washing away. I felt lightheaded, and the details of the room were disappearing in a foggy yellow light. The bathroom door opened and Vann looked at me. It had come on so suddenly. How does it do that, I wondered. I took a breath. Then another.

"Did Malovitch have it done?" I said in a controlled voice.

"I don't think so," he said, "I'm not sure. Maybe, but I don't think so."

"Explain."

"They were supposed to. Like the guys from Millennium. It was all set."

I had the feeling I wasn't going to believe this.

"And?"

I could feel his reluctance.

"It was already done when they got there to do it. They saw two guys coming away from your brother's house. He didn't know who they were, but he described the two guys we got from Millennium before he saw them here. We talked to him at Vann's before bringing him downtown. He and the one Vann shot waited 'til the other two left and checked for themselves, saw the job was done, so they took off. They were sure the first pair we got had done it. End of story 'til Mr. Malovitch tells them to do you. I, I'm pretty sure."

I wondered how many fingers backed it up. If not Malovitch's guys and not Salio's from Millennium, that left only Wolf. Maybe he figured it was only a matter of time before Marty got hold of the studio sheets and figured out the skimming. I wished I'd thrown the little bastard off the balcony at the GMW meeting. But Wolf would never have had his guys make it look like suicide. Look at the trouble that was causing. It was clear his guys were inept, but could they have messed up that much? Or maybe he just told them to do it and never figured they'd get creative. Make it look like suicide. Actually that made sense. There was no reason to think Wolf did this on a regular basis, so it might not have occurred to him that these guys would try to cover their tracks and in doing so, inadvertently void the Key Man insurance. Or was Malovitch more resourceful than I was giving him credit for? Had more than the two guys we knew about been doing his dirty work?

"Did you ask him about his instructions?"

"About you?"

"No, Marty. Were they supposed to make it look like suicide? Or a break-in?"

"Suicide. He admitted they cleaned out your brother's briefcase."

Looking for the co-release agreement. But what difference would how have made to Malovitch? He just needed Marty dead. How didn't matter. Unless it was out of vindictiveness. Punish GMW with the loss of the insurance money. Could he have known about it? Maybe through Weiselman? I thought about what Colin Peters had said: "Malovitch is a very petty man - vindictive." I could see him relishing the sort of two-for-one coup that would represent. Lots of payback. There's a point where patience comes to an end. I thought of something Phillips had said: "Don't let your grief become an obsession." I knew I was already there. I was working on the next step. Rage. It just kept building. I had no proof of anything, but I knew what I knew and keeping it in was suffocating me. I wanted to grab Malovitch and Wolf by the hair with one hand and their power neck ties with the other and pull back their heads and tear out their throats with my teeth. Spit it in their faces. Let them feel their lives running out with each heartbeat. The thought soothed me. I could picture it clearly. I smiled to myself. How did matter. Guys like Wolf and Malovitch, their first thought wasn't about blood. I'd heard enough.

"Remember I said I wanted to see if I could make something work?" I reminded him.

"Let's hear it," he said.

It was 2:15. I took Winters' card from my wallet. Dialed the home number he'd written on the back. "Don't use it," he'd said. He was going to love this.

Chapter 31

MONDAY

———◦◦◦◦———

Vann and I were at Il Fornaio when they opened at six. After showering, we'd gone by her place so she could change clothes and leave her bike there. I'd like to say I hadn't slept well because she thrashed around too much, but it was because the chair wasn't very comfortable. I'd set it up the way she had the night before, but it didn't work well for me. It hadn't worked that well for her. I'd thought about climbing in with her, using her excuse, but it hadn't been particularly cold, so I didn't. I had toast and a de-caf latte. She had a fruit bowl, cheese omelet, toast, croissant, coffee and large grapefruit juice.

"You on an expense account or something?" I asked, impatient to get going. I hadn't planned on a banquet.

"Keep your shirt on. I haven't eaten much since this thing started."

She wiped some fallen jam off her plate with the last of the croissant and finished off the coffee.

"I'll get the check and pay while you finish."

She smiled at me and hurried to swallow so she could tell me, "You're better than an expense account." She gave me the Groucho eyes.

At 6:55 we pulled into the underground garage at 81436 Ocean Avenue. It was already warm, the ocean pale blue and flat as a board. The palm trees in the park across the street seemed resigned, braced for a day without an off-shore breeze for relief. Wolf's guys had picked us up as we left Il Fornaio. There were so few cars around that early they couldn't exactly blend in. It was clear from their hang-back approach that Wolf was unaware that his GOD file had been breached. Vann and I walked out of the garage on the Arizona Street side and around to the front entrance. I gave Wolf's guys a little wave to where they were parked across the street. Pantomimed a golf swing. The driver mouthed something to me. Maybe, Good luck to you. Maybe not. I gave him a wide-eyed toothy smile. Probably too far away for them to see it, but what the hell, it made me feel better.

"That's cute," Vann said.

"They probably been up all night," I said nodding towards them, "seem a little out of sorts."

"You're pretty chipper," she said as we entered the lobby. She took my arm and smiled warmly.

Bud was at the desk. He started to wave us through, but I wanted to sign-in. He and Vann exchanged a look, shrugged. I signed and handed the clipboard to Vann. We were the first ones in this morning. I'd hoped we would be. The bong of the elevator as we arrived at the Penthouse had a less ominous sound to it today. I gave Vann the keys and asked her to wait for me in Marty's office. I went down the hall towards Wolf's office. I wanted to see the size of the smaller Conference Room. I poked my head in. It would do. They'd be crowded, but it would do.

Vann's sandals were on the floor near the coffee table and she'd stretched out on the couch. The curtains and the sliding door to the balcony were wide open, the air still and warm but with the reassuring smell of the ocean on it. She was wearing a new pair of snug fitting Levis and a woman's large necked over-sized crew T-shirt with a linen waist jacket with 3/4 length sleeves. She'd had her pistol and holster attached to the back waist band of the jeans and the jacket hid it, but now she'd taken the jacket off and lying on the gun must have been uncomfortable, because it was on the floor next to her, within easy reach, mostly hidden by her sandals.

"In about fifteen minutes, Ron should be here. Would you meet him at the elevator and escort him and our guests to the big Conference Room? Maybe help him ride herd?"

"You want me to go?" she sounded injured.

"No. Just listen for the elevator. I need to get on the phone. I'll be a while."

"You want me to go? For your calls?"

"No, you're fine."

I pulled the papers from the little briefcase and spread them on the desk. Most of the numbers I'd need were there on the list of invitees, but for any that weren't I had his address-appointment book out. I planned to twist arms and use Marty's name shamelessly, if necessary. Whatever it took. I called Colin Peters first.

I was on the phone when Vann responded to the elevator and got Ron settled in the big Conference Room at 7:15. I got off the phone with Colin at 7:35. Ronnie Hook came in shortly after that and I gave her a quick summary of what I wanted to happen and how she could help. I poked my head out the door. Vann had taken up a position outside the Conference Room doors near Ronnie's desk and they were chatting. I looked into the Conference Room. Ron had things under control at the east side of the room, out of sight from the hallway. All things considered, they didn't look too bad.

I was on the phone for nearly two hours more. I made sure Goodman had gotten the will and my note about the urgency of getting me confirmed. He was confident it would be official before noon. Winters would be in court about the autopsy this morning, and all I'd told him last night was to meet me at GMW when he got done. That maybe we could move Wednesday up. When I was sure he was unavailable, I lied to his secretary, Roxanne, told her he and I had agreed at the last minute that she should talk to Malovitch's secretary, Elaine. Have her, with Ronnie, set up a conference call Malovitch should be prepared to take to discuss with Winters and the GMW partners the signing of the separation agreement he'd given me Saturday morning. That it could be concluded today. That due to an emergency situation concerning me, Winters would act on behalf of the estate. To say nothing more about me. I hoped he'd think the emergency meant his guys had succeeded. If he'd seen me at Marty's or heard I was there, he'd think they got me after. I was sure Malovitch would fall all over himself to make himself available. Only, Winters didn't know anything about it.

Thom Reynolds at United, and Aaron Dinwiddie at Paramount had agreed to come pending a call from Ronnie. It had taken less arm twisting then I thought. Marty's name was enough. I called Victor, then Phillips. Then Besser. Then Sutton and Cooper and Faustini to settle our differences. There was a lot of complaining, but with the expectation that they were going to get what they wanted, each of them was willing to meet with me. I was an outsider. I didn't want trouble. I just wanted to get this wrapped up, I told them. This wasn't my town or my business or my life, and I wanted to get back to my own.

I heard Miriam's voice outside the door. It was imperial and angry.

"Mr. Wolf will not hold a partners' meeting in the small conference room. You can tell Mister Goldman he has no authority to use..."

It was going to begin, and this was as good a time and place as any.

"Miriam, just tell Mr. Wolf that I have a series of meetings planned and the small conference room won't do. I'm sure he'll understand."

"He will not understand!" she said.

She turned at the sound of Winters and Thorne rounding the corner and approaching. Thorne was all smiles. Winters looked tired and irritable.

"What's the problem, Miriam?" Thorne asked.

The guy was on a roll. I didn't want to think about it, but he must have gotten the court order for the autopsy.

"Mr. Goldman thinks he's going to tie up the big Conference Room.

All day! We have a partners' meeting in ten minutes; we've been waiting for your return."

Thorne gave me a contemptuous, dismissing look. Vann got off the corner of Ronnie's desk, reached back and slid the holster with the gun in it from the back part of the waist band to her hip, where her little jacket no longer hid it. She had a playful smile, but standing in front of the doors to the Conference Room, the message was clear.

Winters took one look at her, the gun, then me and rolled his eyes and grimaced, grinding his teeth. He put his briefcase on Ronnie's desk so he could put both hands on his hips and ask me, "What's going on here!?" with the appropriate amount of disbelief in his posture and voice.

Thorne put his arm around Miriam's shoulders and walked her down the hall towards Wolf's office, the fresh white gauze bandages over metal splints binding the injured fingers to the adjacent ones on each hand. It made an attractive contrast to his finely tailored dark suit.

"Let's not start the morning worrying about him. He's just not going to be a problem." He gave me a nasty smile as he escorted her away.

"Inside, mister," Winters said without preamble.

We went in Marty's office. He had a pasty, no sleep look that he was clearly pinning on me. He rubbed his eyes with the heels of his hands.

"They got the court order."

He looked at me for some reaction. A shudder went through me. Now wasn't the time. I stifled it, turned it into a shrug.

"Did Rosen reach you?" I asked him.

"Yes."

"And you raised my objections?"

"Yes."

"And?"

"And nothing. The judge said he was sympathetic, but had no choice but to grant the request. The autopsy is to be conducted," he looked at his watch, "soon. Thorne expects to have the results tonight or tomorrow at the latest."

I thought if he weren't tired and mad at me about it, he would have said he was sorry. Maybe not. But it had gone as he'd expected and my objections had been useless. I should have signed the request to begin with as far as he was concerned.

"So why the hell am I here? And who in the world is that girl with the gun!?" Before I could answer he added to the list, "And where do you get off telling my secretary to make calls on my behalf? God dammit, I've just about had it with you!"

"Sit down, Bob." I led him to the couch. He put his briefcase on the floor next to his feet and sat back into the soft cushions. He had already gone from pink to red. He locked his fingers together on top of his crew cut and tried to head off purple. "You may think it's Monday, but for us it's Wednesday," I told him. "We're gonna have to do this piecemeal. A lot's happened since Friday." He blew out his breath, preparing to hear me out.

"I'm all ears," he said with enough sarcasm to let me know I was wasting more of his time and that he was prepared, probably inclined, to disbelieve anything I had to say.

I told him Vann was a friend and licensed to carry. I told him someone had tried to run me down, then tried to shoot me, but Vann killed him. He looked at me like I was mad. He closed his eyes. It was the only immediate way he could make me disappear. I told him there were guys linked to Wolf, Malovitch and Perry at Millennium who'd been following me and Marty before me. He kept shaking his head like I'd truly lost my mind. I told him we were going to defuse things. That one way or another everyone was going to get what they wanted, or at least what they deserved. He opened his eyes. I told him to humor me if he didn't believe me. We'd take it one step at a time.

I put the separation agreement Malovitch had tried to foist off on me on the coffee table before him. He sat forward and looked it over.

"So?"

"Now look at this."

I gave him a copy of Marty's calculations, the copy of the co-release agreement with Jack Jacobs and another of the initialled memo between Marty and Malovitch and Donald Diamond. He flipped through the separation agreement, then back through Marty's figures. He jaw muscles were clenching and unclenching. He was slowly shaking his head the whole time. This kind of deceit in these professional circles just didn't happen. It was new to him at least.

"Christ almighty! Jesus Christ almighty! Have you shown this to anyone?"

"No."

"He's trying to screw you out of at least $5 million!"

"Over six if you figure in GMW," I said.

Not to mention my life. Maybe Marty's.

I told him what I wanted to do.

The partners were gathered together in the small conference room. It was crowded. Wolf and Miriam, Bob Thorne, Hamilton, McCord, Marshall, Weiselman, Cox, Woodman and Davidson were all there. Miriam was in a folding chair next to Wolf. There was one empty regular chair. I pointed to it for Winters. I whispered to Ronnie to get herself another folding chair. I'd stand.

"I'd prefer he didn't join us!" Wolf growled at Bob Winters. "You can represent him here."

"He has every right to be here. I expect you're going to be glad he is," Winters responded.

More or less, I was thinking.

Wolf waved a dismissing hand. When pigs can fly, his look said. But he had more important things on his mind. "We've discussed the court order. Bob says we'll have the autopsy results tonight or tomorrow." His eyes met mine. He was relishing his victory. "We'll hit the insurance company with it Wednesday noon at the latest." And by his calculations, they'd have a check by Wednesday night.

Right.

"First American Bank has served us with a Preliminary Notice of Default. They've served us jointly as Goldman Marshall & Wolf, and individually. Of course this is not good." There were looks and comments exchanged and a sense of gloom and doom building. They hadn't expected the bank to act so quickly. Wolf tried to restore order. "Quiet! We've got more than a month at the very least before they can step in." He looked at me. "What we need is the money that DBS owes us!" He looked at Winters. "Can you tell us anything on that score?"

Ronnie went around the crowded room and passed out the copies I'd had her make. The skylights were open slightly, but with this many people and the warm day, the room was heating up. When everyone had one, Winters took over.

"This is what Mr. Malovitch proposes. It is based on 12% of 40% of Marty Goldman's client deals done while at DBS. There are no provisions for any monies in relation to client deals created by Ms. Cox, Mr. Davidson or Mr. Woodman or Mr. Weiselman."

Cox already knew, but Davidson and Woodman were both flabbergasted. Mel didn't say anything but it showed. Woodman sputtered and protested in all directions. Weiselman was quiet. His eyes met mine but he quickly looked away. Wolf looked it over. The Music side receptionist came in and whispered in Miriam's ear and left. Miriam waited for Wolf to finish what he was saying.

"This will go a long ways towards solving our problems. A long ways. How soon can we get the $300,000?" he asked Winters.

Miriam whispered to Wolf.

"Right away," Winters said, "if the estate were willing to sign the agreement."

Miriam whispered to Ronnie, who then whispered to me, Malovitch was waiting in the reception area. Apparently, for what he expected to be my capitulation, or capitulation on my behalf by Winters, he decided he could schlep all the way out here to the beach. Wolf and Thorne looked at each other, then me. Wolf said through clenched teeth, "But you're not?"

"No, we're not."

Thorne could stand it no more. "You're jeopardizing the future of all these good people! You're compromising the future of GMW and Roberta's future! You're out of line, mister! This is clearly a breach of your fiduciary duty! I'll have the court remove you as executor so fast your head..." pointing one of his gauzed fingers at me.

Wolf interrupted him to inform the others, "Malovitch's here now.

Miriam, bring him in. I want that agreement signed now!" He looked around at the lack of seating, looked at me as the culpable party. "God dammit, what in the hell are we doing in here!" He looked at McCord. "Get yourself a folding chair. We'll let Mr. Malovitch sit up here next to me." McCord had half risen when Winters stopped him.

"Hold on, hold on," Winters said raising a restraining hand. "You need to see this." Bob took his copy from his briefcase and signalled Ronnie to distribute the next set of copies. Ronnie told Miriam to wait, then passed them out. When everyone had had a few minutes to study it, there was a slow dawning. The outrageous disparity between Marty's calculations and the agreement offered by Malovitch was sinking in. The temperature in the room went up ten degrees.

"That fuck!" Wolf said. "That no good kike fuck!" he added, either oblivious or unconcerned with the religious affiliations of some of us. "There's more than a $700,000 difference!" A change came over Wolf. I was no longer the rotten-apple of his eye. Malovitch was in the cross hairs now.

Thorne piped in, "How in god's name did he think he could get away with this?!"

I was watching Weiselman squirm.

Tina said, "Evidently, Barry didn't think Kurt had access to Marty's files." She shot Weiselman a look. Warm and subtle as an IRS Audit.

Winters looked at his watch. "Mr. Malovitch is expecting to discuss his settlement proposal. Mr. Goldman has another item that will be pertinent to that discussion. Ms. Hook. He's also prepared to let you and Mr. Thorne participate in the negotiations insofar as they relate to monies owed to GMW. Is that acceptable?"

"Completely," Wolf brimmed with good will towards me and Winters as he prepared to rip Malovitch's beating heart from his chest.

Ronnie passed out copies of the co-release agreement. Wolf devoured it like a snake swallowing a rat whole.

"We've got the son-of-a-bitch by the balls with this!" Wolf gloated. He looked at me. "Good work!"

I gave him a modest little nod. Sort of, don't mention it, glad I could help, thinking, this tanned and well manicured rancid breath of evil was most likely Marty's assassin.

"I think Mr. Winters and I and Bob can take it from here. Why don't the rest of you get on with your work. We'll get together later for an update. Bob," he said to Winters, pals now, "shall we have Ronnie show Mr. Malovitch in?"

As Ronnie went past me to get Malovitch, she paused just long enough to look me in the eye and give me that little hint of a smile of hers, then gave my forearm an affectionate squeeze. The others started to file out. As Tina was leaving, I caught her eye and she nodded at me. She was ready. I heard her exchange a curt greeting with Malovitch just outside the door.

"Tina!" his voice sparkled to his favorite former associate.

"Hello, Barry. Sorry, can't talk; gotta run."

I edged my way farther along the wall to the west, away from the door so that as Malovitch entered, I was behind and to his right. Ronnie directed him to the seat next to Wolf, which was to his left. He entered all smiles, good will, and condescension in equal measures. He stepped to Wolf with an outstretched hand.

"Jaahnnnn," he crooned, "goood to see you. I'm sooo glad we can get this business behind us. Nice little set-up you have out here."

Wolf had a grim smile painted on. "This is Bob Winters, for Marty's estate." They shook hands.

Weiselman was down the table on the side opposite the door.

"Gary, good to see you. It's been a while." Malovitch sat down.

Weiselman was well into one of his spells. His eyes were darting and he was edgy and agitated. His hair somehow got greasier during these episodes and hung over his ears, and in front, across his eyes, giving him a look more furtive than usual.

"Elaine said, what? Marty's brother had some kind of an accident? That's terrrrible! It was serious?" He couldn't hide the pleasure, couldn't keep it out of his voice, dripping at once with false sincerity and innocence and concern. "What exactly happened?"

"Nothing," I said from behind him letting him know I was alive and reasonably well.

He spun around so fast his head looked like it were on ball-bearings, independent of the rest of his body. His phony smile evaporated. "What're you doing here? I thought, I thought - Elaine said an emergency of some kind." For the first time, Malovitch began to sense the hostility in the room.

"Just some emergency meetings; sorry I can't sit in on this one, but I'm sure John and Bob and Bob Winters here can work it out with you." I looked at Weiselman while Malovitch was still watching me with his mouth open, "thanks for everything, Gary." He looked up at me, took one look at Malovitch's clouding face, and began to protest to no one or everyone, but particularly to Malovitch, "I didn't do anything! I didn't say anything. Nothing! I swear!"

"Gary, we can take it from here," Wolf told him.

Weiselman was shaky. His frazzled alter-ego was coming unglued. He had difficulty standing. When he got to his feet, he seemed dazed. Malovitch glared at him. Weiselman's eyes were still pleading his case, but I had the feeling judgement had been passed and a carrying out of the sentence was being planned in Malovitch's mind.

"Before you leave, Barry, there's someone here that would like to meet you. Have Ronnie let me know when you're free," I said as Ronnie and I went out the door.

It was 10:55 when we left Wolf and Winters and Thorne to deal with Malovitch. Tina and Sandy Marshall and Mel Davidson were waiting for me in the large conference room. I poked my head in. Ron and his charges sat quietly, not saying a word. Vann had become sort of an armed doorman.

"They're waiting for you in your brother's office," Vann said to me.

"I'll be right with you," I told Tina and Sandy and Mel.

I went in and asked Victor and Brian Browning to go to the conference room. I'd join them after I made a couple of phone calls. I asked Ronnie to join us and take notes, but as soon as we were finished, to prepare the conference room and greet and usher in the group that would be forming in the reception area.

"This is Victor March, Marty's accountant. And this is Brian Browning, Deputy District Attorney. Tina Cox, Sandy Marshall, Mel Davidson," I introduced them. "At my request, Victor's done some research into the studio sheets as they've been concocted by Wolf and Warner Warner and Carpenter. He's here to explain a problem with them that Marty had suspected, and he's confirmed. Victor?"

Victor spent the next thirty-five minutes explaining how the sheets were supposed to work, what operators were and how they'd been tampered with. The amount of money involved was huge. I kept my eye on Sandy Marshall. He'd been partnered with Wolf for a long time, but I didn't believe he'd known. I'd had Tina bring him here to see his reaction, but more, to bring him and Tina together to see if they could find enough common ground to chart a new course for themselves and the GMW associates. The marriage of Music and Film entertainment law might still work. Between them, maybe they could retain enough clients to regroup. I hoped Marshall would emerge with his reputation, most of his clients and some of Wolf's. And maybe Tina could wrap herself in Marty's mantle until her own talents were appreciated. With the money legitimately coming to them from DBS, even without the insurance money, which I was sure they'd never see, they might be able to make it.

Sandy Marshall's chief reaction was outrage, then relief. Like a dark cloud was passing. He and Tina set up a meeting for Wednesday morning. They'd assess where they stood, and with the others, decide where they wanted to go.

Davidson, gripping the arm rests of his chair, had the look of a shipwreck survivor clinging to a piece of the shattered ship in the middle of the sea.

Brian Browning discussed with him and Sandy and Tina how he intended to proceed against Wolf and WWC. Victor was ready to go and gave Browning a copy of his findings.

"I'll be in touch," Browning shook hands and thanked him.

Browning and Sandy Marshall headed for Marshall's office to continue their conversation.

"Look for me before you go," I asked Browning.

"I will," he said.

I thanked Victor and said I'd call him later. Mel Davidson started to get up, but I put a hand on his shoulder.

"Would you wait for me here please?"

"Sure," he said.

I thought he was relieved not to have to get up.

Ronnie closed her notepad and stood. She caught my eye. That little smile of hers was getting a workout. I returned it as discreetly as I could and she winked at me. I nodded in the direction of the reception area. As she passed me she leaned close and whispered, "Who was it that said 'God is Dead'?" She stood back from me with the first relaxed, at ease smile I'd ever seen from her.

"Nietzsche," I smiled.

She headed for the reception area to tell our guests the Conference Room would be ready in a few minutes.

Tina walked out with me as far as the reception area where I greeted Colin Peters. It was quite an assemblage. Colin introduced me to Thom Reynolds of United, and Aaron Dinwiddie from Paramount. Some of the others I'd seen or met at Marty's house or at the funeral service. There were twenty-six of us, so Ronnie enlisted Vann to help ready the large Conference Room with extra chairs. While we we're waiting, the elevator bonged, the door opened and four men who'd been chatting amiably were suddenly and unexpectedly confronted with a gathering of their most distinguished peers.

"Thom, Aaron, what's your business here!?" demanded a burly, bald man who had to be Faustini, from Ronnie's description of him. He looked like something left over from the '55 Rams. "I thought we were here to settle up about Sutton here," he said jerking his beefy thumb in the direction of a slightly built man of about fifty, "and the bullshit lawsuit." He looked around for someone-me, except he didn't know who I was-to tell him what was going on. Colin stepped up and introduced me to him.

"Mr. Faustini, this is Kurt Goldman, Marty's brother. Kurt, Lyle Faustini. This is Danny Sutton, a client of your brother's. And these are?" He waited for Faustini to introduce the other two. He was too preoccupied with the assembled collection of actors, directors, and producers, not to mention Elias Ginsberg and Robert Roland, the money people Colin had enlisted, men he probably recognized, to be bothered with introductions. There was the stiffening in his posture of a male dog encountering another in territory he took to be his own.

"I'm William Cooper, Mr. Perry's representative, and this is Mr. Salio, our associate."

I nodded, not shaking hands with any of them. Salio had a nasty, playful little smile on his face. This was a guy that would pull just one wing off a fly to enjoy the asymmetry of his victim's agony. Faustini could care less who I was, he wanted to get on with it. Seeing rivals from both Paramount and United, and the pool of talent they all relied on gathered here, was bringing him to a boil.

"I asked, what's going on here, and I want an answer," he growled.

Ronnie and Vann came into the reception area. Vann's attention had instinctively gone to Salio. She hung back and surveyed him with a detached wariness.

"We're ready for you," Ronnie told me, not taking her eyes off of Faustini. She stole a quick look at me, like a mother knowing something was wrong, not liking the color on one of her kids. I asked her to ask Vann to have Ron move our other guests into Marty's office. She went to Vann and whispered. I could feel them both watching me.

Faustini's size was a definite advantage. Even standing, I felt dwarfed. His presence was intimidating. I felt a wave of something - maybe apprehension, maybe fear-pass through me. Maybe it was the onset of the kind of panic attack Blum had warned me about. Maybe it was popping up in me now like he suggested it might have for Marty at Millennium. And I didn't have the Desyrel to blame for it. Just fear. Just how far out on a limb I was sank in. I could just imagine Perry! Bigger, meaner, richer; maybe connected to organized bad guys, and not only used to getting his way, willing to do anything to get it! I had the feeling if this had been the onset, thinking about Perry would turn it into a raging episode. I thought about them ganging up on Marty, dizzy and disoriented from the Desyrel, alone and on their turf. It occurred to me that somewhere, right then, someone was busy cutting him up. I focused on that. Wolf, Malovitch, Faustini and Perry wanting Marty dead, one of them accomplishing it, and now the autopsy a kind of final slash and burn and salting of the ground. I had another of those urges or visions come over me, I could see and feel grabbing a handful of hair and necktie and pulling, exposing necks and ripping out throats with my teeth. It had a settling effect on me. My episode passed. I checked my little pocket watch. It was 12:10.

"You're fifty minutes early. You'll have to wait," I told him.

He took two steps towards me, very quick for a man his size, crowding me with his bulk, looked down on me and said, "You expect me to sit here and wait while you're fucking me over with this crowd! What are you trying to pull? What's going on here!?" He looked around for someone to plead guilty.

"Lyle, take it easy," Cooper said, "we are early."

Sutton had a look that put me in mind of Weiselman. He'd gotten off the elevator smiles and certainty, and now was uneasy and uncertain. The more upset Faustini got, the more worried he became. His grey-brown thinning hair seemed to stand on end a little higher with each word Faustini uttered. He shifted and fidgeted and looked like he wanted to go, to stay, to do something but couldn't figure out what.

Salio had noticed Vann's interest in him. He seemed flattered, unconsciously preening himself. A ladies' man. He had another look for me that seemed to say, have a good time, little man, while you can. The guy brought the room temperature down twenty degrees when he smiled.

"Do what you like," I told Faustini, "Mr. Cooper, Mr. Sutton - later?"

I looked at Salio and tried to tell him with my eyes I knew something about him and his guys that he didn't. Where they were, for starters. I was also wondering how many fingers it would take before he gave up Garvin Perry? A shudder ran through me when I decided ten wouldn't be enough. I tried to return his nasty smile. I didn't do it very well. Vann noticed, caught my eye, and gave me a kind of nice try look. I shrugged. It was the best I could do. Besides, Salio had an advantage: he wasn't acting. Vann left to tell Ron to move into Marty's office.

"Of course," Cooper said.

It was 12:20 when we were seated in the large conference room. Across the street the water was flat and pale blue, the Palms desultory and forebearing. It had gotten hot and Vann or Ronnie had opened the huge sliding glass door. Finally, a slight breeze stirred the palm fronds, giving them hope, and then began to stir the air in the conference room, giving me hope as well. I had shaken off visions and fears of Faustini and Perry. I was struggling with the competing emotions of being bashfully starstruck on one hand, and on the other, wanting to make this thing that was so important to Marty live. My first thoughts revolved around how comfortable these guys were with each other. They were all not only very good at what they did and knew it, they were able to be good quietly, without fanfare or horn-tooting. Like Marty, I thought. It was what they expected from themselves. Any awe or notoriety that others attached to them or their work didn't enter into it. I could see why Marty chose them. They loved the work. The amazing, shocking, surprising event of the creative process. There is something unknowable, even to those that create, about the source, the growth, and the direction creativity takes. No matter how difficult, or stymied, or aggravating a project might become, it's as exciting and mysterious for the artist as it is for those that appreciate the art. I thought that that was as true for these guys as it was for me when I was designing and building. And that's the fun of it. The joy of it. Without that, what was the point? I'd read and understood what Marty wanted from Packard Productions, but seeing these people made me realize he understood the excitement and mystery and seduction of creativity and the need to keep the process open to them.

I was sitting at the head of the table, and all the more self-conscious for it. Colin sensed my unease.

"Kurt called and asked that I contact some of you while he called others. We're all still reeling from Marty's death - we will be for some time I'm afraid-but Kurt has become aware of Marty's desire to create an independent production company, a mini-studio that will allow all of you to do what you are truly capable of. He brought us together to discuss the possible formation of Packard Productions, without Marty."

They all knew why they were there, but to hear it spoken brought a buzz of expectation and excitement to the room. I told them what I knew of Marty's intent for the company and why I thought it could still work. That it hinged more on them and their commitment and willingness to make it work than on Marty's absence. I introduced Mel Davidson. I said I thought he could help make it happen. With Colin's help. Mel was taken aback and dizzied by the sudden prospect of not only being a part of Packard Productions, but a fundamental part. He told them about himself, his work with Marty at DBS and here at GMW, his film school background and love of film. Colin made it clear to the financial backers he'd brought in, Ginsberg and Roland, they could make it happen if they'd trust the talent, the commitment and the artistic sense of these people Marty had chosen. He thought he could guide the company for two or three years while Mel got the additional experience he'd need to take over. If the other backers would sign on, Colin pledged $1 million of his DBS settlement for a five year period. I'd agreed to a $2 million investment on behalf of the estate for an equal period, conditioned on an un-protracted settlement with DBS. I had Ronnie pass out copies of the first four projects Marty had created, the lists of participants and the likely costs, participation percentages and minimum outcome he'd projected.

"These are the first four of eight projects Marty organized. These would serve as models for Mel and Colin as they begin to develop beyond Marty's."

As they looked through the projects, I knew Marty was there with them. For the first time since his death, I could feel the positive presence of his life.

"Why am I here?" Thom Reynolds asked.

"My question exactly," echoed Aaron Dinwiddie.

"Because," Colin answered, "there were rumors when Marty was alive and now they'll spread again as soon as word gets around we want to revive the idea. We wanted the studios represented here so you could see first hand, that it is not an exclusive services situation with anyone; that it's on a project by project basis; and that we will seek distribution deals with you before we would attempt to distribute on our own. That was Marty's intention from the outset. It was never meant to thwart studio productions, just add another creative outlet for these people in an artistically freer environment, on a financial basis the studios could never match."

"What about Millennium? Faustini is here, but not here. What's going on?" Dinwiddie asked.

"Millennium is not invited. Period. I'm meeting with them over matters between GMW and Millennium," I said.

"And Sutton?"

"Not in," I said. "Only those of you here; and a few others who couldn't be here now. Mel or Colin will talk with them later."

Reynolds asked, "Will Millennium be in the bidding for distribution?"

Colin looked at me. So did Ronnie.

"Absolutely not. Not so long as Faustini or Perry are there."

"That will mean certain black-balling for those of us that become involved with Packard Productions," Gene Steadman warned.

"That very well may be," Colin said, "but everyone here is wanted in projects. Your stature is such that if Perry black-balls you, producers will pull their projects from Millennium. They'll bring them to United or Paramount."

"Kurt, I'm Margot Archer. I'm a producer. What I'd like to ask is, Thom, will you go along if Perry puts pressure on you or you Aaron, to go along with his black-balling?"

"Garvin Perry doesn't do much of a job running Millennium. Nothing he says or does, short of buying Paramount is ever going to give him a say or influence over us." Aaron Dinwiddie said.

"Thom?" Margot said.

"It won't be a problem," he promised.

There were more questions, more answers. It was good to see how quickly Mel and Colin developed a working relationship, fielding questions, jointly analyzing and producing responses to some of the legal and financial questions that arose.

I tapped Colin on the shoulder.

"Stay as long as you need to. I've got another meeting. I'll check back with you, or you can stop in before you go; let me know where we stand."

"I'll tell you where we stand, Mel and I will get Packard Productions incorporated and in business by the end of the week. Ginsberg and Roland and their money are in. With or without a quick settlement for me or Marty's estate from DBS, we're in business."

His color looked better by far than on the knoll at Hillside. I thought this might be a tonic for him. Hard, good work, with good people. And I thought he could rely on Mel to pull his share of the load.

"That's great," I said. "I'll ask Bob Winters to arrange a meeting with you to spell out the terms of the estate's investment."

"I look forward to it."

It was 1:45 when Ronnie and I left the Conference Room. If Faustini were still in the reception area, I imagined you could probably fry an egg on his fat bald head.

"Ronnie, would you show that slob from Millennium into Marty's office, please? Tell them I'll join them in a minute. And as soon as he gets here, a Detective Phillips will want to join us. Show him in."

Her smile was free and easy.

"As soon as you can, would you type up the notes you took in there? I'd like to have Bob Winters see them before he talks with Colin. Okay?"

"Fine," she said.

"And could you step into the meeting with Malovitch and tell Winters I'd like to see him, if he can get away from there for a bit?"

She nodded and started for the reception area.

"One more thing," I said, stopping her.

"Yes?"

"If you're interested, Colin and I agreed you'd be the perfect choice for Packard Productions. They'd work you ragged. You'd have to handle everything for him and Mel until it was clear where and how the money was going to shake out. You could probably start next week. Or take some time off then start? Interested?"

"Yes," she said. "I'll talk to Colin."

We both turned towards the sound of shouting coming from the little Conference Room. It was the unmistakable New York nasal twang of Barry Malovitch, squealing like the pig he was, stuck, hoisted, whatever, on a petard of his own making. Wolf and Thorne's raised voices could be heard above and between the squealings. Ronnie and I exchanged a smile.

"A marriage made in heaven," I said.

"You're really very much like your brother," she said, "very thorough."

"Same mother," I said.

I waited in the hallway. Ronnie escorted Faustini, Cooper, Salio and Sutton past me to Marty's office. Cooper seemed untroubled, ready for another day at the office, even if it wasn't his office, but Faustini was a churning vat of acid. Salio still basking in his imagined effect on Vann. Not a guy troubled by much of anything. I heard her ask them, and Ron and his charges if anyone wanted coffee or sandwiches from the café downstairs. She took their orders and smiled at me on her way to the small conference room. I would've loved to have seen Salio's face when his eyes met those of his guys. Had a chance to wonder who Ron was and what information the broken fingers had produced.

Ronnie came out of the little Conference Room with Winters. He was all smiles. Ronnie sent one of the young support staff women down to the café. She began to type up her notes on Packard Productions.

"That was a stroke!" he enthused, "turning Thorne and Wolf on Malovitch! They're eating him alive!"

"Where does it stand?" I asked him.

"It's just about over except for the crying. Thorne and Wolf have been beating him up with threats of fraud, breach of contract, the whole ball of wax. In exchange for not suing, and not seeking punitive damages, Malovitch's agreeing to prompt payment to GMW, the estate, and the associates. We agree to the release of the International Distributors funds to DBS so long as payments are made from the escrow trustee directly to the rest of us."

"And he's agreed?"

"They're haggling over small change now, but yes."

"Get Ronnie to type an agreement and get it signed."

He gave me one of his looks. Rolled his eyes. His good will at the turn of events only went so far. "I thought I might have lunch, if you don't mind! Maybe go back to my office and do a little work. You do know I have other clients, don't you? I can have Roxanne type up the agreement for Malovitch to sign."

"If you gotta eat, ask Ronnie or Miriam to have someone get you something from downstairs. It has to be now. Before Malovitch leaves the room. And it has to bind Wolf. He has to be agreeing to accept the money DBS owes GMW as its sole compensation from Marty's settlement with DBS or from the estate or from Marty H. Goldman, A Professional Corporation."

"Wanna tell me why?" he said, hands on hips, then must have read my face. He held up a hand to stop me from saying anything so he could answer for me, "No! no! Let me guess. It's not really Wednesday, so you're not obliged to tell me, right?"

I smiled at him. "Close enough, but soon. Ronnie's typing some notes from a meeting I've just held with some of Marty's clients. I'm committing estate money as a prudent investment in something called Packard Productions, like Marty's will authorizes me to do. I'd like you to arrange a meeting with a man named Colin Peters and Mel Davidson to discuss it."

"You can't just meet with people! You can't commit the estate to anything! You're not legally the executor yet!"

"John got the letters testamentary from the court at 11:00 this morning. I'm it."

"Gee, since you're planning the rest of my agenda, why don't you schedule the meeting and just let me know when to show up! How about that!"

"Touchy touchy touchy! Look, if you could work up the agreement for Malovitch and Wolf to sign while Ronnie's doing the notes, she could turn around and do the agreement while you get a look at Packard Productions. Simplicity itself."

"Oh for Christsakes! Alright! I'll go into your brother's office and..."

"Sorry, I'm meeting with some people in there," I checked my watch, "for maybe the next twenty minutes or so. After that, I'm going to move it into the big conference room with some of the others. I sort of need you in there too."

"Oh? Really? And just how am I supposed to do all three of these things at once?"

I thought about it for a moment. "Tell Thorne and Wolf you want the agreement drawn up and signed before any one goes anywhere. Malovitch may squawk, but Thorne and Wolf should back you up. Maybe hammer it out with Wolf's secretary Miriam, and she or Ronnie or both of them can work on it until you've reviewed it and are satisfied. And it's signed. That's a must. Once the process is started, you could join me in Marty's office. I'm meeting with that Faustini guy from Millennium, and Perry's assistant Cooper and another fine fellow named Salio. You don't want to know what he does. In any case, I'm going to need your help."

"You're doing pretty well so far."

I thought he meant it.

"We'll see. One more thing..."

"Now there's a surprise. What?"

"Tell Malovitch there's no deal on the release of the International Distributors money unless the trustee is also authorized to pay Colin Peters the judgement he's already won against DBS."

"Oh for godsakes!" he groaned, "that's none of our business!"

"It is now. Malovitch should be pleased as punch to be getting off so easy. How much do you think punitive damages would have cost him? Rub his face in that!"

"Okay, okay, I'll try." He went back down the hallway to the little conference room and entered the fray.

I interrupted Ronnie and told her I was expecting Michael Besser. Before he got here, she should tell Colin that we'd need the conference room. If he and the Packard Production guys weren't ready to call it a day, maybe they could go down to the café for a late lunch break? I'd need about forty-five minutes, and then they could have the room back. When they cleared out, and Besser arrived, to show him into the conference room and to buzz Marshall, Cox, Woodman, and Davidson and ask them to join us in there.

I walked up the hallway to Weiselman's office. I knocked but there was no answer. I opened the door. He was on the phone with his back to me.

"No I can't come see you now! It's, it's no! Impossible! I'm sorry. Yes you matter! Too much is happening, that's why! It's just not the time."

He half turned and saw me standing there. "I've gotta go," he said abruptly, and hung it up. "Ever heard of knocking?"

"I did."

"What do you want?" His hair was combed and his eyes weren't as wild as they'd been when he left the partners meeting. He wiped at his nose and sniffed like a man with a cold.

"I'm meeting with some people in Marty's office and I'd like you to join us."

"Fuck you!"

No equivocation there. I smiled at him. Decided to do a little name dropping. See if it moved him to reconsider.

"Mr. Cooper and Faustini and Salio will be disappointed," I shrugged and began to pull the door closed, sealing him in.

"They're here?!" his voice rose. His eyes darted around his sparse office maybe looking for a place to hide. Maybe wishing he'd spent more of his decorating allotment to make it possible.

"As we speak," I said. I gave him a smug little smile for good measure.

"Okay, okay," he said, straightening his tie and slicking back his hair. He looked up at me like I was supposed to say you look fine. What I wanted to tell him was his appearance was the least of his worries. What I wanted to do was sing a few bars of Stormy Weather or A Hard Rain's Gonna Fall, just to sort of set the stage, but instead told him, "Go on in, I'll be right there." He walked past me and I pulled his door closed. He walked down the hall ahead of me and went into Marty's office.

Ronnie looked up from her typing and told me, "Detective Phillips called from the lobby. He wanted you to know he's on his way. He's going to get a coffee at the café, then come right up."

I looked at my watch. 1:55. I needed him up here. "Great," I mumbled, hoping they didn't have donuts down there. I looked at Ronnie's slightly troubled face. "When Phillips gets here, would you leave off that for a minute and come in with us? I'd like you to be there."

She looked more troubled.

"It'll be okay," I tried reassure her. Or maybe myself.

I was really just stalling for time until Phillips got there, maybe give Weiselman and Sutton and their pals from Millennium a chance to catch up, renew old friendships, but more, out of a nagging curiosity I went back up the hallway to Weiselman's office and let myself in, closed the door behind me. I went to his phone and pushed the Redial button. The LCD screen showed the number he'd called last. Marty's house on Seascape. I went back into the hallway and closed the door.

Chapter 32

The elevator bonged and I saw Phillips step into the reception area, coffee in hand, take a wide-eyed look around, then spot me.

"Gonna let me in on it?" he asked.

"Won't be long now," I smiled.

We walked down the hallway together. When we got to Ronnie's work station, I asked her, "Ready?"

"If you are," she said uncertainly.

I took a deep breath and we entered Marty's office.

Cooper was out on the balcony. It was 2:05, still hot, but the breeze had picked up, rippling the water and the bright sun sparkled off it. Faustini had let himself get sucked into waiting for nearly two hours and he was furious. I had the feeling if not for Cooper he'd have been long gone.

"What the fuck! What the fuck you pulling here!" he boomed, leaping from the couch and moving towards me so fast I'd barely gotten the door closed behind Ronnie and Phillips. The guy was amazingly fast for his size. Vann and Ron and the three guys were sitting on folding chairs across the room west of Marty's desk, but Ron got to his feet and was next to me in an instant. Faustini eyed him disdainfully, but would have to have been blind or stupid not to feel his power and resolve. Sutton was in the arm chair, Weiselman and Salio had been sharing the big couch with Faustini.

What's the fuss, I thought about asking him. Vann and Ronnie had placed more folding chairs around the close side of the coffee table, so it wasn't like they'd had to take turns sitting.

I noticed Cooper watched, but made no move to come in, distancing himself. Good. Salio seemed to be a little less pleased with himself now. I had the feeling there hadn't been a lot of chit-chat in the room. Maybe Vann wasn't returning his inviting little smiles. Maybe his guys in Ron's charge didn't make him look to good to Faustini or Cooper.

Faustini hovered over me again. "We're here to clean up this mess your fucking brother made with Sutton. We came to wind it up and you keep me waiting two hours! Who the fuck you think you are? And who the hell are they?" he jerked his thumb in the direction of Ron and Vann and the guys, "And this guy?" he said looking at Phillips.

"Detective Phillips of the LAPD, meet Mr. Faustini."

Faustini whipped his head around from me to Phillips. I had the feeling Weiselman and Sutton would be raising their hands any minute to be excused for a trip to the bathroom. Eyes wild and with no escape, they were rats cornered. Salio was no longer focused on Vann. He was shooting his two guys visual death threats, if I was any judge. He must have wondered who the third guy was.

"I've heard a lot about you," Phillips said pleasantly. "Why don't we all sit down?"

He seemed to be enjoying himself, letting me take this where I might. This was his town and these guys may own it, but they didn't run it. I'd felt that about him every time we'd met. I thought these smug self-appointed movers and shakers were a joke to him. He probably lumped Marty in with these shitheads, but I'd forgive him for the time being. He and I stepped past Faustini and I introduced him to Weiselman, Sutton and still on the balcony, Cooper.

"This is Ron Lawton, and you've met his associate, Vann Quintana."

Vann smiled warmly and nodded at Phillips. A knife in Salio's hopeful heart, I thought.

"And the others?" he asked, noticing their hands for the first time. He wrinkled his brow and made a face at me as though to say, this better be good.

"We'll get to them in a minute." I gave Cooper a look. A smile. We were going to work this out, I wanted him to know. Maybe he'd like to stay out on the balcony. I sat in Marty's chair at the desk. Ronnie pulled up a folding chair and sat to my left.

"Mr. Salio," I asked him, "who do you work for?"

An oily confident smile came to his face, his eyes telling me I was dead meat. "I'm, I'm a consultant to the studio." He exchanged a look with Faustini and Cooper. Faustini's fat mouth confirmed with down-turned corners. Evidently he thought that a fair description. Cooper stiffened. Gave him a look. He knew where this was going.

"But do you report to Mr. Faustini here, or Mr. Perry? Or maybe to Mr. Cooper acting for Mr. Perry?"

"I don't think that's any of your business," he said, looking to Faustini for approval and finding it. They shared a little laugh. Cooper wasn't amused. His eyes bore into Salio. "Well, actually, Mr. Faustini, if you must know." Faustini was about to object until his eyes met Cooper's.

"Since Gary and Mr. Faustini are the only lawyers here, and there's no one representing them or any of the rest of us, and I wouldn't want to put anyone in an awkward legal position, let me just state a hypothesis.

Is that okay with everyone?" My eyes met with Cooper's.

"You've got your fucking nerve! You think I'm gonna sit still for this?" Faustini yelled as he got to his feet.

"SIT DOWN!" Cooper barked from the balcony. "Let's hear him out."

I nodded to him.

"You were at Millennium and negotiated with my brother over Mr. Sutton's original contract, right?"

"So what?"

"And when Mr. Perry bought Millennium and discovered expensive contracts he thought were unjustified, he suggested you renegotiate them?"

"So?"

"So when you came after the Sutton deal, my brother told you it was a valid contract and to shove it. That wasn't an answer you could take to Mr. Perry, especially since you were responsible for it in the first place, so you decided to prevail upon Mr. Sutton to voluntarily renegotiate the contract. Maybe you were aware of certain bad habits, and either pandered to them, supplied him, or suggested how it would be in his best interest as far as future work at your studio, or any other, that those habits not be made public. Maybe you pointed out his health was at risk."

"That's outrageous! I'm not going to sit…"

"Don't move!" Cooper interrupted Faustini.

I nodded again to Cooper. He was making this easier than I thought it would be. I figured I'd have to rely on Phillips' authority to keep them in their seats. I smiled at Sutton. He was as fidgety as a thirteen year old choir boy being invited to stay on a few more years. Weiselman too.

"It seems like you had his complete attention, and got his complete cooperation. And when he insisted on having the contract renegotiated, Marty had little choice. But to sweeten the deal for yourselves, maybe to raise your stock with Mr. Perry, you decided to prevail on Mr. Weiselman here, who suffers from the same bad habit, convince him that it would be in his best interest to ignore certain changes in tax considerations from the original draft Marty had approved. Led Sutton to believe he could go after Marty and the GMW partnership for more than the difference. And you got the compliant Mr. Weiselman to submit the altered drafts directly to Mr. Sutton to keep my brother from seeing the changes. Maybe you gave him reason to believe you were in a position to help him out of the financial troubles his bad habit had created. Or maybe you convinced him his health was a factor too. "

Somehow, Cooper was keeping Faustini and Salio in their seats with a threatened invisible death ray. His jaw muscles were tight, his arms folded across his chest. Hell, if they'd listen, I'd keep on talking. Phillips was fascinated. Ron was beginning to like it, and Vann, well Vann wasn't smiling for Salio.

"But when Marty and his insurance carrier decided to fight back, you got your consultant, Mr. Salio, to kill Marty."

Ronnie's hand flew to her mouth. Salio was as unresponsive as a French waiter.

"That's absurd!" Faustini bellowed. "You can't prove a thing! I'm not going to sit here and listen to this crap without a lawyer!" He started to get up again.

"Sit down Mr. Faustini," Phillips said quietly. "Please. No one has asked you to comment on any of this. I'd appreciate your staying." He smiled at Faustini. Faustini sat back down. "Thank you," Phillips said.

"Mr. Lawton has gained the confidence of the men Salio sent to do the job." I nodded to Salio's guys to my right. They have stated un-equivocally that Salio sent them to kill Marty. Later, me. They insist that Marty was already dead when they got there. Ron believes them," I said. "I'm not so sure. But as it happens, there was a witness to their presence at Marty's house at about the time he died." I nodded to Malovitch's guy. "He and his partner, recently deceased while trying to kill me, were there to kill Marty too."

"Oh dear God!" Ronnie moaned, hand covering her mouth again.

"What!?" Phillips said in disbelief.

"He also claims that my brother was already dead when he and his partner arrived. He claims that these two were there, just leaving when they got there. They checked, saw that Marty was dead, assumed these two did it and took off. Maybe these two told Mr. Salio they'd done the job. This guy and his former partner had been instructed to make it look like suicide. Salio's guys like a break-in or robbery gone bad. So maybe they stuck around longer than he says and put the finishing touches on the suicide even if they didn't kill him."

"We never!" Malovitch's guy started to say.

"Shutup!" Ron said.

He shut his mouth. He looked at the floor and shook his head, mostly for Phillips' benefit, I thought, but had no intention of testing Ron.

"Instructed by whom?" Phillips demanded.

"We'll get to that. But for now, I'd like to suggest that even if Marty was dead when Salio's guys got there, they were there to do it. Attempted murder. And Salio works for Mr. Faustini here. Conspiring to commit murder? And Mr. Cooper?"

He looked at me from the balcony. He raised his eye brows in re-sponse, but said nothing. A cool customer.

"It could be argued that Mr. Faustini and Salio acted without your knowledge. Or Mr. Perry's. That to undo his embarrassment at having negotiated the original contract with my brother, Mr. Faustini was going to extremes to curry favor with the formidable Mr. Perry. Could that be?"

Cooper smiled ever so slightly.

"Just a fucking minute!" Faustini protested.

"Don't say a word," Cooper warned him. "We'll get you representation. Mr. Perry will look into this, I can assure you," he said to me and to Phillips.

"I would also be willing to believe that, although he's acted with unbelievable cowardice, Mr. Sutton here had no idea the lengths to which Mr. Faustini was willing to go. I think he was a pawn, manipulated by Mr. Faustini. I think if given the opportunity, he'd gladly withdraw any suit he's contemplated against my brother, his professional corporation, his estate, or Goldman Marshall & Wolf." I looked at Sutton. He had the look of a turkey not chosen for Thanksgiving. "Is that so?" I asked him.

He looked at Faustini and Salio and was unable to speak. He looked like he might cry from the stress. He looked at Perry's man Cooper, and saw where his best interest lay. Not to mention his health.

"Yes," he stammered, "of course. I never wanted, I never thought..."

"Mr. Cooper?"

"Yes?" he said pleasantly, knowing where I was going.

"Mr. Besser will be here shortly. He represents my brother's malpractice insurance carrier. If it's necessary to sue Millennium over the deleted tax provisions of Mr. Sutton's renegotiated contract, on behalf of my brother's professional corporation and his estate I will, Mr. Besser will, and I believe the GMW partners now will. I was hoping we could avoid that, now that you know what's been done in Mr. Perry's name. Are you authorized to sign an agreement representing him and the studio?"

"Yes I am."

"And you agree that it's appropriate."

"I do."

"Then I'd appreciate it if you'd wait for me and some of the GMW partners in the Conference Room. I'm sure they'd like to get this settled.

"Ronnie, would you escort Mr. Sutton and Mr. Cooper to the big conference room? And show Mr. Besser in as soon as he arrives. And if you know where he's working, ask Bob Winters to join us?"

"Yes." She looked at Sutton like the worm he was. At Cooper like a dangerous, but interesting snake. Wondering if Faustini had acted without his and Perry's knowledge.

"I'd like to confer with Mr. Perry. Is there a phone I could use?"

"Use Mr. Weiselman's office down the hall."

Weiselman didn't bat an eye. Why should he? He wasn't going to need it.

Cooper said, "I'll join you in just a moment." He gave Faustini and Salio a look that dared them to move a muscle. They didn't.

Ronnie left with Sutton. Phillips was shaking his head.

"This is just too much," he said.

"There's more," I promised him. "Do you know Brian Browning?"

"Of course, what about him?"

"He's here on another matter. I'd appreciate it if you'd stay and discuss the situation with him, about these guys," I said, "all of them."

"You gonna tell me who this one works for?"

"Soon," I told him.

It was 2:45 when Ronnie came back with Bob Winters. He looked tired but had a reassuring smile on his face. He took one look around and didn't like it.

"What the hell is this?"

I made the introductions. Told him Mr. Sutton and Cooper were going to meet us in the conference room.

"Where do we stand with Malovitch?"

He smiled. "Done. Miriam worked with us, and with her assistant got it together."

"And you're satisfied with it?"

"Yes."

"He's signed?"

"Yes."

"And Wolf?"

"Yes."

"You've got it in your hot little hand?"

He reached into his briefcase. "Once you sign it, it's law."

"Excuse me," I said to Phillips. I motioned to Winters for the agreement. He laid out three copies before me, all signed by Malovitch and Wolf. I was reading my way through it. "What about Colin Peters?"

"Section III, paragraph..." he reached over and flipped through the pages, "six. Malovitch really needs that release!" he smiled.

I signed all three copies. Gave them back to him to give to Malovitch and Wolf. Asked him to have Malovitch come to Marty's office to meet someone. Ask Wolf to join us in the conference room. Millennium was prepared to approve the original draft of Sutton's agreement and Sutton was prepared to agree to drop his suit against GMW.

"How in the hell??" Winters sputtered. "Wolf will love this. Even Thorne might wanna shake your hand, bandages and all."

Don't bet on it, I was thinking. Cooper poked his head into the room and said he'd meet us in the conference room.

"I'll be there in a minute. This is Bob Winters, for my brother's estate. Ronnie, I'd like you to wait here with me for a moment; then join them and help Bob prepare the agreements."

"Of course," she said.

I buzzed Sandy Marshall's office. Asked him to round up the partners for a meeting with Sutton, and Cooper from Millennium, to settle all outstanding issues. Asked him to ask Browning to come down to Marty's office.

Browning came in, saw Phillips and went right to him. Phillips stood, a wry smile on his face, and they shook hands.

"What're you doing here? This isn't exactly your beat, is it?" Browning teased.

"Nor yours, really." Phillips countered. "Mr. Goldman has an amazing hypothesis I want you to hear; unbelievable really, but it's beginning to look like something."

"Like?" Browning asked.

"Sit down, Brian, you're gonna love this."

Maybe Winters had forgotten to ask him, or maybe Malovitch wasn't taking my calls, so to speak. In any case he hadn't shown.

"Before you begin, I'd like to suggest that you ask Mr. Malovitch to join us."

Browning turned to ask me, "Who's Malovitch?"

Phillips answered for me, "A former partner of Mr. Goldman's brother. Marty Goldman? Died last Wednesday? Malovitch is with...?"

"Diamond Bernstein and Silver," I filled in.

"How does he figure in?" Phillips asked.

I pointed to the guy, "He hired this one and his partner. To kill Marty, then me."

"What!" Browning's professional veneer of bonhomie vanished. "What's he talking about!?" he asked Phillips.

"Sit down Brian. I'll go get this Malovitch guy."

"What does he mean, kill?" Browning demanded. "It was suicide!"

"I'll be right back," he told Browning. Then to me, "Where is he?"

"In the small conference room at the far end of the hallway."

At 3:10 Phillips opened the door, held it open and waited while Wolf and Malovitch, in the hallway, shook hands, exchanged no-hard-feelings pleasantries. Marshall, with Cox, Davidson, Woodman, McCord and Hamilton came down the hall and stopped, waiting for Wolf to finish saying his good-byes and go in with them. Wolf was basking in his glory, having snatched victory from disaster. Put GMW back in the black. He and Malovitch held onto each other's hands, all phony smiles, like fathers of the bride and groom, detesting each other, but putting a good face on it. Wolf stretched it out in front of his partners, seizing the opportunity to rub Malovitch's face in it with what I thought he imagined was aplomb.

"Barry, it's worked out for the best. I can't thank you enough for your cooperation."

"It's good to get this settled. It's time for all of us to move on. Marty's death is a tragedy, a real tragedy, but life must go on!"

"You're right, absolutely right."

"Mr. Malovitch?" Phillips reminded him.

"Right away!" he told Phillips with a patronizing, dismissing, off-hand wave. "Gotta go," he told Wolf and the others, like maybe the Maître d' had called his party. "Tina, Mel, good to see you; glad this worked out so well!"

He'd just been shorn of $6 million, eight and a quarter, give or take if you counted Colin Peters's money, and the guy's glad it worked out so well. As long as he's happy, I was thinking, what the hell. Even though things now pointed to Wolf, I couldn't shake the feeling Malovitch seemed more like the guy to have had Marty killed.

"Mr. Malovitch?" Phillips repeated.

Malovitch turned on him like a hungry Rottweiler, "Just a fucking minute!" he snarled.

Malovitch and Wolf exchanged one of those looks like, "Whatta ya gonna do?" when small children demand your attention.

As Malovitch stepped into Marty's office, Wolf's eyes followed him, a question in them when he saw Browning and Weiselman, maybe got a glimpse of me and Ronnie, Ron, Vann and the hired hands. I didn't think he knew who Browning was, or Phillips for that matter, but I had the feeling after his victory over Malovitch, and seeing him go into what must've seemed in that momentary glimpse to be the lion's den, he was smirking deep down inside that mean little chest of his, that it was a fitting end, whatever.

Phillips closed the door with a firm thud behind Malovitch. Malovitch took one uncertain look around and was all smiles again. I remembered wanting to wash my hand when I first met him at Marty's on Thursday. Now I wanted a shower. A long hot one. No one was returning his smile.

"Ronnie!" he tried. No sale.

"Mr. Malovitch," she nodded.

He looked at me and his lips compressed. I sensed he was harboring thoughts about just leaving.

"This is Brian Browning," I told him, "from the District Attorney's Office. This is Detective Dave Phillips, LAPD."

He looked past me and for the first time noticed Ron and Vann and the guys. But they might as well have been furniture for all they had to do with him. His head must have been swimming. DA, cop, hard guy types. I watched as it registered. It took him a while to see them as people. As separate individuals. When he did he went white. His guy gave him a sad little smile. I thought Malovitch was going to faint. The kike. I wished it were Perry.

"These are the people I wanted you to meet. Ronnie? Let's go. Detective Phillips, I'll let you explain to Mr. Browning. Mr. Browning, I think we'll be in touch."

"Sit down, Mr. Malovitch, please." Phillips said.

Malovitch the lawyer emerged. "What's going on here? Am I being detained!"

"No," Browning said, "we'd appreciate your cooperation for a few minutes, that's all; better here than downtown, okay? Dave?"

"Barry?" I said.

"Yes?"

"Thanks for schlepping all the way out here," I gave him what I hoped he'd recognize as one of his own insincere smiles.

In the hallway outside Marty's office as we were walking to the big conference room, Ronnie reached out and grabbed my arm and stopped me. I turned to see what she wanted. She had tears in her eyes and a smile.

"Thank you," she said.

"What?"

"For asking me to stay; to stay this week; to stay just now to see Mr. Malovitch get what's coming to him. Thank you."

I could feel one of those waves threatening to rise up and close my throat. Now wasn't a good time. I just nodded to her in response. I felt the grip loosen. "Miles to go before we sleep."

Chapter 33

—◦◦◦—

Ronnie and I entered the big conference room. Winters had taken charge, working from the original agreement Marty had drafted. He and Marshall and Cox together seemed to be taking the lead in hammering out the details of the agreements between GMW and Sutton and GMW and Millennium. They sat on one side of the table, backs to us as we entered, along with Davidson, Woodman, and McCord. Wolf was at the head of the table, back to the ocean, Marshall next to him on the other side, then Hamilton, Sutton and Besser. Thorne sat in the chair down the long table opposite Wolf. Near him, alone in the northeast corner of the room, Cooper stood. Still distancing himself. Wolf sat back listening with an air of confidence and detachment befitting an incumbent Senator, unopposed on election-day eve, indulging a few unhappy constituents. The table was overflowing with pages from those long yellow pads lawyers favor. Miriam was next to Wolf, on one side of Winters, with Tina Cox on the other. They were organizing the yellow pages into something Miriam and Ronnie could work from.

Cooper, with a little smile on his lips, nodded a greeting. I had the feeling he was conceding a round, but hadn't decided to throw in the towel. I had the feeling he was contemplating my future. I was looking forward to leaving before he made up his mind about it or Perry made it up for him.

"Tell me," he said pleasantly from across the room, "have you somehow enlisted Thom and Aaron in your brother's putative plan to create his own, what -studio? - with that inspiring array of talent you had here today? Will they be leaving Mr. Wolf and the others?"

I liked the putative part.

Wolf didn't. He didn't like any of it. His complacent smile drifted off on the breeze and his face hardened. He came forward in his chair and looked at me over Winters head. Took a look at Cox as the most likely co-conspirator. I couldn't see her face, but it must have been telling him, not me buster. He found my eyes again.

"What's he talking about?" he demanded.

I was tempted to check my watch. Ours had been a short friendship, maybe a record.

"No offense, but it's none of your business," I said.

"If you're pirating clients or deals away from us, it sure as hell is! Who was here? Why wasn't I told!?"

"If you're undermining GMW, you're undermining Roberta! You won't get away with it!" Thorne chimed in.

Cooper was pleased with the dissention he'd stirred. Turn about being fair play, I couldn't really object.

"All of that talent will seek and find representation one place or another. Packard Productions' projects will be a closed loop. No outside representation. You'll have to get more information next week from Colin Peters."

"What's he got to do with it?" Wolf barked.

"He'll be running it."

"Along with me," Davidson spoke up. Surprising himself as much as me, I thought.

Tina whipped her head around towards Davidson. Then gave me an injured, betrayed look.

Davidson continued, "This is going to be my last GMW partners' meeting. I'll formally withdraw from the firm by the end of the week. Sandy, can we get together?"

"Of course. I'll be sorry to lose you Mel," Sandy Marshall said.

"Shutup Sandy; he's not going anywhere and he's sure as hell not taking any of our clients with him," Wolf snapped.

"John," Sandy began.

"Keep out of it! I want to know which clients are involved, I want..." he was about to continue, but Winters interrupted.

"Mr. Wolf? Mr. Wolf! Let's finish the business at hand. You can bicker amongst yourselves as much as you like, but you're wasting my time. And I don't like it. If you can't save discussion of your internal problems for later, I'd like you to leave this meeting. Please."

"I don't know who you think you're dealing with..." Wolf began, but a loud tapping of a coin or car keys on the glass door behind me interrupted him and turned all heads. The unexpectedness of it silenced everyone.

It was Phillips. He entered. "Mr. Wolf?" he said looking around the room.

"What do you want!" Wolf demanded.

"Mr. Browning would like to see you now."

"I don't know any Browning; who is he? And who the hell are you? And where do you get off just floating around here?"

"Detective Dave Phillips, LAPD."

Wolf was a little less certain now. "And Browning?"

"Deputy District Attorney, Los Angeles County."

"Tell him to make an appointment," Wolf said, looking away from

Phillips, as if that would end it.

"He'd like to talk to you now, in Mr. Goldman's office, without my having to arrest you. Is that understood?"

Wolf colored purple in humiliation and rage. A nice change from that usual Club Med tan of his. I wondered if Winters recognized the color on someone else.

"What the hell are you talking about?! What's going on?!"

I thought I was the only exception to the embarrassed part of an embarrassed silence around the room. Maybe not. Maybe it was just silence. For Miriam it was the apocalypse. I actually felt sorry for her.

"I want to know what this is about! I demand to know!"

"Mr. Browning is the one you need to talk to. Are you coming?"

"You're damn right I am! I'll have the fuck's job! His career is in the toilet!"

Must be something going around, I was thinking. Phillips held the door for him. I watched Wolf head towards Marty's office. Just before he got there the door opened and a uniformed policeman and the other detective, the guy that had taken Marty's gun from me in the parking lot of the West LA Division, led a handcuffed Malovitch, Salio, Faustini and the three guys towards the elevator. The sight must have sent Wolf's nuts to the vicinity of his liver, racing for cover.

At the end of the little procession, Vann and Ron emerged from Marty's office. She looked over, gave me a smile. Ron saw me, gave me a thumbs up. Browning stood at the door waiting for Wolf like the hangman at the top of the stairs. He stepped back to let Wolf in, then Phillips. The door closed.

It was 4:30. "I think we've covered everything," Winters said, "any one think of anything else?" No one did. "Then if you and Ronnie would get this ready for signatures," he said to an ashen Miriam, "we can conclude. How long?" he asked Ronnie.

"Twenty minutes and you can review it," she said, "ten more if there are revisions."

"Good. Thank you."

Ronnie and Miriam left.

There was a strained silence. The air in the room felt heavy and oppressive. In the pit of my stomach there was a dull ache and it had begun to reach up behind my eyes, like the warning signs of a coming headache. I had a slightly disoriented feeling but couldn't pin it down. In fact I couldn't focus on anything. I was aware of being in a kind of mental neutral, but couldn't shift out of it. I went out onto the balcony. I had the feeling of being adrift on water far from land, an incessant rolling making me not quite seasick, but with that wrong feeling that precedes it. A silvery taste under the sides of my tongue. The breeze was warm, but it helped. I watched the late afternoon glare coming off

the water, shimmering, too bright, almost blinding, coaxing the headache out of hiding. Behind me I heard Winters suggest they take a break,
maybe get something to eat downstairs, and meet back there in twenty
minutes. It sounded unreal, like it was coming from a radio or TV with
the volume low. The conference room cleared out. I felt a hand on my
shoulder and turned.

"What a day!" Tina smiled shaking her head, "what a damn day! Could
we have dinner? I'd like you to tell me about," she tried to sort out her
thoughts, gave up and finally just waved her arm encompassingly, "all of
it: what's happening to Barry; why Millennium and Sutton rolled over; I,
my head is just swimming. How did you do it?"

I heard the words and saw her mouth moving, but felt like I were at
the wrong end of a telescope. It didn't have anything to do with me. She
was looking at me funny. I had the sensation of losing my hearing, then
my connection to the things around me. I felt as though I might just
drift off like a kid's balloon set free. But free didn't exactly describe it.

Empty did. And useless did. I had this pervasive sense of futility. But
there was also a nagging signal flashing in the back of my mind. I didn't
know what it was, but it was insistent and was pulling me back. Slowly I
began to focus. My head was clearing and what came into sharp relief
was the realization that Marty was dead and either Malovitch or Wolf or
Faustini were responsible and my maneuvering hadn't determined who.
I hadn't changed a thing. And I knew I'd done all I could. Or thought I
had. Maybe Phillips could take it past the attempted murder for Malovitch
or Faustini. Get one of the guys to crack. But if Ron and the finger
breaking hadn't, there wasn't much chance Phillips could make it happen. What if it were Wolf? He was only up against a grand larceny
charge or something like it, but nothing concerning Marty's death. Since
we'd never gotten our hands on his guys and with their fingers intact,
their instructions from Wolf about me or Marty were still unexplored
territory. Wolf wouldn't be foolish enough to send them after me now.
That had been one of the things I'd been counting on. Exposing him, all
of them, would get them off my back. Maybe I should have dangled
myself in front of him longer. Waited until he found out for himself that
I'd gotten into his GOD files. That would have been more than he
could have resisted. He would have had his guys gunning for me in the
halls of GMW. But now, what would be the point? Revenge? He was
mean, but not stupid. I'd missed my chance with him. The thought
deepened the ache in my stomach. Increased the dizzy disconectedness.

"Excuse me," Vann interrupted.

I looked past Tina to where she stood just inside the conference room,
not coming out onto the balcony.

"Hmmm?" I said. My eyes were trying to focus. "What?"

"Ronnie says there's a call for you. You can take it in here," she said,
meaning the conference room.

She stepped out onto the balcony with Tina, giving me some privacy in the empty room. One light was flashing on the phone. I punched the button and picked up.

"Hello?"
"Mr. Goldman?"
"Yes."
"I'm Doctor Joseph Siciliana."
It rang no bells for me. I was searching my memory and coming up empty. Never heard of him.
"I'm a forensic pathologist."
I didn't respond. I could feel my throat tighten.
"You don't know me," he was saying.
My eyes were beginning to water and I couldn't speak. The tightening in my throat was making breathing difficult. I could feel my chest tighten and heave. I couldn't get enough air.
"Are you there?"
"Yes," came out.
"I've been in touch with Doctor Rosen. He's told me about your feelings concerning the autopsy I've performed. I wanted to talk to you first."
I was biting the inside of my cheek to keep it in.
"As Doctor Rosen has already told you, your brother was in very good health; the autopsy has only confirmed that. I've found nothing that in any way suggests death due to anything but the obvious. I'll be calling Mr. Thorne and sending him my report. I just wanted to speak with you first."
"Thank you," I said.
"Do you have any questions?"
The first thing that popped into my head was the heart disease on my mother's side of the family. I asked about it.
"Clean as a whistle," he said, "I'm about the same age as your brother and I only hope my heart and arteries look so good; anything else?"
"No, thank you for calling."
"I'm sorry for your loss," he said and hung up.
I didn't want to turn around and have to face Tina and Vann. I wished I were on the beach alone so I could let the wave that was trying to swamp me run its course. I took a few measured breaths and wiped my eyes. Before I'd even begun to turn, the phone buzzed. I found the button for Inter-com and pushed it, picked up the phone again.
"Yes?"
"It's Ronnie."
"Yes?"
"There's another call for you. I'll have the switchboard put it on the same line."
In a moment the line flashed again.

The clock near the phone showed 4:50 when I took the call.

"Mr. Goldman?"

"Yes?"

"I'm Florence Mendosa with the INS."

"What's that?" I asked without thinking.

"Immigration and Naturalization Service?"

"Right."

"I'm here with a Maria? Maria Cortinas?"

"I don't know..."

"She worked for your brother; in fact he'd agreed to sponsor her so she could stay in this country and continue to work. Did you know that?"

"No, I didn't; my brother's, he died last Wednesday."

"I'm so sorry, yes, Maria's told me that. The reason I'm calling is that your sister-in-law fired Maria and has terminated the sponsorship. Without it, Maria will be deported."

"I don't know what to tell you. I'm not in a position..."

"Oh no! Maria didn't expect, she just wanted to tell you something before she had to leave. But her English is too poor. So I agreed to call for her."

I waited.

"She said she saw your sister-in-law through the door to your brother's office? She had a piece of paper in her hand. Maria said note. Your sister-in-law saw her and closed the door. A Mr. Weiselman came ten minutes later, then left. Then a Mr. Thorne. Then the police. She was very anxious to have you know that before she left. Does that help you? She wanted to help you."

"Yes, I think it does."

"Well then, good. Maria will be relieved, I'm sure. She was very fond of your brother."

"Thank you. And thank her."

"You're welcome. I will."

Before she could hang up I asked her, "How long before you have to deport her?"

"There'll be a hearing by Thursday or Friday about her lack of sponsorship. When it's clear she has none, she'll be deported early next week."

"Thank you," I said again and we hung up.

"Where's Gary?" I asked Tina.

I stood just inside the room, in the doorway to the balcony where Vann had been. The others were returning to the conference room behind me.

"What's the matter?" Tina asked reading my face.

"Where's Gary?" I repeated.

I was aware of the look on Vann's face over Tina's shoulder.

"I don't know. I haven't seen him since we met this morning in the little conference room."

"He left your brother's office when Phillips cuffed Malovitch. He was coming unglued. Kind of wild-eyed," Vann said.

Behind me no one had sat down yet. They milled around their chosen seats until Ronnie and Miriam came in and passed out copies of the two agreements. It was quiet while they all read. Tina went back in but stood behind her chair watching me. She remained standing while she read, shifting her glace from the papers to me and back again.

On my way through the room I told Winters, "I'll be back."

"Don't be too long. You have to sign too."

"Fine."

Vann had come into the room with me and was staying close. I opened the door and she was right there.

"Where do you think you're going?" I asked her.

"With you."

"You're not invited."

"I'm going. You've got that look like you can't wait to do something stupid."

I didn't want her with me. But I could see she was prepared to make it difficult, so I didn't push it.

"Just keep out of it."

I gave her a stern no-nonsense look. It didn't work. She wrinkled her mouth, yeah, right.

It was 5:10 when I went into Gary's office. Vann closed the door behind us. She stood shoulder to shoulder with me.

"Still haven't learned to knock?" he said with a sardonic grin.

His hair was wet and freshly combed. He'd washed the tell-tale oiliness from his face and other than the distant too-calm look in his eyes, he was just another hard working attorney packing it up at the end of the day. He was standing at his desk, putting papers in his briefcase.

"I've got a question for you," I said.

"Shoot," he said. He smiled at me, a smug, take that smile, and added, "So to speak."

For that alone I would have done it.

"I know you were talking to Malovitch before Marty died. I know you were kissing ass at Millennium. I..."

"You don't know anything."

"I know you're fucked, Gary. You're through here at GMW; Malovitch's not exactly going to be in a position to help you, not that he would; and I think your usefulness to Millennium is nonexistent now. And you got a habit you can't afford. I told you it was gonna rain hard on you."

"Get out of here! This is still my office!" he yelled.

"What I want to know is, how long have you been fucking her?"

"What are you talking about?"

"And what was in the note?" I asked him.

He stopped whatever it was he was going to say and just stared at me. He got that smug smile on his face again. He knew there was no way I could make him tell me. He was sure of it. He kept smiling, prepared to wait me out.

I bumped Vann with my shoulder and while she was off balance pulled her gun.

"Hey!" she complained at the shove, then realized what I'd done. "Give that back!"

It hadn't dawned on Gary what I'd done or why. His attention to detail was slightly impaired. I didn't just get the gun. Because the holster strap had been fixed, I got it all. Vann reached for it and I elbowed her away. It wouldn't be long before she dropped me with some of her razzamatazz martial art stuff, so I pulled the gun free of the holster and pointed it at Weiselman's head.

"Sit down!" I barked.

He hesitated. I was nervous and too excited. I figured I had only one chance to get what I wanted.

"SIT DOWN YOU ASSHOLE!!" Vann ordered him. "CAN'T YOU SEE HE'S OUTTA CONTROL!?"

He sat. I took a look at Vann. She meant me!

"Don't do this!" she said, "this is stupid; you've gotten..."

I turned on her, feeling it come loose, reach my mouth before I could push it back. "WHAT!!" I yelled at her. "Nothing! Wolf? Malovitch? Faustini? They're DOG SHIT I've managed to scrape off my shoe! What the fuck good did it do?" It was all coming loose, all of it, and I couldn't choke it back; sobs and tears escaping so much I lost sight of Weiselman. Vann stepped forward.

"You've made some sense out of it. That's something. That's a lot," she said. "Give me back the gun. Please."

I wiped the tears away. Found Weiselman again. Told Vann no with a shake of my head. I reached across the desk and put the gun to his forehead.

"Last chance, you fucking worm."

"You're crazy! Get him off me!" he pleaded with Vann.

"Bye," I said, cocking the hammer.

"No! No, please! Yes, I was fucking her! I was fucking her; please don't hurt me; pleeeease!!"

"And the note?"

"I never saw it! I swear! She called and told me what he'd done, asked me what to do. I told her about the Key Man policy, what it would mean. When I got there, she must've already taken care of it. I never saw it! I swear!! If there was one, I never saw it. I don't know what was in it."

"You didn't ask her about it?"

"No! I didn't want to know! I didn't want to know anything about it! We agreed she should call Thorne, then I left."

"But Marty knew about you?"

"I don't know! I..."

I pressed the gun into his head.

"He knew she was having an affair. I don't know if he knew it was me. I swear I don't know!"

I took the gun away from his head. My breathing slowed. I regained control. I could smell urine. I couldn't have sworn I'd have done any better but it didn't gain him any sympathy with me either. I looked at Vann. She was making up her mind about me. Considering or reconsidering previous assessments of my character.

"You like the finger bending better?" I asked and handed her the gun.

We went back to the conference room and I signed the agreements. Sandy Marshall took them into Marty's office so Wolf could sign them too.

It was 5:55 when he re-emerged with Wolf and Thorne, Browning and Phillips. I stepped out of the conference room into the hallway so he could see me face to face. Vann didn't let me get more than an arm-lock away from her. Wolf was uncuffed. Being given the favored status of the white collar criminal.

"Wolf?" I hailed him.

Phillips and Browning slowed but kept walking towards the reception area and the elevators. He and Thorne stopped. His nasty unrepentant yes found mine. If looks could kill.

"Time to change your computer password," I said, "Don'tcha think?"

It was 6:15 when Besser and Cooper and Sutton left. McCord, Hamilton, Woodman, Cox and Mel Davidson and Sandy Marshall stayed to discuss what to do about the partnership. Sandy told us that Wolf would be booked, then released on his own recognizance, and Thorne's promise that he would appear for an arraignment, and bail hearing. I wondered if he could post any.

Winters was packing up his briefcase. Snapped it shut and looked at me and said, "You shoulda listened to your mother."

"What?"

"Gone to law school," he said. "You got a minute?"

"For you? Two."

"In your brother's office, then."

"Thorne's got wind of Packard Productions and your commitment of funds."

"So?"

"So they don't like it."

"Tough."

"It's not that easy," he said.

"The will empowers me to."

"Maybe," he said. "I haven't seen it yet; but Thorne and Roberta are claiming that there are inconsistencies and problem provisions."

He was looking at the floor rubbing his hand through his bristle-like hair. I knew I wasn't going to like this.

"What?" I said.

"The bottom line is Thorne thinks he can make a case for Roberta being the only beneficiary."

It didn't register. "You mean her and the girls, right?"

"No, just Roberta."

"What! That's crazy! It's absolutely clear he was dividing his estate between them!"

"He may have intended to, but there are some legal issues Thorne thinks will make Roberta the sole beneficiary. And if that's the case, they don't want you committing any of her money."

"That fucking bitch! She's gonna try to cut his own girls out of his will?"

"That's where they're heading."

I was seething with frustration and rage. When the hell would this end?

I closed my eyes. Tried to think.

"But I'm the duly appointed executor, right?"

"Right," he said warily.

"So I'm going to set up bank accounts and collect monies and payoff creditors, right?"

"Yes."

"And if I put money into Packard Productions, what can they do?"

"Sue you, personally."

Sounded familiar. Worrisome, but now the sting was gone. I smiled.

"Fuck 'em."

"Oh for Christsakes! Use your head! It's gonna get ugly," he moaned.

"You gonna quit?"

"Would it change your mind if I did?"

"No."

"I didn't think so. Why don't you think about it?" he said tapping his temple with a finger. "I'll talk to you, say, Wednesday! Now there's a concept! You let me know if you really want this kind of trouble. It could go on for years! What about your own life?" He raised his brows, hoping for some common sense. "You do have one, don't you?"

I thought about that. Me and Jason. Then about Marty and the girls. "Fuck 'em," I said.

Chapter 34

———◈◈◈———

I signed out at 6:45. Thanked Eric for his help and went out the front door. Wolf's guys weren't there. I hadn't expected they would be. I jay walked across Ocean Avenue to the park, meandered along the pathway under the palms as far as the California Incline, and down to the Pacific Coast Highway, crossed it to the beach side, took off my sandals and walked towards the water. I sat in the warm sand on the slope a little above the water line and listened to the small waves whoosh across the wet sand, then drain away.

If Weiselman could be believed, Roberta was the only one who might know for sure if Marty killed himself. What Maria saw might or might not have been a suicide note. If it was, Roberta knew, and what she'd done was obvious. If it weren't, it was possible he killed himself and didn't leave a note; or someone killed him, made it look like suicide, and Roberta found him and assumed it was. Then called Gary who alerted her to the insurance problem, then Thorne.

The dull ache in my stomach was gone, and my head was beginning to clear. How I loved the sound of the ocean. I thought again of how different things might have been if only he'd come here and listened a while. I laid back in the sand, hands behind my head and looked at the endlessness of the pale blue sky.

I wondered if he would have killed himself over her infidelity? If it played a part, or how large a part? Maybe it was just the last straw. And when he told Roberta, I don't want to live like this, it wasn't just the problems at GMW or with Malovitch or Millennium he had on his mind. I thought it was more the stomach churning, mind numbing, unrelenting pain of having been betrayed by those closest to you. All of them. Even if he could solve the problems, he must have been overwhelmed by a sense of hopeless, disappointed fatigue. A sense of, what's the use? It was surrounding him like a poisonous cloud, coming at him from all sides. He must have felt it like the death of a child. Shocking and incomprehensible. Just sweeping away the desire to go on.

The thing about Marty's suicide that hurt the most, besides the loss of